REALITY
A NOVEL CHECK

karen tuft

Covenant Communications, Inc.

Covenant®

Cover images: *Man and Woman Pinky Lock* by Michael Hitoshi © Flashfilm, Getty Images. *Charm Bracelet* © Covenant Communications, Inc.

Author photo by Michael Schoenfeld

Cover design copyright © 2012 by Covenant Communications, Inc.

Published by Covenant Communications, Inc.
American Fork, Utah

Printed in the United States of America
First Printing: June 2012

18 17 16 15 14 13 12   10 9 8 7 6 5 4 3 2 1

ISBN 978-1-60861-397-7

For my children, who I hope will always stay true to their beliefs despite the prize or the punishment that may await them.

And for Stephen, who continues the journey with me every day.

ACKNOWLEDGMENTS

MANY HEARTFELT THANKS TO THOSE who have helped make this book possible. Thanks to wonderful friends who have continually offered enthusiasm and support, especially Wendy and Jennifer, my ace cheerleaders who stuck with me every step of the way. Thanks to Michele Bell for her generosity of spirit while teaching me the ropes. Thanks also to my editor, Samantha Van Walraven, for her thoughtful and steady hand during my maiden voyage into publishing.

Many thanks to my wonderful family, especially to a few of my nieces who allowed me to use their names in vain in this book. (You do not in any way resemble the characters to which your names are attached.) Special thanks to my son, Stewart, for the dinners he willingly cooked while I was busy writing, to my daughters Lauren and Holly for daring to read something their mom wrote and offering their sound opinions, and especially to my daughter Rebecca, my literary pal and personal in-home editor.

And most importantly, deepest thanks to my own soulmate, Stephen, for not just listening to my dreams but doing everything in his power to make them a reality.

This above all: to thine own self be true,
And it must follow, as the night the day,
Thou canst not then be false to any man.

William Shakespeare, *Hamlet*

CHAPTER 1

"ALL RIGHT. I CAN TELL the two of you are up to no good." Lucy Kendrick popped her hands onto her hips and grinned from the doorway.

"Lucy!" her friend Allie squealed from her comfortable, sunken position in an old beanbag chair. "I'd get up, but I just painted my toenails." She wiggled her feet to illustrate the point then waved as compensation.

Lucy laughed and bent over for a hug, careful of the nail polish brush Allie still wielded. Lucy didn't need a streak of heartbreaker red on her shirt.

"You're home!" Grace leaped up from her computer desk and made it a group hug. "We weren't expecting you for another couple of days."

"Finals are over. I am officially a college graduate." Lucy dropped down onto the couch and used her toes to push off her sandals. It felt good to be back with her best friends, where she could relax. "So what's up? Are there plans for the afternoon, or are we chilling?" she asked as Grace headed back to her computer.

"So far, the only plans we've made have been glam toes for me, geek time for Gracie," Allie said.

"I downloaded all the videos I took of us last summer and over Christmas break," Grace explained. "Now I'm splicing them together and adding graphics—that sort of thing. I want to make a DVD for each of us in celebration of your graduation and Allie's wedding."

"Aw, that's nice, Grace. Do we get to have a sneak peek at it this afternoon?" Lucy asked.

Grace turned her head and smiled. "I could be talked into it . . . for a price."

"Hey, Gracie, show Lucy the part you showed me this morning. Her Olympic diving moment," Allie said as she finished applying a second coat of polish to her toes. "It's classic Lucy."

"Olympic diving moment?" Lucy had to think for a moment before the light went on. "Those guys from Colorado at the resort—" She gasped. "You videotaped *that?*"

"I did." Grace grinned. "It's great. And Allie's right. Classic Lucy."

"Okay, no more Mr. Nice Guy. Let's see it. Now." Lucy gave Grace a steely eyed look.

Grace wasn't fooled for an instant. She simply laughed and scrolled through the footage.

Allie carefully extricated herself from the beanbag and hobbled over on her heels to join them.

On the computer, Lucy watched three hunky guys dive into the pool at the resort Grace's family owned. It was a large, deep pool, and the guys, aware of their female audience, were laughing and trying to outdo one another with each attempt. Then Lucy coolly walked out onto the springboard, did a full summersault with a twist, and slipped into the water with hardly a ripple. After that, things got really serious.

"Nice form, Luce," Grace commented, her eyes twinkling.

"I can't resist the lure of competition, I guess." She watched as a muscular male launched himself from the board like a rocket and jackknifed into the water, only to come up sputtering as one of his buddies snagged him underwater and started a wrestling match.

"Only *you* would see a *competition.* I saw *guys,*" Allie said. "The blond one was really hot."

On-screen, Lucy performed a handspring off the board as the men stood by, arms crossed over their chests, and watched. "Check out the looks on their faces," Grace said. "Worship. Sheer worship."

"A diving board is a lot like a pedestal, isn't it?" Lucy asked, grinning, enjoying herself. "Those guys reminded me of Craig and Andy."

Allie rolled her eyes. "You've got to be kidding. Those amazing specimens were in total alpha male mode, and they reminded you of your *brothers*? Are you *blind?*"

Lucy threw up her hands in mock surrender. "It was like déjà vu. There were Craig and Andy, disguised as these guys from Colorado, showing off, so I had to give them a little power demonstration. It was a knee-jerk reaction."

"Instead of diving into the pool as if you were one of the boys, you should have flirted with them." Allie shot Lucy a saucy smile and wagged her fingers, displaying her engagement ring. "That's how I caught Ben.

You need to play the game differently, Lucy. Flirt and tease and have a little fun. Opportunity lost."

Allie had never had trouble attracting guys, not in all the time Lucy had known her. Lucy, on the other hand, had grown up surrounded by brothers and all of their friends, and they'd continually given her flak anytime she'd as much as batted an eyelash. "Okay, I'll be the first to admit that I'm no good at the whole flirting thing, but, honestly, I'm not interested in playing 'the game' right now, Al. Or even dating, for that matter. There are things I want to do first. Find a job, earn some money, travel. Anywhere. New York, Paris. Disneyland even. Maybe buy a ticket and just be surprised when I get there. And maybe stay there until I earn enough money to buy a ticket to come home. But I need to find a job now to buy the first ticket." She paused while that particular thought took root. "Hey, Grace, can I use your computer for a few minutes?"

"I suppose so." Grace closed the program she'd been using and slid out of the seat. "What for?"

Lucy clicked on the icon to open the Internet browser. "To hunt for jobs and fill out applications. Mom said Brigham's taking an online high school class this summer. He needs our home computer more than I do."

Allie groaned. "Your first day back and you want to fill out job applications. Okay, Gracie, that means your toenails are next."

Grace settled onto the couch. "Not red though. I want something more neutral."

"You got it. But, Lucy, when her toes are dry, we're out of here."

Lucy grinned. "Deal. And thanks, you two."

"Yeah, yeah, yeah," Allie replied. "What are best friends for?"

* * *

"Look at this dress. It's amazing."

Lucy looked at her watch and then at her friends. Time had flown. Grace had had a pedicure *and* manicure and was now flipping through the latest celebrity magazine while Allie thumbed through a fashion catalog.

Grace leaned over Allie's shoulder to check out the picture. "Wow. She must have used an entire roll of double-stick tape just to stay in it. Show Luce."

Allie held up the magazine for inspection.

Lucy studied the picture then resumed typing. "I wouldn't trust my modesty to a strip of double-stick tape. That dress is a wardrobe malfunction just waiting to happen."

"Party pooper," Allie said, tossing the magazine onto the end table. "Anything interesting in that rag you're looking at, Gracie?"

"Not much."

"Let me see."

Lucy glanced up again as Grace handed the magazine to Allie.

"Hmm. It says Vanessa Delgado and Ty Castleton are dating now. Lucky. That is one gorgeous man. I could totally go for him."

"Allie!" Lucy laughed in mock disbelief. "You do remember you're engaged, don't you?"

"Of course I do," she replied. "And I *adore* Ben. But being engaged doesn't mean I've suddenly gone blind. Gorgeous is still gorgeous, Lucy."

"If you keep saying things like that and Ben finds out, he's going to lose it," Grace warned. "I deleted a few scenes from the diving video, you know, where you and the blond Colorado guy—"

"I *know*." Allie sighed dramatically.

"—got pretty flirty yourselves," Grace finished.

"Nothing major happened. We were only having a little bit of fun. And it's not like Ben had actually popped the question at that point. But some things are better for everybody involved when they're not caught on tape. So thanks."

Lucy tuned out the conversation and started another online search. There were a few more websites she wanted to explore before her friends lost their patience completely.

"Whoa, whoa, whoa! Check him out."

Despite her best intentions, Lucy looked up once again from the monitor. "Him, who?"

Allie closed the magazine, a finger between the pages to mark the place, and smiled innocently. "Hmm? Oh, nothing. An article about some new reality dating show called *Soulmates*, so you wouldn't be interested, considering you're not into that sort of thing right now." She made a shooing motion with her hand. "Go on with what you're doing, and ignore us." She opened the magazine, holding it close so only she and Grace could see its contents. "Check him out, Gracie," she said in a low voice.

"Holy cow," Grace breathed.

"Yeah," Allie practically purred.

"What?" Lucy demanded, narrowing her eyes, suspicious now. "You're just trying to mess with—"

"Listen to this," Grace said, holding up a hand to silence her. "Ethan Glass, successful entrepreneur, founder of Glass Enterprises, and self-made millionaire, is the man looking for love on the new reality show *Soulmates*. Glass, who has a reputation for loving the ladies, is seldom seen without a beauty on his arm. Why, then, has he agreed to become the first *Soulmate*? In his words, he is a Glass 'half empty'—"

"Oh, come on," Lucy said. "It doesn't really say that." She jumped from her seat and snatched the magazine. "Where were you—oh, here: he is a Glass half empty and thinks the format of the television series will give him the best chance of finding that special woman—the one who will fill his heart." She snorted. "Give me a break." She started to toss the magazine at Allie before pulling it back to stare at his picture. "Oh, whoa. That's him? No wonder there's always a woman on his arm."

"Yeah." Allie sighed. "And he has two arms. One is constantly going to waste."

Lucy continued reading. "Hunky millionaire Glass says his recent celebrity status has been both a plus and a minus. 'While I don't deny it has given me the opportunity to meet the most beautiful women in the world, it has not afforded me the one thing I desire—true love. I see this show as an opportunity to meet the woman I'm looking for. I know she's out there, looking for me too.' Who writes this stuff?" Lucy shot a last glance at Ethan Glass before she turned the page. But there he was again, tall and dark-haired, escorting a swimsuit model to a premiere in one picture and disappearing into a limousine with a sultry actress in another. Lucy sighed, plopped the magazine in Grace's lap, and returned to the computer.

"Aren't you done yet?" Grace asked, tossing the magazine onto the growing pile on the end table. "I'm starved. Let's take a break and go get a bite to eat."

"Okay, you guys win. I'm done for now." Lucy closed the browser. "Online applications are great. Makes life so much easier. You fill them out, attach your résumé," she held up her flash drive to demonstrate, "and presto! Instant job app at your fingertips. So far I've sent them off to anything I could find that might consider a BA in English. A few museums at the Smithsonian, a couple of New York ad agencies that need copywriters. Whatever. Wherever. And then we'll see who bites."

"Anything local?" Grace asked hopefully. "If you got a job here you could move in with Allie and me."

"Yeah, a few places." Lucy wasn't planning on taking one of the local jobs unless she really had to, but she didn't want to disappoint Grace. "I applied to a couple of insurance agencies and the *Daily Journal*. News!—hang on a sec." She opened the browser again. "I didn't even think about news stations or television networks or cable channels. Think of the jobs they'd have—working on television shows. That would be so cool."

Allie flopped back onto the cushions of the couch. "Get comfortable, Grace. It looks like we aren't going to be eating for a while yet."

Guilt flooded Lucy. She hadn't seen Allie and Grace for weeks, and yet she'd kept her nose pressed to the computer monitor all afternoon. That was no way to treat her best friends. "Sorry, guys. I'm being a total bore. What sounds good, Mexican or Mexican?"

"Mexican," Grace and Allie said simultaneously.

"Let's do it. Oh, and Grace—I left a copy of my résumé on your computer desktop. If you can think of any other places, go ahead and send in the app for me, okay? You too, Al."

Allie stood and slid her heartbreaker-red toes into a pair of trendy sandals. "Sure, no prob. Now let's get out of here. We need to eat and then do something *really* important."

"Like shop?"

Allie smiled like the Cheshire Cat. "Exactly."

* * *

Allie dumped her shopping bags on the living room floor of the apartment she shared with Grace and sank onto the couch while Grace continued on to her bedroom, purchases in tow. Allie would drag her stuff to her own room eventually—unless Grace beat her to it, of course. It was the kind of thing she'd do. She was the ultimate neat freak sometimes.

They'd found some pretty good deals at the mall that afternoon. Even Lucy had found a couple of things she liked before returning home.

"I really like that black skirt you bought," Allie called after Grace. "You going to let me borrow it?"

Whatever Grace replied was muffled and unclear, which was probably a good thing since it was most likely a no, and if Allie didn't hear the no, she could pretend it was a yes or at least a maybe.

She rested an arm against the back of the couch and propped her head against her hand. "I ran into Mike Sessions the other day," she said when Grace came back into the room. Grace had had a crush on Mike Sessions since . . . basically, forever.

"Mike's great," Grace said neutrally, carefully smoothing and folding her now-empty shopping bags.

"Doesn't he work for your dad now? Isn't he a bigwig in the resort's business office?" Allie's dad worked at Grace's family's resort, and as a result, the girls had been friends since they were kids. Now Grace worked at the resort as well.

"Uh-huh. Dad thinks he'll go far in the company."

"He took Lucy to a party once, right?"

Grace got a glass out of the cabinet and filled it with water. "She went out with him over the holidays. Lucy said she thinks Mike's nice, but there wasn't any spark."

Allie caught the forced objectivity in Grace's voice. She idly reached for the celebrity magazine still sitting on the end table and started flipping pages. "I don't understand how any girl who's even half alive can see Mike Sessions and not feel a spark. Most girls would say it was more like they'd been struck by lightning, wouldn't you?" She looked up and pulled a comic, all-knowing face at Grace.

Grace only glared back and turned on her computer. "Will you please take your stuff to your room?"

"Sure, in a minute." She turned another page of the magazine.

Grace puffed out an exasperated breath, picked up Allie's bags, and marched down the hall. Allie grinned to herself. Grace was so predictable.

She flipped another page and found herself looking at Ethan Glass once again. Grace stalked back into the room. Allie glanced up and gave Grace her best innocent look. "I was getting to it."

Grace just shook her head and sat down at the computer.

"What are you doing now?" Allie asked.

"Finishing the video. I want Lucy to have a copy before she packs up and leaves for good."

"You don't really think that will happen, do you?"

Grace shrugged. "You heard her. She wants to see the world. She doesn't want to settle down yet, especially here in Eagle Bluff. And if Mike isn't tempting enough to keep her here, then nothing is."

Poor Gracie and her crush on Mike. Allie wanted to laugh. Instead, she sighed melodramatically. "Mike *is* the best catch in Eagle Bluff, that's for sure."

"I'm telling Ben you said that."

"Ben *was* the best catch in Eagle Bluff, but now he's caught. I'm talking about single, *available* men."

"Whatever. The point is, I don't want Lucy to leave Eagle Bluff."

Allie sighed. "I know. Me neither. Maybe if she got a little travel out of her system, she'd be happy to come home and stay."

"Where did Lucy say she wanted her applications to go?"

Allie looked down at Ethan Glass. He smiled up at her. It was a great smile, she had to admit. A really great smile. "Hmmm? Pretty much anywhere. Why? I thought you were going to finish that video."

"I changed my mind. Help me brainstorm places for Lucy so we can tell her we did. Maybe we can find something local she'll be interested in."

Allie started to close the magazine then stopped. She turned the page. Ethan Glass and the swimsuit model were walking down a red carpet; she was wearing some slinky silver thing that Allie wished was hanging in her own closet. He was wearing black—including sunglasses—and that killer smile of his that was all white teeth and male confidence. "Um, didn't she say something about news? And TV?"

"Oh, that's right."

She could hear Grace typing away, but Allie's attention was fixed on the next picture of Ethan Glass, which showed him climbing into the limo. He really was one gorgeous man. Even Lucy had thought so—Lucy, who'd sworn off guys until she'd traveled the world or something ridiculous like that. Allie's mouth quirked into a half smile. "Gracie, do a search for *Soulmates*, will you? I've got an idea."

Grace glanced over at Allie. "You think they have openings for production assistants or something?" She saw the devious look on Allie's face, and her own turned decidedly suspicious. "You don't. You have something else in mind."

Allie jumped off the couch and nudged Grace over so she could share the edge of her computer chair. "Just type in *Soulmates*, and let's see what we get. There it is. Gracie, it's perfect! Forget production assistant, we're going to sign her up to be a contestant. Yeah, this is perfect."

When Grace opened her mouth to comment, Allie held up her hand. "Listen. All Lucy wants is a chance to travel, right? A little adventure. They're probably taping in Southern California, but sometimes these shows go to exotic places. Plus, it's *him*"—she stabbed her finger at the photo in the magazine—"and even Lucy went nuts when she saw his picture. Nuts for Lucy, that is. And you know how competitive she is—even if she doesn't want to win, she'll put in a good effort for a while. She'll have a great time. And she'll get this out of her system and come home ready to stay."

"I don't know, Al. It isn't exactly what she meant when she asked us to submit job applications for her. And—"

Allie cut Grace off again. "Technically, Lucy said if we thought of any *places* to send her application, to do it. She didn't actually say *jobs*. Now, let's get busy." She clicked the link for the information for contestants. "Oh, man, we nearly missed the deadline for entries. It says videotaping is set to begin in just over two weeks. Contestants chosen need to arrange their schedules in order to be free for up to six weeks. They will also need to sign a bunch of release forms and a contract."

She stared determinedly at Grace. "If we do it, we need to do it today. Tomorrow might be too late."

"Allie, I don't think—"

"Look, Grace, the chances of her being picked as a contestant are so slim it probably won't even happen. We'll tell her what we did and have a big laugh over it. And even if she's chosen, she can turn it down if she wants." She kept up the stare, and Grace's shoulders started to slump. Allie shook with mischievous glee. Grace was weakening.

She picked up the magazine and held it in front of Grace's face. "Look at him, Grace. Ethan Glass. Even Lucy—Lucy!—was melting when she saw him. Every woman's dream man."

"Not Lucy's, not completely, unless he passes the religion test."

Allie rolled her eyes. She knew how devout Lucy and her Mormon family were. She herself didn't get it, but, whatever. "Yeah, well, she can cross that bridge if she makes it that far in the competition."

Grace sighed and clicked on the link to the contestant application. It was pretty straightforward: name, address, birth date, e-mail address. Allie and Grace knew all that stuff. A current photo. Grace had several on her computer, so that was easy too.

"The last page of the application is a questionnaire, Al. Maybe we should call Lucy for the answers. We don't have to tell her why we want them."

"Hey, who knows her better than we do? We'll just do it." She grinned. "Let's be outrageous when we answer them! That would be so funny."

"No!" Grace glared at Allie. "If we're going to do this to Lucy, we're going to represent her as honestly as possible. Don't even think about it."

Allie shrugged. "Fine."

They answered the questions and found themselves at the button marked Submit. Giving each other a look—Allie's mischievous, Grace's wary—they both reached up and clicked the mouse together.

CHAPTER 2

"WHO WRITES THIS STUFF?" ETHAN Glass tossed the celebrity magazine onto his desk and returned his attention to the documents he'd been reviewing earlier. "'Glass half empty' stopped being clever by the time I was in third grade."

Curt Myers, the executive producer of *Soulmates* and Ethan's longtime friend, slouched in his chair and grinned. "I don't know; some flunky in publicity, probably. The point is, the more press we get for *Soulmates*—and that really means you, by the way—the better our potential ratings. You're the golden ticket on this little venture, and I want that gold to be the highest market value possible."

"Right. Then we tie up the loose ends on this media deal—"

"And make me a very rich and happy man and you an even richer and happier man."

"Uh-huh." He set the papers aside for the time being and looked up. "I know you have a lot riding on this, Curt, and I agreed right from the start to be the first *Soulmate*—and I fully intend to hold to my part of the bargain—but I won't make any guarantees."

Curt casually hooked his foot across his knee, but Ethan knew him well enough to know he was preparing for battle. "We've already established that you don't have a problem with looking for love on the show."

"No."

"And we've discussed the format of the show often enough. Only *our* format allows us to virtually handpick the best women out there for you. Our edge, as you know, is all the compatibility tests we're using to narrow down the field of applicants, which will give you all the info you could possibly want to cross-reference against your own gut. *Plus*, Dr. Lindstrom will be on hand to offer consultation. So I don't see the problem, bro."

Dr. Berta Lindstrom, psychologist and relationships expert, had signed on not only as show advisor, but she had also expressed an interest in providing her services for the proposed Internet venture. Curt rubbed his hands together. "The show's success will give us the exposure we need to kick off the online personals website. Search engines, personality tests, dating services, networking, more seasons of the TV series—"

"Curt." Ethan's patience was wearing thin. He didn't blame his old college friend for getting off the subject at hand. He himself understood the blood-pumping thrill that accompanied the brokering of a big deal. This was Curt's first opportunity to really go for the big time. And Ethan himself recognized the potential in this venture. But that wasn't the point. "I didn't get to where I am without being a risk taker. That isn't my concern. It's the women.

"I have faith in the product you've put together. But despite the compatibility tests and your confidence in my gut instincts, I won't guarantee a positive outcome. Don't get me wrong; I'm committed to this. I'll be giving it my best effort. But the track records for success among dating reality shows is poor, to say the least. We expect better odds with our approach and format, but they are still long odds that my *Soulmate*, as we've termed her, will be in that group. Long odds for happily ever after."

"Not a problem, bro," Curt repeated.

"Really?"

"Sure." Curt leaned forward and braced his forearms on his thighs. "How many women have you dated over the years?"

"Plenty."

"Seriously, romantically interested in?"

"A few."

"Ever proposed to anyone?"

"No."

"Ever considered the possibility of marrying, settling down, kids, the works?"

"Sure. Usually when my folks remind me how badly they want more grandkids while they're young enough to enjoy them." Ethan exhaled heavily. For years he'd been focused on building his business. There'd been a few nice women during that time whom he'd genuinely cared about. But not cared about enough, apparently. Considering where his priorities had been, he'd probably saved himself a bundle in alimony instead. He'd literally worked around the clock, seven days a week.

The past couple of years, with his high-profile success, he'd found himself surrounded by a different kind of woman—the opportunistic kind. They were beautiful, convenient, and temporary. And starting to become more than a little tedious.

"Okay," he said, getting back to Curt's question. "I'm not opposed to the idea, or I wouldn't have accepted the gig in the first place."

"Exactly. Now, it's a foregone conclusion that most of these reality dating shows don't end up in happily ever after. We've already established that. They have a happy-for-now finale, the viewers get their little thrill, and then they move on to the next reality show or reruns of *Seinfeld*. They *forget*. We only need you to have a relationship with the *Soulmate* winner for a few weeks, couple months at most, until the show finishes airing. Things don't work out, fine. It ends like any other relationship that doesn't pan out. Nobody really expects happily ever after to last forever these days. Neither do the women on the show. We'll amend the contract to make it clear to the women that there is no guarantee of a long-term outcome for the winner if you think it needs to be there. Just give me a happy-for-now finale. That's all I ask."

Ethan had heard this spiel from Curt before. The show was primarily intended to draw business to the Internet products they were developing. They needed to demonstrate that *Soulmates'* personality tests and compatibility questionnaires would garner results. Ethan Glass finding his soulmate on prime-time television was the means to achieve those results. But Curt was blowing too much smoke for Ethan. It wasn't Curt's head on the national chopping block, after all.

If Ethan found the right woman, he'd consider marriage. But what did that even mean? Did the *right woman* even exist? He wasn't sure, and he hadn't met the woman yet who'd changed his mind. And *soulmate*? That word conjured up only romantic myths and impossible expectations. As a result, he'd initially said no when Curt had asked him to be the male sacrifice on prime-time television.

Ultimately, Curt had argued a strong case about Ethan's name recognition and its marketing potential, and Ethan had committed to the gig. He'd taken the personality tests, the compatibility quizzes, the astrological readings—whatever nonsense the lady shrink had set up. He'd be as open to the experience as he could possibly be. For the women involved, he would at least take the high road.

Curt leaned down and picked up his briefcase. He pulled out a thick manila folder and tossed it onto Ethan's desk. "These are the top applicants," he explained as Ethan began to thumb through the papers inside. "These sixty women screened to the top for various reasons: your general preferences in appearance, IQ test results, personality, career similarities, backgrounds, interests—you get the picture. I'm taking these over to Dr. Lindstrom to select the top twenty-five. The more diverse they are, the better the show, and I'm going to remind her of that fact. We begin notifying the contestants tomorrow. I thought before I handed them off you might enjoy a peek."

Ethan blew out a breath he hadn't realized he'd been holding and returned to the top page of the stack. Each page had a picture in the upper left-hand corner. Across from the picture, the applicant's name leaped out at him in bold type, with her vital statistics listed beneath. Denise, applicant number one, was a five-foot-seven, dark-haired beauty with brown eyes and was from Atlanta. Southern belle, then. The next applicant was a petite blonde with narrow eyes and a nose proportionately too long for her face. But she'd graduated magna cum laude from college and had an expressed interest in Renaissance art—a particular interest of his. If he ran into her at a club, he wouldn't look twice at her. But, he admitted reluctantly, if he'd read this beforehand, he'd at least have given her a second glance, especially after the date he'd been on yesterday.

The network publicist, in an effort to promote him and the show, had set up tickets for a movie premiere with the stunningly gorgeous Raven MacDowell, an aspiring actress. Ethan had been excited to meet her. But he'd quickly discovered that the stunningly gorgeous Raven was mind-numbingly dull. By the time the limo had reached the corner, Ethan had decided he would have preferred a color photograph of the actress reclining against the limo seat rather than the real woman.

Then her endless ramblings about herself had taken an unlikely turn in his direction. She'd actually asked him if he was anybody important. Not that he had a particularly lofty opinion of himself, but he'd figured the publicist would have filled her in on the personal details of her date. Of course, the publicist hadn't told him much about Raven either. Unfortunately.

He'd replied, very sincerely. "I am to my mother."

"I mean, like, are you like a director or something?" she'd asked.

"Well, I suppose in a sense I direct the people I employ, if that counts."

She'd looked confused for a moment, an interesting combination of total blankness, supreme vanity, and layers of black mascara. Then he'd watched the light gradually dawn, which he confirmed with her next question. "Does that mean you, like, own your own company?"

And he, like, wouldn't even have hired her for the mail room. "Guilty as charged."

"Have I heard of it?"

That had to have been a trick question. After all, he'd introduced himself to her using both his first and last names. "Possibly. Glass Enterprises."

Well, she *had* heard of Glass Enterprises. She'd begun gushing. She hadn't *realized* her date for the evening was *that* Mr. Glass. And if he'd had any doubts about it before—which he hadn't—it had been confirmed once again that, while he figured he was an okay looking guy, money in and of itself was very, very attractive.

Raven, newly motivated, hadn't wasted any time. With a discreet nudge of her toe, she'd slid across the seat of the limo with the slick intensity of a shark on the scent. Ethan had almost sworn that he'd heard a cash register inside her head go *cha-ching*. He'd sighed, taken hold of her hand as it had started finger walking up the lapels of his jacket, placed it in her lap, and patted it like a kindly brother. He'd sat through the premiere mentally working through the projects sitting on his desk and afterward had informed a—by now—pouting Raven that he had an early start the next day.

After that evening with Raven, considering he'd initially been excited to meet her, he knew he needed a better way to evaluate the contestants than just his masculine reaction to them once taping began.

He continued to thumb through the applications. Many of the women were pretty; all were unique. And in roughly two months, one of these women would be someone he would, if the theory held, be calling his *Soulmate*.

As a kid growing up on his father's ranch, he'd dreamt of striking out on his own, taking a different direction. He'd wanted to make his own mark and be successful doing it. The gangly ranch kid makes good. He reflected that, as the top prize on a reality dating show and in a wholly unexpected and surreal way, he'd blown the top off his own expectations. Shutting the folder, he shook his head. "Well, good luck to Dr. Lindstrom. I don't envy her the task."

Curt took the folder from Ethan, snapped his briefcase shut, and rose from his chair. "I wouldn't say that. Her task is the easy one, screening the applicants down to twenty-five. They aren't her potential soulmates; they're yours, bro." He grinned.

Ethan shot him a bland smile. "You owe me on so many levels, Curt."

Curt clapped him on the shoulder and laughed. "Really, I envy you, Ethan. Millions of men do. The hard work has been done. The women have all been collected, sorted, and categorized. These ladies are handpicked for you. You get to go on exotic dates, do exciting things with gorgeous women all trying to woo you. All you have to do is enjoy the pleasant company and weed the women down from twenty-five to one—and then keep that one around for a few weeks." He grinned again and waggled his eyebrows. "Have fun."

Curt paused when he got to the door and lifted his hand to indicate the briefcase he was holding. "There are some beauties in there, Ethan. You could pick any one of them and make it a show. I'll shoot you the final itinerary by Friday." He gave Ethan a jaunty salute and left.

Ethan shut his eyes and ran his hands over his face. He didn't want Curt's ambitions for the show to outstrip his common sense. Ethan knew he owed it to Curt, the network, the producers, the crew, and the contestants to be as committed to this venture as possible. He hoped the women were prepared to handle the risk and any potential heartbreak when the time came.

Because when all was said and done, the only person he intended to be true to was himself. He would not commit himself to someone if he wasn't absolutely sure he was being true to himself first. Soulmate or not.

CHAPTER 3

Lucy lugged the last box of college stuff she'd procrastinated unloading out of the backseat of her car and gave the door an energetic shove with her hip to close it. Arms full, her purse threatening to slip off her shoulder, she gingerly made it to the front porch and poked at the doorbell with her elbow.

Unsuccessfully.

She gave the door a couple of forceful kicks.

It swung open, and her brother Brigham appeared. "Oh, it's you. Why didn't you ring the bell?"

Lucy pulled a face at him.

Brigham laughed and reached for the box then nimbly took the stairs two at a time to her room to deposit it. She sighed with something close to envy. He was only fourteen and the baby of the family. Her other brothers—Craig, two years her senior and married now with a child, and Andy, two years her junior—had egged her on since almost before she could walk, daring her to try things, prodding her to compete with them. They'd goaded her into tricycle races and then, when she was older, into racing against them on their bikes. They'd bullied her into zooming up—and hurtling off—skateboard ramps. As teens, they'd hooted at her attempts to bench press their weights. Her vanity had only survived intact because she'd at least been able to beat Brigham.

Obviously not anymore.

Oh well. She grinned affectionately at him as he came back down the stairs and took the last six in one giant leap. "Thanks, Brig. You using the computer? I want to see if I've heard back on any job applications. Maybe you can help me think of more places to apply."

"Okay." He sprawled on the sofa with a yawn and grabbed the remote to the TV.

She slid into the chair at the computer desk in the family room. "Where's Mom?"

"Running errands, I think."

She logged onto her e-mail account. There were six new messages. Holding her breath, heart racing, she opened the inbox. And slumped.

Joke e-mails and spam.

She'd sent a couple dozen applications over the past week, but she'd only heard back from three so far. All negative. *Thank you for your application. We currently have no available positions. We will keep your application on file for future consideration.*

Reminding herself that patience was a virtue, she stood and stretched. A celebrity news story was airing about the reality show *Soulmates*, and it caught her eye. She was suddenly face-to-face with the guy in the magazine she'd seen at Grace's apartment the other day. Ethan Glass.

He was even more gorgeous on TV than he'd been in the photographs. "Ahem."

Lucy spun around to see her mother, Linda Kendrick, watching her, arms crossed, an amused look on her face. "Oh! Hi, Mom. I didn't hear you come in."

Her mom laughed. "Obviously. I thought for sure I'd find you glued to that computer, looking for a job."

Lucy followed her into the kitchen and slid into a chair. "I was just checking before you walked in, but no takers so far." She sighed and propped her chin on her hand. "Rejection bites, even over the Internet."

Her mom sorted through the day's mail. "It's early yet. You need to give people time to sort through candidates and evaluate things."

"I know. I'm just ready to move on to the next phase of my life now that school's finally over."

"It will happen sooner than you think and a whole lot sooner than I want to think about. In the meantime, enjoy your time at home with us. Let's see—bills, bills, and more bills. Oh. Here's something addressed to you, Lucy." She handed her a large, thick envelope that had been under the grocery store mailers.

Lucy straightened quickly, examined the envelope, and then let out a shriek. "It's from a television network, and it's too thick to be a rejection letter."

Brigham, alerted by the noise, came in and hovered over her shoulder.

"I asked Allie and Grace to send my application to some networks— you know, working on sitcoms, news, whatever jobs might be available there. I wonder what this could be." Shaking with impatience, she ran her finger under the glued flap and drew out the enclosed papers.

"Dear Ms. Kendrick," she read aloud, "we are pleased to inform you that you have been selected as a contestant on the upcoming reality dating series *Soulmates*. Taping is scheduled to begin—"

"Wait a minute," her mom interrupted. "Did you just say *contestant?*"

An uneasy feeling curled in the pit of Lucy's stomach, replacing her euphoria. She quickly scanned the rest of the letter then flipped the page up to see what was in the stack of papers beneath. It included a basic itinerary, a suggested apparel list, disclosure and privacy agreements, contracts. Now she was shaking for an altogether different reason. Her eyes returned to the cover letter, and she started reading it aloud again.

"Dear Ms. Kendrick, we are pleased to inform you that you have been selected as a contestant on the upcoming reality dating series *Soulmates*. Taping is scheduled"—her jaw dropped—"it's in less than a week." She stared at her mom, her mind working, then she continued reading. "We have provided an envelope for the overnight express return of the enclosed contracts . . . Upon receipt of these documents, a courier will deliver your airline tickets. We look forward to having you join us on the debut season of *Soulmates*. Yours sincerely, Curt Myers, Executive Producer." She dropped the letter into her lap and looked up in astonishment.

"Cool," Brigham said.

"Did you just say *contestant?*" Her mother repeated. Her voice had been a little soft and shocked sounding when she'd started the question but had reached a pretty high pitch by the time she'd said the last syllable. "What on earth is this all about, Lucy?"

Lucy didn't immediately answer. Her mind flashed back to that afternoon when her two alleged best friends had agreed to send her application out wherever they could. Allie had been in the beanbag chair, Grace on the couch thumbing through a magazine with an article about the millionaire who was going on a dating show. Then her mind flashed to the news story she'd just watched about Ethan Glass. She reread the cover letter in disbelief.

"Lucy?"

"I'm not sure, Mom," Lucy said as she grabbed her purse and dug for her car keys. "But I have a sneaking suspicion that Allie and Grace have some explaining to do."

* * *

A few hours later, sitting in her car outside her home, Lucy found herself facing a dilemma. When she'd confronted Allie and Grace and told them she'd been chosen to be a contestant, Grace's jaw had dropped and Allie had squealed. Then they'd jumped up and down hysterically for several minutes, pulling at Lucy to get her to jump up and down with them. Then they'd pored over all of the documents together.

Allie had given Lucy a pep talk with an endlessly long list of reasons Lucy should do the show. She'd started with Lucy's acknowledged Achilles' heel: the opportunity for travel and adventure. She'd be going to Hollywood and staying in a mansion. If she made it past the first episode, she might bungee jump or skydive or ride in a helicopter. They did those kinds of things on reality TV. And if she didn't make it past the first evening? Then, Allie had argued, Lucy could do what she'd said she was going to do after she graduated from Arizona State—go to Disneyland. Lucy had laughed at that. Allie had skirted around the issue of the *Soulmate* himself, knowing that vying for the affections of some celebrity millionaire held less appeal to Lucy than the other arguments. Her chances with the guy were practically nonexistent, so it was only a secondary consideration anyway.

Then Grace had taken her turn at Lucy. She'd pinned Lucy down on the fact that she hadn't gotten anywhere with her job searches yet. She'd reminded her that this reality show was temporary and would give her some time—some fun time—while her job applications were reviewed. Grace's logic had closely paralleled her mother's earlier observations. Eight weeks was the full time required for the entire taping schedule, if by some miracle Lucy made it to the end of the competition. It would probably take a couple of weeks to hear back from the companies she'd contacted, and that matched closely with how long Lucy figured she would last as a contestant.

What to do? Ironically, once she'd talked to her friends and gotten past her shock and annoyance over the stunt they'd pulled, she was intrigued by the idea. She had no intention of really competing for this guy, this Ethan Glass. What could they possibly have in common? He played in the big leagues. She was a small town girl, a Mormon girl no less, who only wanted to spread her wings a little before she married and started a family. She also wanted someone who understood the word *forever* when it came to marriage and family, and she was certain that person wasn't Ethan Glass. "Forever," where she came from, was a lot longer than "'til death do us part."

Lucy grabbed the packet of documents sitting on the car seat next to her. Privacy agreements, preliminary shooting schedules, suggested wardrobe essentials—and less than a week to pull it all together. It was a good thing, Lucy thought wryly, that she had a couple of good friends—good and *guilty* friends—who had assured her they would be more than willing to help her pull everything together if she decided to do it.

She would run it past her folks first before making her decision.

As she walked through the kitchen door, Brigham's voice broke through her thoughts. "Here comes the TV star!"

David Kendrick, Lucy's father, looked up from the newspaper he was reading. "I think Mom made a plate for you, Lucy, and put it in the fridge. She wasn't sure how long you'd be."

Lucy brushed a kiss on the side of her father's face, stuck her tongue out at her grinning brother, and opened the fridge.

She'd just placed the plate of grilled chicken and broccoli into the microwave when her mother walked into the room. "Oh! You're finally back," she said as Lucy set the timer and pushed the start button. "As you can see, we waited for you just like one pig waits for another."

"That's okay. Years of having Brig as a little brother have taught me to love pigs." She heard a grunt and only had a moment to react before an unidentified missile flew from the family room into the kitchen. She ducked as a white athletic sock, expertly rolled into a ball, barely missed her head and slid across the counter. She grabbed it, stretched it with both hands, and walked into the family room, which was connected to the kitchen by an island with barstools.

She snapped her brother's backside with the sock as he lay sprawled on the sofa, laughing and cringing and dodging her. Then Brigham grabbed her arm and tossed her to the floor, trying to tickle her.

Nearly out of breath but still laughing, she managed to escape and plant a big smacking kiss on him, making him splutter in mock horror, then gave him a cocky look and swaggered back to the kitchen to retrieve her dinner from the microwave.

Yeah, she still had it, baby brother. Take that.

Her dad, who'd intentionally ignored the entire uproar, folded his paper and laid it on the kitchen table. "Mom says you got some interesting mail today."

"Uh-huh." She stabbed the chicken breast and sliced off a bite. "Definitely unexpected, that's for sure."

"Yeah." Brigham piped up from the sofa, where he'd resumed his couch potato status. "She's going to be on a new dating show. Only I think they made a mistake. She was really supposed to be freak of the week on *Circus World's Secret Oddities*."

Lucy looked up from carving off a bite of chicken. "You're a genius, Einstein. Now be a good boy and let the grown-ups talk, or I might have to take you down again." She followed up the threat by making smooching sounds at him.

"Sick! Okay, okay!" He laughed and started channel surfing with the volume down low enough that he could still hear their conversation.

"Where'd Mom go? Oh, good, you're here," Lucy said as her mother walked back into the room. "I want to talk to you and Dad about this TV stuff. I looked over the papers with Allie and Grace. They confessed to their crime, by the way. The show is called *Soulmates*, and the big masculine prize is some guy named Ethan Glass."

"Ethan Glass?" Her dad was suddenly interested. "As in Glass Enterprises?"

"Ethan Glass—as in I don't know, but he's some millionaire celebrity hotshot. Allie said they had to fill out my basic info, attach a photo, and answer some questions about me. Gracie said she made Allie answer them like they thought I would. Apparently," Lucy added wryly, "*I* did a good job of answering those questions because I was chosen to be one of twenty-five women who will compete to become Ethan Glass's so-called soulmate."

Lucy's dad's eyebrows drew down in thought. Her mom glanced at him then at Lucy. Her fingers knotted together on the kitchen table. "You aren't actually considering doing this, are you?" she asked.

"I don't know. Maybe. I mean, what's the harm? Chances are, I won't last beyond the first day. And I think it would be really cool to see what it's like behind the scenes on a television show. Seeing it all firsthand would be amazing. And if I actually make it on any dates with this guy—which I highly doubt—I might get to do something I wouldn't dream of ever doing otherwise—"

"That's what worries me," her dad muttered.

"Like skiing off a glacier or something." Lucy shot him an exasperated look. "I probably won't last a day or even a week, but it's a week to experience something new." She turned to her mother. "But I want to know what you and Dad think."

Her mom cleared her throat, and glanced at her dad. "Well, honey, I think I can understand its appeal to you. I know how much you want to experience life and explore the world around you. I have to admit, I'm more than a little hesitant about sending you off to do this, competing for the affection of a total stranger, especially where there will be cameras documenting every move and every word. I've watched some of these shows—" She shot a warning look at Lucy's dad when his eyebrows rose. "Don't say anything, David. It's not like I watch them all the time." She turned back to Lucy. "And I know they're going to be looking for drama and controversy. They might try to stir the pot a little at your expense." She smiled ruefully. "What can I say? I don't want to see you get hurt."

"Oh, Mom." Lucy rose from her chair and hugged her mother. "I love you too."

Her dad cleared his throat. "I have to echo your mother's concerns. I'm your father. I'm the guy who likes to polish his shotgun in the living room when your dates come calling." Lucy's eyes rolled skyward. He'd never done anything like that in his life. "I'm not crazy about the idea of sending you to Hollywood to deal with people who won't have your best interest at heart, and the loss of privacy makes me uncomfortable.

"Bottom line though: you have to do what you think is right for *you*, honey." David leaned forward and clasped his hands together on the kitchen table. "We can express our opinions, and we hope you would consider them as you make your decision. But we've also raised you to be a responsible, moral young woman. We trust you. I know"—he looked at his wife—"*we* know you want to experience some of the great, wide world outside of Eagle Bluff. We understand that. Heck, it's normal. If I were your age, I'd want to do it too. And if you think this opportunity is a way to do some of that, then fine. If it's the first step on your journey toward building your future, then do it. All we ask is that you do what we've always taught you to do first, ever since you were a little girl. Go over the facts, the pros and cons. Ask us any questions you want. Listen to what your heart is telling you. And then—"

"I know. Study it out in my mind, ask in prayer if it's right, then wait for the Lord to answer. Seems kind of strange, praying about something that's basically a glorified vacation, but if it'll make you and Mom feel better, I'll do it."

Her dad smiled affectionately and gave her hand a squeeze. "That's my girl."

* * *

Ethan slid into the saddle and nudged Raphael forward. The Appaloosa tossed his head and nickered. "Easy, old friend." Ethan reached down to pat the horse's neck. "You'll get your chance to stretch your legs. Let's deal with the family first." The morning sky was the vibrant blue he remembered; the air was infused with a crisp bite of pine and the pungent scent of livestock. He took a deep breath, filling his lungs with fresh air.

Raphael picked his way along the dirt path for a while. A pair of squirrels skittered past on their busy search for breakfast. A light breeze riffled Ethan's hair and moderated the morning sun's attempt to heat his shoulders.

He could finally see a couple of horses grazing near a copse of trees just ahead. His father and brother would be at the stream that lay behind them, getting in a little fishing before they started the day's chores. He dismounted, leaving Raphael to forage with the others, and made his way through the trees.

When Ethan found them, his father and brother were lounging silently on the bank, watching the movement of the water as well as the movement under the water. Seated between them was a small girl gripping a child-sized pole in her hands and wearing a ball cap that sported moose antlers on the sides.

Ethan brushed aside a branch and stepped into the clearing. His niece's moose-antlered head spun around at the noise, a no-nonsense scowl scrunching her tiny features.

"Shh!" she whispered, whipping a finger up to her puckered lips. "You're scaring away all the fish!" Ironically, her words were delivered with a dramatic crescendo, and Ethan had to cough back laughter.

He stooped and kissed her puckered lips. "Hey, Beans. Catch any good ones yet?"

In a flash, she grinned, dropped her pole, and wrapped both arms around his leg. "I just caught *you!*" she cried, disregarding her own words of warning. Ethan's brother nimbly snagged her pole before it slid into the creek. Ethan sat down next to his father and pulled Brianna onto his lap.

"Does this mean you're done fishing, Beans?" Jacob Glass, Ethan's brother, asked his daughter.

She was busy cramming her moose hat onto Ethan's head. "Nope."

"You're up earlier than I expected you to be," Jedediah Glass said. "Word is, you got in pretty late last night."

"I booked a later flight than I'd originally planned. There were a few loose ends at work I wanted taken care of before taping for the show begins."

Jake snorted. Ethan kicked him.

Jedediah Glass, family patriarch, removed his beat-up cowboy hat, scratched his head, returned the hat to its original spot, and said nothing. Brianna experimented to see if her moose hat would look better on Ethan if it were on backward. The morning was silent except for the rumble of the creek and the humming that escaped from Brianna as she tipped her head from side to side, evaluating her handiwork.

"What do you think, Beans?" Ethan asked.

"I think your head's too big," she said matter-of-factly.

Jake snorted again.

Ethan grinned, but he still took advantage and kicked his brother again.

The silence returned. Ethan knew the routine. His father spoke when he spoke, in his own good time, with as few words as possible. "I think you've got more freckles now than when I was here last," Ethan said to Brianna.

"I do not!" The scowling, scrunchy face was back. "Freckles are yuck."

Ethan glanced at Jake, who only shrugged. "Well, I love freckles, especially yours. Let's count them and see if I can find extra freckles to love." Ethan placed his forefinger on her cheek. "One," he said. "Are you going to help me count?"

"One," she grumbled.

He moved his finger over slightly to the next freckle. "Two." He waited for her to join in.

"Two."

"Three," he said.

A pouty lower lip stuck out farther. "Boys don't like freckles."

Ethan looked at his brother again. *Where is she getting this?* he tried to ask telepathically. *She's only four.* Jake grimaced and shook his head. Old Jed didn't move a muscle.

"That's not true, Beans. I just told you I love your freckles."

"You're not a boy. You're *old.*"

She looked so serious he bit the inside of his cheek—hard—to keep his expression neutral. After all the women he'd met the past couple of years and all of the fawning and flirting he'd been subjected to, it had taken less than ten minutes for his niece to put him in his place. He had a big head. He was old. He was not a worthy male in her eyes.

Wound to the heart.

"Any boy who doesn't like everything about you, including your freckles, doesn't deserve you."

She seared him with a look that clearly said she thought he was an imbecile. But Ethan Glass had never shied away from a challenge. He leaned close to her and whispered in her ear, "You *do* know what freckles are, don't you?"

She looked up at him with her terrifyingly intelligent, big, brown eyes. "What?" she loudly whispered back.

"Angel kisses." He drew out the word *angel* to make it sound magical.

Her face began to scrunch again.

"They visit you at night to make sure you are safe while you sleep. Some children are so special," he gently tugged a pigtail, "that the angels can't resist kissing them good night."

"Then the angels must *really* love Sally Hinsdale because she has freckles all over, even on her *legs*. And the boys call her Freckle Freak, and Danny Garrity pushed her down after snack time, and she skinned her knee, and it *bled*—"

Uh-oh.

Ethan looked at Jake, but he looked as clueless as Ethan felt. Old Jed still hadn't moved. The old man was no fool. He was leaving Ethan to get out of this mess on his own.

Brianna continued. "So if the angels *love* Sally so much, why do they let the boys call her Freckle Freak? Why didn't they stop Danny from—"

"Brie, let's you and me go ask your mama about that, now that we're all done fishing," Jake said.

"But I wasn't done fishing!"

"You are now. I think Uncle Eth here wants to talk to Grandpa about other stuff. Let's head back to the house and get some breakfast." He stood and brushed the dirt from the seat of his jeans.

Brianna was temporarily silenced. Then she turned her full attention to Ethan. "What other stuff, Uncle Eth?"

Ethan felt a crazy urge to hug her until she squeaked. He settled for kissing the end of her nose. "*Old* guy stuff."

"Ohhhh," she replied with all the wisdom of the ages.

Ethan started to lift her off his lap, reluctant to give up the innocent joy of holding her but relieved that he didn't have to answer any more of her questions.

"What old guy stuff?" she asked.

"Brianna Lynne, mind your pa. Go on with him now."

Jedediah had spoken.

"Okay." She planted a kiss on Ethan's cheek and then threw her arms around Jed's neck. "Bye, Poppy. Can we come fishing again tomorrow?"

"We'll see, honey. Now, go on with your pa." He ruffled her hair.

She planted a smooch right on the old man's kisser and then jumped up and grabbed Jake's hand. Ethan felt a stab of something that felt suspiciously like envy.

Ethan and his dad watched father and daughter disappear through the trees. Jed slid his hat back from his face. "That one's a pistol. Mind's always working." Ethan could see the slight upward slant of his mouth. "Keeps us on our toes, that's for sure."

"She's something else, all right."

"One of life's great blessings, grandchildren."

Ah. Here was the warm-up for the real subject.

More silence.

"Fish aren't biting this morning," Jed added.

Ethan picked up a pebble and studied it, rolling it around in his hand. He waited. Then he tossed it into the dirt, leaned back onto his elbows, and stared out across the creek to the meadow beyond.

Jed scratched at his cheek. "You really think you can find love on a TV show?"

And there it was.

"Anything's possible."

His father made a grunting sound that conveyed a healthy amount of skepticism.

"Heard the show's called *Soulmates*."

"You heard right."

"That what you're looking for?"

And there was the million-dollar question. "Right now, I'm looking to make the show a success for Curt. I'm looking to be open-minded about the women I meet on the show and the selection process we put in place. Whether I find a soulmate remains to be seen."

"Didn't ask you if you planned to find one. Asked if that was what you were looking for."

That stopped Ethan short. "Why wouldn't I be?"

His father turned and looked him square in the eyes for the first time that morning. "Because you haven't been, up 'til now."

Ethan returned his gaze. "Is it practical to look for something that may not even exist?"

"Is that what you think?"

"I don't know what I think. What does it mean? *Soulmate*?"

"Probably means different things to different people."

Ethan had expected his father to deliver part two of the pep talk he'd gotten from his mother—something along the lines of "It's past time you settled down and started a family"—not this cryptic conversation. "What do you think it means?"

"Doesn't matter what it means to me. Matters what it means to you."

"Is Mom your soulmate?"

Jed looked off into the distance. After a long pause, he answered. "Maybe."

His reply was ambiguous but still alarming. The part of Ethan who was the son of Jed and Ellen Glass, basking in the security of their long and stable marriage, reacted. "What do you mean, 'maybe'? Is everything okay between you and Mom?"

"Everything's fine. Just want you to make sure you know what you're looking for now that you've decided to look at all. So think about it some before you're surrounded by all those women."

Ethan nodded then stood and collected the fishing gear. Jed adjusted his hat to shade his eyes and then rose from the ground with agility uncommon in someone his age, and yet Ethan spotted stiffness in his movements that hadn't been there before. Age was catching up to his father, and it hurt to see it. His father was a good man and had always been Ethan's rock—even when Ethan hadn't wanted to stay home and work the ranch like he knew his father had hoped he would. "Got any advice?"

Jed looked at him, and Ethan saw a glimmer of something in his eyes before the crusty old cowboy demeanor slapped back in place. "A successful man like yourself doesn't need advice from an old hayseed." He paused. Ethan waited. "All you need to do is what you've been doing to be that successful man. As your father, I would add one thing: you've got to know how you want to spend your life before you can know who you want to spend it with. Whether or not you consider that woman your soulmate, only you can decide." He stopped then said, "Those horses are probably wishing they could stretch their legs a bit. What say we stow this gear and take them for a good run."

CHAPTER 4

OF ALL THE DAYS TO feel like someone is banging on a garbage can in my head, this is not the day, Lucy thought as she squinted at the bright California sky.

She'd hardly slept the last few nights. After talking to her parents just over a week ago, she'd gone to her room and had pored over the details in the packet. The network had needed her confirmation returned ASAP, which hadn't given her any wiggle room. She'd recognized her parents' concerns, but she'd also been admittedly intrigued by the whole thing. Really, how many people got a chance like this? It wasn't one she'd ever dreamed would happen to her. She was also a realist. The chance of anything happening romantically between her and this Ethan Glass was remote at best.

Her dad had done some research on Ethan Glass and Glass Enterprises, and he'd filled Lucy in on the basics. Mr. Glass was raised in Montana—on a ranch, no less—with his parents and younger brother. He'd gone away to college, apparently putting the rural life behind him. His younger brother managed the family spread, and relations with his folks and sibling were solid. Her dad had acted relieved when he'd told her that part. Ethan Glass wasn't exactly the guy next door, but family values counted for something, at least as far as her dad's peace of mind had been concerned.

Glass had flown through college on scholarship, a fact that had made Lucy jealous, and gotten his MBA as well. Then he'd turned a small nest egg into a modest investment and a modest investment into a lucrative deal. That deal had mushroomed into something even more substantial. Several million times more substantial. Her dad had scratched his head in wonder. A lot of people had business acumen, he'd said, but they didn't necessarily parlay it into something the magnitude of Glass Enterprises.

The information had reinforced Lucy's opinion that a man of Mr. Glass's power and savvy would not look twice at a small-town girl whose ambition at the moment was to visit Disneyland for the first time.

Ironically, the fact that she was no match for Ethan Glass was what had made her consider actually being on the show. It had freed her. With no expectations for romance, it had become an opportunity to travel while she waited for something more solid to appear on the horizon.

One final step though. One final, supremely important step. With that in mind, she'd knelt next to her bed. *Get on your knees and take it to the Lord*, her parents had always taught her. *If the decision is a good and right one, He will let you know in your heart. It will burn with rightness. If it's not, you'll know that too.*

So Lucy had prayed. She had poured out all of the pros and cons of the situation, her parents' concerns, her longing to spread her young adult wings and fly, her desire to do the right thing. It had taken a long time, but she had expressed it all in the prayer. And then, still on her knees, her head cradled on her crossed arms, she had waited.

She'd heard the wind blowing outside her bedroom window and the soft hum of the air conditioner. So she'd cleared her mind and listened with her heart instead. She'd felt herself relax. And then it had happened, as it had happened to her on other occasions.

It had started as calmness, a peace that had spread from her core like a pebble gently dropped into still water. Then a warm feeling had begun, a glowing ember that had grown warmer, stronger, and had made her heart leap. It was a perfect paradox—peaceful serenity coupled with a quiet, burning intensity.

She had received her answer.

So while on her knees, she'd prayed again—to say thank you. And then she'd stood, certain of her decision and grateful for the reassurance.

And then she'd overnighted her signed contracts back to the network.

So here she was in Southern California. She should be used to the brilliance of the afternoon sun; it wasn't so different from Arizona, after all. She put a hand up to shield her bleary eyes and squinted, looking through the crowds until she spotted someone holding a sign that said *Soulmates*. She hurried over to him.

After making her decision, she'd had to shift into high gear. She'd started by recruiting her mother, Allie, and Grace. She'd had to scramble to put together a wardrobe like the one suggested in her packet: a dozen cocktail dresses, formal and semiformal, playwear, swimwear, the list went on and on. They'd scavenged thrift stores and clearance racks, Allie and Grace had each donated last year's styles to the cause, and Lucy and her mother had spent hours altering everything. The cutting and unpicking and fitting sessions had gone on until late into the night and then begun again early each following day. Additionally, the network had e-mailed a variety of in-depth questionnaires to her with instructions to complete them and send them right back. One was a personality test, one assessed IQ, and one was a multipage, comprehensive questionnaire about all personal aspects of her life. Allie had told her that she and Grace had filled out something similar when they'd submitted her application, but theirs had been on a much smaller scale. Lucy had filled the questionnaires out as quickly and completely as she could, faxed them back, and returned to the unpicking.

Unfortunately, even with Allie and Grace pitching in, Lucy and her mother had worked nearly around the clock the last three nights to complete all of the alterations. Lucy was exhausted.

She dozed on the plane, but it had only taken the edge off her fatigue. Besides, it had been her first time on an airplane, so she'd found herself glued to the window, watching tiny cars and people and finally carpets of clouds beneath her, until sleep had eventually won. But it had been a short flight and, therefore, a short nap. Wishing she'd packed some ibuprofen in her purse, she hoisted it onto her shoulder and followed the young man with the *Soulmates* placard through the terminal to her waiting ride. He had beautiful bronze skin and was dressed in black, his glossy black hair tossed by the hazy blasts of exhaust the traffic spewed as it constantly sped past. He opened the door of the hybrid SUV parked at the curb, and she slid into its dark, cavernous interior.

Ah, but the tinted glass and air conditioning felt wonderful! Lucy sank heavily into the leather seat, closed her eyes, and sighed. If they'd included a cold glass of lemonade and some soft music, she would have called this heaven.

They wound through Los Angeles into the hills, past elegant homes surrounded by huge walls. Despite her fatigue, she was mesmerized by what she saw. Before she knew it, they were driving through a large iron gate that swung open as they approached. As the SUV proceeded along the drive, a sprawling mansion came into view. It was multilevel with a modern design and seemed to go on endlessly. The formal entrance had a portico that blended with the architecture, and large terra cotta pots overflowing with exotic flowers flanked the double doors. It took Lucy a moment to realize that the SUV had come to a stop.

"Here we are, Ms. Kendrick."

The young man with the black hair had stepped out of the car and was now holding the passenger door open for her. Grabbing her purse and summoning up her flagging courage, she slid across the seat and reached for his outstretched hand.

"Thanks. Please call me Lucy. And you're . . . ?"

"Kyle," was all he said as he ducked behind her to retrieve her bags from the back of the SUV.

Lucy turned to face the entrance, straightened her shoulders, and started forward. As she neared the steps, the doors opened, and a woman stepped outside. She was petite, with dark framed glasses and short, sleek hair the color of ripe raspberries. She was all Hollywood business, in a biscuit-colored skirt with a tiny black T-shirt, too-tall stilettos, and gobs of gold jewelry. Clutching a clipboard, she strode over to Lucy and stretched out her hand.

"You must be Lucy Kendrick. I'm Melanie Carlton, Curt Myers's associate producer." Her handshake was firm, brief, and all business as well. "Mr. Myers is the executive producer of *Soulmates*," she added as she turned and strode briskly up the steps to the portico, motioning for Lucy to follow. She opened the front door and beckoned Lucy inside.

The foyer was modern, spacious, and stylish, with lush foliage in planters that softened the overall effect. Lucy noticed cables coiled discreetly behind furnishings and stretched tightly along the floors against the walls. She could hear the humming of women's voices coming from somewhere, smooth talk punctuated by exclamations and laughter. Still all business, Ms. Carlton referred to her clipboard and glanced back at Lucy. "You're our last contestant to arrive, and with the party tonight, things are getting a little hectic. Let me give you a quick tour of *Soulmates* House and a rundown of our taping schedule for the next couple of days while Kyle gets your luggage, then you can freshen up and meet the other women."

She led Lucy into a large living room with Oriental furnishings. "Just so you are aware, official shooting begins this evening, so plan accordingly. The cocktail party is after dinner, and that's where all of you will be introduced to Ethan Glass.

"Mr. Glass will be sending ten of you home at the end of the evening. Nothing is scheduled for tomorrow morning, so you will have time to relax—*if* you're still around." She gave Lucy a cool assessing look.

Apparently Ms. Carlton assumed Lucy wouldn't make it past tonight's introductions. And despite the fact that Lucy had convinced herself of the same thing, it irritated her that this woman she'd barely met thought so too.

"This is the living room. We've arranged for a catered dinner this evening as a kind of kickoff celebration. You'll be meeting Mr. Myers and Dane Esplin, our director, and others of the crew. We will be taking you through some orientation then as well. After this evening—assuming you are still here, of course—you will each be responsible for cooking your own meals, together or separately. We will keep the kitchen and bar well stocked, and if you have any specific requests, just post a note on the fridge. We aim to make your time here pleasant."

Ms. Carlton's last line sounded rehearsed, like a dentist offering the ever-comforting "this won't hurt a bit."

"There are a few items we need to discuss, in case you missed them when you read the contract. You signed a confidentiality agreement. Anything that occurs during the production of the show is to be kept confidential. That is especially important, since the show is scheduled to begin airing while we're still in production but women will continually be eliminated from the show during that time frame.

"As a result, electronic devices are off-limits during your stay. Cell phone? Laptop?" She gave Lucy an inquiring look and put out her hand, palm up. Lucy handed her phone over. "Anything else? Good," she added when Lucy shook her head. "Also, remember you are restricted to *Soulmates* House and its grounds unless you are on a scheduled date or have made arrangements with either Curt or myself. And *that* should be considered only a rare exception to the rule. Now, through here is the kitchen . . ."

The kitchen was spacious, with professional appliances and an entire colony of gadgets. Over the center island hung assorted top-quality cookware. It was an airy room, with light natural woods and a large window overlooking the grounds. Cables snaked against the back wall and behind a large hutch, and a couple of small cameras hung near the ceiling, strategically aimed at the cooking area and dining table. Through the window, Lucy could see several women lounging and playing in a swimming pool that sparkled in the sun. The surrounding landscape looked natural and inviting, a tasteful balance of lawn and woods, openness and privacy.

"And through here are the laundry facilities; that door, there, is the main-floor bath. Through there is the formal dining area, and that"—she waived vaguely behind Lucy's shoulder—"is the game room and home theater. And now, if you'll follow me upstairs, I'll show you to your room."

Ms. Carlton strode quickly back to the main foyer and up a wide staircase. Lucy glanced around her, taking in the attention to detail in the design. Everything was perfect except for the cables and cameras. Too perfect, really. This wasn't anyone's home. No great person lived here, and the furnishings were probably rented for the show. It was a set, a make-believe part of reality TV.

Straightening her shoulders, she marched up the stairs behind the professional Ms. Carlton. "This is your assigned room for now. Don't unpack—other than what you'll need for tonight—until we know that you will be staying with us." Again, the assessing look. "You are sharing this room with"—she glanced at her clipboard—"Sara, Ashley, Lauren, and Rachel." Luggage and all manner of totes and travel bags cluttered the room. Her own bags stood just inside the door. "After tonight's cocktail party, the fifteen remaining women will be assigned permanent sleeping arrangements." She checked something off on her clipboard and smiled briefly. "So there you are. Make yourself comfortable. Do you have any questions?"

Probably, but Lucy's head was starting to throb again, so she just smiled and shook her head.

"Well, if you do, or if you need anything, let me know. And good luck, Ms. Kendrick—"

"Lucy."

"Lucy, then. Welcome to *Soulmates* House, Lucy. Make yourself at home."

Lucy looked around the bedroom after Ms. Carlton left. She knew she should pull her dress out of her suitcase to see if it needed ironing, but first she had to do something about her headache. Grabbing her overnight bag, she headed for the bathroom.

Except it wasn't simply a bathroom, not by Lucy's standards. It was a huge dressing room and wardrobe. The other girls had already taken advantage of the space, and fancy dresses and all manner of stockings and lacy things hung on the racks. Just beyond was the actual bathroom, which had a jetted tub, a glassed-in shower, and a vanity that could seat several women at once. Skylights and a high panel of windows that ran just below the ceiling gave the room a bright, airy feel. Lucy hunted through the overnight bag for her ibuprofen. She popped a couple in her mouth, cupped her hand under the running water of the faucet, and drank. She felt a little foolish lapping up water like a dog—it shouldn't be a big deal to head to the kitchen for a glass—but she wasn't up for any more encounters just yet. She needed a few minutes to recoup before she had to put her game face back on and meet the other girls. Just a few minutes, she thought, as she settled on a corner of one of the beds and curled up with a pillow.

* * *

Melanie Carlton escaped out the door, pulled her cell phone out of her pocket, and checked her text messages. There were three texts from Dane, and she'd only been gone for half an hour with the last contestant. She ran her fingers through her hair. They were all here—finally!—catering was set for tonight, and the temps were arranged for that as well as for the cocktail party. She'd been running since her feet had hit the floor this morning at six, and she wasn't close to being done yet. Dr. Lindstrom was due to arrive within the hour, and Curt had left the coddling of *Soulmates*' resident expert up to her. That was in addition to keeping Dane soothed and anticipating Curt's expectations—Curt, her boss, in fact, who was a great visionary but lousy detail person, in her opinion. Melanie knew full well who on this crew would be keeping the proverbial plates spinning through the taping of the show. She would.

She had been thrilled when she'd landed the job as associate producer of the new reality show, even though Curt was new to television. After he'd offered her the job and she'd accepted, he'd informed her that they were producing a reality *dating* show—he'd neglected to mention that little detail before—and the next words out of his mouth had been, "I'll be relying heavily on your background and experience." Not good, considering she'd embellished her résumé a bit.

She'd told herself it would be fine. Then she'd discovered that "relying heavily" meant she was expected to stay on top of a never-ending list of organizational details to keep everybody happy. Everybody—an inexperienced producer, an intense director, a shrink, a millionaire celebrity, and a houseful of bloodthirsty women—with a depressingly small staff at her disposal.

No problem.

Her phone buzzed. It was another text from Dane. *Tell J to recheck the lighting in the solarium.* Between Curt's delegation of *all* details to her and Dane's intense micromanaging, she was on the brink of losing her mind—even before they'd started taping. Another buzz, this time a text from Curt. *Is the fruit basket in Berta's room?*

Yes, for the hundredth time, she wanted to text back, *the fruit basket is there, the imported chocolates are there, the flowers are there.* Melanie knew there was pressure to keep Dr. Lindstrom happy. Curt had explained that the show's success hinged on a successful outcome, i.e., true *soulmate* love, which in turn hinged on all of the compatibility tests the contestants had taken and Dr. Lindstrom's interpretation of those results. He'd also explained that the show's success was just a launching point for the Internet personals package they were developing.

Her phone buzzed again. Dane again. *Is Glass here yet?*

Somebody please shoot me now, she thought. *Please.*

Dane knew as well as she did that Mr. Glass was a half mile from *Soulmates* House at the rented bungalow he was using during the taping. Mr. Glass had made it clear he would arrive at nine that evening and was not to be disturbed until then. But Dane was antsy.

Yeah, sure, keeping everybody happy was going to be a piece of cake.

She ignored the text and walked across the grounds to the guesthouses. How had it come to this? She was young, bright, and had a degree in journalism under her belt. She'd wanted to work her way into network or cable news and had fought for any job she could find that would help her chart that course. She'd had to kiss a little booty along the way too to try to earn favors from various people in power. But things had taken a decided turn south, and now she was here, working on a reality *dating* show, of all things. She was spending her days *not* digging into hard-hitting news stories, *not* honing her own on-air skills, wearing holes in the soles of her Manolo Blahniks. And now she had a houseful of females adding to her list of daily headaches—females who were either looking to land a hunky rich guy or get their fifteen minutes of fame, in her not-so-humble opinion. As the person who was busting her chops to make life even easier for them, it didn't sit well.

She hadn't introduced that last contestant to the other women in the house. But Melanie had already put in a full day's work and was facing at least another ten hours overseeing any and all details for the cocktail party, so she wasn't about to worry if the last girl to arrive had to meet people on her own. Especially when odds were she wouldn't even be here tomorrow.

Thankfully, the guesthouse was empty of crewmembers at the moment. She walked into her room and flopped down onto her bed, toeing the pumps off of her suffering feet. She had a break coming. Probably about a hundred breaks, considering how few she'd taken the last couple of weeks, not counting overtime. It was time for the crew to set up in the house, and they could live without her for thirty minutes. They were double-checking lighting and marking camera angles; Curt and Dane were busy fine-tuning questions for Glass and the women. There would be on-camera interviews as well as a couple of floating cameramen whose sole purpose was to catch anything that could be developed into good on-air drama. Curt had also told her to watch for potential story arcs to drive each week's episode.

Like she didn't have enough to do already.

Well, she thought grimly as she relaxed into her pillow and threw an arm over her eyes, she would do whatever it took to make this reality dating show the most talked about new show of the season. She would earn her place with the networks, no matter what. That was what would make *her* happy. People in the business would be speaking of this show—and her—for years. She felt her eyelids grow heavy. Yes, they would have drama and controversy, and those who really knew how things worked would know it was because of her efforts, her brilliance. She smiled to herself as she settled quickly into her power nap.

CHAPTER 5

LUCY AWAKENED WITH A START and realized she wasn't alone in the room. Struggling out of her sleep-induced fog, she focused on her watch and groaned. She'd slept for three hours. She'd only expected to close her eyes for a few minutes when she'd curled up on the bed. Still, ibuprofen and some shut-eye had done wonders for her headache.

A power-blonde glanced up from her suitcase and narrowed her eyes at Lucy. "We haven't met, have we? I'm Sara, and she," she pointed to a petite girl with curly hair, "is Lauren."

"I'm Lucy. I just got in this afternoon." She pulled herself into a sitting position and stifled a yawn. Open suitcases littered the place, and tops and shorts flew off bodies while someone yelled first dibs on the shower. Still groggy, it took Lucy a moment to adjust to the scene as the women tossed dirty clothes aside and grabbed clean ones, laughing and shrieking with excitement.

"Over there is Rachel," Sara added as Rachel waved briefly. "Ashley is the one in the shower."

"Nice to meet you all." It felt like the first day of college, except with a big dose of Hollywood glamour. The girls were gorgeous. Lucy's college experience had started in the dorm, though, not a sorority, and as a general rule, her roommates had been the quiet, unassuming types who haunted the library.

She quickly found herself caught up in the frenzy of the moment and joined in as they held dresses up for feedback from each other. Soon they were all sharing makeup, testing perfumes, suggesting eye color, fixing each other's hair, and trying on jewelry. Allie would be having the time of her life here, Lucy thought, and her brothers would be rolling their eyes and dragging her outside for a game of pickup basketball.

She was putting on earrings when Sara gave her a critical once-over. "That's an unusual dress." It was a little Oriental thing Grace had found, and Lucy had instantly fallen for it. It fit nicely and was comfortable, with short sleeves, a Mandarin collar, and a row of decorative fasteners down the side. The fabric was a gold silk embroidered in a deeper gold with a small Chinese motif. The midcalf hemline had a fun little slit on the side that went to her knee. When she'd tried it on at home, her mom had said she looked like she'd stepped out of an old war movie. Here, alongside these girls, with her long, straight hair pulled up in a sleek twist and held in place with a funky gold clip, she felt exotic, at least for a girl from Small Town, USA.

Until Sara put her under the microscope.

She flipped her long, platinum hair over her shoulder and shook her head. "Lucy. It's Day One of *Get the Rich Guy*. Ethan Glass is even financing the show, from what I heard. You'll have a better shot at staying in the game by strutting your stuff more—unless you're trying to make it easy for the rest of us. I mean, the guy dates actresses and models." She laughed and looked at the other girls, who had stopped what they were doing to listen.

There wasn't a thing in Lucy's wardrobe that would strut her stuff the way Sara thought she should strut her stuff, the way Sara was presently strutting her own stuff. Even now she was smoothing her stretchy little dress down her curves and checking herself in the mirror. But Lucy's personal modesty was important to her—and that could easily translate into *invisible* in this situation.

She had gone the rounds with Allie and Grace as they'd thrown together her wardrobe. With time working against them and with Ethan Glass and a television viewing audience as motivators, Allie and Grace had been particularly vocal about what they thought she should wear. But Lucy had held firm on any modesty issues that arose. Her modesty had meant altering outfits, which in turn meant finding mix and match items, hunting through consignment shops and thrift stores, all while Lucy and her mom ripped and measured and brainstormed and sewed.

"I think your dress is cute, kind of like you're a Chinese nun or something," Lauren said. "Well, not *exactly* like a nun," she added when everyone stared at her.

"Are there Chinese nuns?" Ashley asked.

"Oh, probably." Sara smiled, obviously happy with what she was seeing in the mirror. "I guess you'll have to find your own edge with Ethan wherever you can tonight."

There was a soft knock at the door, and Lauren opened it. Kyle, the quiet, dark-haired, bronze-skinned guy who'd brought in Lucy's luggage, stood there. He cleared his throat. "It's time for dinner," he announced.

Lucy smiled at him. He gave her a shy smile in return and glanced at each of the girls before turning and walking down the corridor. His cheekbones and the tips of his ears glowed pink. Had he actually blushed? That was kind of sweet, Lucy thought.

"He is *so* weird," Rachel said.

"He never says anything to anyone—have you noticed that? And he's always staring at us." This from Ashley.

"He's been nice to me," Lucy said. A snort from Rachel only made her more emphatic in her defense of him. "I think he's shy."

Rachel tossed her head and checked her lipstick one last time. "Whatever." She ignored Lucy and turned toward the others. "Shall we go, ladies?"

Lucy straightened her spine and joined the other girls as they followed Kyle down the hallway. *It all begins right now*, Lucy thought. Time for her mantra. *This is an adventure. Only an adventure.* An opportunity to try something new, meet new people, see new places. She leaned on the assurance that she was supposed to be here for some reason. She would discover what that reason was. She would have fun. There would be tense moments, she knew. Throw twenty-five women together to compete for the same hunky prize and there were bound to be tense moments. But she intended to focus on making new friends and memories that would last a lifetime because she knew Ethan Glass might look once, but he would never look at her twice. And if she looked twice at him, it was only because he was so handsome. What red-blooded girl wouldn't? It didn't mean a thing.

She walked down the hall toward the dining room and the real beginning of her adventure. She had no strategy that involved strutting her stuff or otherwise. This was all about meeting new people, experiencing new things, and enjoying herself. And finding the answers to two questions: Why had she felt so strongly that she was supposed to be here? And when would she be visiting Disneyland?

* * *

"You ready, Eth?"

Ethan glanced over his shoulder at Curt, who was leaning against the doorframe, then returned his attention to the mirror and straightened his tie. Despite Curt's relaxed stance, Ethan could tell he was humming with excitement. "As ready as I'll ever be."

"Good. The girls are pumped, Ethan. Really excited to meet you. We went over the rules with them at dinner. The crew's ready and in place. We're just waiting for the man of the hour."

"And Dr. Lindstrom?"

"She's here. She'll be watching the monitors in the trailer and taking notes. She'll also be feeding questions and suggestions to Melanie for the on-camera interviews. At the end of the evening, when it's time for you to cut the ranks, the good doctor will meet with you, review the girls' scores, and share her observations. Any questions?"

"Not too many at the moment." He grabbed his suit coat and headed to the door. He already had a preliminary list of his top fifteen candidates in his head. He was using tonight's party as a means of confirming, or refuting, his initial decisions. He was fairly confident in his selections but would reserve final judgment until the end of the evening. He had a lot of experience reading between the lines of résumés. He'd hired enough employees over the years to know that interviewing—in any form—was an important step in the process. It was one thing to look at a picture and read biographical data and another thing entirely to talk to the person. And this wasn't about hiring an engineer or accountant; he was looking for his so-called soulmate. It couldn't be done on paper, despite Dr. Lindstrom's battery of tests. It had to be done in person. Tonight was about chemistry and connection.

"It's almost nine now. We're giving you until midnight to get to know the women, although we can stretch that a little if necessary. Introductions will take place in the atrium." He rubbed his hands together briskly and grinned. "This is it, Ethan. We're on our way."

"Uh-huh. You're on your way to fame and fortune. I, however, am on my way to the gallows—the firing squad, the electric chair, the gurney with that tragically lethal needle . . ."

Curt didn't bite. He just laughed. "More like you're on your way to the buffet table or the candy store. And the women are half in love with you already."

"Wow," he deadpanned. "You think so?"

Curt grinned, not catching Ethan's sarcasm. "Look in the mirror, old friend. What's not to love?" He checked his own reflection and smoothed down his hair with a casual hand. "Besides, they knew you were the *Soulmate* before they applied to be on the show. That says something."

"I'm messing with you, Curt."

But in reality, he wasn't convinced there was a single woman out of the twenty-five who was there for the real Ethan Glass. Not Ethan Glass, the complete man. That man currently came with some pretty dazzling trimmings, the type that tended to blind people.

Curt stopped in the doorway and put his hand on Ethan's arm. "Look, we've been friends a long time. A *long* time. I know it's your head on a platter. You're the *Soulmate*. I get that that puts you in the crosshairs." He paused briefly in his comments as they strode down the steps toward the waiting limo. "But it's my name at the top right next to yours. I'm in it neck and neck with you."

He looked over Ethan's shoulder at some unknown horizon. "I won't lie. I want this to succeed—like, man, I can taste it. This is my big shot. I already owe you for giving me that much." He reached for the door handle and paused. "The product's good, Eth. We've done our homework. If you're looking for her, there's a good shot she's here. Your soulmate. But if she's not, no pressure, okay?"

If you're looking for her. It brought to mind what Old Jed had said. *Didn't ask you if you planned to find a soulmate. Asked if that was what you were looking for, because you haven't been, up 'til now.*

Curt pulled the door shut behind them after they climbed into the limo, and it started down the drive. "If things on *Soulmates* don't work out like I think they will, like I have *confidence* they will, you'll be old news by summer reruns. You can end things with her after the show airs. People will forget, you'll move on to greener pastures, and our online personals website will still live happily ever after."

"Curt," Ethan said, sounding fairly patient, he thought, all things considered. "I'm committed to the project. If she's here, I'll find her. If she's not, I'll consider options that are in the best interest for everyone involved, including the success of the show. Now relax. Anyone would think you were the one expecting to be married at the end of this."

The limo pulled into the gated drive of the mansion. It was ablaze with light—not the warm, inviting light that tended to glow from windows at nightfall but the artificial daylight of an amusement park. Crew were still dragging cables, adjusting equipment, and yelling last-minute directions at each other. Ethan could see Dane Esplin, director of *Soulmates*, speaking and gesturing to Curt's redheaded assistant about something and her nodding and writing furiously on a clipboard. Dane glanced in their direction, recognition and relief washing over his manic expression before he turned and headed briskly toward them.

Ethan shot a look at Curt, who had targeted a cameraman wielding bulky equipment as a means of escape, and hissed so only Curt could hear, "Coward!"

Curt shot a standard thumbs up and grinned before jogging off in the cameraman's direction. Ethan turned back and smiled a polite greeting at Dane.

"Glass! Good, you're here. We can begin." He extended a hand to Ethan and pumped it vigorously. "Melanie!" he yelled over his shoulder. "Find Rick." Rick Madison was the series host. "Come with me, Glass. You're set up in the atrium. I want the two of us to touch base with Rick and Dr. Lindstrom. Berta is . . ." He looked frantically in the redhead's direction and mouthed "Lindstrom." Even from a distance, Ethan saw her roll her eyes as she pointed at a large trailer at the far end of the drive.

Dane Esplin was a man in high octane mode at the moment and seemed to thrive on it. "I've already spoken with Dr. Lindstrom," Ethan said. "Thank you. You said the atrium was located . . . ?"

"Ah, yes. Follow me."

They headed along the north side of the mansion, which was less brightly lit, and followed a stone path past the swimming pool and patio toward a glassed-in room with open French doors. The stage lighting inside created a soft halo over the glass enclosure as it filtered through the dense foliage within.

He and Dane walked up the couple of steps and through the French doors into the atrium. To his left, he could see a display of tropical plants and flowers. Water bubbled softly and drew his attention to a small fountain nestled into the greenery. It was beautiful, serene, and lush—a veritable garden of love. Like where Adam met Eve. Soulmates.

The greenery and lighting were arranged to create the spot where he would meet the women tonight. The opposite wall from where they were standing was the entrance that connected to the house. Those French doors were propped wide open and were disguised with more plants.

To the right of that door and opposite the backdrop of plants was a spray of opaque umbrellas set to soften the lighting for the cameras. Electrical cables coiled around them like snakes. *Even in this little Eden*, Ethan thought wryly, *there appear to be snakes*. It would pay to keep that in mind. Then he realized Dane was speaking again.

"Each woman will enter there," he gestured to the entry from the mansion, "descend the stairs, and walk toward you—here." He pointed to the spot Ethan had already identified. "You introduce yourselves, blah blah blah, and she will exit the atrium—there." He pointed to the exterior door through which they'd entered. "You need to keep the introductions pleasant and short so things seem natural. I had Ms. Carlton come up with some ice-breakers—questions you can ask if you find yourself running dry. It'll keep you sounding fresh meeting that many women."

"Good idea."

"We'll be over there, next to the lights, watching the action. Once each woman is videotaped, she'll return to the house. We have additional cameras set to capture their reactions after meeting you. We are also going to shoot them as they mingle with each other, waiting for you to join them. Excuse me, won't you?" Dane stepped away from him, pulled on a headset, and began a rapid stream of instructions to someone.

Ethan wandered over to the set and ran his fingers through the fountain, fingering a smooth, wet pebble. His life was taking an odd turn toward fiction. What had started as a simple business deal had put him on a crazy path. But that was the way things went sometimes. He would approach his role as *Soulmate* with his usual business acumen. He would keep his head, and—Curt was right—they'd find success one way or another. He'd make sure of it.

Rick joined them, and he and Rick were quickly blocked for the opening scenes of the first episode. Dane and Melanie moved over behind the lights, and Dane said, "Quiet, everyone! Three, two . . ." His outstretched fingers mimicked his countdown. One finger. He pointed at Rick.

Rick smiled warmly at the camera. "Good evening. I'm Rick Madison. Welcome to *Soulmates* . . ."

Ethan watched Rick glide through his performance, shift his focus from camera one to camera two for different angles, and deliver his lines with charisma and credibility. Then it was Ethan's cue.

"And now, let's meet our *Soulmate*: Ethan Glass." Rick shook Ethan's hand after he walked on-camera to stand by Rick. Director Dane smiled and nodded encouragement, like Ethan had performed some brilliant feat with those simple moves. He looked at Rick, remembering not to glance at the camera—camera one, to be exact—and waited for the questions from Rick to begin.

"Welcome to *Soulmates*, Ethan. How're you doing so far?"

"Thanks, Rick. I'm good. It's great to be here."

"As you know, there are a lot of reality TV shows out there, including reality dating shows. What was it that impressed you about this particular show and convinced you to become the first *Soulmate*?"

"Well, I was intrigued by the show's premise, which included using various compatibility tests to find women who might be well suited to me and vice versa."

"And this is unique?"

"It is—at least on television. Some matchmaking companies use the concept to a certain extent. *Soulmates* takes that concept even further by incorporating a large array of tests for the women to take and comparing each woman's scores with my own."

"Sounds a little scientific for a dating show. Isn't *Soulmates* supposed to be about romance?"

"Absolutely. The tests, of course, are only the beginning. How much easier would it be, Rick, if you walked into a room, into a social gathering, and knew at a glance which women there had common interests with you or similar life goals to your own?"

Rick chuckled good-naturedly. "Well, my lovely wife might complain. But I can see where a single man would find that to be an advantage. And a single woman."

"Exactly. And that is the intent of this particular show, to demonstrate that a little knowledge can make finding that special someone a lot easier." He paused then puffed out a half laugh. "I hope!"

Rick added an all-knowing grin and nod. "I'm sure you do!"

"That does not, however, relegate *Soulmates* to the oatmeal excitement of an arranged marriage, at least I certainly hope not. I will be looking for the woman with whom I also feel electricity and chemistry, and where common interests create a solid foundation upon which to build the romance."

"The science and the art of love combined."

"Yes. I am looking forward to meeting these women, finding those connections, and exploring the possibilities."

Rick turned to face camera one. "We'll learn more about these compatibility tests, how the women scored, and what that all means throughout this season of *Soulmates*. And later, we will meet Dr. Berta Lindstrom, our relationship expert, who will be helping Ethan find his *Soulmate*."

Camera two. "The contestants are just as excited to meet him and explore the possibilities as he is. Let's introduce them to Ethan now."

* * *

Lucy was contestant number seventeen. They'd drawn numbers at dinner, and she'd pulled seventeen. Not an ideal spot. The first contestants to meet Ethan might make a great initial impression. The final ones had a chance at staying in his memory. Instead, she would be part of the potentially unmemorable middle of the pack. And since her non-stuff-strutting dress wasn't about to wow Ethan Glass, apparently, picking seventeen had lowered her odds even further. That meant she needed to relax, decide if she wanted to ride Splash Mountain or Pirates of the Caribbean first tomorrow, and simply enjoy tonight's adventure for what it was. Amazing how her stress level dropped at the thought of Minnie Mouse waving to her in the morning.

Or maybe not.

She'd prayed and felt confident in the answer she'd received about being here. The funny thing about prayers and answers to prayers was they didn't always come with clear explanations or full instructions on how to proceed. She only knew it had felt right when she'd decided to be here—once she'd gotten over her initial shock at what her friends had done, that is. But the prayer and the reassurance she'd felt as a result could mean anything. Connections to a job that would put her on a solid career path, making new friends, having the chance to share her beliefs with someone.

And who was to say it might not introduce her to her soulmate? Yeah, that was the reason, all right. Ethan Glass was going to remember contestant number seventeen. Chances were, he'd be so overwhelmed by designer perfume and estrogen by the time they met that his eyes would be glazed over and she would only be part of an indecipherable blur of anxious femininity.

She'd met a lot of guys: friends of her brothers, to be exact, and she was comfortable around them. So it was crazy to feel so nervous right now. Except that meeting a good-looking millionaire on a national television show was a bigger deal than meeting some guy under the basketball hoop hanging on her garage at home. Go figure.

The women waited in the living room at the front of the mansion for their turn to meet Ethan Glass. Kyle and a production assistant named

Zack each took five women at a time through the house to the atrium. Each woman was then supposed to descend the stairs into the atrium while on camera and introduce herself to Ethan Glass. Ethan. Mr. Glass. Lucy wasn't sure what to call him. She supposed he'd clear that up when they met. She wiped her damp palms on the skirt of her dress. If she could remember what he said afterward. If she remembered to breathe in the meantime. If she didn't trip in her four-inch heels as she went down the steps. If she didn't trip over her tongue trying to speak simple English.

Concentrating on not tripping, sweating, or sounding like an idiot in front of a camera was a little more challenging than she'd expected it to be. And Zack had just taken his second group of five. Lucy glanced at the clock on the wall. They'd been waiting in the living room since eight forty-five. It was almost ten. The air in the room had all but vanished. Ninja butterflies were battling each other inside her stomach. She had to get a grip, and the sooner the better. Kyle would be back any minute, and as bad as tripping over her tongue or her feet would be tonight, throwing up on camera would definitely be the worst. She caught herself pacing and forced herself to stand still and examine the painting above the fireplace. It was a seascape done in oranges and deep purples but strangely managed to work with the décor, she thought abstractedly. She focused on the brush strokes and tried to settle her thoughts. This was a good moment to offer another prayer, she decided—a silent prayer to calm her nerves so she wouldn't hyperventilate in front of several million viewers.

By herself, in front of the painting, she briefly shut her eyes and sent a silent plea for help. Then, after taking a cleansing breath, she decided she should mingle and looked around for familiar faces. She wished she knew more of the girls' names. They were clustered in small groups and everyone, of course, was speaking about Ethan Glass.

"Did you know he's been dating Raven MacDowell?"

"Wasn't she the actress who got slashed in the speedboat in *Cut to the Chase*?" a blonde asked.

"That movie was such a turkey," a redhead in a black dress said.

"Yeah, but she's gorgeous," someone added in a depressed tone. "How are we supposed to compete with someone like Raven MacDowell?"

"I heard he went to the Caribbean with the princess of that little European country," a tall brunette said. "You know which one I mean?"

"Princess Angelina was on vacation there when he was, but apparently they're only friends," the redhead in black responded. That led to a discussion about how good of friends they were and if they were really *just* friends.

"His family owns a ranch in Montana," Lucy offered. That particular bit of info didn't get much play from anyone.

"All of his past girlfriends have been brunettes." This comment came from a decidedly dark-haired beauty.

"Not if you count the swimsuit model. You know who I mean—Heather somebody? I read they were together for a while last year." This from the blonde again.

A small noise at the door drew everyone's attention. Kyle was there, looking flushed. "It's time for numbers sixteen through twenty."

Oh no. Kyle's announcement brought the ninja butterflies roaring back into fierce combat. Two women checked their appearance in a mirror near the doorway, one woman actually *giggled,* and Lucy silently ordered the combatants in her stomach to cease and desist. They refused to listen. *Time for that prayer to be answered. Please.* Time once again for her mantra: *It's an adventure. Pirates of the Caribbean. Minnie Mouse.* Lucy repeated it in her mind as they walked down that very long, but at the same time very short, hallway leading to the atrium. The mantra didn't work as well as it had earlier in the evening.

The light from the atrium spilled through the open doors into the hallway like a bride's veil. Kyle stopped them about ten feet back and held a finger to his lips. He was wearing a small headset hidden by his glossy, dark hair. Bending his head so he could concentrate on the instructions he was getting through the earpiece, he motioned for the woman in front of Lucy to proceed. Number sixteen was on her way.

Lucy took a deep breath. *Adventure, Pirates, Minnie Mouse. Don't stumble, don't sweat, smile. No matter what, don't throw up. He's a normal guy, just like your brothers. A normal guy.*

Kyle nodded his head and motioned for Lucy to go. *It was time.* The ninjas were attacking like it was the end of the world.

Somehow, she made her feet move forward.

The veil of light grew larger; the atrium doorway loomed. Lucy paused a few feet shy of it, took another cleansing breath, and ventured forward.

Don't stumble.

She stood at the doorway, allowing herself a moment to adjust to the light and the scene in front of her. To her left were the cameras. The contestants had been instructed not to look at the cameras.

Right at that moment a memory flashed through her mind. She was in her room at home, on her knees. She could almost feel the silkiness of her comforter on her fingertips. And with that memory, a warm feeling started inside her and spread. It soothed the warring ninja butterflies and settled her shakiness. Reassured that her prayer was being answered, she straightened and was able to take the steps a bit more steadily than she'd expected to just a moment before.

To the right was Ethan Glass.

Holy cow.

He stood there, tall, dark, and handsome—it was a cliché, but it was true—in a suit that looked like it had been made specifically for him. He smiled.

She started to sweat.

Don't sweat.

"Hello," he said. Lucy watched a very large, very square hand reach for hers. A beautiful hand. A masculine hand.

She shook it firmly. *Smile.* "Hello. I'm Lucy."

"Lucy. I'm Ethan."

Okay. Ethan, not Mr. Glass. She'd remember that.

"Am I remembering correctly that you're from Arizona? Phoenix?"

"A small town outside of Phoenix, actually. Eagle Bluff." She was surprised that he knew that about her. The man had done his homework, even on contestant number seventeen.

"I grew up in a small town too. In Montana. A ranch, actually, outside of town. Nothing as large as Phoenix for miles."

"It sounds nice. Quiet and beautiful. I'll bet you love being there."

"It is. And I do. Although a couple hundred head of cattle aren't as quiet as you might think." The side of his mouth quirked up into a half smile. "So tell me, Lucy, if you were to invite me to Eagle Bluff, what would we do?"

"Oh, we could golf or swim, the typical resort stuff. Or we could check out the ghost towns. There are some cool ones not far from where I live. Or we could hike or fish, if you prefer."

He looked her over briefly. "You hike and fish?"

"I even bait my own hook." At his look of surprised amusement, she added, "Three brothers, and they're the double-dog-dare types. I was baiting my own hook by the time I was four."

He chuckled. Then, glancing discreetly over her shoulder, he smoothly wrapped things up. "I'm looking forward to getting to know you better later."

"Thank you. Me too."

He leaned in and placed a friendly kiss on her cheek. "Later, then."

She nodded and walked out into the muggy night air. That was it. That was all it took. She hadn't sweated too badly, hadn't tripped at all, and had remembered to smile and speak clearly . . .

She'd had two minutes to introduce herself to Ethan Glass, and she had spent the time talking about baiting her own fish hook. Brilliant.

Splash Mountain, here we come.

CHAPTER 6

LUCY WALKED ALONG THE STONE pavement to the pool area and took a deep breath. The turquoise glow of the pool lights, the scent of chlorine—so much like home—were oddly soothing. She would take a few quiet moments to herself here to collect her wits and calm her jumping nerves. She was expected to return to the house with the other contestants, but this was a chance to be alone for the first time since she'd awakened from her nap that afternoon.

What a day it had been!

This morning she had bid her parents good-bye and boarded a flight to Los Angeles. She was twenty-four, and it had been her first time on an airplane. Then she'd ridden in a fancy SUV through the rolling hills of Southern California to a mansion. Now she was in the middle of a reality television show. Her time with the other women had been a strange mix of mutual support and barely suppressed rivalry. That, and a couple of suspicious encounters, had revved up Lucy's competitive streak.

Plus, after meeting Ethan Glass, she'd suddenly realized she wouldn't mind hanging around for a few more days and getting to know him better.

Number Eighteen had spotted her by the pool and was hurrying over. So much for alone time. Eighteen squeezed Lucy's arm with the force of a tourniquet and squealed. "He is *so hot*!" She didn't let go of Lucy as they headed across the patio back to the house. "I mean, I *knew* from his pictures he was hot, but he is *so hot*! I could just *die*!"

Lucy's arm was going numb from lack of circulation. Smiling as best she could, she pried Eighteen's fingers loose.

Ms. Carlton intercepted them at the doorway and led them to a small room set up with a chair, more lights, and more white umbrellas.

The cameraman, a tall guy with bushy orange hair, stood by. Ms. Carlton motioned for Lucy to sit in the chair, and the cameraman hoisted his camera into position. The power light blinked on.

"What are your impressions after meeting Ethan?"

Oh, great. The camera was rolling, Eighteen was grinning at her like a lovesick idiot, and the only words Lucy's brain could form were *Ethan was hot* and those weren't even *her* words. *Think, Lucy, think.*

Nothing. *Nada.*

Ms. Carlton gave the camera guy the signal to cut, and Lucy shot her a pained look. "Sorry. My mind went blank. Give me a minute?"

Ms. Carlton muttered something unintelligible, flicked her wrist up, and stared deliberately at her watch for a long, drawn-out moment before giving a brisk nod and saying, "Hit it, Rogan." The light of death blinked on again.

Great. "Ethan was . . ." She paused. She glanced from Ms. Carlton's tense expression to Eighteen's loopy grin. "He was not what I expected. He made me feel comfortable, which he didn't need to do, since it's our job to win *him* over." It wasn't a brilliant comment, but it was better than saying he was *hot.*

Melanie gave the signal to cut. "He reminded me of my brothers," Lucy suddenly added just before the little light went off. Her eyes shot open in horror. Where had that come from? He reminded her of her *brothers*? How much more dull and platonic could she make him sound? She could almost hear Allie lecturing her like she had about the guys from Colorado.

The camera guy was choking back a laugh. Wonderful. Ms. Carlton maintained her professional Botox look, although her eye had developed a twitch. "That's all. You can go join the others."

Lucy had been dismissed. As she walked down the hall, she could actually hear Number Eighteen squeal again. Lucy didn't stick around to hear the word *hot.*

* * *

Melanie watched the last contestant float out of the interview room. She tossed her clipboard onto the floor and groaned. "That was about as exciting as watching paint dry." Rogan didn't say anything. He just smirked the way he always did. She'd learned that about him. He didn't talk much.

"I have to find some angles for this show, or we might as well be shooting an infomercial for beauty products." She tapped her chin with her fingers. Rogan had a reputation in the business for getting the shots he wanted, and he'd freelanced for the tabloids for a while. They could use that to their advantage. They were going to get huge ratings no matter what it took. With his help, she could spice things up. She might have to leave Esplin out of the loop, but so what? And Curt would be ecstatic.

"Okay. Back to business, then. Time to plant some ideas in a few soft female brains. You get ready to tape whatever happens as a result."

"Whatever you want, Red." He tugged on her hair.

She brushed his hand aside and then wondered whether she'd get better cooperation from him playing the boss or the flirt. For now, hard-to-get would read as either. She stared coolly at him. "Yeah, remember that. Whatever I want."

She strode out the door and ignored his low chuckle.

* * *

Ethan was having an undeniably *great* time. The introductions had gone well, and now he was basking in the attention of twenty-five lovely women. What guy wouldn't dream about being in a situation like this? Everywhere he turned there were beautiful women smiling just for him, vying for his attention, trying to please him. It was only temporary, but it was sweet.

He imagined himself as a Roman emperor being fanned with palm fronds and fed grapes from the fingers of gorgeous serving girls. Move it up two millennia, and he was lounging on a plush sofa with willowy, bright-eyed, smiling women on either side, while another asked if she could "borrow" him for a few minutes. And he allowed himself to be borrowed. He had limited time in this fantasyland before he had to announce his decisions, but he only had a few questions to work out in his mind before finalizing his cut to fifteen, so why not? He was in a field of beautiful flowers, and he saw no reason not to enjoy the moment, savor the fragrance, and linger over each blossom.

He'd enjoyed meeting the women. Introductions told him a lot about a person. But the introductions had also reinforced the unique position he was in—that of keeping a cool business head to weigh the pros and cons, balanced with his personal reaction to each woman. It wasn't like the gut read he got with job applicants. He hadn't ever anticipated having an intimate future with any of the employees he'd hired.

But if things went according to plan—and Curt's fervent hopes—one of these women would be his so-called soulmate. And there was nothing more intimate than the soul, was there?

He enjoyed his work; he enjoyed his success. It had taken all of his energy and time. Was that how he intended to live the rest of his life? His father had said he needed to know how he wanted to live his life before he could know who to live it with.

He knew what his parents had and what his brother, Jake, had with his wife, Megan. Ethan thought he wanted something like that. They worked hard, but they worked together. And that sounded like something else old Jed would say. They were life partners, the real deal through thick and thin, to the end.

Was that different from having a soulmate?

He would ponder that later. For now, he was going to bask in the evening's pleasure a while longer.

There had been a couple of interesting moments with the women so far like when—which woman had it been? Ah yes, April—had nearly crawled inside his suit jacket giving him a friendly hug. *Friendly* being loosely translated. She wasn't going to make it through the first cut, so he'd rolled with it. And he'd been caught off guard a while later when perky little Kelly had impressed the group with her gymnastic abilities—a detail that hadn't appeared on her application. And he *had* been impressed. She'd done things that would make a Chinese acrobat proud, with her elegant blue evening gown hoisted nearly to her hips. He wouldn't have chosen this setting for that particular performance, so he wasn't sure if she'd earned points for guts or lost them for poor judgment. Kelly was a borderline pick, so he'd have to evaluate her against the other borderline contestants as the evening progressed.

And then there was Lucy. She was a mystery. She'd matched him remarkably well on the tests, and he'd liked something about her picture, although she hadn't been the flashiest contender in the pile of applications. But there had been something about her that had intrigued him, and he hadn't been able to put his finger on it. She came from a devout religious background, which had raised a yellow flag in his mind. His own mother was fairly religious, and he was traditional enough to consider religious values a plus. But he wasn't religious himself, despite his childhood upbringing, and he didn't really foresee changing his ways anytime soon.

That had made Lucy a borderline pick—until he'd seen her this evening. In the atrium, she'd been a breath of fresh air.

Knowing these weren't like job interviews and that he was also evaluating his attraction to each woman had made him acutely aware of bare shoulders and legs, plunging necklines, and slinky dresses. Not that he was complaining. This was a guy's heaven.

And then Lucy had stood in the doorway, staring at her feet and looking flustered. She'd worn a gold Oriental-style dress. No bare shoulders and legs, no plunging neckline, but it had flattered her slim shape and had been surprisingly appealing.

He'd watched her find her bearings. Then she'd looked up and glanced around the room. He'd seen her face—and caught his breath.

She had glowed. She'd honest to goodness *glowed*.

Her hair was a deeper version of the gold of her dress, and that could have been the reason. The lighting in the room was soft, and that might have accounted for it. Except no one else had glowed, not like that.

And then their eyes had met. He'd nearly laughed out loud. He wished he had a picture of the stunned look that had crossed her face at that moment.

She'd recovered quickly and been friendly and direct with him, not aggressive, not coy. That had been a pleasant change from the usual too. And then she'd confided that she baited her own fish hooks, and he'd nearly lost it again.

She was one he would be watching tonight too. He would keep the religion issue in the back of his mind; it wasn't a total deal breaker. And the glowing thing intrigued him. He wanted to see if she glowed in the rest of the house as well.

Careful, Glass, he thought with an amused laugh, *you sound like you're searching for paranormal activity instead of a soulmate*. He turned his attention back to the ladies at hand.

* * *

Lucy sat at the bar with Lauren, sipped her ginger ale, and watched the action unfold. A couple of women were making a play for time with Ethan. The redhead named Tiffany won, and Ethan walked out onto the terrace with her. The loser, Kaitlin, stalked over to them. "Tiffany came and took Ethan away from me. Wasn't it obvious he didn't want to go? He was, like, totally into me."

With uncanny instincts, Ms. Carlton was there with the orange-haired cameraman in tow. "Kaitlin, tell us about your chat with Ethan." The camera's on button instantly lit up, and Lucy and Lauren were stuck as background while Kaitlin vented on tape about Tiffany. Aware of the camera, Lucy sipped her soda and tried to act casual.

Suddenly, and without warning, Kaitlin burst into song. "Ethan's so much more than a date," she belted, "He's my uh-uh-uh-ohhh, forever soulmate." Lucy choked on her soda. Lauren's eyes bulged before her head dropped to the counter of the bar, her shoulders shaking with suppressed laughter. She glanced at Lucy, croaked something that sounded like "bathroom," and rushed off.

A few women wandered over to listen, and Kaitlin, aware of both audience and camera, pumped up the volume for a big finish. "Uh-uh-uh-ohhh, it was a twist of fate, whoa, whoa, I found my lovinnnnn' forever soulmate!" Whistles and applause followed. "It's even better with the guitar," she gushed. "I put my career as a singer/songwriter on hold when I learned that *the* Ethan Glass was going to be the *Soulmate*."

The group gradually disbanded, and a few intrepid women headed out onto the terrace to flush Ethan out. Kaitlin flounced off after them, spouting warnings about Tiffany.

Lucy picked up her ginger ale and wandered across the room. Some of the women were comparing their Ethan experiences and giving each other pep talks. All eyes followed Ethan's every move.

Ethan had circulated all evening. He seemed comfortable in his own skin, smiling, talking, taking the occasional woman aside for a personal conversation. Mr. Esplin and Ms. Carlton were constantly on the move, issuing orders to the several cameramen who were always nearby.

Lucy settled into a leather club chair, set her soda on an end table, and glanced at her watch. It was getting late. She watched Ethan take Lauren out onto the terrace. She was smiling at Ethan, nodding in agreement to something he'd said.

Lucky Lauren. Lucy hadn't had a chance to talk to him yet.

The bar had stayed busy all evening. It seemed to Lucy like a deliberate ploy by the producers to loosen everyone up, and it was working. A few people had become well lubricated as the night wore on. Voices were getting louder, behavior more outrageous. Cameras and crew buzzed around like hornets.

A woman with turquoise eyes and a dress to match grabbed Ethan's hand as he returned from the terrace and pulled him to the middle of the room, leaving Lauren in the doorway with her mouth gaping. Tiffany was doing a slow burn on the other side of the room, watching. The woman, Alison, danced sensuously to music playing only in her head and encouraged Ethan to join her. But Ethan led Alison into more traditional dance moves, ended with a big dip, and then invited a few others to each take a spin with him as well.

"Have you had a chance to talk to him yet?" a woman seated on the couch next to Lucy asked as they both watched Ethan get pulled outside again. "I'm Chelsea, by the way."

"I'm Lucy. And no, not yet. Every time I think he might be heading in my direction, somebody grabs him."

"I know. It's so frustrating! I'm ready to yank *that* woman's hair out by the roots." She gestured toward a tall brunette with a killer figure who was wearing a tie-dyed, backless dress that made her look like Mother Earth and Bond Girl combined. Someone had called her Woodstock Barbie earlier. "I've seen her drag him off four different times tonight. She stole him away from me. What do you say when Ethan comes back inside we go together and head him off."

It sounded like they were planning to round up a stray bull. Lucy grinned at the mental image it created. Should she go get her lasso and spurs?

She was about to respond when Rick came into the room. Ethan and Woodstock Barbie were with him. "Ladies, it's time for Ethan to consult with Dr. Lindstrom now." He gestured toward the doorway, and both men left. A collective sigh sounded through the room.

Lucy tried not to feel disappointed that she hadn't talked to Ethan again. In the beginning, she'd been excited simply to be here and maybe visit Disneyland. But she *was* disappointed now. Her big adventure in reality TV—and if she were honest, her chance to get to know Ethan Glass a little better—was most likely coming to an end.

She succumbed to a sudden need for self-torture. "What do you think of him? Ethan, that is," she said to the redhead, Tiffany, who was standing next to her. Tiffany pulled her gaze from the door and looked at Lucy and Chelsea. "He's everything I've ever dreamed of. He's rich, he's hot. He's magnetic and powerful. He knows how to make a woman feel special. At least he made *me* feel special. I don't know about you." She smiled at them in a mocking way and sauntered off.

Twenty-four years of taunting from Lucy's brothers rushed back at full speed. *I bet I make it to the top of the hill before you're even out of the parking lot. You'll never hit that bucket from here like I just did. You're a baby and that makes you a big chicken. Waack, waaack!* Razzing like that had had her climbing to the tops of the pine trees on camping trips, zooming at breakneck speed off skateboard ramps, and holding her

60

Karen Tuft

breath underwater at the pool. She'd nearly passed out doing that one—but she'd outlasted Andy, and Craig had rewarded her with a laughing high five and a double-double chocolate shake at Betty's Drive-In. Andy had gone along, scowling and nursing his wounded pride, and Craig hadn't let him live it down for months.

Now, here she was, ready to throw down the gauntlet once again and show Tiffany a thing or two. Old habits died hard.

"Ooh, I want *her* for my new best friend," Chelsea said. "Maybe we should go to the ladies' room and check for footprints she may have left when she walked all over us. 'He's rich; he's hot,'" she added in a breathy voice. "'He's everything I've ever dreamed of.'"

Lucy laughed in response, but the urge to beat Tiffany at her game still burned. It didn't help that Tiffany had the advantage. She'd spent time with Ethan, and Lucy hadn't. Ethan had made Tiffany feel "special," while he'd only given Lucy a friendly kiss on the cheek, like he was meeting his great-aunt Alice. It was a depressing thought. "I have three brothers," she said. "My bet is Ethan Glass puts his pants on one leg at a time just like they do. Even in dreams."

* * *

Ethan strode into the small office the crew had affectionately dubbed "the war room." Dr. Lindstrom was already there, seated at a table that took up most of the room's space, reviewing her handwritten notes. She flapped a hand in a loose welcoming gesture without bothering to look up. "Come in, come in. I'll be right with you."

Truthfully, Ethan had enjoyed the evening so far—once he'd gotten used to the cameras and Esplin's constant hovering, that is. Dane Esplin was talented, ambitious, and high strung. His focus was on creating drama; Ethan's was on finding his soulmate. Eventually, Ethan had simply ignored the guy and done things his own way.

Curt's assistant, Melanie, poked her head through the doorway. "Excuse me."

Dr. Lindstrom looked up over her reading glasses for the first time.

"Is there anything I can get for either of you?" Melanie asked. "Anything, Mr. Glass?"

"Ice water, if it's no bother." He smiled at her. Melanie nodded, and the door clicked shut. "Let's get down to business, Dr. Lindstrom. What pearls of wisdom do you have for me after watching the women this evening?"

Dr. Lindstrom chuckled. "Truthfully, Mr. Glass of Glass Enterprises, you're a man who knows his own mind. You've tolerated my questionnaires, and you may even consider my 'pearls of wisdom' helpful, but my value here will be minimal in terms of what you decide."

The door opened again, and Melanie handed them each a tall glass of ice water. "Thank you," Ethan said. When the door closed, he turned back to Dr. Lindstrom. "Let's talk shop."

She slid her reading glasses back into place and pointed to her notes. "I'm ready. And, please, call me Berta."

"Berta, then. And I'm Ethan. Now, will you *please* explain how Whitney actually made the cut of twenty-five? Whitney, of the one-word vocabulary? I never want to hear the word *hot* again, even in reference to weather or frying pans."

Berta laughed. "Oh dear. The answer to your question, Ethan, is *priorities*. Mr. Myers made it clear that while it was important to identify women who had scored highly on the various tests, it was equally important to include women who could add variety and dramatic interest to the show."

He leaned forward and looked squarely into her face. "Are you telling me that my already tragic odds for romantic success here were reduced in favor of *ratings*?" It was a pathetic attempt at intimidation, he knew, foiled mostly by the grin he couldn't control.

The irony in his comment hadn't been lost on her. She smiled and patted his hand soothingly. "I would never do that to you. All of the girls selected scored well overall and very highly in at least two categories. Whitney's strong category was in career. She made a small fortune from a yoga DVD infomercial, so your entrepreneurial similarities should be obvious."

She sat back in her chair, more serious now. "Ethan, I have learned in my years of practice that while questionnaires may inform us, ultimately, it's the heart that guides us. I did my professional best to select the strongest matches and the widest variety I could so you would have as much depth and scope to choose from as possible. The rest is up to you. Now, tell me what you're thinking."

Ethan briefed her on the contestants he planned to eliminate so far and why. She was thoughtful and objective, her comments direct. He was about to discuss the few women he still had questions about when they were interrupted by a soft tapping sound.

Kyle poked his head through the door and cleared his throat. "Pardon me for interrupting, Mr. Glass. There's a small matter that needs your attention."

Ethan rose. "Excuse me, Berta. I'm sure this will only take a moment."

He left and followed Kyle out of the house through a small service entrance. The women were holed up in another part of the mansion. They walked silently along a paved path to a driveway hidden by shrubbery. It was dark there. The bright photographic lights were only a soft corona around the house from this angle, and through the shrubs, the pool and patio lights twinkled like distant stars. It was quiet, with only an occasional car engine humming from far away. Ethan stopped and shoved his hands into his pockets.

"Pardon me for interrupting, Mr. Glass?" Ethan mimicked questioningly as he laughed.

Kyle grinned. "I was going for meek and subservient. Oh, before I forget, my mom told me to tell you *again* that she thinks you've lost your mind for good this time. Those aren't her exact words, but I think you get the picture." Kyle's mother, Terri, was the housekeeper at the ranch in Montana and had been for years.

"Good old Terri. She already gave me an earful when I was home last week. You'd think she'd be thrilled, considering how much I'm paying you to be here. If you don't do something stupid like blow it all on a weekend in Vegas, the money could get you through grad school."

"She thinks I'm here as cheap labor for the show since I needed a summer job. I didn't tell her you're paying me to play 007."

Ethan had hired Kyle to help him out in a way no one else could. He and Jake had grown up with Kyle on the ranch, and Ethan trusted him like a brother. "I like knowing you have my back, Kyle. Dr. Lindstrom will only see the women when they're on-camera, but people are on their best behavior when the cameras are rolling. You're my secret weapon, my eyes when the cameras are off. That means you'll be providing me with valuable information I won't be able to get any other way.

"As to your mom's opinion, I prefer to think of myself as someone who's willing to take a calculated risk as opposed to someone who's lost his mind." He grinned. "Besides, she's thought that about me ever since I tried riding that unbroken colt the summer I turned eleven."

"I was only four, but I still remember," Kyle said almost wistfully. "One minute I'm in the kitchen helping her make bread, and the next I'm watching you fly through the air straight into the corral fence. It was cool."

"She made me cookies every day for two weeks." He laughed. "Of course, she ripped into me every afternoon in the kitchen while I ate them. If you call her, tell her I may be crazy but I haven't been thrown yet. So tell me, 007, what have you learned?"

Kyle quickly filled him in on some of the antics he'd observed. Most of them were minor and involved women Ethan was planning to send home tonight anyway, so he mentally checked them off. Kyle cleared his throat.

"What?"

"I'm not sure what you're thinking, you know, or who interests you at this point. So I'm kind of following my gut."

"I trust you, Kyle. That's why you're here." He glanced at his watch. "But we're going to have to wrap this up so I can get back. What is your gut saying?"

"I've been here a couple of days, shuttling women from the airport and playing gofer. Most of them talk *at* me. They ask me to turn on the hot tub jets or get them towels or drinks. Some don't talk to me at all." He shrugged a little. "I'm playing a role, you know? The lowly hired help, so I'm invisible. But a few of them notice me anyway."

"Like?"

"Like Denise and Lauren."

"Denise. She's the brunette from Georgia. And Lauren, you said."

"Yeah. And Lucy."

"Lucy."

"Yeah, Lucy."

"Hmmm." He'd attempted to speak with her a couple of times this evening, but other women had successfully intervened. In fact, some women had aggressively pursued him, while others had not. Lucy had been one of the latter. Frankly, he wanted a woman who was willing to *try* a little—he didn't want to drag the effort out of anyone, glow or no glow. "Well, keep your eyes open. I'd better get back." But then, glow or no glow, if Lucy had been nice to Ethan's Native American brother, she might be worth the time to get to know a little better.

* * *

If her brothers thought holding her breath underwater had been a feat, they should see her now. She was sure she hadn't taken a single breath since they'd been summoned for the elimination ceremony. The women had been allowed to freshen their makeup and hair while Ethan conferred with

Dr. Lindstrom. Now it was nearly two in the morning, and Mr. Esplin had put them in a staggered arrangement for the best camera shot. What was it about cameras that seemed to raise the stakes so much? Rick was off to the side awaiting his cue, while a young woman adjusted his tie and powdered the shine from his nose.

Ethan stood across the room from the gathered women and began methodically naming his choices. Lucy simultaneously waited to see if she fainted from a lack of oxygen and to hear if Ethan eventually called her name.

So far he'd chosen Chelsea and Lauren and Amber and Kaitlin. As each woman's name had been called—with sighs of relief (Chelsea) and/ or suppressed squeals (Kaitlin)—she'd walked forward (with looks of anxiety and envy from everyone else), and Ethan had asked her if she would continue the journey with him. Each had said yes. Who wouldn't at this point? He'd been hugged and kissed, and the ninja butterflies in Lucy's stomach had returned for a rematch.

Jena, Tiffany, Sara. Each name Lucy heard that wasn't her own burned into her memory. Denise, Sienna. Ethan gave each of the chosen women a silver bracelet with a charm. From a distance, the charm looked like a tiny teardrop that sparkled in the light. "It's not much," he explained wryly as the cameras rolled. "Just a small piece of Glass."

Rachel, Kelly, Alison. Lucy watched him fasten the bracelet on Alison's wrist and ask her to continue the journey; then she watched Alison give Ethan a very proprietary kiss and mentally prepared for Disneyland. Twelve girls down, and only three spots remained. Poise and dignity were the way to go, but those pesky ninjas must have had black belts in the martial arts if her upset stomach was any indicator.

"Lucy."

Did she really hear her name? She glanced from side to side. Everyone was looking at her. Ethan's eyebrows rose. She put her hand to her chest in a questioning gesture. Ethan smiled and nodded. *Don't sweat, don't trip, don't throw up.* Somehow, she managed to walk the few feet from where she stood to where Ethan was. He took her hand and slipped the bracelet around her wrist. His hands were warm. Hers were cold and clammy, like a landed trout. She sucked in the deepest breath she could as quietly as she could manage. Her brother Craig owed her another double-double chocolate shake. She was sure she'd beaten her previous breath-holding record. She could barely hear over the pounding in her ears.

"Thank you," she managed, and Ethan Glass pulled her in for the requisite hug. She wasn't leaving yet after all. As the hug ended, she held up her wrist. The charm caught fire under the lights.

"Even a small piece of glass can be multifaceted and brilliant," she quietly observed, mostly to herself.

"I'll take that as a compliment," he replied.

He'd interpreted her impulsive comment as referring to himself. That was okay with Lucy, since it sounded more intelligent than her fish hook confession had.

Stacy, Kim. Ethan made his final two selections, and Mr. Esplin cut the action, sending Zack and a cameraman off with the departing women. Lucy looked at the bracelet on her wrist and its tiny glass pendant. She hadn't been eliminated. Ethan hadn't spoken to her all evening, but she was still here.

"Ladies, Ethan," Mr. Esplin said, interrupting her thoughts. "Let's shoot this final scene, shall we? Then you can mingle while we wrap up some details."

Someone handed Lucy a flute of champagne. She took it without much thought. When everyone had one, Mr. Esplin spoke again. "Okay, everybody, back into position. Ethan, do you know what you're going to say for the toast? Quiet, people! Okay. Ethan, on one." He held up his hand, four fingers, three, two . . .

"Thank you all for going on this journey with me. Here's to finding true love and a *Soulmate*." He raised his glass, all the women raised theirs, and so did Lucy. But she didn't drink when everyone else did. "Cut," Mr. Esplin shouted, and she deposited the glass on the nearest table.

Eventually, Ethan excused himself from them and made a smooth exit. As the sighing and good-byeing from the women subsided, Lucy was finally able to survey the remaining women who were her competition. There was no way to know how she fit into the mix. She still couldn't believe she'd survived the first round.

She had a lot to think about. She had felt strongly that she was supposed to be here for some reason, despite the long odds of making it to the end. She wasn't convinced Ethan Glass was interested in someone like her. It was simple math: celebrity hotshot millionaire plus small-town Mormon girl just didn't add up to happily ever after in her calculations.

She thought again that maybe her reason for being here was simply to make friends. Maybe it was for the learning experience.

She also thought about the champagne toast. She hadn't been expecting it, and she realized that a lot of simple, even innocent actions she made were going to be observed—and judged—by a lot of people. Maybe her reason for being here was as simple as standing by her beliefs and values. That was okay; she could do that. She'd done it all her life, so it should be easy now.

CHAPTER 7

LUCY AND SEVEN OTHER WOMEN were on their first group date with Ethan—at a rodeo. Ethan would meet them at their destination, a small fairgrounds in the foothills outside Los Angeles. The group included Lauren, with whom she'd become friends, Sara, country singer wannabe Kaitlin, a shy blonde named Kelly, a not-so-shy blonde named Jena, a premed student named Amber, and the redheaded siren Tiffany.

They'd been told to wear jeans and to bring a change of clothes. Jena had opted for khaki trousers and an argyle sweater. Ethan arrived wearing Levis and a snug black T-shirt and looked like a million bucks.

They spent the afternoon exploring the fairgrounds—looking at livestock, riding carnival rides, playing games of skill on the midway, and vying for Ethan's attention.

Tiffany and Kaitlin clung to him like Velcro, and the rest of the women hovered close by, waiting for their chance to attack. Living with brothers had taught Lucy to loathe clinging. If competing for Ethan Glass meant *clinging* to him, she was going to lose, no question. She smiled and joked with the others, tossed baseballs at milk bottles, shot mechanical ducks on the firing range, and tried her luck swinging a mallet hard enough to ring the bell (Ethan rang it on his first try). She did her best to ignore the cameras that had been pointed at them ever since they'd slid into the SUV that morning.

"Next up," Ethan said, waggling his eyebrows. "The kissing booth."

The girls squealed.

Unlike most booths, which usually looked like something Lucy from the *Peanuts* cartoon would sit behind hoping Schroeder would walk by, this one was small and enclosed, with an entrance covered by a burlap curtain. Across the top was a large pair of red plywood lips with the words *Kissin' Korral* spelled out in rope.

Kountry Kaitlin rushed into the Kissin' Korral first. The rest of them milled around outside, with the ever-present cameramen recording it all for posterity. And then Kaitlin was back and grinning like a fool.

Did Lucy want to kiss Ethan? Maybe. He was attractive. It was only a silly kissing booth. No big deal, right? Except that there were seven *other* women right next to her who were eager to kiss him, not counting the ones back at *Soulmates* House. Kissing should be something special shared by two people interested in a relationship with each other, not some sort of audition. And that's what this felt like, an audition. She rubbed her damp palms down the legs of her jeans. She was getting a case of performance anxiety.

Tiffany went second and strode through the burlap curtain. A few minutes later she emerged, looking coolly smug, although smug seemed to be her default expression. The others followed one by one, and Lucy concentrated on a flock of noisy gulls scavenging for food rather than the reactions of the women as they exited the booth. She told herself not to think about what was happening inside the booth with Ethan. This was only a silly kissing booth kiss, not an audition, she reminded herself firmly. It wasn't like she was in love with the guy or anything.

She ended up being last by virtue of her attention to the gulls, but there was no avoiding it now. Mr. Esplin was waving her over to the booth as Lauren exited, bouncing up and down like a winner on *The Price is Right*. Lauren was the excitable sort, but still.

Lucy took a deep breath and tentatively drew aside the curtain. Ethan was sitting on a metal folding chair behind a low counter framed out of two-by-fours. The counter itself was about eight inches wide. The orange-haired cameraman was standing in the corner. The booth's dimensions couldn't have been more than four feet by four feet, so with the narrow counter, a couple of bigger than usual guys, and a camera, it was cozy, to say the least.

She stepped inside and let go of the drape.

Natural light was plentiful, as the plywood structure didn't include a roof in its construction. The cameraman, Rogan, started taping. Ethan smiled and beckoned her to sit on the empty folding chair opposite where he was sitting. Lucy sat.

They'd been told at least a thousand times not to look at the camera. That was easier said than done. It was the *Soulmates* equivalent of the all-seeing eye, and right now she felt as conspicuous as she had when Mike Scofield had kissed her good night after a date and she'd caught her dad peeking through the living room curtains right before the moment of impact.

"Are we saving the best for last?" Ethan asked.

She saw Tiffany's and Lauren's and Kaitlin's faces in her mind. She doubted they'd gone for silly kissing booth kiss. They would have gone for serious audition kiss. "I doubt it," Lucy muttered then blushed. "Maybe if we were arm wrestling instead of kissing."

He laughed and leaned forward, resting his arms on the makeshift counter. "Do you have a quarter? It costs twenty-five cents a kiss here in the old Kissin' Korral."

Why would she have brought any money? The show paid for everything. Maybe she could use this as a way to escape the inevitable audition kiss. She wasn't exactly feeling ready to perform on cue. "Uh-oh, I'm afraid you've caught me a little short on cash."

His eyes started to twinkle. She wasn't sure she trusted that. "What, no quarter?" he asked.

She shrugged and tried to look sheepish. "Guess it's not my lucky day."

"Maybe, maybe not," he said, and sticking his hand in the pocket of his jeans, he fished out a quarter. "I have an idea. *I'll* pay *you* for a kiss, instead of the other way around. That will make it a lucky day for both of us." He pushed the quarter across the narrow countertop with his index finger.

She wished she'd paid better attention when Allie was coaching her in Flirtation 101. It was impossible to get the image of the seven previous visitors to the old Kissin' Korral out of her head. She nudged the quarter back in his direction. "Thank you, but . . . I can't accept. I don't kiss on a first date." She smiled apologetically.

"You don't really think of this as a first date, do you?" He leaned on the counter and rested his chin in his hand. "Not after the cocktail party the other night."

"Yep, I'm pretty much thinking that, actually."

"Hmmm. Fair enough. Do you have other dating rules I should know about? And what numbered date would your kissing date be, according to those rules?"

This teasing, T-shirt and jeans version of Ethan Glass was new and unfamiliar. "Not so much rules as guidelines," she said evasively, hoping he wouldn't notice that she hadn't answered his questions.

"So then, Lucy, tell me: would those first date *guidelines* of yours apply if I were to simply kiss your hand?" He reached over the barrier between them and took her hand, lifting it just short of his lips. He looked at her, his eyebrows raised in question.

She shook her head. He smiled and pressed his lips lightly on her fingers then released them. He nudged the quarter back toward her. "Payment." He tipped his head, studying her. Then his mouth curved up on one side, and she swore she could almost *see* the lightbulb go on above his head. She went on full alert. Reaching again into his pocket, he pulled out another quarter. Lucy sat up straight in her folding chair.

"So kissing your hand was within the guidelines. What about on the cheek, Lucy? What about a friendly little first-date kiss on the cheek?" That untrustworthy twinkle was back in his eyes.

He was double-dog daring her! Swap the Kissin' Korral for a basketball and hoop and he was no different from her scoundrel brothers, except the stakes were higher. But since this was something she recognized and understood—now that the tingly sensation in her fingers had begun to subside—she didn't feel quite as far out of her depths. "I'm very cautious about any lips I let near my cheek." She looked directly at his mouth to make the point and realized too late it was a tactical error. He had ramped up to full-wattage grin mode, all white teeth and humor. To recover lost ground, she went for the three-point shot. "I mean, you just *never know* where they've *been.*"

Rogan's camera started bobbing up and down in time with his shoulders, and Lucy vaguely wondered if Mr. Esplin would be happy with kissing-booth-during-earthquake footage.

Ethan looked stunned, but he quickly recovered and looked straight at Rogan's camera (only bobbing slightly now) with a comically deadpan expression. He had to realize he was breaking one of Mr. Esplin's cardinal rules by doing that.

"Ouch!" he exclaimed and heaved a sigh. "'The course of true love never did run smooth.'"

She knew that quote. She *absolutely* knew that quote; it was from *A Midsummer Night's Dream.* He turned back toward her with all the innocence of a sneaky little boy. His expression had shown on her brothers' faces often enough for her to recognize it on sight. Who would have believed it of Ethan Glass? He'd not only remembered she'd majored in English but had *literally* done his homework. "Don't you think spouting Shakespeare is pouring it on a little thick?"

"Not a chance. He echoes my thoughts exactly. Here's another good example: 'The lady doth protest too much, methinks.'" He smiled, a little too slyly.

"'Some Cupid kills with arrows, some with *traps*,'" Lucy countered. "And that quote echoes *my* thoughts exactly, hence the *guidelines*."

"But this is a *kissing* booth, Lucy, yet you're here, even though it's against those so-called first-date guidelines of yours. That's sending mixed signals at best and is unfair to me under the circumstances, don't you think? So what can you suggest that would be fair to both of us?"

There was no way Lucy was going to answer that one.

"Let's try what you mentioned before," he suggested. "We'll arm wrestle. If you win, I'll give you another quarter. If I win, you give me a friendly little kiss on the cheek." He patted his cheek as if he needed to identify its location for her. "Deal?"

There was that twinkle again. Was "in for a penny, in for a pound" a Shakespeare quote? It should be. Or, in her case, a quarter instead of a penny. "Deal," she said, knowing she was a fool to be taking his double-dog dare, and planted her elbow on the counter. Some things were simply too ingrained, especially when one had grown up with brothers like Craig and Andy.

Looking inordinately pleased, Ethan took her hand and made a few angle adjustments to allow for a fair fight. He invited her to give the go-ahead to begin because, as a gentleman, he said, he wanted her to have the advantage.

Okay, if he wanted to give her an advantage, she'd take it. She knew she'd need it.

"On your mark, get set, GO!" she said at the speed of light so that even to her own ears it sounded more like "onyermarsego." She had him pressed halfway to the counter before he rallied.

But rally he did. He forced her arm back to its starting point, and then down toward defeat. Lucy clenched her teeth, aware that she probably looked like one of those cartoon people whose faces balloon and turn fire-engine red right before steam shoots out of their ears. It was time to call in reinforcements, specifically her other arm and her upper body, but to no avail. He laid her arm flat on the counter.

Ever the modest winner, Ethan patted his bicep fondly and said, "Honey, a good cowboy always packs an extra set of guns. Right here."

Lucy groaned, laughing, and buried her fire engine face in her aching arms.

"Now, just to show you how fair-minded I am, I'm giving you this quarter anyway," he continued. She looked up. "And you can put that friendly first-date kiss right here," he patted his cheek again, "like the good sport you are." He leaned forward over the counter, tipping his head to position his cheek directly into firing range.

It was her own fault for agreeing to this. She took a deep breath, leaned in, ready to make good on her part of the deal, puckered up, and right as she kissed him he turned his head, catching her square on, mouth to mouth, his lips curved up in a grin.

Lucy pulled back, several seconds slower than she would have expected or preferred—especially when she saw the victorious gleam in his eyes. "Hey!"

"'Though this be madness, yet there is method in't,'" he said and winked at her.

Shakespeare again. *Hamlet.* She glared at him.

Ethan laughed and held out his hand to her as she stood. "Whew. I don't know about you, but I'm relieved that we got those first kiss guidelines all ironed out. Let's go join the others."

Lucy exited the kissing booth fifty cents richer and wondering if she would rather punch Ethan Glass or kiss him again.

Punch him. Definitely.

Maybe . . .

The group headed toward the rodeo arena. Ethan told the women he was leaving them temporarily and that they should follow Kyle, which they did. The rodeo was already in progress. Instead of taking them to seats in the arena, however, Kyle led them past a public barricade toward a rodeo official who was standing with Ms. Carlton and a cameraman. He, in turn, herded them all into one of the empty chutes at the side of the arena.

The official, middle-aged and leathery, with a paunch resting on his silver belt buckle, pushed his cowboy hat high on his brow and smiled politely. "Welcome, ladies. You will all be participating in the next event. But don't worry, it's just good old-fashioned fun. While you're being introduced over the PA system, you need to run on out into the arena and wave at the crowd. Everything will be explained to you then." He gave Jena the once-over and took in her country club getup. "Hope you're not too partial to those duds you're wearin', honey."

Jena looked at him with alarm.

He glanced over at the scoreboard. "Shoot, I gotta go. Well, good luck, ladies, and may the best woman win." He tipped his hat in a courtesy gesture, gave Jena another quick appraisal, chuckled, and left. Lucy watched him approach a grizzled old cowboy who nodded at something he said and then headed in their direction.

Lauren sidled up to Jena. "I think he liked you," she teased. "He couldn't take his eyes off of you."

"Ha ha." Jena smoothed a stray piece of hair and wandered over to the gate that led out into the arena, ignoring the cowboy who was now positioned behind her at the gate latch.

"In fact," Lauren continued, "you could say—" but whatever she was about to say was interrupted by the shrill whine of feedback from the loudspeakers.

"Ladies and gentlemen, please give a big country welcome to television's *Soulmate*, Ethaaannnn Glass!" The crowd roared. The voice booming over the PA system continued. "He's on a quest to find love, and he's here today to ask for our help." Lucy, who'd moved over to the gate beside Jena, watched as Ethan, on horseback, rode the circumference of the arena. His T-shirt and Levis had been replaced with old faded jeans, scuffed-up boots, and a shirt that could have been the original property of Butch Cassidy himself. He waved his cowboy hat in welcome and then reined his big horse in at the center of the arena as though it were something he did every day of his life. "Are we going to help him?" the voice asked. The crowd erupted in the affirmative.

"Let's meet some of the ladies who want to win his heart!"

The old rodeo hand opened the gate, spit, and said, "That's yer cue." The eight of them scrambled out into the middle of the arena.

They stood there while several hundred spectators yelled and cheered. Lucy glanced at the others. Tiffany had her arms crossed and looked wary, while Jena nonchalantly studied her manicure. Kaitlin waved and blew kisses to the crowd. The others were huddled together like quail, Kelly looking ready to faint at any moment. Lucy herself felt like one of those Christians from Roman times waiting for a hungry lion to make an appearance . . . in a strange sitcom sort of way.

A grinning Ethan made his way over to them, tipped his hat, and trotted off to disappear behind the gate through which they had just entered. Rodeo hands rolled short barrels out onto the far end of the arena. Kelly moaned.

Good old-fashioned fun, the guy had said. Good old-fashioned fun doing *what* was the question.

They didn't have to wait long for the answer.

The PA system squawked. "A man enjoying the single life and trying not to get caught can be as slippery as a greased pig," the announcer said. "Am I right, gentlemen?" The audience whooped with loud male agreement. "We're talking survival skills here, after all." A distinctly female booing and hissing followed that remark.

"But it appears our *Soulmate* is planning to get caught. That being the case, he wants to make sure these pretty ladies know how to do that, right and proper. So the first woman to get a greased pig into her barrel will be joining Ethan for a special romantic evening, Western style. Folks, let's cheer these ladies on!"

The crowd roared.

They were supposed to catch a greased pig.

"You've got to be kidding me," Jena muttered. Lauren busted out laughing. Lucy grinned at her, her own mind frantically searching for a strategy. She needed to think, and fast.

"On your mark! Get set . . ." Bang! And with the firing of the gun, a dozen startled, squealing pigs thickly coated in lard frantically raced from a chute in every direction, with eight women pursuing, hoping to be the first to wrestle one into her barrel at the far end of the arena. Make that seven women. Out of the corner of her eye, Lucy saw Jena casually jogging toward the barrels. "Somebody explain to me," Lauren panted at Lucy, "why we have to chase greased pigs, but the other girls get to go sailing—on a *boat*—for their date tomorrow?" She shrieked as a pig streaked between her legs, taking her feet out from under her.

Lucy pushed her hair out of her eyes, laughing, and gave Lauren a hand up. "Good question. Hold on, I need to . . . catch . . . this . . ." But the wiggly critter she'd almost snagged zipped through her arms and darted off. Lucy darted off right after it.

The audience laughed and roared and stomped and cheered. Lucy could barely hear the announcer's voice over the din. "Which woman will get her pig first?" A couple of pigs sprinted next to the arena fence, with Sara and Amber in hot pursuit. The announcer droned, "Hope Ethan isn't as eager to escape as these pigs are!" The audience roared again. "I got him!" someone yelled. Panicked, Lucy glanced up. Kaitlin was hunched in the dirt like a running back protecting a recovered fumble, but a split second later, the squealing pig shot out from between her legs. She face-planted into the dirt then scrambled back to her feet and dashed after it.

Lucy wiped her slimy hands on her jeans and looked around. How was she supposed to hang on to a squirming pig when the grease made its skin so slippery?

But wait. Not slippery pig's skin. Slippery *pigskin*.

She knew what to do. Her brothers (and Kaitlin's running back stance) had given her the key to the answer. She was going to get a pig into her barrel and be the first to do it.

One summer when she was a kid, they'd had monsoon-like rains, and her brothers and their buddies had taken full boyhood advantage and reveled in several days of mud football. Lucy, of course, had been pestered into playing as well. Everything had been slippery: slippery pigskin, slippery ground, slippery players. Lucy could remember all the tricks she'd had to come up with to hang on to the ball, stay on her feet, and keep away from her brothers.

She could totally do this.

Chasing the pigs had taken her closer to the barrels. It was time to make her move. One wild-eyed pig had changed its course and was headed toward the barrels. He was caked in dirt and grease and was galloping straight at her.

She got ready, waited for the right moment . . . and lunged. Thirty pounds of frantic pig were now under her, hooves churning up dirt into a brown cloud around her face. Coughing, Lucy slid one arm over the pig's shoulder as fast as she could and the other around its flanks. Snuffling and grunting, the pig bucked and shifted into reverse. She quickly wedged one of her legs between its hindquarters so it couldn't slip out from behind. Now on her knees, Lucy sucked in a breath and looked around.

She was still a good fifteen feet from her barrel.

Gripping the pig in the armlock as tightly as she could, she staggered up to her feet and into a crouch. The pig, sitting astride her thigh, grunted and squealed, its snout just inches from her ears, shrill and indignant over the roar of the crowd. It arched its back and twisted, hooves flailing. Lucy lurched forward, trying to keep its hind legs apart. Its tail ground painfully into her hip; her arms burned from exertion. She was sweating, and her hair was in her face. She had no idea if anyone else had caught a pig or had made it to a barrel. She didn't care. She only knew that her barrel was now in front of her and this pig was going into it, so help her.

She was almost there.

She hurled herself at the barrel, leaning against it for support and using her knee for leverage, and heaved the pig up to the rim. As its hindquarters slipped over the edge, the indignant pig screamed and lashed out with a hoof, catching her on the shoulder. She didn't even feel it. She was only aware of the pig tumbling down into the barrel and bouncing onto a cushion of hay.

She'd done it. Nothing else mattered right then.

She hung on to the rim of the barrel, trying to catch her breath. Gradually, she tuned in to noise around her. The other women were standing nearby, clapping. Ethan had reentered the arena on his horse and had nearly reached her. The PA crackled. The crowd was on its feet, cheering and whistling.

Ethan dismounted and walked toward her. Giving her a wink, he grabbed her by the waist and tossed her onto the back of his horse. She clutched the saddle horn with her greasy hands, hoping to keep her seat in the saddle, while Ethan took the reins in hand and walked her around the arena for a victory lap.

The PA announcer boomed. "Well, folks, I'd say that that little gal, Lucy, surely knows how to go after what she wants. Looks like she's headed for a romantic evening with our *Soulmate*." Lucy looked down at herself. She was filthy, she was dripping with sweat, and she stunk. Definitely romantic.

Ethan pulled off his hat and waved at the crowd before settling it back on his head. "Did they happen to mention that, traditionally, the prize for winning the greased pig contest is the pig?"

Her feet didn't reach the stirrups, and her grip on the saddle horn kept slipping. She rubbed her hand on the cleanest spot of her jeans, but it still felt greasy. She hoped she didn't fall off the horse. "Then if I were you, I'd be insulted."

He laughed and patted the horse's neck. "In this case, you won two prizes. The pig is the pig, and the romantic evening with me is, of course, the real prize."

"Of course." She grinned at him.

"Wave to your adoring fans."

Lucy waved. "Did I really win that pig?"

"Yup."

They'd circled the arena and were making their way through the gate. Mr. Esplin was waiting for them. "We have you set up for a little more taping over here," he said.

Ethan lifted Lucy off the saddle and handed the horse off to a waiting rodeo hand. Mr. Esplin pointed them toward a lot filled with empty horse trailers. Lucy's barrel sat there with high-pitched squeals emanating from it.

"Oh," Lucy said, walking toward it, "I'd know that sound anywhere. It's the reason for my current hearing loss." She looked inside. Her thirty-pound nemesis stared back at her with little black eyes, noisily protesting. "Poor guy. He's not happy."

Ethan peered into the barrel. "Do you always have this affect on others? Get them all riled up like this?"

Lucy put her hand in just far enough for the pig to snuffle at it. "Not intentionally. Only if they're surprised to discover that I'm a force to be reckoned with."

"Okay, Mr. Glass," Mr. Esplin interrupted. "Let's get some footage with the pig." He looked at Lucy and grimaced, making her wonder if he'd meant her when he'd said that. "Ooh, darling, you stink to high heaven. We'd better get that taken care of ASAP and get you looking civilized as well, otherwise tonight's romantic rendezvous will be a bust."

His comments were hardly flattering, even if they were true at that particular moment. It took something away from her victory and left her feeling deflated. If Ethan sensed anything, he didn't let on, and she wasn't about to clue him in either. She smiled brightly, they joked about her pig chase for the camera, and then she was escorted to a trailer where a shower and her clean clothes awaited.

CHAPTER 8

Lucy dragged herself out of bed the next day around midmorning. It had been late when she'd returned to *Soulmates* House after her date with Ethan. She tugged on her tank swimsuit, threw some loose sweats on, and headed to the kitchen, pulling her hair into a ponytail as she went. She wanted to snag a piece of toast and some OJ before heading out for a swim and a soak in the hot tub. Her muscles ached, and her shoulder and hip throbbed where the pig had taken potshots at her.

Kaitlin and Kelly were seated at the table sipping coffee when she got there. "Do you want coffee?" Kelly asked her. "It's fresh."

"No, thanks. I'll just grab some juice."

She tugged the refrigerator door open and located a carton of orange juice. She grabbed it and a loaf of bread and shut the fridge door.

"Glasses are in there." Kelly pointed to a cupboard as she refilled her own cup and returned to her seat.

Lucy stifled a yawn and dropped a slice of bread into the toaster. "I suppose the other group date has already begun."

"You just missed them," Kaitlin said. "They left about a half hour ago."

"I hope they have to do something embarrassing like we had to do," Kelly added. "It only seems fair, don't you think?"

Lucy poured orange juice into a glass and unconsciously rubbed her sore shoulder. "Where is everybody else?"

"At the pool. Your toast popped." Kaitlin rinsed her cup and put it in the dishwasher. "You got in pretty late. We've been dying to hear how it went with Ethan last night." Kaitlin smiled, but her eyes were saying that she hoped the date had seriously tanked.

Lucy located a jar of peanut butter and spread a thin layer on her toast. Talking over a bite, she said noncommittally, "We had a nice time."

"Hey, you're finally awake!" Lauren and Sara bounded into the kitchen in their swim attire, followed by Jena and Amber. Lauren plopped into the seat next to Lucy's and propped her chin on her hand. "Spill it. What was it like?"

"We want to hear *everything*," Sara added.

Lucy drank some juice and collected her thoughts. "Well, after the greased pig competition, I needed time to clean up."

"Tell us about it," Sara said. "I threw my clothes away. They were disgusting."

Tiffany entered the room and busied herself looking through the pantry cupboards. Despite her studied nonchalance, it was obvious she was tuned into the conversation like a satellite dish.

What was Lucy supposed to say? Here on *Soulmates*, they were all dating the same man like it was the most normal thing in the world. It was turning out to be a lot harder than she had imagined. And was she even interested in Ethan? Maybe a little bit after last night. She'd enjoyed being with him. But were the feelings mutual? Was Ethan interested in her? He was charming, definitely funnier than she'd expected for someone with a reputation for being tough, and an easy conversationalist. Was he that way with everyone? She didn't have a clue. Plus, she wasn't about to lose her heart to someone who didn't believe as she did. There was too much at stake.

"We're waiting," Kaitlin crooned, enthusiastic singer that she was. "You got cleaned up, and then . . ."

"We went to a barbecue. It was your basic barbecue—fried chicken, corn on the cob. Square dancing."

"*Square* dancing?" Jena asked in a tone that suggested she placed square dancing on par with dumpster diving.

"Square dancing. As in the I-haven't-done-this-since-fourth-grade kind of square dancing." She wouldn't mention that Mr. Esplin had made her wear a gingham skirt for it. Blue and white checked, with so many net petticoats attached that the thing had stuck out one hundred and eighty degrees in all directions. They could wait for that bit of info until the show aired.

Jena took an empty seat and stole a drink from Kelly's cup. Kelly looked startled and pushed it toward her. "Do you want this?" she asked.

"No," Jena replied and turned to Lucy. "It sounds so romantic. I'm dying of jealousy," she added with a heavy dose of sarcasm.

Lucy took another bite of toast and tried to ignore Jena.

"Then what happened?" Lauren asked.

"Yeah, do we have to drag this stuff out of you?" Sara asked. "You went square dancing, and then . . . ?"

"Sorry. Um . . . Kyle brought Ethan's horse back—the one from the rodeo. We rode up the canyon—"

"On horseback? On *one* horse?" Jena asked, a groove appearing between her eyebrows.

"Finally, we're getting somewhere!" Sara exclaimed.

Ethan had slid into the saddle, and then Lucy had been given a leg up so she sat in front of him. The crew had been all over the place, watching them like hawks, and the main camera had been smack dab in front of them. But even still, it had been surprisingly cozy seated there in front of him, with his arms around her while he held the reins. At one point he'd lowered his face to whisper in her ear, and when she'd turned her head to hear him better his eyes had been right there on her. She'd gone tingly and had thought he was going to kiss her, but then she'd wondered if, after his teasing about her kissing guidelines earlier, it would be a good thing or not. But he hadn't kissed her, the moment had passed, and she'd wondered if she'd imagined it.

"Yes, on one horse. We rode the horse a little way up the canyon. It was pretty, with lots of pine trees and—"

"Wait a second! Back up." Sara interrupted, studying her closely. "Did you two kiss?"

Lucy didn't want to answer that question. If she said yes, it would feel like a breach of trust to Ethan somehow. But saying no went against her competitive instincts around these women. Something must have shown in her face, though, because Sara's eyes grew huge, and she grinned like she'd just learned she had a winning lottery ticket. "You didn't kiss!"

"You were both on the same horse, he had his arms around you, and you didn't *do* anything?" Jena looked shocked. "You didn't even make a move? You are *so* lacking."

"*I* would have," Sara said. "I would have laid a big one on him and made it last for about fifty years."

Tiffany shook her head. "You aren't going to last long around here, Lucy. You don't pass up opportunities with Ethan Glass like that." She laughed in disbelief. "I don't believe it. You're such an idiot."

Lucy was getting annoyed and was equally determined not to let it show. She stood, rinsed her plate and glass, and put them in the dishwasher.

"You know, we had a great time, and we're getting to know each other. Things need to happen naturally, and it's twice as hard when the camera is there every minute—"

"It wouldn't be for me," Jena said.

"Me neither. I don't mind the camera," Kaitlin added, tossing her hair for emphasis.

"Well, I'm afraid it was uncomfortable for me." Despite having clenched teeth, Lucy tried to appear apologetic. "So if you're looking for juicy details, there aren't any. Sorry."

Tiffany gave her the Tiffany look, which translated as smugly superior. "Ethan won't bother to keep you around if he thinks you're not interested in him romantically. Not that I have a problem with that, personally."

Lucy was done talking. "I'm going out to do laps in the pool. How's the water?" She didn't wait for a reply; she walked through the door and made her way down the path to the back of the house.

A good swim would help her muscles recover from the pig ordeal. Working off the steam she'd built up listening to the others was an added bonus and would keep her from doing something violent to Tiffany and Jena. Forgive seven times seventy, she told herself grimly as she marched to the pool. She quickly stripped down to her swimsuit and dove in. The water was a cold shock, but as she settled into a rhythm, it felt soothing, and she allowed herself to let go of her irritation. With her body now on autopilot, her mind shifted back to her date with Ethan.

They'd eaten strawberries under the stars. Fresh strawberries with dipping chocolate. They'd talked and eaten while the cameras had rolled and Mr. Esplin had shouted directions. It had been the strangest thing she'd ever done, playing a romantic scene staged by others, because it *was* staged, but being expected to be herself. The pig chase and kissing booth had at least been spontaneous.

And then he'd dunked a huge strawberry into the chocolate and had held it to her lips. Feeling self-conscious, she'd managed to take a bite, though not gracefully, and had gotten chocolate on the side of her mouth. Before she'd been able to grab a napkin, Ethan had wiped it away with his thumb. Then that thumb had traveled down the corner of her mouth and across part of her lower lip—and had paralyzed her. His eyes had caught hers and held, flashing with something Lucy couldn't name. The cameras and crew and Mr. Esplin had evaporated from her awareness like smoke. Ethan had leaned in closer . . . closer . . . just bare inches from her face . . . she'd held her breath, mesmerized . . . and then he'd licked the chocolate from his thumb and grinned at her.

He'd been teasing her, egging her on like he had with the arm wrestling trick! He'd also successfully proven to them both that she *wanted* to kiss him—and wasn't *that* embarrassing after her big no-kissing speech just that afternoon?

And then there had been champagne. Again. She'd had no choice but to decline it with the cameras rolling. She'd wished she'd been able to explain herself to Ethan in private; it would have felt less awkward.

But to her surprise, he'd only nodded and said, "No problem," and Kyle had brought her a bottle of water. Ethan had clinked his glass against her bottle, and while she sipped, he said, "Here's to your unique first date guidelines."

And she'd choked and spit water all over him.

Ethan had thumped her on the back and mopped the front of his shirt while fighting back laughter—along with the crew. So much for romance. She'd resorted to humor.

"My turn," she'd managed in between coughing spasms. Taking a few breaths to clear her lungs, she'd held up her bottled water and clinked it against his glass.

"To Ethan," she said, "a cowboy who is definitely well armed." And then she'd poked his bicep with her finger.

Ethan had laughed outright. And then he'd yelled, "Dane! We're done shooting for tonight." He'd grabbed Lucy by the hand, hauled her off the blanket and onto her feet, and had tugged her up the hillside away from the crew and the lights.

There, above the California foothills, the stars had been vast and brilliant, like diamonds generously strewn on velvet, and had seemed close enough to touch. Ethan's hand had been warm in hers, and he'd carefully led her over the uneven terrain to the summit. They'd sat together on an outcrop in blissful solitude.

"Enjoying yourself?" Ethan had leaned back on his forearms and gazed at the sky.

She'd nodded and waved her hand in the direction of the sky and stars. "They're magnificent up here."

"It's one of the things I like most about home—the ranch, I mean." He'd dropped onto his back, his arms under his head. "When we were boys, our father would take us out on the range, away from the house. He'd point out the constellations and help us find them."

She'd lain back on the outcrop, her feet dangling over the edge next to his, so she could see the stars better. "I can find the Big and Little Dippers." She'd pointed them out as she spoke. "But I don't recognize anything else."

"It's been years, but, let me see . . . Okay, look to the right of the Little Dipper—not right next to it, but . . . yeah, right about there," he'd said as she'd adjusted the angle of her gaze. "See the bright stars that form a sideways *W*? That's Cassiopeia."

And she'd been able to find it. "Have you ever wondered how the ancient astronomers were able to look at the sky and see people and animals in the stars?" she'd asked him.

"Yes. Considering their primitive technology, they would only have been able to see the brightest stars. It was a clever and effective way to organize what they saw—using animals and characters from their mythology. Simple. Inspired, really."

Lucy had agreed. "I saw a news story online once, with photos from the Hubble Space Telescope. It was a picture of deep space, as deep as humans had ever been able to see. They called the picture a 'pencil beam' shot, because it focused on such a narrow visual field—narrow in width but deep in scope. They compared it to looking at the sky through an eight-foot-long drinking straw. There were at least ten thousand *galaxies* in that one picture. Ten thousand!"

Lucy had turned onto her side to face Ethan. "Can you even fathom how many 'drinking-straw' pictures it would take to photograph the entire sky?" She'd gestured at the sky above her. "And then do the entire thing again from the Southern Hemisphere? How many galaxies that would be?"

"It boggles the mind."

"Then I think about the nearest star to the sun and how distant it is. And it's just in our Milky Way galaxy. *Just!* How many other worlds like ours could there possibly be among the billions of stars in *just* our own galaxy? And then how many more than that could be in all those other galaxies? It makes you wonder, doesn't it?"

"It makes a person wonder and ponder a lot of things," he'd said.

He hadn't said anything more, and Lucy had caught him studying her. They'd quietly looked at the stars for a few more minutes, and then he'd stood and helped her to her feet. "Come on," he'd said. "The crew is waiting to take us back."

Lucy finished her swim laps and pulled herself from the pool. She settled into the bubbly heat of the hot tub next, rested her head on the edge, and sighed. She should have asked Ethan more about himself. She shouldn't have gone all *Star Trek* on him. He'd been polite but quiet on their return trip back to *Soulmates* House. She'd been left at the door without even the slightest suggestion of a kiss—the teasing kind or otherwise.

Today he was sailing with the remaining women. They would be flirting and vying for his attention. One of them would spend a lot of time with him this evening.

And Lucy realized she didn't like the sound of that at all.

* * *

When the sailing girls returned from their group date early that evening, sun kissed and ecstatic, the rodeo girls discovered they'd spent their day on a luxury yacht. Denise, a Southern belle from Atlanta, had won the privilege of spending time with Ethan because of her unmatched skills on a jet ski. They hadn't had to do anything dirty and undignified like chase a greased pig through the dirt. And that made Tiffany and Jena fighting mad.

Lucy realized that *she*, on the other hand, was fighting panic.

Ms. Carlton shooed them all into the living room. Tomorrow was an elimination day, she told them. How did they feel about that? Who had a good connection with Ethan so far? Who did they expect would be leaving? Who did they want to see leave? Why?

"You got time alone with Ethan, Lucy," she said to her from her off-camera angle. "Does that give you an advantage over the others?"

If discovering that she liked being with Ethan and was attracted to him was an advantage, then, yes. If discovering she could really fall for the guy and there were fourteen other women—amazing women—trying their hardest to make him fall for *them* and not her, then not so much. "Spending time with Ethan means he's gotten to know me better. That could also mean he knows all he needs to about me." She attempted a smile at Ms. Carlton, who didn't smile in return. Although, considering what had happened the first time Lucy had been interviewed on-camera, it felt like an improvement. Plus, she'd sounded levelheaded—hadn't she?—and not bothered in the least that someone named Denise might be nibbling strawberries and chocolate from the fingers of Ethan Glass at that very moment.

Was she bothered?

And what had Ms. Carlton just asked her? "I'm sorry, I missed that question."

"What I *asked*," Ms. Carlton said slowly and with emphasis, as if she were addressing an imbecile, "is, what are you planning to do with that pig you caught?" She raised an eyebrow.

It was a wholly unexpected question and safely removed Lucy from dangerous emotional territory. Lucy relaxed a little. "It just so happens I do have a little something planned for that pig—and, of course, it involves Ethan—but I'm going to need help pulling it off." She raised her own eyebrow in an answering challenge. "Are you with me?"

Ms. Carlton stared at her. They were in a showdown of wills. Finally Ms. Carlton said, "Stop the camera." And to Lucy's surprise, she smiled the tiniest bit. "Tell me what you're thinking, and I'll tell you if I'm in or not."

* * *

A successful businessman was something of a gambler, a man used to high stakes and taking risks. But Ethan also understood that a successful businessman—or gambler—didn't reveal his hand until he had a chance to read the other players and calculate his odds of winning. It had worked for him before and would work for him now.

It helped that he had an inside source. Ethan trusted his instincts, and his recent meetings with Dr. Lindstrom confirmed many of his initial impressions of the women too. But Ethan wasn't completely satisfied. He'd conducted too many job interviews and met with too many business associates who smiled and said everything they thought you wanted to hear to your face.

Ethan wanted to know what the girls were saying when he wasn't around to hear.

Kyle sauntered into the café and pulled off his sunglasses then spotted Ethan sitting in a booth near the back and headed in that direction. He slouched into the seat opposite Ethan, scowling and squinty-eyed. "Do you think you could have found a dive any more off the beaten path? Carlton will be all over my case if I'm gone too long. I swear she had someone plant a GPS tracking device in me when I was asleep—oh, wait, I never have a chance to sleep."

"I got you a cheeseburger, extra cheese, and a double order of fries."

"They'd better be good, considering all the hassle you put me through to get here."

The waitress arrived with a large soft drink she placed in front of Kyle and an ice water for Ethan. "Your burgers will be right out."

"Thanks, Rosa."

Kyle sipped his drink. "You've eaten here before?"

"A couple of times." Ethan ran his finger over a hole in the laminate tabletop. "The food's decent."

"If you say so. I'm sending you the bill for the ER if you're wrong though."

Ethan laughed. It felt good to laugh. "Let's get down to business before the warden discovers you're missing."

Kyle started to mutter, but their burgers arrived in the nick of time, sparing Ethan a review of Melanie Carlton's latest crimes against humanity.

"Now we're *talkin'*!" Kyle exclaimed. The cheeseburger was roughly the size of his head, but apparently that wasn't a deterrent. He took a huge bite and made growling noises like a starved wolf. "Mmm. You were right. Good burger. The caterers at the house keep bringing us these little chicken and veggie wraps. And tofu," he said around another mouthful. "Not real food like this stuff. So what do you want to know?"

Ethan picked up a fry and popped it in his mouth. "I spent some time with the doc today."

Kyle wiped a blob of mayonnaise from his mouth. "Yeah?"

"There are some great women here, Kyle. Bright, beautiful women."

"You got no argument from me on that, Kemo Sabe."

"Which ones stay beautiful when the cameras stop rolling?"

Kyle grabbed a bunch of fries, shoved them into his mouth, and chewed. "Which ones are you *hoping* stay beautiful?"

Ethan shook his head. "I'd rather hear what you have to say first."

Kyle ate another clump of fries, chewed thoughtfully, and chugged his soda. Then he took a big bite of his cheeseburger, extra cheese . . .

Ethan sighed. "I own a multinational company; I terrorize lesser mortals with only a look. You don't flinch. I can't even get you to stop chewing long enough to answer a simple question."

"It's not a simple question. And you didn't answer mine either."

"You have more of your mother in you than you know," Ethan grumbled. "Okay, there *might* be a frontrunner. *Might*. But I mean it—that's *all* I'm saying at this point. It's too early in the process."

Kyle snorted. "A *frontrunner*, Ethan? You romantic devil! I can just hear you: 'Mom, Dad, I'd like you to meet my *frontrunner*. She only used to be a *contender*, but she outflanked the other *participants*.' Maybe you could put it on a valentine."

"You're enjoying this way too much. Fine. I genuinely like some of the women. I'm strongly attracted to some of the women. There might be a woman—or *two* or *three*—I'm drawn to more than the others. But it's too early in the process; there are concerns that need to be addressed." Rosa was approaching with a pitcher of water, so he lowered his voice. "That's all I'm saying."

Rosa refilled Ethan's glass. "Can I interest either of you in dessert?"

"Not for me," Ethan said. "I'm sure the bottomless pit here will have something though."

"How about one of those brownies I saw in the case out front? A la mode."

"You got it." Rosa headed toward the dessert case.

"With an extra scoop," Kyle called.

Rosa waved over her shoulder in acknowledgment.

"If I guess who your frontrunner is, will you tell me if I'm right?"

"No."

"That's what I thought." Kyle polished off the last of his fries. "Let's see . . . who would Ethan Glass consider a *frontrunner*?" He looked at Ethan speculatively. "But is it the business mogul Ethan Glass who is doing the considering or the bronco-busting pale face I grew up with?"

Ethan eyed him suspiciously. "Have you been talking to Old Jed?"

Kyle laughed. "No, but maybe I should. How about . . . Sara? She's a babe. I'm thinking Malibu Barbie, man."

Ethan picked up a fry from his plate, dunked it in ketchup, and kept his expression neutral.

Kyle continued. "Okay, let me think. The mogul Ethan might like . . . hmmm . . . Jena or maybe Tiffany. You know, the kind who wears a tiara into the bathroom." He glanced at him to get a read, but Ethan kept his poker face firmly in place.

"Now, the bronco-busting Ethan, he'd go more for Denise or Lauren . . ." Kyle was studying him too closely, "or Lucy." He gave the last name emphasis.

Ethan took a sip of water. He could outstare Kyle, he was certain.

Kyle slapped the table. "Man, I'm right. I'm totally right."

Ethan couldn't help it. He laughed. "You don't know anything, and I told you, at this point, I'm not saying. It's too early in the game. Give it up for the time being. Now, I answered your question; you answer mine. Which of these beautiful women remain beautiful when the cameras stop rolling?"

Kyle shrugged and dug into a mountain of vanilla ice cream. He pointed with his spoon. "You need to give that Rosa a big tip, Ethan. And for the record, you *didn't* answer my question." He shoveled another bite of ice cream into his mouth. "Don't be such a stiff about this. It's *me*, you know."

"I know. But if there is a frontrunner—and I'm only saying *if*," he held up both hands to make the point, "until I put her and the others through a few more paces, I want to play this close to the vest for another day or two. Keep to my strategy."

"Hearts don't usually stick to strategies."

"Is that some sort of ancient Lakota wisdom, frat boy?"

Kyle grinned. "Nah, it's just me . . ." he tapped his chin thoughtfully with his finger, "although maybe it ought to be."

"The strategy is sound. It will get everyone through this process with the least amount of heartbreak."

Kyle turned surprisingly serious. "Just watch your step, and watch your heart."

Ethan snagged one of his last remaining fries. "Don't worry, Kyle. I'm on top of this, and you're going to help me stay there. Between the doctor, you, and me, we've got it covered."

"I'm sure you're right." Kyle shoveled a bite of brownie into his mouth and took a moment to chew and savor it. "But . . . today, instead of telling you anything I've collected on the women so far, I'm going to tell you something my mother always tells me." He grinned crookedly. "Coming from Mom, I guess that makes it *ancient* Lakota wisdom, in a way. She says: *Wa chay kay ya yo.*

"So that's what I'm saying to you: *Wa chay kay ya yo, Hunka ate.*" He threw his napkin down on the table and stood just as Rosa reached the booth. "He's getting the bill," he told her. "Make sure he gives you a big tip. The guy's a gazillionaire."

"Hey, come on! Aren't you at least going to tell me what it means?" Ethan asked, chuckling and shaking his head.

"Nah, that's *all* I'm saying at this point," Kyle replied, tossing Ethan's words back at him with a laugh as he headed for the door. "I'll be in touch."

CHAPTER 9

LUCY HAD SURVIVED THE SECOND elimination. Of those who'd gone on the rodeo date, Amber and Kelly had been cut. Kelly was lovely but, Lucy suspected, too timid; a man like Ethan would eat six of her for breakfast. But Amber, the med student, had been a surprise. Lucy had figured someone with the brains and ambition to become a doctor would appeal to a successful man like Ethan.

Of the women who'd gone on the sailing date, the only one to leave was Stacy. Lucy hadn't known her, had barely been able to put a name to a face. All totaled, twelve of them remained: Jena, Tiffany, and Kaitlin (Lucy couldn't understand how smart, pretty Amber had been eliminated, but those three hadn't), Sara, Lauren, and herself from the rodeo date. From the sailing date, Chelsea, Kim, Alison, Sienna, Rachel, and Denise.

Each woman had also received another charm for her bracelet. The sailing girls had received dolphins. Tall, gorgeous Denise with the smooth Southern accent had gotten a dolphin *and* a palm tree with tiny pearl coconuts. Lucy hadn't heard the particulars of her one-on-one time with Ethan. She hadn't wanted to appear too curious when Denise had talked about it with the others. She remembered Tiffany's tactics all too well during her own post-one-on-one inquisition. Besides, in some ways, it was better not to know. There was something to the old adage about ignorance being bliss.

The rodeo girls had received a charm shaped like a cowboy boot. Lucy also got a pig charm. When Ethan had given them to her and invited her to "continue the journey" with him, he'd leaned close to her ear and whispered, "It was a toss-up between this pig and a pair of lips. I couldn't decide what was more memorable, your first-date guidelines or your livestock-tackling methods." His teasing had felt good—until she'd watched him whisper in Denise's ear and watched her smile and flirt back. And, anyway, what did it say about Lucy that Ethan had chosen the *pig*? Lucy wasn't sure she wanted to pursue that line of thought too closely.

This week they were being divided into three groups for three different dates. The kicker was that, at the end of each one, Ethan would send someone packing, so these were pressure dates. The first one was today, and the group that included Denise, Jena, Kaitlin, and Rachel was accompanying Ethan on a wine-tasting excursion.

Lucy was glad she hadn't been assigned to this one. Even though Ethan had seemed accepting of her refusals to drink alcohol, she wasn't sure how he really felt about it. By not being on this date, she figured she'd dodged a big elimination bullet. Obviously, Ethan was comfortable drinking. Most people were. But abstaining from alcohol was a part of her. That difference alone ought to caution her away from him—and it did—but not entirely, and that realization surprised and unsettled her. She needed to think about it.

Plus, it was Sunday. She hadn't expected to have any Sundays free while she was here. They'd signed away their rights to nearly everything: cell phone, Internet, anything they might potentially use to contact someone. Every aspect of the taping was guarded to prevent leaks prior to the airing of the show. The women were required to stay at the house. Still, it was Sunday, she wasn't on the date, and they weren't taping the girls left behind. She decided to ask the producers if they would bend enough to let her go to church somewhere. Anonymously. If she took a vow of silence, under penalty of torture.

It was worth a shot.

Ethan had arrived at the house looking GQ in a polo shirt with casual slacks. And then he and the four women had left in a limo.

"Ethan will see right through Jena and Kaitlin in no time," Chelsea said, her leg draped over the arm of the chair she was lounging in and swinging back and forth. "Kaitlin's only looking to land a recording contract. She said so again last night."

"Yes, but she also said that finding out Ethan was so cool was making her rethink her plans," Lauren added.

"And Jena made it perfectly clear that there are very few men on this planet who meet her high expectations, and Ethan Glass is one of them," Sara said. "Daddy would definitely approve," she continued in a dead-on imitation of Jena. "Of course, Ethan's family roots are a little rustic, not very blue blood, but he does have an advanced degree from a suitable, if not exactly Ivy League, university. His financial successes definitely compensate for *those* personal weaknesses."

Chelsea chimed in, mimicking Jena like Sara had. "Besides," she droned, "Ethan Glass is *exactly* what I need to make Michael Hensley, the *reptile*, realize what he lost when he dumped me for that little blonde witch."

Lucy slipped out of the room. Maybe they were right, and Ethan would see through Jena and Kaitlin, who definitely had ulterior motives. But Lucy didn't think Ethan would simply dismiss Denise and Rachel. The two women were a matched set: tall, brunette, and blessed with the looks and figure of a Victoria's Secret model. Next to either one of them, Lucy felt like the proverbial kid sister.

If Lucy were honest with herself, her own motives for being on the show could be considered suspect. She'd had low expectations about the whole thing, figuring, at most, it would amount to a free vacation or provide leads for a job. Getting to know Ethan had changed things for her, like they had apparently done for Kaitlin. The other women's motives could change just as easily as hers had and for the very same reason: they were starting to develop feelings for him.

Watching him with the other women was like having a sliver—it got under her skin and was a lot more painful than she would have expected.

Why was she here? Why had coming here felt so right? She didn't want to contemplate the day she'd be leaving and hitting the Magic Kingdom anymore. She wanted to be *here*, getting to know Ethan better. She wasn't ready to trade him for Donald Duck or even Prince Charming at this point.

Conversely, she *didn't* want to be here watching Ethan date the other women. She didn't want to spend the day wandering around *Soulmates* House with little to do except wonder what he was doing and with whom and feeling anxious about it. She needed something to get her mind off of things for a while and give her a better perspective, and she knew just what that was.

She found Ms. Carlton in the kitchen, supervising Kyle and Zack as they stowed groceries in the cupboards and refrigerator. "Who knew a bunch of skinny girls could eat so much in a week," Zack said.

Ms. Carlton didn't even look up from her clipboard. "Yes, and most of them probably just throw it up anyway." She saw Lucy out of the corner of her eye and had the decency to look embarrassed. "Hello, Lucy. Was there something you needed?"

"Things are quiet around here, and—I know our contract says we're required to stay at the house, but . . ." Kyle and Zack stopped putting away groceries and were now listening as well. "Well, it's Sunday, and I wondered if I could go to church." Zack rolled his eyes and went back to unloading produce from a box. Fresh spinach. "If I promise not to talk to anyone about the show or try to get in touch with anyone from home . . . ?"

Ms. Carlton studied Lucy. Kyle's eyes shifted from Ms. Carlton to Lucy and back to Ms. Carlton. Her pen tapped against the side of the clipboard. Finally she said, "I'll need to check with Curt, and probably Dane too. I'll see what I can do."

Lucy smiled. "Thanks. I appreciate it."

Ms. Carlton pulled out her cell phone and started texting. "Don't thank me just yet."

* * *

Lucy sat near the back of the chapel, listening to a teenage boy speak on the subject of faith. Kyle slouched next to her with his arms folded over his chest and his eyes shut. Lucy wasn't sure if he was asleep or not but figured she could nudge him if he started to snore or drool. He'd knotted a tie around his neck, so she hadn't bugged him about his jeans. She, on the other hand, had gone through her suitcase in search of the least cocktail-party-looking dress she could find. She was sure they'd raised a few eyebrows as they'd walked into church together.

Ms. Carlton had allowed Lucy the use of her laptop to locate a meetinghouse. They'd found one only a dozen miles away with a sacrament meeting beginning at eleven. Conditions had been laid out in no uncertain terms by Mr. Myers, the producer, and Kyle had been recruited as driver, aka babysitter. He'd raised a ruckus when he'd learned that church normally lasted three hours, until she'd agreed that they could leave after the first one.

Kyle had proceeded to pepper her with questions as soon as they'd slid into the back bench: Where's all the stained glass? Where's the cross? Why isn't there a cross? Where's the altar? Which one is the pastor? Where is his collar? Was there going to be a collection plate? Was she sure there wasn't? How much would it cost him if she was wrong about that? When he'd finally run out of things to ask her, he'd relaxed into the bench and left her alone to collect her thoughts.

He'd been quiet through the first part of the services until they'd gotten to the sacrament; then he'd gestured toward the row of teenage boys in white shirts and ties who'd stood and moved to the front of the chapel after the congregational hymn. Kyle had whispered, "Altar boys?"

"Kind of, but not exactly," Lucy had whispered back.

He'd looked like he wanted to ask something more, but she'd smiled and mouthed, "Later." He'd nodded and turned away, content for the moment to simply sit and watch as the boys passed the sacrament. It had given her a few minutes of peace to collect her thoughts before she proceeded to listen to the speakers. She'd wanted to answer his questions, but it had also been distracting. She needed peace and answers herself.

The youth speaker concluded and returned to his seat on the podium, and a woman stood next. The subject was once again faith. Lucy tried to concentrate on what was being said, but her thoughts wandered.

What reasons might explain why she'd felt so strongly about being on the show? Because truthfully, she *had* felt strongly about it. In fact, when she'd learned that her friends had filled out the *Soulmates* application for her and she'd been chosen to be on the show, she'd been appalled. It wasn't until after she'd read all the info, talked to her parents, and *prayed* that she'd really felt at peace about the whole deal. So why, she asked herself again, was she here? Why had the prayer felt like a virtual green light? And why, oh why, was she beginning to think the answer might lie with Ethan and not with the friendships she was making with the others? And why was that thought so disturbing?

Kyle jerked a little, like he was dozing off. The movement brought Lucy out of her reverie in time to catch part of a scripture the woman was quoting. It was a familiar one about dispute not because you see not, for you receive no witness until after the trial of your faith. Something like that. She would look it up in the small set of scriptures she'd brought with her when she got back to the house that afternoon.

Was that what this was, a trial of her faith? A test of her belief in her prayers and the answer she'd felt in her heart?

Or was this all wishful thinking, based on feelings for Ethan that she could tell were getting stronger?

Organ music filled the air as the introduction for the closing hymn began. Lucy reached for the hymnal, and Kyle straightened and rubbed a hand over his face. "Is it over already?" he asked with a drowsy sigh. "That didn't last very long."

Despite her serious thoughts, Lucy nearly chuckled. Maybe she should ask him if he would like to stay for Sunday School as well.

* * *

"I wasn't surprised to see Kaitlin go," Sienna said the next morning when the women gathered to hear about the date. "She's a Gemini. It would never have worked between them."

Lucy had no idea what that meant, but Sienna seemed absolutely certain.

Rachel scoffed. "It was either that or the fact that her singing was making his ears bleed. I know mine were."

A few women snickered. Lucy wasn't exactly sorry to see Kaitlin go, but Rachel's comment was harsh. She opened her mouth to say something, but Sienna, taking offense for a totally different reason, bristled. "You can make jokes, but the stars don't lie. They tell it like it is."

Obviously Sienna had missed the point of Rachel's barb. But Lucy was struck by what Sienna had unintentionally said. During their evening together, she and Ethan had looked at stars in a heaven that went on forever. The stars do tell it like it is. Sienna was right about that, at least. How could a person not believe in forever when the stars proved it every night?

Denise, Jena, and Rachel had each received a charm, and Denise held out her arm so everyone could see their latest addition. It was a little cluster of grapes made of amethysts, and it was breathtaking. Not like a pig at all. "We took a private jet to this lovely little winery up near Carmel." Why was it that everything Southern belle Denise said sounded like it could be poured onto pancakes? "I've never been in a private jet before—it was heavenly. And the wines! Just wonderful."

"Yes, at least Ethan knows his wines," Jena added approvingly.

Ethan knows his wines. Lucy drank Welch's grape juice.

Denise continued. "And that man! I fall a little more in love with him every day. I wanted to keep him all to myself."

Lucy could feel the burning question coming and waited to see who would do the asking. It was Tiffany. "Does that mean you kissed him? Did any of you kiss him?" Lucy glanced around. Denise smiled demurely, Rachel looked victorious, and Jena acted aloof. Elementary, my dear Watson. He'd kissed *both* Denise and Rachel. And wasn't that just spiffy?

"Spill it." Tiffany added.

Lucy didn't want to hear what spilled, but she heard it anyway. A Mrs. Butterworth sigh flowed out of Denise, all sweet and warm and—

sweet. "It was *so* romantic, just the two of us, out on the veranda." The *veranda*. Not the patio or deck or balcony. *Vuh-rayan-dah*. Could Lucy pull off words like *veranda* as well as Denise did? Nope. "It gives me shivers just thinking about it. He made a toast . . ."

"What did he say in the toast?" Sara asked, looking disgustingly dreamy-eyed.

"Oh," Denise murmured, "he said, 'here's to finding love, and here's to a lovely woman.' Bless his heart. Isn't that sweet?"

Sweet wasn't the word Lucy would have chosen, but she wasn't surprised that Denise had. It was a lovely *veranda* kind of word. Personally, Lucy felt queasy, as if she'd just eaten too much—like pancakes maybe.

"And then we talked and talked like we'd known each other forever."

Forever. There was that word again, except it sounded like *foh-ray-vah* when Denise said it.

"What did you talk about?" Lucy ventured, hoping she'd struck the right balance between friendly curiosity and nonchalance.

Before Denise had a chance to answer, Sara interrupted. "Never mind all that. Tell us about *the kissing*."

Denise blushed prettily. How did she *do* that? She'd probably blushed prettily out on the *veranda* too. And Ethan probably found it irresistible. "A lady doesn't kiss and tell."

"Well, *this* lady does," Rachel proclaimed. She looked at the other women and smiled in a way that said, "Game, set, match."

That was enough for Lucy. She didn't wait to hear the rest. She left the room and ran laps around the *Soulmates* House property.

The next group date included Kim, Chelsea, Alison, and Sara. They headed to Las Vegas with Ethan for some glitz and gambling, and the women didn't return until nearly dawn. Vegas was a city of the night, after all.

Lucy sat up in bed with a start. She'd awakened to a crashing sound, followed by some thumps and muffled talking. The gray light of dawn filtered through the window. In the hallway, the thumping and talking got louder.

"Wha's goin' on?" A drowsy Lauren pushed herself up on her elbows, her curly hair completely hiding her face.

"They're back," Lucy whispered.

"Who? Oh yeah . . ." Lauren collapsed back into her pillow and started snoring gently, making little puffs and snuffling sounds.

Heaving a sigh, Lucy eased her legs over the side of the bed. Maybe she'd catch a nap later by the pool, once the Vegas girls were sleeping off their excitement.

She opened the bedroom door and stepped into the hallway.

In the dim light, Lucy could make out three figures. They tromped up the stairs, breaking into giggles and shushing each other. The one in the middle—Lucy thought it was Alison—whispered loudly, "I have to take these off before I fall." She turned suddenly, sending the other two off balance and grabbing at the walls for support. More giggling. Alison plopped down onto the step and reached for her shoe. Sliding it from her foot, she tossed it down the stairs toward the entry, where it clattered onto the tile floor.

"Shh!" one of them—Sara?—said and giggled some more.

The other shoe noisily followed the first. Alison groaned as she hoisted herself off the step, holding tightly to Chelsea and Sara. "That feels *so* much better! Now I wanna go to bed, and—"

They all shrieked simultaneously when they saw Lucy at the top of the stairway. That startled Lucy into shrieking too.

Sara clung onto the stair rail for dear life. "Don't you *ever* do anything like that again!" she said to Lucy between gasps and giggles.

"I could say the same to you!" Lucy managed in between her own deep breaths.

Alison, normally a cool temptress with her auburn hair and exotic blue eyes, was grinning at Lucy like the village idiot. "I tripped and landed in the potted plants."

Lucy heard noise behind her. She turned and saw sleepy faces peeking from bedroom doorways. "Kim's gone," someone observed.

Sara slid into a sitting position on the landing with her back against the wall. "Poor Kim. When it comes to Ethan, she gambled and lost." She snickered and shook her wrist at them. Her bracelet now included a charm shaped like a pair of dice. "Pair of dice, pair of dice," Sara crooned in a drunken singsong way until the words ran together. "Pair of dice, paradise. Vegas was paradise! But not for Kimmie." Lucy's eyes widened in shock. She hadn't ever seen funny, good-humored Sara like this. Actually, she hadn't seen any of them quite like this. They were completely wasted.

Lucy liked Kim and was sorry she'd been eliminated. She wasn't classically pretty like a lot of the women here, but she'd been friendly and funny and amazingly smart. Someone Ethan would appreciate, Lucy thought.

Kim had joked that she intended to write up her *Soulmates* experience, call it "What I Did for My Summer Vacation," and use it as her master's thesis. "Do you think my professors will be impressed?" she'd asked Lucy, almost managing a straight face.

"I suppose it depends on what you're studying," Lucy had countered. "Abnormal psychology?"

"Chaos theory was more what I was thinking," Kim had replied. They'd had a good laugh.

"And then we cashed in our chips and went to this dinner show," Alison said to her growing audience. Her words slurred. "There was this musician"—she giggled—"I mean *magician.* He asked for volunteers—"

"Except they'd already arranged for *us* to be the volunteers," Sara said, taking over the telling of the story, although she wasn't in much better shape than Alison. "Chelsea got sawn in half."

Everyone looked at Chelsea, who'd been quiet so far. Her forehead was resting on her knees, but at the mention of her name, she looked up at everyone and nodded, bleary-eyed. Her head immediately returned to its resting place.

Alison spoke up again. "I got levistated—legitated. Hmm." She looked puzzled, but then she shrugged. "I floated in the air."

"What did Ethan do?" someone asked.

Sara flicked a hand in dismissal. "Oh, he only had to walk around the stage and wave a wand and say abracadabra and stuff. I got changed into a tiger and then back again."

"What about Kim? Did she do a magic trick?" Lucy asked.

Sara and Alison looked at each other and then burst out laughing. "Kim vanished!" Sara said.

Alison nodded. "She vanished into thin air."

"In a puff of smoke," Sara added, giggling.

"Someone who's supposed to be a genius like Kim ought to know that Vegas is all about the party." Alison grabbed the stair rail and pulled herself up. "Now I'm going to bed to have me some sweet Ethan dreams."

"Me too." Sara teetered for a minute before she found her balance. "Mmm, Ethan is so tasty, he's delish—"

"Don't say tasty!" Chelsea jerked herself off the floor suddenly. "Don't say anything food! Arrgh!" She fled down the hall. "I'm going to be sick!" Lucy started to go after her to see if she was going to be all right, but Denise was already on the way.

"We want to hear more about Ethan," Tiffany said, ignoring Chelsea's plight and focusing her patent bare-lightbulb-and-rubber-hose glare on Alison, the person who seemed most likely to crack under the strain of the moment.

But Sara grabbed Alison's hand and pulled her, stumbling, to their shared bedroom. She poked her head out the door and shot a goofy grin back at the others. "We're not saying anything else for now," she crowed, "except that the fight for Ethan is *on.*" The door slammed, and the remaining girls were left with the sound of Chelsea moaning as she threw up repeatedly in the bathroom.

* * *

"What are the story arcs we've got so far?" Curt asked. Melanie looked up from her laptop to glare at him. How could such a fantastic looking guy be such a clod at times? Oh wait. That was exactly why.

He'd called this clandestine meeting with her because Ethan was gone today, attending to "urgent business"—Curt had finger-quoted when he'd told her that—before the Mexican date tomorrow. She'd spent the morning playing nursemaid to three whining women, doing online searches for hangover remedies, and sending assistants here and there for vitamin water and bananas and Gatorade, in addition to her regular work.

She wasn't being paid enough to play Florence Nightingale, especially since she'd had to handle too many of the details for the Carmel and Vegas trips because Curt had had an "emergency" of his own. She finger-quoted the word in her mind. She could believe Mr. Multimillionaire was attending to urgent business, but Curt had probably had a week at a spa scheduled and couldn't change the dates. His absence had left her with a boatload of the work. They were sparsely staffed to begin with, and she'd been swamped coordinating the crew and keeping Dane Esplin from rupturing an artery. "I don't do story arcs or windows." She wouldn't tell him she'd been doing research of her own. Not yet anyway. "Maybe you should talk to Dane."

"Dane's worth squat. He makes me nervous. When this is over, I'm going to remember who recommended him to me and have them shot." He poured on the charm. "Mel, I trust you. And I really need you to tell me what you see going on so we can push the edge on this thing."

The next time Melanie thought a job looked like a great career move, she was going to haul on her Nikes and run away as far and as fast as possible. "You know, Mr. Myers—"

"By now, shouldn't you be calling me Curt?"

"Probably not." If he became Curt instead of Mr. Myers, she was positive she'd be taking care of his dry cleaning and giving him pedicures along with everything else. She ignored his hurt puppy dog look; she didn't believe it for a second. "I already do the work of five people. I average four hours of sleep a night. I've been covering your sorry backside all week. I should complain to a union rep. I'm going to Mexico tomorrow only because I plan to sit under a big umbrella in a little bathing suit with a tropical drink in one hand and a dime store novel in the other. I've earned it."

"I agree. You have earned it."

Sympathetic words from Curt? It was undoubtedly the threat about the union rep that had done it. All the same, he ought to win an Oscar; he almost sounded sincere. "I deserve more than a day in the sun; I deserve a medal for putting up with a boss who's referred to as Voldemort by the US Department of Labor."

Curt only chuckled. Annoying man. "Ouch!" he said. "I think I'm bleeding. I tell you what—starting tomorrow, I will be the model employer." He had the audacity to place his hand over his heart. "In the meantime, just for today . . ." He let his words linger in the air, giving her his patent charm-your-socks-off look.

She felt herself caving and cursed her weakness. Why did her internal fortitude collapse so easily with this guy? "Okay! Okay. I can't promise I'll be of much help though. My sleep-deprived mind only wants to focus on a Mexican beach and some fictional guy named Raoul—he looks a lot like Antonio Banderas, by the way—who is massaging the knots out of my shoulders while the sea breeze lulls me into the sleep of the dead." She glared at Curt for emphasis.

"Yeah, yeah, forget Raoul. Help me here and now and I'll arrange for a whole army of masseuses to come in later this afternoon to beat you to a pulp if you want." He slid over into the seat next to hers. "Just tell me what you've noticed when you're around Ethan and the women. You're right there in the middle of them more than anyone else."

Melanie rubbed her temples. "Story arcs. I don't know. Let me think." She glanced at him. "You'll really bring someone in to give me a massage?"

"I said I would, didn't I? So what have you noticed about the women? Have you picked up on any particular vibes? Who's really into Ethan?"

"They're all into Ethan. That's the whole point of the show."

"How do they get along around the house?"

"Tiffany and Rachel are out for blood. They even scare me sometimes, and in case you haven't noticed, I don't scare easily; Lucy and Lauren are the *nice* girls, if such a creature actually exists. Take one gigantic step past nice toward the sugar bowl of sweetness, and you have Saint Denise of the Southern Belles. Don't get me started there."

Melanie moved her head to stretch the tightening muscles in her neck. "Chelsea is basically boring. Sara and Alison are in it for the game, since the prize for the winner is a millionaire and his bank account. Same goes for Jena, with extra bonus points for snob value. And Sienna has yet to land on planet Earth."

Curt leaned back and put his feet on the table, crossing them at the ankles. "So we have a couple of pit bulls, some gold diggers, a few nice girls—one who gives you diabetes when she smiles—and a wild card."

"That about covers it."

"And what about the girls who've been eliminated?"

Melanie scowled. "What about them?"

"We still need to flesh out the story arcs for the first few episodes. They're being edited right now so if you can add any insights, now's the time to do it."

Melanie sighed. Again. "I don't remember anything about the ten who left the first night. Sorry. But since then, let's see: Kelly, Amber, Stacy. Nice, nice, nice. Kaitlin. Nice, but annoying with her whole singing career obsession. Kim. The walking encyclopedia . . . but nice again." Her brow wrinkled. "Hmm. Isn't that interesting. He's getting rid of nice girls. Funny, Ethan Glass doesn't strike me as the type to go for bad girls."

"He's not." Curt got serious, an abnormal state for him, and Melanie wondered what he was thinking. The silence stretched before he finally spoke. "He's up to something; I'm not sure what. He wouldn't jeopardize the success of the show—that I know for a fact. But he *is* up to something." He looked at Melanie. "I think I'd better go to Mexico tomorrow and check on things personally."

"Sounds like a good idea," Melanie said, "because, *Curt*, I'll be there reading my dime store novel and sipping my tropical drink."

Curt tugged on a few strands of her hair as he stood and headed to the door. "With an attitude like that, I guess I'll be rethinking that fat bonus I had planned for you. Especially if someone named Raoul really does show up."

CHAPTER 10

LUCY WRIGGLED INTO THE ONE-PIECE bandeau swimsuit Grace had found online for her before she'd left for California. Allie had complained that Lucy's standard racers made her look like an amoeba with legs and that she needed an upgrade. So Lucy had relented, and they'd found a couple of fairly modest swimsuits online that Allie had conceded didn't actually make her look like she was preparing for the Summer Olympics. The Summer Olympics of 1952, that is.

There was a knock just as Lucy fastened the straps of the suit behind her neck. "Are you decent?" a voice called.

She opened the guest room door. Lauren stood there, golden and glowing in a tiny leopard print bikini with a sheer cover-up, her curls bouncing around her head from her barely contained excitement. "It's time to go." The two of them, along with Tiffany and Sienna—and Curt Myers, Dane Esplin, Melanie Carlton, and the cameramen and most of the crew—had traveled with Ethan by private jet to Baja, California, where Ethan had a very rich friend who owned a very large (and conveniently unoccupied) hacienda near the Sea of Cortez, complete with its own private airstrip. They'd been told to dress for hot weather and pack swimsuits and casual evening wear.

Lucy pulled on her cover-up and grabbed her tote bag and sunglasses. The two of them headed outside to find Tiffany and Sienna already there with Ethan. Cameras were already rolling. Tiffany had a territorial grasp that still managed to appear flirtatious on Ethan's arm. Sienna stood nearby, making deliberately subtle adjustments to her clothing in an attempt to draw Ethan's attention away from Tiffany. Since her clothing consisted of three tiny scraps of neon-pink fabric and a cover-up that made her look like she'd been caught in a silver fishing net, it was nearly impossible for anyone to ignore what she was doing. Ethan glanced up as Lucy and Lauren approached. Politely extricating himself from Tiffany's clutches, he walked over to greet them. The cameras followed him.

"You look great," he said to Lucy. Lucy watched as he regarded her from head to toe, moved to survey Lauren, and then glanced back at Tiffany and Rachel. "All of you." He smiled. She silently thanked Allie and Grace for insisting she buy the new swimsuit. At least she didn't feel like an amoeba on legs. The other three women's suits combined could have been made from her swimsuit with fabric to spare. And it was patently obvious that Ethan—and everyone else—was as aware of that fact as Lucy was.

The Mexican air was hot and dry and reminded her of home. The sun burned white in the sky, and she could feel the heat of the pavement through the soles of her sandals as she climbed into the idling SUV.

Ethan followed and settled himself between Lauren and Lucy, who were in the very back seat. Sienna and Tiffany were sitting in the seat in front of them, which had been installed to face backward. A cameraman rode shotgun, his camera already recording the action. Between the relentless Mexican heat and the number of passengers, the air conditioning's efforts did little to lower the temperature.

"I'm ready for some fun," Ethan said. "José, let's get out of here."

"*Sí*, Señor Ethan," the chauffeur said.

They turned onto a road that headed toward the Sea of Cortez. "This area is known for its great snorkeling," Ethan said. He glanced at them to gauge their reactions. "Anyone interested?"

Happy squeals and clapping seemed to give an affirmative.

The Sea of Cortez was breathtaking. It rippled and shimmered under a cloudless sky, and the barren rocks and hills bordering it made it even more dramatic where they occasionally broke through the water's surface offshore. For a moment, Lucy simply took in the view. She'd seen it flying in, of course, and it had been beautiful. But right now, looking through the window, she allowed herself to drink it in and savor it.

The road led to a secluded beach. They piled out of the SUV and headed in the direction of a local resident who was waiting to instruct them in the use of snorkel equipment. Lucy had always wanted to try snorkeling because she loved to swim. *This is why I agreed to be on this show*, she told herself, *so that I'd have experiences like this.*

After they'd been taken through the essentials, the group waded into the sea for some shallow water practice. To her delight, Lucy adjusted to the snorkeling equipment easily. She couldn't see much underwater, except everyone's feet at this point, but she didn't care. She was exhilarated by the prospect of the adventure to come.

Ethan turned out to be an old hand at the sport. In fact, someone let it slip that Ethan had his scuba certification, although he personally downplayed the fact. He spent a lot of time helping Sienna, who couldn't seem to get the hang of it no matter what Ethan or the instructor suggested—much to the chagrin of the other women.

After a couple of trial runs in the shallow water, they made their way to a waiting boat and cruised through the turquoise waters of the Sea of Cortez, stopping about a hundred feet from a small, rocky island. Ethan dove in first, with Lauren and Lucy quickly following. Tiffany opted to slip over the side of the boat and push away from the hull.

Sienna, however, planted herself on deck, shaking her head. After enduring several minutes of haranguing from Mr. Esplin, who was standing behind the cameramen on the deck, she got up the nerve and made it to the bottom of the ladder. Then she froze again. Ethan swam back to the boat.

"Come on, Sienna," Ethan coaxed in soothing tones. "You can do it. I'll catch you."

Ethan promising to catch her was apparently all the motivation she needed. She let go of the ladder and lunged for Ethan then scrambled up his body and locked her arms around his neck.

"Loosen your grip, Sienna," Ethan rasped, his face starting to turn red. "Relax and let the water carry you. I won't let go. Trust me." Sienna continued to cling to him like seaweed. "Come on, honey. If you choke me, we'll both drown."

He sure was patient, Lucy thought a little enviously as she treaded water and watched him gradually get Sienna to relax the stranglehold on his neck.

Lauren swam up to Lucy, her naturally curly hair coiling into springs around her face. "Lucky Sienna, huh. Check out Tiff," she whispered and gestured with her head toward Tiffany. "If looks could kill . . ."

With her red hair wet and glistening against her flawless features, Tiffany should have looked like a sea goddess or the subject of a Botticelli painting. Instead, she had all the soft allure of a villainess from a graphic novel. Right then, Ethan turned his face and smiled at them, and Lucy watched Tiffany's face magically transform from shrew to siren. Amazing. Not to mention spooky.

Sienna maintained a white-knuckle grip on Ethan's arm, and there were a few welts on his neck, but at least his face had returned to its natural color, which meant he was taking in oxygen again. He pointed to the island. "We're heading there. It's one of my favorite spots for diving and snorkeling." He gave Sienna a concerned glance. "Are you ready?"

Sienna, brave little soldier that she was, nodded reluctantly. Ethan helped her adjust her mask. Tiffany scowled again. Lucy could actually relate to how Tiffany was feeling.

She told herself he was only being solicitous of Sienna and her clingy-vine fear of the water, ignoring the little stab that went through her middle. *I'm here for the adventure*, she reminded herself sternly. *Not for the guy.*

If only she still believed it.

She nudged Lauren. "Last one to the island is a rotten egg."

"You're on," she replied, quickly jamming the snorkel into her mouth and taking off through the water.

Lucy yanked her mask in place, cleared her snorkel, and followed, determined not to let Ethan's attention to Sienna ruin her day in Mexico.

And then real magic happened. Below her, the liquid blue world took shape, and she forgot all about racing Lauren and being a rotten egg. Schools of fish darted past, angelfish and species Lucy didn't know but that were colorful even in their turquoise environment. The sea wasn't very deep at this point, and although the sun didn't make it to the bottom, she could make out the ghostly outlines of sea urchins and starfish in the shadows. A turtle swam past her, intent on its business. She spread her arms wide and floated blissfully along with the current and watched a manta ray rise from its resting place on the sea floor, stir up clouds of sand in the process, and flutter off. It was glorious.

Too soon, she reached the island. Lauren had gotten there ahead of her and had perched on a rocky ledge. "You win," Lucy said once she'd hauled herself up next to Lauren and removed her snorkel and mask.

"You're a rotten egg," Lauren replied, staring out at the water behind Lucy. "But I think we both lose," she added grimly. Lucy looked back over her shoulder. Tiffany was trying to start a water fight with Ethan, while Sienna clung to him, screaming and ducking her head to avoid getting splashed. Two cameramen shot footage from a dinghy near them, and another was treading water nearby, shooting as well.

Tiffany shoved water in Ethan's direction. Sienna shrieked.

"You know," Lauren said, "I remember Sienna spending time in the pool back at the *Soulmates* House. Don't you?"

"Besides the hot tub? I'm not sure."

"I'm positive I've seen her swimming in the pool."

Lucy shrugged. Sienna had never really been on her radar. She remembered seeing her lying by the pool and doing a meditation-type ritual on the lawn nearby, but she'd never paid enough attention to know if she'd gone for a dip afterward. "Maybe she has a phobia of sharks or something."

Lauren snorted. "Yeah, that's it. She's afraid of sharks. It bugs me that she's getting extra time with Ethan this way, especially when I'm positive she really does know how to swim. Doesn't it bug you?"

The part of Lucy that grew up trying to outdo her brothers was honest enough to admit that it did bug her. A lot, actually. "If she's faking this, then, yeah, it bugs me." Another part of her was beginning to admit that seeing him with *anybody* was beginning to bug her.

"Lucy, how good are you at holding your breath underwater?" Lauren asked.

"I'm way better than good."

Lauren grabbed her mask and pulled it on. "What do you say we go liven things up for Ethan, Tiffany, and the chicken of the sea?"

Lucy wriggled her mask into place and grinned. "I say you're on."

They slid into the water covertly, taking advantage of the fact that Ethan had a female on either side of him demanding his attention. When they were about ten feet away, Lucy and Lauren took deep breaths and went under. Lucy could see Lauren to her left and three pairs of legs kicking straight in front of her.

The target was in sight.

She also noticed that a cameraman with an underwater camera was down there with them as well. He wore dive skins and a tank. Even more fun.

She swam up behind Ethan and ran her fingers over one of his ankles just above his fin and up his calf a few inches. His foot twitched, and he kicked out in reflex, like he'd caught a loose frond of floating seaweed. Dodging his kick, she resumed her tickling, down his calf and around his ankle. He kicked again.

Lucy fought to hold back laughter and lost the battle. Bubbles of escaping air surrounded her face. She broke the surface and gulped a few breaths. Strangely, as she looked around at the choppy water, she couldn't see anyone nearby. Suddenly Ethan emerged from the water, pulling Sienna up from below the surface; she was coughing and spluttering in gasping sobs.

Uh-oh. Something had happened, and unfortunately, Lucy knew who the culprit was.

Lauren popped up between Tiffany and the cameraman, who had also surfaced. They watched a concerned Ethan help Sienna into the dinghy. Lucy turned to Lauren. "By 'liven things up,' I didn't think you meant forcing Ethan to perform mouth to mouth resuscitation on anyone."

Lauren smiled sheepishly at Lucy as they swam to the island.

"Oops," was all she said.

* * *

The crew had set out a picnic lunch of fresh fruit and seafood under beach umbrellas—mangoes, pineapples, avocados drenched in lime juice, and mounds of shrimp and shellfish on beds of ice. The women nibbled and relaxed—as much as it was possible to relax when surrounded by cameras. They also flirted with Ethan. Later, he would take them one at a time for some snorkeling and exploring. A cameraman had been assigned to tape the women who remained behind each time.

Sienna went off with him first.

"It's not fair that Sienna gets more time with Ethan; she's been glued to him ever since we landed in Mexico," Lauren complained as she stretched out on her beach towel.

Lucy made a noncommittal noise and tugged the brim of her hat down over her eyes. She was full, sun warmed, and sleepy, and not in the mood for this type of conversation. Tiffany ignored them both and smoothed tanning lotion evenly over her skin.

A half hour passed before Ethan returned with Sienna and left with Tiffany. Sienna picked up her towel and moved it several feet away from Lucy and Lauren. No big surprise there, especially after the dunking she'd taken earlier.

Lucy rolled onto her stomach and peeked out from under the brim of her hat at Lauren. "Will you put sunscreen on my back, please?"

"Sure." Lauren sat up and squeezed lotion onto Lucy's shoulders in squiggles then proceeded to rub it in. "You don't want to wait to let Ethan have the honors?"

Lucy snorted. "No. Besides, I'll turn into a lobster if I wait any longer."

"Just asking."

"I can't believe you pulled Sienna under the water," Lucy whispered, darting a glance at Sienna.

"I know I shouldn't have, but I couldn't stand the idea that she might be faking," Lauren whispered back. She sighed. "If Ethan finds out, I'll be toast. Not that I had much of a chance with him to begin with."

"Lauren?" Lucy lowered her voice even more in case Sienna's hearing was particularly good.

"Hmmm?" Lauren rubbed the excess lotion off her hands and stretched out on her towel.

"What do you think of Ethan? I mean, really think of him."

"I think he's freaking amazing. It wouldn't take any effort to fall for him, and hard."

Lucy knew she shouldn't have asked. She had no idea what to do. It wouldn't take much for her to fall for him too. Her competitive nature was battling her practical side. Millionaire guy versus Mormon girl. Fight for Ethan, fall on the sword. Be aggressive, be reserved. Care, don't care. Her emotions were in constant upheaval, soaring one minute and plummeting the next, going from elated to depressed to confident to insecure. She made friends and then became jealous of them. Ethan alternately made her feel like the only woman he could see—and then invisible.

And it all stunk because as much as she didn't want to admit it, Ethan had turned into her reason for being here. He made her want to climb the pine tree, figuratively speaking.

Underlying it all was the dilemma that, for her, a real soulmate would be a man who would want to be married to her forever. As in temple-marriage forever. Was there even the remotest possibility of that happening here? The odds were beyond bad. Should she bow out and make room for someone who wouldn't have those types of concerns? She didn't want to.

"What about you?" Lauren asked.

"What about me?"

"Are you falling for him?"

Lucy propped her chin on her fists. *Fight for Ethan, fall on the sword. Be aggressive, be reserved. Care, don't care.* "He's definitely not what I expected."

"I know! It's crazy to even think about falling for a guy who can't tell any of us how he feels. It's crazy watching him date other women." She rolled to her side and supported her head on her hand, facing Lucy. "But

I can't help it; I've never dated anyone like him before. You know—good looking, loaded, smart, loaded, funny, loaded . . . he probably rescues kittens from trees and is able to leap tall buildings in a single bound." She paused. "You're supposed to be laughing. You're not laughing."

Lucy smiled. "I am too laughing. This is me laughing on the inside."

Lauren fell back and threw her arms over her eyes. "Yeah, but it's not funny, is it? Not really."

Lucy glanced over at Lauren. Her hair had dried into a funky mass of curls that she'd simply finger combed into perfection. She was also starting to burn, giving her spray-on tan a slightly pink cast. The only thing wild about Lauren was the leopard print on her swimsuit; she was bright and bubbly with a girl-next-door quality about her. She would be a great catch for Ethan—and religion wouldn't be an issue.

"And now—here we are," Lauren continued, "a couple of crazy girls dating the same guy. Putting it all on the line and hoping it's worth it. That he's worth it, in the long run." She looked down the beach, shading her eyes with her hand. "They're back."

She jumped up from her towel and waved as Ethan and Tiffany walked up to join them. Lucy rolled over and sat up—just in time to watch Ethan give Tiffany a brief kiss and invite Lauren to go with him. Lauren gave Lucy a hopeful thumbs up as they left.

Sienna hadn't moved a muscle during the entire exchange, so Lucy decided she'd better wake her up. She might not like any of them very much at the moment, but she'd hate them for sure if she ended up with third degree sunburns.

Tiffany stretched out on her towel and sighed dramatically, like a lioness that had gorged on some poor, unsuspecting wildebeest. Lucy prepared to endure some gloating about her time with Ethan, but all Tiffany said was, "Make yourself useful and put sunscreen on my back."

Good old Tiffany. She made Miss Manners look like a slacker. "In a minute, Tiff. I need to wake up Sienna before she fries." Tiffany scowled, sat up, and began slapping lotion on herself with deliberate movements that telegraphed her annoyance. Lucy's eyes rolled heavenward.

"Sienna, wake up." She nudged her shoulder. "You're starting to burn."

Sienna moved a little. "I don't burn," she murmured sleepily, "I have good karma." Lucy nudged her again until she sighed and rolled over. At least now she wouldn't fry for a while, good karma notwithstanding.

And speaking of good karma, Lucy thought, she needed to give herself a pep talk before she went with Ethan. She wanted to have as much fun with him as she could. There would be a lot to think about afterward though.

* * *

"How are your diving skills?" Ethan asked Lucy. "I want to show you something."

They'd been snorkeling on the opposite side of the island, shadowed by cameramen and crew. Lucy was getting more comfortable having them around and even waved at the cameraman shooting underwater footage. She wished she had a camera so she could shoot underwater pictures too. The view was amazing; she was finally having one of those new experiences she'd longed for all her life.

"They're solid," she replied. "Lead the way."

Ethan smiled and took her by the hand. The shore where they'd been snorkeling was mostly beach, with an easy slope that went out a ways before dropping off steeply. Ethan led her away from the beach, toward some cliffs. "We'll have to climb a little," he said, "but it's not too bad."

He went first up a rocky incline, pointing out footholds to her along the way and then taking her through a narrow passage that opened onto a cliff. Lucy walked over to the edge to investigate. Below her was a lagoon surrounded on three sides by sheer rock. Part of the crew was down there, waiting for them in the dinghy.

"The water is deeper here," Ethan said. "Deep enough for diving and protected from the stronger currents and a few of the more terrifying predators."

From where they were, about thirty feet above the surface, the lagoon looked both peaceful and dangerous. The cliffs cut gray slices of shadow through the sapphire water. Lucy felt a flash of empathy for Sienna. Cliff diving, even from this modest height, was something she'd never done, and the high dive at the resort back home wasn't in the same league as this at all.

"The cliff here runs straight down, even underwater. All you need to do for clearance is jump forward a little, and you'll be fine. After you jump, head to your right. I'll go first, and you follow behind me. Ready?"

Thank you, thank you, Craig and Andy, for all the years of skateboard ramps and rooftop challenges. She swallowed and nodded. "Ready."

He studied her face; apparently satisfied by what he saw there, he turned, took a couple of running steps for momentum, and dove. Lucy didn't stop to think; she took a deep breath and followed. The free fall was terrifying and exhilarating, and she hit the water more inelegantly than she would have preferred, but without the bodily trauma of a total belly flop. Ethan reached her as she was still gaining her bearings. Grabbing her hand, he kicked toward a rocky shelf that glinted in the filtered sunlight. The underwater cameraman soon joined them.

As they got closer to the shelf, Lucy could see that it was covered—*covered*—in starfish. Dozens and dozens of starfish. They were of all different shapes and sizes and varied colors. A few inched slowly across the algae-covered rock face, their movements barely perceptible.

She was hooked.

Ethan gestured upward, and she nodded, following. Her lungs were ready to burst. They reached the surface, gasping for breath and grinning. "Another galaxy of stars for you," he said.

Wow.

"Come on, let's check it out again." Taking a deep breath, he descended once more. She was right behind him.

It took a few more returns to the surface for breath before Lucy had seen everything she wanted to see. A couple of puffer fish, startled by their presence, inflated right before their eyes, while a small school of disinterested damselfish darted past without a care.

When they'd seen their fill, Ethan asked her, "You up for another cliff dive?" His eyes glinted behind his mask.

Lucy was more than game now. "Oh yeah!"

"Great. Let's do it." They pushed themselves onto the rocks and climbed back to the top of the cliff.

"Do you think you can do a summersault?" he asked.

She looked at him then looked at the water. She'd done summersaults off the diving board at home; heck, she'd taught those boys from Colorado a serious lesson with her diving stunts. It was time for this cowboy to learn a thing or two. She cocked an eyebrow. "I know I can. The real question is, can you?"

"No question at all." He grinned and gestured toward the ledge. "Ladies first."

All righty, then. She backed up several feet, ran, and jumped. Her stomach leaped inside her as she twisted and flew in the air. And it felt glorious.

They dove a few more times, trying to outdo each other with their aerial stunts, until Ethan told her it was time to return to the others.

Lucy grabbed her towel and began drying her arms and legs. "This has been the best afternoon," she said, smiling at Ethan. She relinquished her towel when he reached for it, distracted momentarily when his eyes caught hers and held them.

Still looking at her, he reached behind her and wrapped her in the towel. "Thank you," she said, but it came out sounding hoarse. Her heart started to pound.

He held on to the edges of the towel and used them to pull her closer. "You're welcome," he whispered. "But what you really meant to say was that this has been the best *third date* you've ever been on. Am I right?"

Oh. That was probably why her heart was pounding. He brought her even closer, and his face lowered to hers. Lucy waited, not moving, barely daring to breathe. His lips met hers. They were cool from the water, his cheek rough with sand and stubble. The sensations were as pleasant as they were surprising.

He raised his head an inch and looked at her. "Yes," he said, "definitely the best third date ever." And then he kissed her again.

Her stomach leaped inside her, and she flew. And it felt glorious.

And somewhere in her dazed, exhilarated mind, she knew she'd taken another leap—one just as real as the ones she'd taken from the cliff.

CHAPTER 11

"How's the dime store novel?"

Melanie opened her eyes, squinted through the bright afternoon sunlight at Curt, and wondered how long she'd been dozing. She needed another twenty, thirty more hours before she'd feel human again. "Riveting. Thanks for asking." Where was her book? Oh yeah, she'd stuck it back in her bag when the siren call of sleep had become more compelling than the sci-fi murder mystery had been. "So have you been able to figure out what our boy is up to?"

"I have a working theory." He sat down on the edge of her towel, forcing her to make room for him under her beach umbrella. It was just like him to do that, she thought as she scooted over, wishing the beat-up cargo shorts and faded T-shirt he wore made him look more like a slob instead of carelessly chic. "I'll be watching him closely tonight. I reread the remaining girls' applications last night to see if I could pick up on anything." He brushed sand off his legs. Tan, muscled legs. "I know who I'd send home if it were me though. Is Sienna for real, or what?"

"Ah," she said, reaching for her water bottle and taking a sip. "What did the resident earth goddess do this time?"

"Nothing too serious. Only put Ethan in a headlock and nearly drown him, pretending she couldn't swim. But get this: She was on her college water polo team. I remember it specifically because it was *water polo*, and I'd never met *anyone ever* who'd played competitive water polo before. When I cornered her about it this afternoon, do you know what she said? That in a former life, she'd been a passenger on the *Titanic*, and they'd never recovered her body. And because it was such a *recent* past life, the vivid memories of it still distress her, especially in deep water."

Melanie snorted. "Well, of course. I'd avoid the open seas too if I'd drowned on the *Titanic*. Heck, I'd even avoid ice cubes if I were her."

"I don't care if she's Cleopatra; I don't need anyone trying to drown the star of my show. I also know Ethan, and he's not going to put up with someone who might suddenly go into hysterics because she remembers being tortured by the Spanish Inquisition."

Melanie smirked. "But . . . *Curt* . . . think about it. It does make for one of those great story arcs you're looking for." She smiled slyly at him.

"Not at the risk of sending the show's insurance premiums sky high. If I could afford that, I'd hire myself a second assistant."

That stung. Melanie resisted the urge to drown *him*.

He crossed his feet at the ankles. "I'll relax more when I know what Ethan's up to."

He already looked pretty relaxed to her. Of course, *she'd* been the one constantly running around like a crazy person twenty-four seven, so why shouldn't he? "So what's your working theory?"

"I think he's already picked his *Soulmate*. And I think he's trying to hide it by his elimination choices. You don't enjoy the success my buddy Ethan has without knowing how to cut through the facts and make up your mind fast—and how to trust your instincts in the process."

"You really think the Great and Powerful Ethan Glass has fallen in love with one of the women?"

"Yep."

"Really. After only three weeks?"

Curt stole her water bottle, took a swig, and grimaced. "How can you drink this? It's warm. That's the whole point of the show, in case you didn't get the memo. And Ethan promised me from the beginning that he was one hundred percent on board with this. So yeah, knowing Ethan, it's totally possible. Why?"

"Well, I don't know, Curt. Maybe for the exact reason you gave: that he's cut through the facts and made up his mind—and his mind says 'none of the above.' Or maybe his strategy is only to get rid of the women he finds the most annoying first and put up with the least annoying woman at the end until the website is launched."

"You know, Mel, you're a cynic when it comes to love. But if I'm right, and he's already chosen his *Soulmate*, then we're home free. We push this show for drama to get the best ratings possible. He announces his *Soulmate*. The future installments of the show and the personals website make us a fortune. We have our happy ending."

Melanie knew she wasn't included in the "us" making a fortune, so Curt Myers, executive producer, must be referring to himself in the royal plural. "If I'm cynical about love, then you're mercenary. And I really hate to say this, but I think this is all wishful thinking on your part. Why does it matter anyway? He'll pick who he picks, and you'll still have your show *and* your fortune."

He took another swallow of water and immediately spit it into the sand. "Ugh, I forgot. Nasty." He handed her the bottle. She rolled her eyes and tossed it near her bag. "I don't really care if he dumps her a few months down the road, as long as we have a happy ending for the show. That's what I told him. And drama's good for ratings. But the web products depend on a perfect, romantic ending, and Ethan notoriously does what he wants to do and doesn't always feel like he owes me an explanation. I don't like flying blind here, so when I really know what he's up to, I'll sleep better."

She *really* didn't want to talk to Curt about sleeping better—or sleep at all, since he'd just interrupted hers. She needed sleep a whole lot more than he did. "So what are you watching for tonight? And who do you think he's chosen?"

"I don't have any idea. That's why I went through the applications again last night. Lindstrom's added notes and adjusted some of the compatibility scores."

"And?" she asked.

He shrugged. "I don't know. It's too close to call." He stood up, and Melanie had to crane her neck to see him. "In the meantime, watch Ethan's every move. The minute you think you know anything, tell me. *And* I want you to find any drama and controversy you can so we can push the envelope on this thing."

"It would help if I read those files. It would give me some idea of where to start."

"I'll arrange it. In the meantime, pay attention and think like a girl."

He strode off before she could ask him what he meant by that comment.

* * *

That evening, Lucy and the others dined at a small local grill rented for the occasion. Its white stucco exterior and red-tiled roof provided the perfect exotic backdrop for taping. The whitewashed interior was accented with rich woods and bright vintage posters advertising bullfights and old Latin movies. Large strings of dried chilies hung on the walls.

Additional lighting had been added, but the effect was softer and more romantic than it had been for the cocktail party the first night at *Soulmates* House. The white walls, dark woods, and bright splashes of red and yellow retained their sense of drama even in the subdued lighting and added to the ambience.

They had shrimp cocktails and seviche for an appetizer. The waiter served everyone margaritas, although Ethan opted for a Mexican beer. Lucy ordered a pineapple soda to go with her spicy fish tacos.

A mariachi band joined the guitarist, who'd serenaded them through dinner and performed as they ate desserts of caramel flan and fruit empanadas. The band wore black outfits, studded with silver along the seams of their pants and the cuffs and breasts of their jackets. Their shirts were crisp and white and accented with red bow ties. The crowning touch, of course, was each musician's black sombrero, its wide brim heavily ornamented with looped gold braids. Lively trumpet and violin melodies expertly wove in with the strumming guitars.

Standing, Ethan extended a hand to Tiffany, who was seated next to him. "Would you like to dance?" he asked her, making Lucy's heart nearly leap to her throat and choke her.

Tiffany nodded, obviously pleased, and he led her to a small open area in the restaurant reserved for that purpose, the serenading mariachis following behind. Lucy worked to suppress her jealous reaction. She needed to get a grip. He'd finally kissed her—really kissed her—but it only meant that and nothing more. She had no idea if the kiss had changed things for him like it had for her.

She clapped along with the band and watched them do something that resembled a polka, and then each woman got a turn to dance with him. Lauren pretended to be a bull while they attempted a *paso doble*. Everyone laughed. Ethan was a good sport about it, dodging her as she charged after him with her hands raised to her head, fingers pointed out like horns. Maybe Lauren had indulged in a couple too many margaritas, Lucy speculated. Someone handed Ethan a napkin, which he flourished like a matador's cape. At the end of the dance, Lauren died dramatically, having been "run through" by Ethan with a salad fork, earning applause from everyone, including the waiters and kitchen staff.

When it was Sienna's turn to dance the band performed a fast-paced number. Ethan was into the spirit of things by then and spun her around and in and out. Lucy had to give Sienna points for keeping up with him and staying on her feet.

Lucy danced with Ethan last. The music shifted down in tempo, and Ethan swept her into a slow Mexican waltz. Surprised, she glanced at the other girls, who looked as surprised as she was by the change in music. Sienna wandered back to the table and sipped her drink. Lauren's eyes were huge with wistfulness, and Tiffany glared at them with her arms crossed.

"I enjoyed myself today. Did you?" Ethan asked, leaning in toward her.

"Mmm hmm," she answered, right before she tripped on his foot. He caught her and smoothly maneuvered her into a spin she knew was meant to cover her mistake.

"I'm not quite as confident a dancer as I am a swimmer," she confessed.

"Even with all those available dance partners hanging around your house?"

"Unfortunately, dancing with a little sister doesn't provide the same incentive for brothers that daring her to try idiotic stunts does. By the time they figured out that knowing how to dance would win them points with the girls, they had girlfriends to practice with."

He smiled and swung her around again. She tried to concentrate on her feet instead of his smile or how good he smelled or how his ear had such a nice shape . . . Ethan held her close, and soon she forgot about her feet and the other women and simply waltzed.

He brought her even closer, his mouth right next to her ear. "What makes you different?" he murmured.

"Different?" Lucy wasn't sure what he meant by that, and his proximity was affecting her ability to think.

"Different from the other women. What is it?"

"I'm not sure I understand what you're asking me."

"I'm not sure I do either," he said and laughed like he was laughing at himself. "Maybe we'll get a chance to explore it more later."

Lucy's heart leaped into her throat again, but with hope this time. Maybe she wouldn't be going home tonight. She wasn't ready to leave; she was certain about that, though she wasn't certain about anything else.

As the music came to an end, he spun her around slowly and took her into a dip. When he raised her back up, he took her hand to his lips and kissed her palm. His eyes were warm, intense, without the teasing sparkle she'd seen in them at the kissing booth. Had something changed for him today too?

The band started to play again, a number with the spirited tempo of the earlier dances. Still holding Lucy's hand, he kept her on the floor and gestured to the others to join them. Soon they were all dancing together, clapping high above their heads, clapping low, swishing their little American skirts, and Lucy wished hers was long and full and covered in colorful rows of ruffles and ribbons. The dance came to a frenzied conclusion, and they all clapped and cheered.

Their table now held pitchers of flavored coffees and hot chocolate. The band took a break, leaving only the guitarist to once again serenade them.

They'd barely returned to their seats when Mr. Esplin approached Ethan and whispered in his ear. Ethan paused with his cup halfway to his mouth and then nodded before taking a sip. He waited for Esplin to leave then set his cup down and rose to his feet. Lucy watched him take a deep breath and exhale slowly. "Lauren," Ethan said, "will you join me outside for a moment?" The mood at the table plummeted.

Lauren attempted a brave face. "Of course." She turned to Lucy, who was seated next to her, and Lucy's heart sank when she saw her face. Lauren set her cup of hot chocolate down, unable to drink. "Good-bye," she whispered so no one else would hear except Lucy.

"I'm so sorry," Lucy whispered back.

Lauren shook her head slightly and smiled reassuringly, but her eyes glistened with tears that threatened to fall. "Stay in touch, okay?" Lucy nodded and watched as she walked away from the table to join Ethan, and then the two of them left, followed by Mr. Esplin and a cameraman.

"Whew," Tiffany said to the group as soon as they were gone. "I'm glad we finally got that out of the way."

"Lauren had two strikes against her," Sienna added, sipping from her cup. "First, her Venus sign isn't compatible with his at all. And second, it's obvious that she's not even close to the same level of spiritual enlightenment that he is, or that *most* of us are, for that matter." Sienna looked pointedly at Lucy and arched an eyebrow when she said that last part. Apparently, she was still angry at the two of them for the dunking she'd taken.

Lucy was feeling a little raw herself; she'd just said good-bye to one of the best friends she'd made on the show. Now her spiritual nature was being maligned, although she wasn't certain she'd understood what Sienna had actually meant by her comment. "What do you mean, not the same level of spiritual enlightenment?"

"I *mean*," Sienna replied with all the patience of a kindergarten teacher, "that Lauren hasn't learned enough from her former lives to be a balanced partner in this one for Ethan." She patted Lucy's hand, which was totally weird, not to mention condescending. "I know you've gotten to be friends with Lauren. I'm not trying to be mean, simply honest. Ethan is too advanced to tolerate someone like Lauren and her silly pranks. She pretended to be a *bull*, for heaven's sake."

What was this about former lives? Lucy had missed something somewhere along the line. "Huh?" she asked, realizing after making the noise that it made her sound like she did need a kindergarten teacher after all.

"Lauren has not attained the level of enlightenment she would need in order to be a successful soulmate for Ethan. One doesn't really need to know *who* she's been to figure that out." Lucy looked at Tiffany to see if she was getting any of this; Tiffany only rolled her eyes and stared out a window. "Although it wouldn't have surprised me," Sienna continued, "to learn that she was formerly one of the Three Stooges."

"Now, wait a minute," Lucy said, suddenly feeling testy. "That's crossing the line. It's one thing for you to claim spiritual enlightenment from past lives or even feel you have answers from Venus or whatever it was you said. I'll discuss it with you anytime you want. I know how it feels to believe strongly in something and want to share it. But don't use it to hurt people. Lauren is sweet and—"

"Lauren tried to drown me!"

"No, she didn't. It was a prank. She'd seen you swimming in the pool and thought you were faking things to get extra attention from Ethan."

Tiffany's head swung around. "What?" She glared at Sienna accusingly.

Lucy continued. "You were in no danger of drowning, and you know it. Lauren was right too, wasn't she? You do know how to swim, don't you?"

Sienna looked uncomfortably toward the camera and then realized she'd broken one of their cardinal rules and looked away. "I can swim, but I have issues with open bodies of water."

"Let me guess," Tiffany scoffed. "In a former life, you were attacked by the kraken."

"No, I—" Sienna started indignantly.

"The point," Lucy interjected before things digressed horribly, "is that you were never in any danger, and Lauren was right."

"Yes," Tiffany added, doing an impressive *Law and Order* scowl as she stared at Sienna. "Lauren *was* right. And that makes you pathetic."

Ethan returned with Mr. Esplin then, effectively ending the conversation. Lauren was gone. "Ladies," Esplin said, "we'd like to set up for this next shot on the dance floor." On cue, Ms. Carlton came forward to direct them into position for the cameras, while the crew set up the pedestal for the small velvet-lined tray bearing the bracelet charms they'd receive. Ethan watched the process from behind the scenes until it was time to begin taping. His face was carefully blank, and Lucy wondered how things had gone when he'd said good-bye to Lauren.

Her own emotions were a mess. She wanted to beat Tiffany and Sienna in their little games. She wanted Lauren to be here. At the same time, Lucy was relieved to still be here herself, and her senses buzzed from the things Ethan had said to her during their dance.

Mr. Esplin called action, and the cameras focused on Ethan. "Thank you for a wonderful day here in Baja California," he said. "I enjoyed getting to know each of you better and couldn't have asked for more. Unfortunately, I had to send someone home this evening, and that person was Lauren.

"That said, I am thrilled the three of you are here with me, continuing the journey." He picked up a charm and walked over to give it to Sienna, then repeated the process with Tiffany. As he approached the tray the last time, he slid his hand into his pants pocket.

He picked up the last charm from the tray and approached Lucy like he had Sienna and Tiffany. "Will you continue the journey with me?" he asked her.

"I'd love to," Lucy replied. Her heart shouldn't be pounding this hard, but explain that to her heart.

He reached for her hand and turned it palm up. He'd kissed that palm after their waltz, and she wondered if he was remembering it now, like she was. This time he stroked a finger down the center of it, sending chills through her, then placed the charm there and closed her fingers over it. Still holding her closed hand, he used his free arm to pull her in for a quick hug, like he'd given the others. But as he backed away he gave her a look that held a note of caution in it.

She raised her eyebrows slightly in question. He glanced briefly, almost imperceptibly, at her closed hand. She understood then that he wanted her discretion, and it had to do with the charm in her still-closed hand.

When he saw that she didn't intend to open her hand, he nodded slightly and moved away. Mr. Esplin seemed satisfied with what they'd taped, and the women mingled with Ethan for some informal shots. Lucy turned away from the group and the cameras for a moment. She opened her hand and gasped.

In addition to the angelfish charm she'd seen him give Sienna and Tiffany, he had given her another, a starfish embellished with rows of tiny diamonds, and it was stunning.

The symbolism was obvious, the gesture sweet and wholly unexpected. She closed her hand again and turned to look at Ethan. He was talking to Tiffany, but his eyes caught and held hers meaningfully for a moment before turning back to the conversation. She whirled around, facing away again, and tried to catch her breath.

Something had definitely changed between them today, and suddenly Lucy was terrified. This was no longer about looking for adventure. This was no longer about a crush on a man who was beyond her reach. This was about two people who were drawn to each other and were discovering the need to find out what that meant and what it might lead to. She should feel ecstatic.

Instead, she was shaking, because it also meant taking huge risks and facing challenges she knew might be impossible to bridge. And despite what his actions today might imply, he hadn't made any kind of declaration to her, nor should she expect one at this point. There were still eight other women here, and Lucy had no idea how he felt about any of them.

Why make the charm a secret? Had he given one to anyone else secretly? Why give her an additional charm at all? The way he'd gone about it suggested he didn't want anyone else to know—not the other women, not even the show's producers.

And if that were the case, how was she supposed to act? Her only real choice was to wait and follow his lead.

When she'd been at home deciding whether or not she wanted to be a contestant on the show, she had not anticipated this. When she'd prayed for guidance and gotten her answer, she had truly not included Ethan in any of the possibilities.

Things had definitely changed. They'd gotten serious and a lot more complicated.

CHAPTER 12

ETHAN WAS ON A MISSION. He wanted changes in the dates scheduled for the week, and that meant finding Curt.

The original plan for the dates, service projects that included a day at a homeless shelter, one at a local hospital, and one in a nursing home, included randomly dividing the remaining women into groups, with Ethan eliminating three of them at the end of the week. That plan wasn't going to cut it, not now that he had his short list in place.

And his short list was Lucy Kendrick.

What was it about her? Lucy, who'd acted more friendly toward him than flirtatious, whose swimsuit covered more physical territory than his mother's did. Not that she hadn't looked great in it. She had. He'd noticed. He thought she'd probably look great in a potato sack. Then there'd been their little kissing booth encounter at the rodeo. She'd held her own with him, word for word. She'd challenged him in Mexico too, dive for crazy dive. And if their first kiss had been part of a fun game, their second had been drop-dead serious.

What was it about a kiss—not unlike many other kisses he'd had, including several here while taping *Soulmates*—that would change the landscape of things for him so much? On an impulse, he'd called the local jeweler they'd hired and had him include the starfish charm.

It had been a risky move on his part.

He didn't want to show his hand yet, nor could he. He had a commitment to Curt to make this work. Showing a preference for anyone at this point was premature and reckless, not to mention bad for their business objectives.

He wasn't foolish enough to risk it all on Lucy at this point anyway. He hadn't gotten to be where he was by avoiding risks, but a good risk taker always had a trusty backup plan. He'd picked out a couple of the women for that. Now he wanted to observe Lucy and the other short-list women more to make sure his decisions had been sound ones.

That meant spending more time with them without giving anything away to Curt and the others.

He found Curt in the war room with Melanie, who was poring over the women's personal files. He frowned. He, Curt, and Dr. Lindstrom had agreed that all personal info would be strictly limited to the three of them, despite the disclaimers and releases the women had signed before coming on the show. His own info was accessible only to the doctor and himself. Period.

"What's going on?" he asked.

The color drained from the woman's face as she looked up; Ethan knew he intimidated her, so her reaction was nothing new. Curt answered the question. "A little fact verification. Almost done." Melanie glanced at both of them then quickly stacked the folders and set them aside. Curt continued. "Did you need something?"

Ethan didn't like it. "Yes, I do." He walked over and picked up the files. They got the point. "I want to change some of the plans for this week's dates."

"How much change?" Melanie asked, looking wary. Since Curt delegated virtually everything to her, Ethan wasn't surprised by her reaction; undoubtedly, it was going to be her headache to deal with.

"Only a minor change. This is my week to see the women in real-life settings. So I'd like to suggest taking all nine women to the homeless shelter. Based on how that goes, I choose six to go with me to the hospital and then two or three based on the hospital date to take to the nursing home." He waited and watched Curt chew on the idea.

Curt studied him, searching, Ethan was sure, for hidden angles, but Ethan kept his poker face on. Curt turned to Melanie. "What do you think?"

Melanie shook her head. "I don't see any problem. In fact, it might work to add some drama into the mix."

Ethan waited patiently to get what he wanted. Curt was still staring at him, but he eventually shrugged and said, "Okay. If it isn't going to create more work for Melanie, then I don't see why not."

"Great. I'll leave you to the details, then."

Melanie was staring at Curt with an odd, almost worshipful look on her face as Ethan left the room.

* * *

There were a lot of days between dates when the women were stuck in *Soulmates* House together. They had a pool and a gym. They had an entertainment room with a huge flatscreen TV, satellite, and on-demand movies. The entire house had a built-in audio system with an unending selection of music downloads.

And while Lucy was now on better terms with Ms. Carlton, the associate producer had made it clear that her earlier church visit wouldn't happen again. She'd been bombarded by off-site requests from the other women when they'd caught wind of it.

"I told them I'd be happy to let them go to church too if they wanted, but that was the only place they'd be allowed to go," Melanie had said dryly. "I didn't have any takers. Although Denise did actually consider it for a minute . . ."

But the bottom line was that the women were contractually obligated to stay at the house, and that was that.

The days had become routine, with never-ending leisure time. They tried on each other's clothes, modeling them for each other. Lucy had thought her outfits, thanks to Grace and Allie and her mom, were fun and stylish. The women in the house were less enthusiastic, questioning her lack of strapless gowns and short shorts, especially in a competition where she was supposed to catch a man's eye.

Certain people had been less tactful about it than others. Jena had smirked and told her that some women's looks improved the more they were hidden from view. Rachel had wondered what Lucy's mother was wearing all month if most of her clothes were here with Lucy.

On the flip side, Denise and Chelsea had made her try on some of their things and had even suggested she borrow a few. The outfits *were* really cute, Lucy had to admit, although they were a little too revealing for Lucy's comfort. She'd sighed and declined their offers.

Now that they were entering week four, the latest movies and long naps by the pool had lost their appeal, as had playing dress-up and beauty parlor. Lucy started spending time alone working out in the gym, writing in her journal, and reading. She also spent time studying her scriptures.

She wasn't reluctant to discuss her beliefs; she and Sienna had had an interesting conversation after Mexico, and a few of the others had asked questions over the weeks in *Soulmates* House. Lucy had learned at a young age that when people found out she was Mormon, they responded in one of basically four ways: (1) they were intensely curious, with lots of questions; (2) they were mildly curious, looking for short, simple answers; (3) they were indifferent; or (4) they were hostile. The women—and the crew, for that matter—had seen her with her scriptures and had stumbled onto her occasionally when she'd been praying. They knew she didn't smoke (a couple of the girls discreetly smoked off-camera and away from Ethan); she didn't drink alcohol, coffee, or tea; and they knew she'd gone to church while she was there. Short, simple answers had been enough for most of them. Sienna, amazingly, had been the exception.

Sometimes Lucy could sense the elephant of her religious beliefs in the room—it was a feeling she'd experienced often enough over the years. But it boiled down to the fact that while the women liked her, they considered her to be different, and they were right. She was different in some respects. And the differences had often made her feel isolated. Alone. And here, that feeling was compounded by the tenuous emotional balance that existed among them due to their shared interest in Ethan Glass.

So it was a great relief for everybody when Rick showed up bright and early to announce on camera that they were all going with Ethan to visit a homeless shelter. This was a big departure from anything else they'd done, and while it wasn't exactly an exotic adventure, everyone was game. Everyone was ready to get out of the house, even if it meant they'd be working all day long, as well as fighting for individual time with Ethan.

The head cook at the shelter, Bonnie, welcomed them and instructed each of them to put on an apron and hairnet. Lucy tied what was essentially a pup tent around her waist, picked up something that must have been spun by a giant mutant spider, and tucked her hair into it.

"Check out the pirate," Denise whispered to Lucy, her voice all soft and Southern, like the fuzz on a Georgia peach. "Mercy, but I *do* love pirates." Ethan had successfully avoided the mutant spiderweb look by tying a bandana on his head. Add a few dreadlocks, an earring . . . and Captain Jack Sparrow would definitely have some competition.

"Pirate, cowboy, hotshot businessman," Lucy whispered back as she pushed her sagging hairnet off her forehead. "Ethan Glass could publish his own calendar."

Denise chuckled. "I'd buy a copy." She sighed and patted her own hairnet. "I surely wish I didn't look like my great-aunt Tildy right now."

If Denise looked like her great-aunt Tildy, then Great Aunt Tildy would be ecstatic, hairnet notwithstanding. Lucy felt more like a member of the Addams Family.

They spent the morning doing prep work—peeling and chopping carrots, mixing gallons of instant potatoes, and dicing a small mountain of onions. Ethan the Kitchen Pirate helped set up extra tables and chairs; when that was done, he went around to each workstation and assisted. He peeled carrots with Denise, helped Chelsea and Rachel mix a bathtub's worth of gravy, and patiently showed Tiffany a dozen times how to use the industrial can opener, while Tiffany smiled and managed to convince him a dozen times that she couldn't get it to work whenever she tried it.

Lucy dumped the diced onions into a barrel-sized mixer that already had a steer's worth of hamburger and a half bushel of oats in it, the end result supposedly being meatloaf, and wished she were clever enough to make incompetency come off like a talent.

Lunchtime came way too soon, and the dining hall doors opened. People poured into the room and kept right on coming. "Apparently, word got out that a television crew was taping here today," Denise told Lucy after a quick check on the action. "The lines go down the street at least three blocks. I don't know about you, but I've got a feeling we're gonna need a lot more food ASAP."

Just then Bonnie, the cook, came in and made it official. They made more of everything until the supplies ran out, then they resorted to opening every can and jar they could find. Bonnie hustled around the kitchen, hurling directions at everyone and pointing out the locations of tools and supplies.

Lucy was hurrying to the convection oven with an emergency tray of frozen chicken nuggets when she heard Ethan say, "No one goes away hungry, Bonnie, not today. Do what you can with what you have, and we'll pick up the slack." He gave her a reassuring look and yelled, "Zack, Kyle! Grab Esplin and get over here."

And just that quickly Ethan organized the crew—everyone not holding a camera, that was, because Mr. Esplin held firm on that point—and Zack and Kyle left to buy anything edible they could find ASAP. The kitchen pirate wasn't afraid to assume the role of captain.

A day that had started out fun and busy became a fast-paced pressure cooker. The kitchen was furnace hot, between the ovens and the steam from the dishwashers that ran constantly. Dishing up portions in the dining hall was easy work by comparison; the hall was a comfortable temperature, despite the number of homeless people who'd shown up. Lucy didn't want to name any names, but certain ladies managed to spend the majority of their time avoiding the kitchen inferno. She, Denise, and Chelsea weren't those certain people.

The doors to the dining room finally closed late in the afternoon, everyone fed (the last ones through the door chose between burgers and fries from Mickey D's or drumsticks from KFC). Lucy crawled into the limo along with the others. She wanted to shower and collapse—after having her feet surgically removed. Why was it a person could walk around all day and be fine but standing all day killed? Tiffany and Sara sat next to Ethan in the limo, both chattering on about the heartbreaking plight of the homeless. Doing charity work had made them feel *so good*, and doing it by Ethan's side had made everything *so special*.

Lucy felt a headache coming on.

Tiffany was practically glued to him and punctuated each point she made by putting her hand on his knee and, when she felt bolder, leaving it there. Ethan didn't seem to mind. Lucy tried not to grind her teeth since it would only make her headache worse. She was too exhausted to talk and too grouchy to say anything nice. It took all her energy to ignore the annoying hand resting on Ethan's knee and hope that her complacent expression masked her real feelings well enough. Maybe whoever surgically removed her feet could cut off Tiffany's hand as well. She would probably regret having such mean thoughts tomorrow, but at the moment, she was too tired to care. She would repent after a good night's rest.

Maybe.

"And what about you, Lucy?" Ethan asked.

She tried to remember what the conversation had been before her mind had taken such a violent path. Was that a knowing glint in his eye? She checked to make sure her attitude of nonchalance hadn't slipped. Sara's hand crept up to play with the ends of Ethan's hair. Maybe Lucy could arrange a third amputation . . .

"What about me what?" Wow, *that* was an intelligent response, not to mention snappish enough to give herself away. The corner of Ethan's mouth quirked up slightly. Lucy groaned silently. "I mean, I guess I missed what you were talking about. I'm a little tired."

"We all are; that's what we were talking about and whether anyone has ever felt more tired than we do right now. Sienna claims to have had a few experiences—" he paused like he wasn't sure what to say next, probably because Sienna's experiences hadn't actually occurred in *this* life, "and Denise has run a few marathons," he smiled at her, "and is of the opinion that today might have actually been worse. I feel like *I* ran a marathon today. So what about you? Anytime in your past when you felt more tired than we do now?"

She was really tired of watching Tiffany and Sara maul him, but obviously that wasn't what he meant. Because she *was* really tired, it took her a minute to come up with an answer. "It would have to have been the women's pull."

"What's that?" Sara asked. "Some sort of tug-of-war?"

"No, not a tug-of-war. When I was sixteen, the youth group in my church did a kind of reenactment of the pioneers crossing the plains. At a point along the trail, it was left up to us girls to pull—and push—the handcarts by ourselves. The women's pull. That was the most tired I've ever been."

She stopped talking. It was one of those times when the short answer seemed best, especially with a camera running nearby. Besides, she was using all her energy to ignore her aching feet and head, not to mention the urge to kick Sara and Tiffany in the shins, which would only make her feet hurt worse. She shifted in her seat a little to ease her stiffening back muscles.

"Tell us about it," Ethan said.

* * *

Ethan watched Lucy, waiting—hoping that she would tell them the story. He was tired, his smile muscles were sore, and speaking of tug-of-wars, there was the distinct possibility that he'd end up torn limb from limb in a tug-of-war between Tiffany and Sara. The upside of that nuisance was that Lucy seemed more than a little disgruntled by their attention to him and was having trouble hiding it. He tried not to smile.

He couldn't imagine pretending to be a pioneer and spending a few days pulling a wagon around in the sticks for fun. He'd put in some long hours doing hard labor growing up on the ranch, but they'd always had modern comforts at the end of the day.

All eyes were on her. The camera was on her. She hesitated.

"Please," Ethan said.

She nodded and took a breath. "Early on, the pioneers used covered wagons to cross the plains, but wagons and ox teams were expensive, and many people were too poor to afford them. So they used handcarts instead. Starting near the Mississippi River, they walked a thousand miles, pushing and pulling the handcarts the entire way.

"So for our reenactment, we dressed like pioneers—no T-shirts and shorts. Long sleeves, long skirts, bonnets, bloomers."

"Bloomers? And bonnets? You can't be serious!" Rachel said, grimacing. "I wouldn't be caught dead wearing stuff like that."

Ethan was intrigued, however. "It sounds like you were going for authenticity," he remarked.

Her face lit up. Literally. How did she do that?

"Yes, exactly," she answered. "The boys wore long-sleeved shirts and long pants with suspenders and substituted cowboy hats for their aviator sunglasses. No iPods, no phones—"

"It sounds like life at *Soulmates* House," Sara quipped, earning a few laughs.

"Except for the wardrobe," Jena added, smoothing the fabric of her designer blouse.

Why would a person wear a silk blouse to work in a soup kitchen anyway? Ethan wondered.

"True," Lucy said. She looked at Ethan and smiled. "Early in the morning, they put us on buses that took us out to the middle of nowhere, and we started to walk.

"We walked about fourteen miles the first day, a bunch of us so-called city kids pushing and pulling handcarts loaded with all of our provisions. Those carts were heavy, let me tell you, and it took all of us to keep them moving along the trail. Not that there was much of a trail, really." Lucy had everyone's attention. "It was hot, and I was sweating like crazy in all those clothes. We were thirsty and dirty—there was dirt in my ears and in my nose; even my teeth felt gritty from all the dust flying around us. It was a long, hard day.

"The sun was going down, and we were expecting to set up camp soon, desperately hoping to, really, when we heard a bugle call. None of us knew what was going on, so we stopped. I was exhausted. A man dressed in an old military uniform marched up, pulled out a document, and read from it. Essentially, they were orders from the government for all the men to fall out and form a battalion to help in the war with Mexico."

Lucy stopped speaking. Everyone was quiet. Ethan found himself anxious for her to continue. "Technically, the battalion business happened when Brigham Young took the first groups west in wagons. Most of the handcart companies crossed a decade later. But our leaders wanted us to understand the loss of physical support the first groups felt when those men were required to enlist and to know what it was like to be separated from each other after we'd struggled and worked together all day.

"The guys were taken to the top of a hill that we'd stopped right in front of. They were lined up at attention and ordered to watch, not to move, and not to speak. And then the women—I mean, we were just girls, really—were instructed to get the handcarts up the hill."

Ethan felt a stab of helpless frustration at the scene Lucy was describing and even anger. He could picture Lucy at sixteen—slim and strong but still just a kid. "They couldn't help you? They had to stand there and *watch*?"

Lucy nodded. "They were ordered to stand at attention and watch. Some of the girls were also told not to help—they symbolized those who had died on the trail. Some were told to ride in the handcarts—representing those who were too sick to help. They were really upset—one girl said it was bad enough that they weren't allowed to help, but becoming a burden by riding was too much.

"We'd been pushing and pulling those handcarts all day, and *that* had been tough enough, even with everyone's help. Now the sun was going down and those of us who were left had to do it alone.

"We started pushing. After the first few steps, I knew I couldn't do it. It was too hard; the cart was too heavy, and the hill was too steep. I concentrated on my feet, thinking, *One more step, one more step*. Sometimes the cart barely moved an inch. I had to rest a lot, and I would look to see how much farther we had to go. The top of the hill was still so far away that I eventually stopped looking." She paused again, hesitating like she was suddenly deep in thought.

Ethan could feel his heart swelling within his chest; the atmosphere around him pulsed in a way he couldn't describe; something unusual was happening, tangible and intangible, but he wasn't exactly sure what.

Lucy came to some sort of resolution. She glanced at the camera, turned away from it as much as the crowded limo would allow, and spoke, but in a softer voice. "I started praying for help. I couldn't do it alone. We couldn't. There was nothing else we could do.

"I could hear the boys crying. Tough high school boys. They couldn't stand to watch us struggle, not when they'd been by our sides all day, pushing and pulling with us. But they'd been ordered not to move. After a while, a couple of them couldn't take it anymore, and they ran down and helped as many of the carts up the hill as they could. I glanced up sometimes to see what was going on, but mostly I watched my feet and kept taking one more step. And I kept praying.

"And then suddenly, it got easier. The cart felt lighter. I looked up to see if one of the boys was helping, but no one was there." She paused and took a breath. "And we made it to the top."

In that moment, the world as Ethan knew it ceased to be. The air around him felt heavy and sweet and warm. His heart pounded. Everyone was silent, even the cameraman, his camera still pointed at Lucy. Could they feel what he was feeling? He was reluctant to speak for fear he'd break the spell that had been cast over the limousine.

"That night we slept in makeshift tents," Lucy continued. "I had a sleeping bag with a pad, but I was still cold, and the ground was still hard. The pioneers didn't have those things. I imagine most of the people we fed today probably don't either.

"So if we were the angels who helped lift their load a little and got them one step farther up that hill, then today's tiredness was worth it."

Ethan's mind shifted from a slender teen in a bonnet to a little girl in a moose-antlered cap. *If the angels love Sally so much, why do they let the boys call her Freckle Freak?* He wondered how Lucy would answer that question.

"Angels," Ethan repeated softly to himself.

CHAPTER 13

KYLE HAULED A HUGE, HEAVY box of toys down the hospital corridor. Melanie had sent him out with a laundry list of things to buy, and it had taken him all morning to round everything up.

A young lady wearing Hello Kitty scrubs and a big smile stood near the nurse's station. "You must be Kyle," she said. Hello Kitty had never looked better. "I was told to expect you. We have a room ready for you to use. Follow me."

Sure thing, baby. Kyle watched her ponytail swish back and forth like some crazy hypnotic pendulum. She glanced over her shoulder to make sure he was behind her, and she was still smiling at him. Man, dimples were now his favorite thing, right after big blue eyes and swishing ponytails. Right after Hello Kitty.

"Can I help you with anything?" she asked when they reached the room.

"If you have time to help me organize all this stuff . . ." Kyle tried unsuccessfully to read her ID badge, "I wouldn't say no." Not in a million years. "Especially since I have a couple more boxes to bring in."

"I'd love to! Oh, I'm Erin, by the way. Sorry about that. We are *so* excited to have the *Soulmates* cast here today. The kids are really looking forward to it. Oh wow! A Hogwarts robe! That must be for Baylee. She's going to *love* it." Erin beamed at Kyle like he'd done something spectacular instead of just a little toy shopping.

By the time they'd emptied the last box, the room looked like every kid's Christmas fantasy. There were stacks of storybooks and comic books and coloring books and crayons and markers and pencils in every color under the sun. They'd made one pile of stuffed animals and another of dolls. There were balls, cars and trucks, and an array of action figures. There was also a heap of princess dresses and superhero costumes, crazy hats and wigs. Kyle had gotten a few funny looks as he'd cleared the shelves of rhinestone tiaras and feather boas—and fairy wings—at Toys "R" Us, but Melanie's list had been comprehensive. Very comprehensive.

And speak of the devil . . . Melanie poked her head into the room. "Good. I found you." She came in and shut the door, offering her hand to Hello Kitty Erin for a brisk handshake. "Melanie Carlton, associate producer. You must be Ms. Stearns. Thank you for helping us today. We're creating a huge disturbance to the routine around here, and we appreciate what you're doing to assist us."

"I'm happy to help, Ms. Carlton. We all are. This is going to brighten the day for our little patients, and that will certainly help with their healing. Or, at the very least, give them a day to forget their illnesses and just enjoy being a child."

There was a yellow princess dress on top of the heap. Kyle watched Melanie run the fabric between her fingers before turning her attention back to Erin. "Kyle will be working with you to coordinate things behind the scenes. In addition to organizing the toys by patient, we'd like you to identify each child's needs for us so we're sensitive to them during the visits."

Wow. The *Soulmates* Nazi might actually have a beating heart after all. And Kyle was going to be working with Erin Hello Kitty Stearns all day. Compared to his day at the homeless shelter, this was going to be heaven. Compared to almost *anything*—oh man! Erin's dimples flashed again—yep, this was going to be heaven.

He spent the next hour happily sorting toys—and flirting. They had just dug into the last pile, a bunch of movie-themed stuff, when he noticed Ethan leaning against the doorjamb.

Kyle grinned stupidly. "Hey, Eth." Play it cool. Aw, forget it, this was Ethan. "This is Erin Stearns," he said. "She works here." Duh. He was a real Einstein today. Maybe he should have said, "This is Erin Stearns, and my IQ dropped fifty points this afternoon when I met her." As if Ethan wouldn't have guessed that already.

"A pleasure, Ms. Stearns," Ethan said, reaching to shake her hand. "Actually, it's you I came to find. The producers want to coordinate some final details with you."

"Oh! Okay." She looked at Kyle, which was awesome because no one ever noticed him when Ethan was around. Not that it bothered him;

he'd grown up with it, and Ethan was a brother. But she'd looked at *him*. Kyle. "I'll see you later?" she asked *him*. Kyle.

"Yeah. Definitely. See you later." As the door shut behind her, he turned and stared at Ethan. "Don't. Say. Anything."

Ethan laughed. "Relax, hotshot, you have my blessing. Just keep your eyes open while you're here . . . and on more than just your new friend." He wandered around the room, inspecting the piles of toys.

"Heat starting to get to you?" Kyle joked.

"Not at all." Ethan eyed him with a cool, expressionless CEO gaze.

Uh-huh. Sure. "So anything or anyone in particular my eyes should keep open to, *boss*?"

Ethan picked up a football and rifled it at Kyle, who deftly caught it and lobbed it back. "Everything. All of them. The six who are here anyway."

"And what exactly am I looking for?"

He put down the football. "This stuff is great—oh, I need this guy." He picked up a Mr. Spock action figure. "Maybe he can do the Vulcan mind meld on everyone, and I'll have my answers." He returned Spock to the pile, setting him next to Optimus Prime.

Kyle shook his head and picked up the patient list Erin had left. Maybe now was a good time to figure out what kid was supposed to get the lightsaber. He obviously wasn't getting anywhere with Ethan at the moment.

Ethan raked a hand through his hair. "Before I bare my soul, tell me what you've observed since the last time we spoke." He glanced at his watch. "Hold on." He opened the door a crack. "Excuse me. Hi. I wonder if you'd go find Mr. Esplin—he's the director, that's right—and tell him Mr. Glass will be unavailable for fifteen minutes. Thanks." He turned back to Kyle. "Okay. Shoot. Recent observations."

"Recent observations. Let's see . . . Tiffany is . . . I understand the attraction, man. She's smoking hot, with all that red hair and vavoom. And she's totally into you. I get that. But she doesn't play nice with the other women. She's not going to win the Miss Congeniality award anytime soon."

He watched Ethan process that bit of info. "All right. Next."

"Here's a good one: Jena put together a list of names. They might be for a future Baby Glass. Lucky you, man. But since Sea Siren and Aquasition"—Kyle couldn't help rolling his eyes at that one—"are on the list, my guess is she thinks a yacht would make a nice little engagement present. But she's also mentioned some dude named Michael, an ex-boyfriend maybe."

Ethan waved his hand in dismissal. "Forget Jena. She'll be gone at the end of the week." He picked up one of the baby dolls. "Kyle, what do you think about kids?"

"Huh?" Talk about a weird segue, although he *had* mentioned baby names—if a yacht could be considered a baby. It probably could to a lot of people, especially someone like Jena. He shrugged. "I like kids. I think kids are great, especially when they're somebody else's kids."

"That's what I used to think too." He tucked the baby doll into the crook of his arm like a football player might. Like a father might. Crazy. "I've thought a lot about kids lately. I've thought about a lot of things since agreeing to this *Soulmates* business. Marriage. Kids." He looked down at the doll. "Ugly little thing, isn't it? One of the patients really wanted this?"

"Uh-huh. Marriage and kids . . ." he repeated, hoping Ethan would continue. He'd never heard him talk about this stuff before.

"Marriage and kids, Kyle. It's what my folks have, what Jake has. Lately I've found myself envying them."

"They probably envy you."

"I don't think so. They're happy for me, happy for my success. But I don't think they envy me because they have what makes them happy. And that's what I envy."

"Aren't you happy? You're rich, successful—"

"Tell me, Kyle. When you met Erin Stearns this morning, did you automatically wonder if she thought your connections could further her career? Or that you were her ticket to a life of luxury?"

"No." He snorted. "More like the opposite. Like if I'm worth the cost of what it will take to put me through grad school. It generally weeds out the ones who aren't into me enough." The light clicked on in Kyle's head. He nodded. "Okay, Eth. I get it. Tell me where you're at in all this so I can really help."

"I'm definitely attracted to the women here and see relationship potential as well."

Kyle dumped a Lego kit he was holding onto a pile and raised an eyebrow at Ethan. "Wow, once again, that was insightful and romantic, like you're forecasting business trends or something."

"Cut me some slack here, will you? And let me finish."

"Sorry. But I gotta say—you really sound more like Joe CEO than a guy on the hunt." He crossed his arms. "Tell me who you *like*."

"I *like* them all."

"Come *on*, Eth!"

There was a knock at the door. "Mr. Glass?" One of the crew poked his head into the room. "We're ready to begin shooting."

"I'll be there in five," Ethan said through his teeth and then waited with a clamped jaw for the door to close.

Hmm. Kyle could count on one hand the number of times he'd seen Ethan lose his professional cool.

"If you haven't figured it out already," Ethan continued tersely, "the short list includes Lucy, Denise, and Tiffany, although after what you said about Tiffany, I'll have to think about that one some more."

"Keep talking." Now that they were finally getting somewhere, time was nearly up.

"That's all you need to know. So any final thoughts?"

"Nope." None that he wanted to share. Lucy, Denise, and Tiffany. *Tiffany*. Kyle shuddered. He'd said all he could there though; the rest was up to Ethan to figure out. Denise was nice enough, except she made Kyle feel like a poodle when he was around her, all "aren't you the sweetest *thang*." He liked Lucy best of the three. She'd gone out of her way to be nice to him from the start. But she wasn't a perfect fit for Ethan either. He wasn't sure she was sophisticated enough for Ethan—especially the Ethan whose picture ended up in the celebrity mags these days.

And then there was the little day trip Kyle had taken with Lucy . . .

"Eth, you know about Lucy and the whole church thing, right?"

"Church thing? Yes, I know about that. I don't see that as a problem."

"She went to church the first week we were here. Curt gave the okay. I was assigned to go with her."

"And?"

"And do you know many people who do that? Arrange to go to church their first free day in Southern California? I'd be hitting people up to take me to the beach or some local hot spot, wouldn't you?"

"If it will make you feel better, I'll keep it in mind." Ethan headed to the door.

"Her church was different, at least different from what I expected," he blurted.

Ethan turned. "Different how?"

"I don't know exactly. I'm not an expert." He watched Ethan's mouth twitch. "Okay, maybe I'm an expert on *different*. Mom's Lakota traditions mixed with the conversations she had with Father Mick are definitely *different*. But Lucy's church was a *different* different. Not, like, weird or anything. Just not what I expected, like you see in the movies."

"Movies being so representative of real life."

"You know what I mean. And it lasted for three *hours*, man."

"What?" His brow wrinkled.

"We only stayed for the first hour, but that's what she told me."

"Three hours. All right. In the meantime, this is how I see things on *Soulmates* playing out: Lucy, Tiffany, and Denise will be my final three, unless something happens to shake things up." He glanced at his watch. "I have to go."

"Are you feeling better now that we've had our little chat?" Kyle couldn't resist asking.

"Don't push it, Dr. Phil." But Ethan smiled and seemed a little more at ease. "I appreciate what you're doing, Kyle."

"Anything for you, Ethan."

He nodded in acknowledgment, rolled his shoulders a little, and moved to open the door. Then he paused, his hand still on the doorknob. "This is meant to stay between you and me."

"I understand that."

"No. I mean this next part really has to stay between you and me."

Kyle felt a tingle run up his spine. "Okay."

Ethan sighed. "I'm not sure how to say this, but . . . there's something about Lucy—I don't know what it is. Do you see it, or is it just me? It sounds nuts. I can't explain it." He shook his head. "Never mind."

Whoa, that was unexpected. And that made it all the more enlightening. "Lucy's special, no question. I'll keep a close eye on her today and see what I can find out."

A brisk knock on the door interrupted them. "Mr. Glass?" Kyle grimaced at the voice. It was Melanie.

Ethan opened the door and instantly turned into the chilly CEO. "Is there a problem, Ms. Carlton?"

The *Soulmates* Nazi actually took a step back in retreat. "No, sir. No problem. We're ready to start if you're free now. We'd like to go over a few of the details with you concerning the kids."

"Thank you. I'll be right there."

Ethan waited until she was gone before turning his attention back to Kyle. "Are we on the same page here?" he asked quietly.

"I think so, Kemo Sabe."

"Thanks again." He clapped Kyle on the shoulder in farewell and headed down the hall, CEO persona solidly in place. He looked like a walking ad for *The Wall Street Journal*; even in the Levis and button-down shirt he was currently wearing untucked, he looked like a force to be reckoned with.

He was a fearless entrepreneur and a hard-nosed businessman who had climbed to the top through study, hard work, a few risky moves, and—maybe—a little old-fashioned luck. Kyle admired him.

Ethan's stride brought to mind the cocky strut of the eleven-year-old Kyle had idealized at the age of four. At the time, he'd seemed grown-up and hero-like to Kyle.

Kyle could see the eleven-year-old Ethan who'd been bucked off a colt and had fought back tears of pain and manly embarrassment while his dad had given him an earful. The fourteen-year-old who'd helped deliver a foal and had whooped in victory when it had stood for the first time. The seventeen-year-old who'd been washing his truck and had decided hosing down his younger brothers would be more fun.

Kyle could see Jake Glass's best man, who'd dashed away an escaped tear when the bride and groom had exchanged vows.

Ethan and Jake were Kyle's brothers. The Lakota had a ritual for binding people together as relatives, people who weren't blood relatives. *Hunkapi.* He and Jake and Ethan hadn't gone through the ritual, but Ethan and Jake were his *hunka ate*, his chosen brothers, just the same. He would do whatever he could for his brothers; he would do whatever he could to help Ethan right now.

Kyle could see the Ethan the world saw these days, the professional man, the CEO, but he also saw his brother, the private man with dirt on his boots and a big heart beating in his chest. They were two sides of the same man. Kyle was afraid the CEO Ethan was on the set of *Soulmates*. The private Ethan had only emerged a couple of times in the past few weeks. And if the women weren't allowed to see through the CEO Ethan to the private one, Ethan would fail—because Ethan wouldn't find his real soulmate any other way.

* * *

"How's the research going?"

Melanie closed her laptop with a snap before realizing it was Curt. "Oh, it's you."

He leaned against the table. "Always a pleasure to see you too." He gestured with his chin toward the closed laptop. "So . . . how's it going so far?"

"It's going," she said.

"Find anything useful yet?"

She reopened her laptop. "Maybe."

He looked over, trying to read the monitor. "Anything you'd care to share?"

"I have a few leads. You're going to have to be patient."

"Sweetie, I don't have the luxury of being patient. We're halfway through taping, and if we don't get something dramatic to happen, the network will yank us off the air by midseason."

Something in Melanie snapped. Maybe it was him calling her sweetie, but she'd been working her tail off, was still working her tail off, and enough was enough. "It seems to me, *Mr. Myers*, that you don't even know what you want. Do you want to convince people that *Soulmates* is the latest, greatest matchmaking product out there, or are you interested in making a soap opera?"

He smirked. "Why can't I have both?"

"If you want both, then give me space to do my job. And it wouldn't hurt you to relax and breathe. You're turning into Dane."

His smirk deepened to a scowl, and she wondered if she'd gone too far with the insult, especially since his scowl had relocated to about six inches from her face. Now *she* needed to breathe. "You think I'm turning into Dane? You'd better find something we can use, and *soon*. We're running out of time, sweetie, and I *promise* you, if this show tanks, my turning into another Dane Esplin will be the least of your worries."

Melanie waited for the door to shut before huffing out a breath. Curt, of all people, had just threatened her. Unbelievable. Except that she did believe him. And wasn't that just great.

* * *

"How are things?"

Melanie snapped her laptop shut a second time. "Dr. Lindstrom! I wasn't expecting you."

The doctor slid into a chair and waved in Melanie's general direction. "Don't let me interrupt."

Melanie wanted to scream, but she only bit the inside of her cheek and reopened her laptop. The demands on her time were bad enough, and Curt had just made them worse. The last thing she needed right now was Dr. Evil nosing about.

She tried to keep working, but it was impossible with Lindstrom sitting there staring at her. She finally gave up. "Was there something you needed?"

Dr. Lindstrom smiled. Therapists must receive specialized training in patronizing smiles, or maybe the doctor just had a particular talent in that area. "Only to make sure you continue to respect the privacy of the contestants' info. I heard that Curt gave you access to the files. He agreed not to do that."

"Uh-huh." She ignored Lindstrom and started typing again.

"I would hate to think that you'd actually try to—"

"Wouldn't dream of it," Melanie cut in, reaching the limit of her endurance.

Curt wanted controversy on the girls for the show, Lindstrom wanted to protect their confidentiality, and Melanie wanted to stop being pulled in every direction. She didn't need the doctor giving her flak about using the women's files. It wasn't as if most of the women hadn't been doing their fair share of self-promotion anyway.

"Anything else?" she asked sweetly, knowing her tone didn't fool the woman for a second.

She actually thought she saw disappointment flicker across Dr. Evil's face. Except that wasn't possible. All she said was, "For now."

* * *

"Are you busy?"

Ms. Carlton slammed her laptop shut and slumped on top of it in obvious frustration. "No. No. I'm not busy at all. Please, come in and take a number."

Lucy looked around for other people, thrown off by the sarcastic comment. "I can come back later if now is a bad time."

Ms. Carlton glared at her. "Just spill it."

The tension in the air was thick enough to cut, and Lucy considered leaving anyway, but she wasn't sure when she'd get another opportunity to talk to Ms. Carlton, so she dug in. "Since tonight's the next elimination, I thought maybe I should talk to you about the pig."

It was obvious by Ms. Carlton's blank expression that not only had she forgotten about the rodeo pig, but she'd also forgotten the plans Lucy had wanted to discuss with her. "The original owners agreed to keep the pig until production was complete." She paused. "Oh, that's right. You wanted me to arrange to send the pig to Ethan's ranch as some sort of gag gift." She slid her chair back from the table and crossed her legs. "Sit down. Let's talk."

"Thanks. I was thinking . . ."

"Think faster. I haven't got all day."

"How do suppose Ethan would react if Hamlet showed up at Ethan's ranch?" she blurted out.

"Hamlet. By Hamlet, I'm assuming you mean the pig?"

Well, so much for thinking Ms. Carlton would find the name funny. "Um, yes. You see, at the rodeo, in the kissing booth, he kept tossing quotes at me from Shakespeare. He remembered that I majored in English and used the quotes to outsmart me and get what he wanted. Where I come from—and with the brothers I grew up with—you just don't let something like that go unchallenged. I figure it's my turn for payback. If he's going to quote *Hamlet*, I'm gonna give him Hamlet. Hamlet the pig. So I was wondering . . . how hard would it be to find an Elizabethan costume that a pig could wear?"

Ms. Carlton snorted. "Well. Good question," she said. "One I can honestly say I never expected to hear asked. Ever." She tapped her chin in thought. "But it just so happens I know someone who might have the answer." She pulled out her cell phone. "Let's see what we can find out." She placed the call and kept her eyes squarely on Lucy. "Paula. Melanie Carlton here . . ."

Lucy felt tense. She glanced around the room, studied her hands, and tried to appear like she wasn't listening to the conversation on the phone. Listening was actually helping her, even if it might seem rude to Ms. Carlton. Tonight was another elimination night, and Lucy was trying hard not to think about that.

Ms. Carlton replied to the person on the phone. "Keep in mind that pigs grow fast, so even if you got measurements today . . . Yes, those balloon-type breeches from Shakespeare's time. And a ruff collar and puffy hat with a feather. Great. Perfect." She gave Lucy a conspiratorial smile.

This little prank might just work. Lucy hoped she would be around to enjoy it. She'd know one way or the other that evening.

"Figure out how much this will cost, and let me know," Ms. Carlton said. "Hold on—I'm going to give you the number for the guy who's got the pig. And we need to work out a timetable." She put her hand over the mouthpiece. "Was there anything else?" she asked Lucy.

"Can you let me know when Hamlet will be sent to Montana? I want to include a card with him if I can. For Ethan."

"The best plan would be to have Hamlet transported right before Ethan takes the finalists there to meet his family. That's your time frame. Now, why don't you go relax before the big evening gets underway?"

Lucy stood. "Thank you. I know you have a lot to do around here, and I appreciate your help with this." Ms. Carlton froze for a minute, like she wasn't sure how to react. Lucy smiled. "Thanks again. And wish me luck tonight."

"Good luck," Ms. Carlton said.

Lucy hoped she meant it, but with Ms. Carlton, you couldn't tell.

CHAPTER 14

L̲ucy̲ w̲as̲ l̲eaving̲ *S̲oulmates̲* H̲ouse̲. A month had passed since she'd first walked through the doors, and it felt strangely poignant to see her time here coming to an end.

She made one final check of the bedroom suite for belongings, looking in drawers, glancing in the shower, rechecking the closet one last time. She tucked her scriptures and journal into the corner of her suitcase and then placed her remaining outfits on top. Satisfied that she had everything, she zipped the suitcase shut, grabbed her purse, and headed down the stairs.

The past week had been an intense one, starting with the group date at the homeless shelter. Her feet still ached when she thought of it. She'd worked hard that day and heard stories that had broken her heart.

Then Ethan had taken six of them to the pediatric ward of a local hospital.

She'd handed out toys, read stories, colored pictures, and fought battles with action figures. She'd helped more than one superhero into costume and several princesses too.

She'd painted a flower on the cheek of one little girl who'd then insisted on returning the favor. That had started a trend, and soon both of her arms had been filled with child-rendered artwork—rainbows and flowers, squiggles and smiley faces. By the end of the afternoon, she'd felt like the tattooed lady at the circus, but the giggling and the mischievous looks on the kids' faces while they'd decorated her would stay with her for a long, long time.

She headed down the stairs to the living room and wandered over to a picture window that overlooked the grounds. From this direction, the production trailers weren't visible, and Lucy could see green lawns, flowering shrubs, and palm trees jutting high overhead. It looked like anybody's home. It had been her home for a month. But it was an on-location set, a theatrical stage. It wasn't reality at all.

Yet it had been her reality for the past month.

Yesterday Ethan had taken only three of them—Sara, Denise, and herself—to a home for seniors. The day had started out well enough. Ethan and Sara had been pulled into a high stakes game of penny poker with some "old geezers," as they'd called themselves. Denise had offered to help a woman touch up her makeup. The jagged eyeliner and wild eye shadow had suggested that either the poor lady's vision wasn't very good or her hand wasn't very steady—or both—and soon Denise had had a line of eager women who'd wanted their turn, including a couple of employees.

Lucy had been sweet-talked into playing checkers with a man named Bernardo, a gentleman with a white fringe of hair, a hawklike nose, and bright black eyes that had twinkled when he spoke. He had also been a flirt, and Lucy had enjoyed every minute of his company, even though he'd beaten her three games to one.

After lunch they'd spent time visiting seniors who were confined to their rooms. Lucy had read aloud to one woman and then been escorted down the hall to visit with another. She hadn't seen Ethan for a while, or any of the others, for that matter. As they'd passed an open doorway, a raspy voice had called, "Hey! Hey!"

The aide had said, "Ignore that. Ada yells all the time. Come on."

But Lucy hadn't been able to ignore it. She'd looked into the room. The woman inside had waved frantically at her while struggling to get out of an easy chair. The aide had hustled over. "Ada, let's sit back down now," she'd said. "There's a good girl."

The woman, Ada, had jabbed her finger repeatedly in Lucy's direction as she'd approached her. "She came! I told you she'd come." And then she'd grabbed Lucy's arm with both hands in a viselike grip. "It's my birthday, and you remembered. I knew you would."

Startled, Lucy had looked questioningly at the aide, who'd whispered, "She thinks you're her daughter, Mary. She thinks everyone not in scrubs around here is Mary." Then she'd addressed the woman. "Now, Ada, you need to let go. Come on. You're going to give her bruises."

Somehow, Lucy had known immediately what she needed to do. She'd knelt next to the chair, which had managed to soothe the woman. She'd allowed Ada to hold her hands in her lap, and the poor woman had stroked and petted them and raised them to her lips to kiss over and over. Lucy had done her best to respond to her nonsensical comments until the aide had finally whispered to her that it was time to go. It had been just as well, since Ada had forgotten they were there and had begun mumbling to herself, things about her daughter and her husband and forever.

Lucy had looked back through the doorway. "Will her daughter visit her?"

"Oh, she comes nearly every week. Mary's a good daughter. She'd appreciate how kind you were to Ada today."

"It's not her birthday, is it?" Lucy had already known what the answer would be.

The aide had shaken her head. "We had a nice party for her last March."

Lucy came back to the present when she heard someone behind her, in the living room, clear his throat. She pulled herself out of the memory and turned away from the window. Kyle stood in the doorway.

"Your luggage is stowed in the SUV, Lucy. We need to leave for the airport now."

"Thanks, Kyle."

He nodded and left.

She picked up her purse and took a deep breath.

This was really it.

Despite going on three group dates this week, she'd barely had a minute alone with Ethan. She'd been a wreck at the elimination ceremony last night. One might think after three elimination ceremonies she'd be used to this, but she'd been as tightly wound as a spring.

Ethan, in the meantime, had been the gracious host, as usual, but it seemed like he'd erected a wall around himself. Had she been the only one to sense it? Was it only in place when he was with her? And then, ironically, after the party had been going on for a while, he'd taken her aside and had asked her how she was feeling about things. The question—or, more specifically, his cool tone when he'd asked it—had conjured up all the emotional ghosts she'd felt since she'd walked in the door of *Soulmates* House.

How am I feeling? she'd thought. *Like I might choke or explode at any moment. Like I need to throw something breakable. Like I want to grab your face and kiss you until your eyes cross. Like I want to shake you out of this cool politeness. Like I want to ask where your teasing spark from the rodeo or the closeness we felt in Mexico has gone.*

That's what she'd been feeling. But the Ethan who'd asked her about *her* feelings hadn't seemed to have any of his own at that moment. So she'd hidden hers. At least she'd tried.

Whatever she'd said in reply, it must have worked because he'd chuckled. That meant his own sense of humor hadn't totally vanished behind his protective veneer.

And then he'd called her *different* again. She'd begun to hate that word. He'd used it in Mexico, but at least then he'd seemed attracted to her, like he'd singled her out as unique to him in some way. "What makes you different?" he'd asked.

Different. Ethan thought she was different. So did the women. So had a lot of guys she'd dated in high school and met in college.

Lucy, you're a great girl and a lot of fun, but you're different. You're too different. It's not going to work out between us. Sorry.

I really like you, Lucy, but hanging out with you is different from what I'm used to. Maybe we should just be friends. Sorry, babe.

The Bible talked about a peculiar people. The dictionary said it came from the Latin *peculium*, meaning "a special possession," God's own possession. But when people heard the word *peculiar*, that wasn't the definition that came to mind.

Weird. Odd.

Different.

She was *different*. All her life she'd been *different*.

With the cameras running and Ethan chuckling and asking her how she was feeling, she'd crossed some invisible line in her mind. Maybe she was the normal one and everyone else was different. "What makes *you* different?" she'd asked, the words out even before she'd realized they'd been there.

His eyebrows had shot up, and he'd been silent. Then he'd replied, "I don't think I am. Different, that is."

Smooth as glass.

And that, ironically, had been when the epiphany had struck her, a flash of inspiration with such clarity it had stolen her breath. If she'd heard a chorus of angels at that moment, she wouldn't have been surprised.

In a backward way, she'd been right, at least as far as Ethan was concerned. He *was* different.

He was different. If the words had been spoken aloud, they wouldn't have sounded any clearer in her head. The impression had stayed with her the rest of the night and through the elimination part of the evening, which she'd survived.

The charm for that week had been an angel with open arms.

And so, now, she was leaving *Soulmates* House. They were all leaving *Soulmates* House.

Only five women remained: Alison, Sara, Denise, Tiffany, and Lucy. The cut to five instead of the planned-for six had nearly halved them and had emphasized that Ethan meant business.

This week they were heading home so Ethan could meet their families. She couldn't believe she'd made it this far. Her parents were going to be meeting Ethan Glass. So were her brothers. She hoped they liked Ethan. She hoped he liked them.

Because, she knew, it mattered to her. Their opinions mattered. Ethan mattered. It was all beginning to matter way too much, in fact.

"Lucy?" Kyle poked his head through the door. "You coming?"

"I'm right behind you." She'd been wishing for adventure and new experiences when she'd signed up for this. It only went to show that you needed to be careful what you wished for because you just might get it.

* * *

Ethan tossed the last of his shirts into his bag and zipped it shut. This was it. Time to start the next phase of the *Soulmates* process. The crew was striking the set at the house, and the women were on their way home by now. Starting day after tomorrow, he'd be meeting five families, starting with Sara's in Tampa, Florida, and working his way back to the West Coast.

Dr. Lindstrom had shown up a few minutes before and was now comfortably settled in an overstuffed chair. "It's been quite a week," she commented.

"I thought you'd be halfway home by now," he said as he packed his carry-on bag with reading material.

"My flight's later this afternoon," she explained. "I heard you cut four women last night."

It had been quite a week, Ethan thought. He'd eliminated four women, whittling the numbers from nine to five, and no one had been happy about it, especially Curt, who'd accused him of playing fast and loose with the production. It had meant pulling a scheduled week of dates and moving everything forward on the calendar. "Are you here to give me grief about cutting the ranks to five? If so, you can relax. Curt already did."

"I see."

Typical shrink answer. "It needed to be done," he said firmly.

She put up her hands in a defensive gesture. "I'm on your side. I just want to hear your reasons for doing it. You didn't give the staff much warning."

"It was a last-minute decision. Compatibility tests aside, I didn't see a future with any of them, so it was better for them in the long run. This week only emphasized that fact."

The homeless shelter had been a good place to start his planned week of charitable activities. Everyone had been enthusiastic, even if the plans had caught them by surprise. The day at the hospital had been a treat, and the six women he'd taken had been terrific. He'd enjoyed seeing the pleasure on everyone's faces, especially the children's.

He'd only taken three of the women to the senior care center. He and Sara had spent the morning playing poker with a couple of self-proclaimed old geezers. She'd flirted shamelessly with them, and it had been just the right touch—for both the cameras and the old guys.

Denise had been a gem. She'd gone off to do girly things with some of the senior ladies. She was beautiful and genuine, and he found her appealing.

Then there was Lucy. Lucy had played checkers with an old flirt who'd obviously appreciated spending time with a pretty woman. And while Ethan had found Sara and the poker geezers only amusing, he'd felt the urge to punch the checkers guy. Considering the fact that the man had to be nearly eighty, it had been an absurd reaction.

Berta glanced at her watch and stood. "I'd better be off. For better or worse, you're down to five, and you're meeting families. Have you decided what you are looking for when you meet them?"

He leaned against the dresser and crossed his arms. "More insight. And the fit, I guess. If they feel like family to me or if the potential exists that they might."

"There will be both positives and negatives."

"I'm counting on it. I want to uncover both, especially the negatives."

"Are you prepared to have the families looking for the same in you?"

He shrugged. "I know I'm not perfect, but I'm also not worried, Berta. I'm a decent catch." He gave her his most charming smile. "I'm the *Soulmate*, remember?"

She chuckled and shook her head at him as she headed out the door. It was something his mother would do. "Berta," he said impulsively.

She turned. "Yes?"

"What do you think a soulmate is?" He hadn't intended to ask her that, but there it was. There was no taking it back now.

She pondered the question and appeared to be choosing her words carefully. "A soulmate can be different things to different people. Some don't even believe such a person exists." She sighed as if she knew her answer was vague and inadequate. "If I were going to put it into words, I might say that a soulmate is someone with whom a person feels an extra bond, a kinship that transcends compatibility and emotional attachment."

He grinned. "Transcends compatibility, Berta? After all those tests you made me take, compatibility isn't enough? I should be looking for someone who *transcends* it?"

"You think I've been hoisted by my own petard? Maybe. But I do believe the compatibility tests have narrowed the field and will ultimately help you in your search. I hope at the end of this you have found someone to spend your life with. Whether that person is your soulmate, only you can answer."

"Do you think it actually has anything to do with a person's soul?"

She raised an eyebrow. "Now you're getting religious on me, and I don't intend to go there. Why are you asking?"

"It's just the word itself, I guess. The name of the show keeps it in the foreground." He shrugged. "It's gotten me thinking, that's all."

She smiled. "All right. Good luck with the families. If you want to talk, give me a call."

He nodded. "Enjoy your week home with Dr. Fred."

Her smile broadened. "He's promised me his homemade lasagna, and he's arranged for his partners to cover his hospital shifts for the next three days."

Ethan laughed. "You'd think the poor guy hadn't seen his wife in almost a month."

"The poor guy's wife misses him too. I doubt I'll let him out of my sight while I'm there." She waved farewell, and he could hear her chuckle as she walked down the hall.

Was Dr. Fred Berta's soulmate? They'd been talking about that very subject, and yet she hadn't mentioned it. It was obvious they were crazy about each other, and he knew they'd been married for several years. Did their relationship "transcend compatibility and normal attachment"? It sounded clinical, just the way a psychiatrist and a hospital pathologist might describe their relationship. He smiled at the thought.

It was time to hit the road. He wheeled his luggage out to the car and stowed the pieces in the trunk. It was time to look forward and—as he got to say on camera frequently—"continue the journey." He slid his sunglasses on and shifted the car into gear.

The past week had been a successful one as far as he was concerned. *Soulmates* objectives aside, he'd found it intensely satisfying to help as many people as they had and to see the women, for the most part, give of themselves.

He had some favorite moments, a few that really stood out in his mind. Lucy's story about her pioneer trek had struck him for some reason. The mood in the limo had changed while she was telling the story. It had felt . . . *different*.

And then he'd stumbled onto a scene at the nursing home . . .

He'd been looking for her. He'd gone to the room where he'd expected her to be, and she hadn't been there, so he'd set off in search of her.

As he'd headed down the hallway, he'd heard voices coming from a room and had recognized one of them as Lucy's. What he'd seen when he got to the doorway had brought him to an abrupt halt.

Lucy had been on her knees next to a woman in a chair, a nurse's aide hovering in the background. The woman had clutched Lucy's hands possessively, caressing them repeatedly, but it had been their conversation that had caught his attention.

"Your daddy's gone, but you're still here, aren't you?"

"I'm here."

"Do you like my birthday dress? You gave it to me."

"You look lovely."

"Your daddy never forgets my birthday."

"That's because he loves you very much."

"You look just like him."

That comment had made Lucy pause. Ethan himself had felt frozen, suspended in time. The air around him had felt warm and thick, like a soft blanket of peace had been wrapped around them all. Like it had been in the limo when Lucy had told her story. He'd felt it, recognized it, but hadn't understood it.

He'd waited to see what she would say.

"Do you think so?" She hadn't sounded in control of her voice. "Maybe that's his way of letting you know that he misses you, and—"

"He said he'd love me forever and ever . . ." the woman's voice had drifted off.

"I'm sure he still does."

The woman hadn't heard Lucy; she'd gone into her own little world, mumbling, "Forever and ever, 'til death do us part. Forever and ever, 'til death do us part . . ." Ethan had suddenly felt awkward, like he'd been eavesdropping on something intimate. Sacred, almost.

At that point, the aide had gestured to Lucy that it was time to go. Ethan had disappeared before they'd noticed he'd been there.

The freeway traffic was congested and slow. Flashing signs warned of road construction. He'd estimated his drive time to the airport with only a slight allowance for delays. It was a rare miscalculation on his part. He checked his watch and consulted the car's GPS. If he followed what the GPS was saying, he should still make it to the airport on time, but his gut was telling him there was more going on than just the road construction.

He threw on his blinker and quickly shifted lanes, heading for the nearest exit. Right now, he trusted his gut more than the GPS.

The same thing applied to his *Soulmates* journey. He had to trust his gut. Despite the fact that he'd decided to take Lucy to the end, he'd be a fool not to follow this journey to its conclusion with an objective eye. So he'd ask the questions and listen to the answers. He'd talk to Dr. Lindstrom some more. He'd meet the families, and he'd spend as much time as possible with each remaining woman. He'd talk to Kyle. He'd listen to his parents' opinions. He'd do it all.

But ultimately, he'd trust his gut. It was what had gotten him to where he was, in business and in life. It would get him through the rest of this journey. And if he were lucky, at the end of the journey, he would find his soulmate. He waved at a driver who made room for him to merge into the exit lane for the airport. Yeah, he'd gotten through life so far on skill, instinct, and luck and had been plenty successful. Now it was time to be lucky in love because he was ready. He was ready for that soulmate, call her what you will, and for the rest of his life's journey to begin.

Forever and ever, 'til death do us part. That's what the poor woman had kept repeating. People said it all the time, but when he thought about it, it didn't actually make sense. It had taken her ramblings for him to really hear the contradiction in the statement.

He'd wondered, on occasion, what happened when a person died. He figured most people wondered at some point. Was it the end? Was it all over? Was there more? There were a lot of different theories and beliefs about it. Even Sienna had talked to everyone about her own take on it.

Ethan had been raised in a Christian home, with a mother who attended church regularly and a father he considered to be a passive believer. He personally tended to believe that there was something after this life, that the soul lived on in some manner. What manner, he wasn't sure.

Lucy had talked to the woman about her dead husband as if he were still alive. *He's letting you know . . . He misses you . . . He loves you.* Present tense. Had she been aware that that was what she was doing? Was the woman's husband somewhere beyond, waiting for her to join him? If the soul continued on forever, did it automatically follow that the love or the marriage would as well?

He'd like to think so, but now the woman's words haunted him.

Forever and ever, 'til death do us part.

CHAPTER 15

LUCY COULD BARELY KEEP STILL. She felt like a jack-in-the-box, wound up and ready to pop. The production crew and cameramen had arrived the day before and were already in place as the rental car Ethan was driving headed up the dirt road. He stepped out of the car, settled a beat-up cowboy hat on his head, and grinned as he walked toward her.

Finally, *finally*, he was here. She ran to him and threw herself into a bear hug while he swung her around.

"You're here," she said into his neck, dizzy for more than one reason.

Still spinning her in the air, Ethan kissed her. A solid, yeehaw, good-to-have-you-in-my-arms kiss. Lucy's toes curled, and electricity flashed down her spine like a lightning bolt. This was the Ethan from the rodeo, the Ethan she'd been with in Mexico. The distant CEO was gone.

He set her down, and his eyes traveled over her, eating her up, drinking her in. She needed to get a grip—*now*—or she'd be a molten puddle of goo before they even made it out of the parking lot. "Lucy," he said, "you look like a million bucks."

"Well, you ought to know," she replied.

Laughing, he laced his fingers through hers and started walking. It took her a minute to match his stride. She needed to keep up in more ways than one. She'd been excited to see him but hadn't known what to expect from him today. He'd had four other women's families to meet this week, in addition to her own, and she couldn't forget how distant he'd been at the last elimination.

"Wow, look at this place," he said.

"I promised you a ghost town if you came to Arizona. Welcome to Ophelia." Lucy could hardly believe Ethan was actually here in this little town not far from Eagle Bluff.

"Ophelia's the name of the town? You're joking, right?"

"Digby Whitlock was an English immigrant who decided to try his luck at prospecting and then found when he got here that selling goods to the other miners was a more lucrative business, at least for him."

"Exactly the type of bold entrepreneur I admire. So you're telling me that this Digby Whitlock, Englishman that he was, named the settlement after his favorite Shakespearean heroine, who just happened to be from *Hamlet*?" He eyed her suspiciously. "Or was Ophelia the name of his long-suffering but faithful English wife?"

Lucy fought back a smile. "Neither. He named the town after his burro."

He stared at her in disbelief. "You're pulling my leg."

"Nope. It's true." She laughed when she saw the expression on his face. "Okay, I confess. It's all true except for the Ophelia part. I couldn't resist throwing a little *Hamlet* at you. Welcome to *Cecily*, formerly a thriving boomtown that, during its very brief heyday, boasted a post office, a general store, three saloons, and seventy-nine permanent residents—as best we can tell from the few sketchy accounts that exist. But those accounts also claim that Cecily was, in fact, his burro."

"I imagine Cecily was deeply honored by the tribute."

"Whitlock said on at least one occasion that she was the only female he'd ever met that he completely trusted."

"Poor man. As one of his species, I have a lot of sympathy for him." He noticed the horses tethered behind her. "Ah, what do we have here?"

"I thought you might enjoy the countryside better on horseback." It was an easy ride on horseback from Cecily to the resort Grace's father owned, where they would be having lunch later. She, Allie, and Grace had ridden this particular trail frequently as kids.

"You thought right." The gray gelding next to him tossed its head and tried to sidestep. "What's your name, my handsome friend?" he asked, patting its neck and allowing it to become acquainted with him.

"His name is Ghost—mostly because of his coloring, and not because of any supernatural abilities he possesses. He can be a handful though. My horse is named Daphne. Say hello, Daphne." The little bay nodded her head, seemingly on cue, making Ethan laugh.

"Daphne and I are old friends; I've ridden her many times, and we understand each other. Ghost and I are only friendly acquaintances. They belong to my friend Grace's family. Grace rides Ghost because she's a better horsewoman than I am and because Ghost is Ghost. I figured you were up to the challenge."

"What do you say, pal?" he asked the horse. "Feel like showing the ladies a good time?" The gray didn't make any objection, so Ethan gave Lucy a leg up onto Daphne and then swung himself into the saddle. Ghost balked for a moment before settling under Ethan's expert touch.

They wandered through the rubble of what used to be Cecily, Arizona, with Lucy pointing out the various landmarks that were hardly more than rock piles and crumbling foundations. There was a small graveyard bordered by a rusty fence made of an irregular hodgepodge of barbed wire, rebar, and some fancy wrought-iron pieces. A few of the locals had made it a point to keep up the graveyard over the years. Old Digby Whitlock himself was buried there, along with an Eagle Bluff ancestor or two.

"We used to come up here all the time when we were younger, my friends Grace and Allie and I. We knew every rock and tree, every hiding place. Sometimes we'd pretend we were archaeologists, like Indiana Jones, hunting for ancient relics. Sometimes we were outlaws, this dangerous band of women who came into town stirring up trouble. When the sun would start to go down, we'd sit by the graveyard—right over there—and make up ghost stories, trying to see who could scare the others the worst."

"Who told the scariest stories?"

"You know how I like to win, but honestly, I'd have to say Allie had the most vivid imagination of the three of us. She'd really get us going, then Grace would panic, and before we ever found out if the bloody hand attacked or the pale crying woman found her lost child, Grace would be hightailing it home, and we'd be racing after her."

"Any scary stories about the residents of Cecily? Ghostly gunslingers dueling at midnight?"

"There was a hanging tree, but like I told you, most of the info on the town is sketchy. Whether they ever used the tree, I don't know. Maybe just having a hanging tree helped maintain law and order."

They wound their way along the trail. Lucy pointed out the old mine, barely visible up on the hillside to their left. A meadow sprinkled with summer flowers beckoned to them on the right. It was a peaceful scene, and the rhythmic swaying of the horses was relaxing.

He talked about his family's ranch in Montana, and Lucy could tell how much he loved the place and missed being with his family. "Are you sorry you're not there? Do you regret leaving to do other things?"

Ethan shook his head. "No, I like what I'm doing; it was the right choice for me. My brother, Jake, takes good care of the ranch. He's smart, and he loves the place. It's a good fit." He glanced at his watch and then over at the camera crew. "Hold on a sec."

He pulled out his cell phone, tapped out a text, and slipped the phone back into his pocket. "What do you say we give Daphne and Ghost a chance to stretch their legs?"

Lucy heard a noise and looked over her shoulder in time to see Dane Esplin throw down his clipboard—rather violently—and stomp off. Lucy couldn't hear what he was saying, but from the looks on the crew's faces, which ranged from terrified to amused, Lucy decided that was probably a good thing. She looked back at Ethan, who seemed unaffected by Mr. Esplin's outburst.

"Dane's not happy with my change of plans," he said, "but he'll get over it. You ready?" He nudged Ghost into a canter, and she and Daphne followed in pursuit.

It was freeing, Lucy thought, her hair whipping behind her, and she mentally said good-bye to the crew and the cameras and nudged Daphne on.

Ethan and Ghost were soon tearing over the landscape at full gallop. Lucy and Daphne tried to keep up, and Daphne did her darnedest to hold her own with Ghost, but they were outclassed. Lucy eased up on Daphne and watched man and horse fly together. It was a magnificent sight.

Eventually Ethan reined Ghost in, and they trotted back to where Lucy and Daphne waited. He was ablaze with joy, and the look on his face took Lucy's breath away. She'd never seen him like this, so totally free and open, and it fit him as comfortably as the faded jeans he wore. This was a side of Ethan she could really fall in love with.

She froze at the thought.

Oh, she was in big trouble. Because, truth be told, there was more than just this side of Ethan she was falling in love with, and deep down she knew it.

But deep down she also knew that falling in love with someone didn't mean the road would be easy. It also didn't mean it was the right road to take.

She needed to remember that.

They headed toward a cluster of pines, where he dismounted and then assisted her. Ghost and Daphne busied themselves foraging, and Ethan and Lucy relaxed in the shade.

His hat came off, and he flopped onto his back. "Thank you for including horses in today's plans. It was perfect."

She leaned back on her elbows and looked at him. "When Mr. Esplin catches up to us, you might not think so. And he'll blame me for providing our means of escape. Do you think he's the type to hold a grudge?"

"For what we're paying him, he wouldn't dare." He shifted on the ground to find a more comfortable spot and then put his hands behind his head. "He got plenty of footage for the show today, and I wanted time away from the cameras with you."

That made her happy until she wondered if he'd done something similar on the previous dates. Probably, or else Mr. Esplin wouldn't have been quite so upset. That deflated her bubble of happiness somewhat. Time to change the subject. "Tell me more about the ranch in Montana and your family."

"The ranch has been in the family for a while, passed down from father to son. It's in a beautiful spot in the western part of the state. Jake's been running the ranch full time since Old Jed—my father—had a run-in with a bull a couple of years back."

Lucy gasped. "Is he okay?" She was certain "run-in with a bull" was an understatement.

"He's fine and as stubborn as he ever was. But he was out of commission for a few months, so Jake took over the day-to-day of the ranch. Once Old Jed was back on his feet, they just left things as they were."

"Where were you?"

"I was in London at the time, tied up in some dicey contract negotiations. I made plans to fly home when I got word, but my mother told me Old Jed's injuries weren't life threatening, and there wasn't anything I could do." He frowned.

She could tell his father's injuries had bothered him a lot more than he was letting on and so had not being there when it had happened. "Why do you call your father Old Jed?" she asked.

He rolled to his side, supporting his head with a hand. "When I was in high school, we hired a ranch hand named Jed. He was a young guy—barely twenty, I'd guess—and green as they come but eager. So our foreman put him to work.

"In the past, if there were two hands with the same name, they got nicknames so there wouldn't be any confusion. In this case, they became Jed and Old Jed."

"But he's your dad. Why do *you* call him Jed?"

He shrugged. "It was my age, I think, being in high school. I worked on the ranch a lot, and I already took guff for being the owner's kid.

Calling him Dad was just asking for more trouble. I started calling him Old Jed when the others did, and it stuck."

Lucy shook her head. She had three brothers, and she didn't think she'd ever learn to understand the male mind. "What did your father say?"

"He never said anything. Of course, to be honest, it usually takes an act of Congress to get him to say anything anyway. He's not much of a talker. And he wasn't old, either, only compared to the greenhorn. The guys thought it was a good joke, especially since he wasn't even forty at the time and he was the best horseman on the ranch. Old Jedediah Glass." Ethan chuckled and ran his fingers lazily over her hand. "Tell me about your parents and your brothers."

"Oh." Concentrate, Lucy. "Um . . . my parents are nice, normal people, really. Dad teaches high school English—"

"The nut doesn't fall far from the tree, then."

"Are you saying," she asked, simultaneously trying to ignore his fingers and feign indignation, "that you think I'm a nut?"

"Your words, not mine." His mouth twitched. "I'm reserving judgment for later."

She laughed.

He grinned. "He won't be coming after me with a shotgun, then?"

"Not with TV cameras all over the place. Hard to beat a murder rap that way."

"Good point."

"My mom tends to be quiet, but don't let that fool you. She's sharp as a tack. She decided long ago to be a stay-at-home mother, and when you meet my brothers, you'll probably understand why. No sane babysitter would have taken them. But it also meant my brothers and I didn't get away with anything." She grinned. "At least not half as much as we tried to get away with."

"I think I'm going to like your parents."

He rolled off his arm so he was sitting next to her, and Lucy shivered when she caught the look in his eye. "Because I find I really like their daughter." She could barely breathe, waiting to see what he would do next.

He lowered his face to hers and brushed kisses on her cheek and next to her ear. Her hand crept to his shoulder. His free hand went to the back of her head and urged her closer, and his lips found hers.

It was Mexico all over again, but better. No other women waited impatiently on the beach for their return, no cameras lurked nearby.

"And then," she managed to say in between kisses, trying to keep her sanity, "there are my brothers."

"Mmm hmm. Brothers." His kisses continued along the line of her jaw. "Miserable things, brothers."

"Horrible beasts."

"I'm going to like them too, aren't I?"

"I hope so. Although I should warn you that TV cameras won't necessarily act as a deterrent in their case."

"Mmm." He stole another kiss and then another before pulling back. "I *am* going to like them. But I can also tell that I'm going to have to watch my step."

She puffed out a laugh and tried to steady herself. "Right now, I think you have more reason to worry about Dane Esplin than you do my brothers."

He rolled his eyes then glanced at his watch. "You're right. It's time we head back to the resort so I can face his wrath." He took a deep breath and gently brushed a few stray locks of hair from her forehead. "Although, right at the moment, I wish we could stay here like this forever." He rose to his feet and offered her his hand. "Come on. Let's go."

She wished they could stay like this too. She was falling hard for Ethan Glass. What worried her was the forever part.

* * *

Melanie watched Dane pace around the resort's private dining room, fuming and snapping at everyone as they set up for the lunch shoot. It was hilarious. Did the guy really believe he had some sort of authority over Ethan Glass? Come on. This was *Ethan Glass* they were talking about. The *Soulmate*. Daddy Warbucks. The signature on their paychecks. Media darling and man with the Midas touch.

Dane was merely a tool Curt needed to get a viable show on the air. Dane had surprised Melanie by actually being competent, especially since he acted like a Chihuahua revved up on caffeine most of the time, but still, he was deluding himself if he thought *he* was the one in charge here.

Now that they were down to five women, Dane had begun pushing for more passion. The three women they'd taped so far this week had been more than happy to oblige, but Ethan's cool CEO exterior seemed to have dropped a few degrees in temperature. Dane's frustration and temper, as a result, had risen to just under the boiling point.

The exception had been Tiffany in Chicago. Mr. Smooth-As-Glass had had to work at deflecting Tiffany and her scorched earth approach to romance. But he had, and Melanie had wondered about it at the time.

At least she'd wondered about it until she'd seen him in action with Lucy today. Watching the two of them riding off on horseback, ditching the crew and the rest of the morning shoot, had been informative. Dane, if he would stop ranting long enough to think, would realize they'd gotten an unexpectedly romantic moment on videotape—two lovers galloping across a meadow of wildflowers—cue the audience sighs, please—and Melanie had gotten a clear picture of who Ethan's *Soulmate* was going to be. She would bet her job on it.

It also meant that the plan of action she'd put into play that morning after Ethan and Lucy had ridden off was going to achieve results. Rocking the love boat a little would heighten the show's drama. If she were lucky, they'd even get some controversy. Controversy would lead to all sorts of great things: interest, chatter, ratings, money. Melanie's career would be made.

The sound of glass breaking drew her attention back to Dane, who was storming off as a kitchen employee now mopped something dark and runny off the wall. Melanie controlled the urge to laugh. Dane hadn't been happy with her either when she'd informed him she and Rogan would be gone for an hour or two. If things went the way she hoped they would, Dane wouldn't be unhappy with her for long. She gestured to Rogan, and they left.

On the other side of the resort, located near the clubhouse, was a small coffee shop that catered to morning golf enthusiasts. At this time of day, however, the hotel guests would be lounging by the pool or indulging in spa treatments rather than golfing. The coffee shop was mostly deserted. Exactly as she'd planned.

Sitting at a table near the back was a curly haired blonde and a sleek brunette, Lucy's best friends. She nudged Rogan's arm.

"Those are our girls. Now, remember—we don't want them getting nervous or suspicious in any way."

They approached the two young women, and Melanie offered her hand. "You must be Allie and Grace. So nice to meet you. I'm Melanie Carlton, associate producer of *Soulmates*, and this is Josh Rogan." She shook hands with Allie, the blonde, and then with Grace, and she and Rogan joined them at the table. "Thank you so much for meeting with us." She leaned over the table in a conspiratorial manner. "I'll bet you two were excited to learn your friend has made it this far." She smiled winningly and searched both of their faces.

The blonde looked like she'd burst any minute from excitement; the brunette wasn't exactly wary but was still reserved. Melanie chatted with them, attempting to put the brunette at ease, and pulled out papers for them to sign and pens to use. "If I can get you both to sign these release forms. There's also a confidentiality clause attached that we'd like you to initial. We like to keep things under wraps until the show airs; I'm sure you understand." She watched as both girls signed the documents and smiled to herself. Melanie had a list of questions ready to go, prepared from the information she'd collected from Dr. Lindstrom's files. Now it was just a matter of getting the right answers to her questions. She gestured to Rogan to start taping.

* * *

Grace tried to kick Allie's leg under the table but missed. She'd never seen her like this. She was always a little outrageous, to Grace's way of thinking, but today she was over the top. They'd freaked out when the lady producer had called. She'd said they were doing in-depth features to give viewers a closer look at the final five contestants, and who better than Lucy's best friends since childhood to provide special insight?

It had made sense at the time, but alarm bells had started sounding in Grace's head the minute the lady and the cameraman had walked through the door of the coffee shop. She wasn't sure why, maybe they were just too Hollywood for Grace's comfort, but it had made her cautious all the same.

The producer had done everything right so far. She'd smiled, shaken their hands, and glided into easy chitchat with them. She hadn't done anything suspicious at all.

The camera guy was sitting there with an easygoing smile on his face, acting vaguely interested in the conversation, but he was more interested in checking out Allie than anything else—but, really, Allie *had* dressed in one of her hottest outfits, knowing it was her big chance to be on TV, and, anyway, he was a guy.

There hadn't been any reason that Grace could come up with for her nerves to have jangled like they had. If Allie weren't acting like an idiot, she'd feel better. Unfortunately, Allie was having a bubble bath in a Jacuzzi moment.

Putting bubble bath in the spa Jacuzzis had been one of Allie's more lame-brained ideas when they were teens, and Lucy and Grace had been stuck with a huge frothing mess to mop up before housekeeping discovered it. Allie had helped, sort of, but mostly she'd laughed and tossed globs of bubbles at them. Maria, the housekeeping supervisor, hadn't been fooled for a minute, but she also hadn't reported them to Grace's father. He'd have blown a gasket if he'd known.

They'd been extra nice to Maria for weeks after that.

Grace wasn't in the mood to mop up after Allie today, especially since any mess she made would involve a Hollywood producer, a cameraman, and the potential to hurt Lucy.

She gave Allie a look to get her to shut up, but Allie simply ignored her and talked on.

Grace glanced at the redheaded producer. She was smiling.

Grace still felt uneasy. She wished she knew what to do.

Now Allie was going on about how Lucy never had any boyfriends but always dated a lot. Technically, that was true, but she needed to be more careful about how she said stuff—she was making it sound as if Lucy went from guy to guy like an alley cat, and nothing could be further from the truth.

Grace tried not to panic.

"So Lucy's never been in a serious, long-term relationship. Why is that?" the producer asked. What was her name? Grace had been so nervous when they'd met that it had slipped her mind.

Allie shrugged negligently. "Oh, I don't know. She's dated some hot guys though. I thought she was nuts. She'd see a guy a couple of times, things would be looking good—you know what I mean—and the next time we'd see her, she'd say it was over. Then some new guy would come along . . ."

Grace winced and looked for the courage to speak up. If only the camera weren't there. She cleared her throat. "Uh . . ." The producer and the cameraman both turned in her direction. She tried again. "Uh, I think they weren't Lucy's type, that's all. She's careful—"

"Too picky, you mean," Allie tossed in.

"Grace," the producer smiled at her like a hungry, redheaded spider. "What do you think Lucy's type is, then?"

"I don't know—"

"Do you think Ethan is her type?"

Grace glanced at Allie. Allie raised her eyebrows at Grace, challenging her to come up with an intelligent answer. She was miffed now that the camera was on Grace. Great. Grace turned back to the producer. "It's possible. She thought he was good looking when she saw his picture. And Lucy is ambitious. She works hard at whatever it is she wants to accomplish."

"*Ambitious*," the producer commented. "Interesting word choice."

Oh no. Grace shook her head. "I don't mean Lucy's ambitious dating-wise, like she's going after Ethan just because or anything like that. She works hard, and he seems like that type too, and—"

The producer interrupted her. "But if it's as Allie says, that she's never had a serious relationship, what would make her decide to be on *Soulmates* to try to win the heart of Ethan Glass? Ambition?"

Allie laughed merrily. "Oh, that's easy to answer." Producer and camera shifted back. She smiled smugly. "She didn't. We submitted her application for her."

Grace's foot connected with Allie's shin this time. Allie jerked. "Ow!" She glared at Grace. Grace didn't care.

The producer went on full alert. "What do you mean? Are you saying you and Grace filled out the application for her? Did she know what you were doing?"

"It was my idea," Allie said. "Lucy said she was looking for adventure, and I thought, what better adventure than a romance with Ethan Glass, the most gorgeous millionaire in America, even if it doesn't last."

"It wasn't quite like that, Allie." Grace tried to do damage control. What was up with her today?

"What was it like, then, Grace?" the producer asked.

"She wanted a job. Something that would get her out of Eagle Bluff. She was really mad at us when she found out that she'd been chosen for the show."

"*Really.*" The producer tapped her French-tipped nails on the table. "And yet, she decided to be on the show anyway. Why do you think that is?"

"If she's smart," Allie said, "it's because she decided to relax and have some fun after pretending to be a prude for so long."

"Allie!" Grace turned to the producer. "She doesn't mean that. It's just that Lucy is kind of religious, you know? She doesn't do a lot of the normal stuff people do, but *that's okay*. It's always been okay with you too," she muttered at Allie. "What's wrong with you today?"

Allie smirked. "Why don't you ask Mike what kind of 'normal stuff' he and Lucy did together? You remember Mike—that guy you've been in love with forever?"

The world around Grace suddenly went gray; her awareness reduced to the pain knifing through her insides and the slimy grin on the cameraman's face. "Lucy didn't do anything with Mike. They only saw each other that one time at Christmas. She wasn't interested in him, she said."

"Believe what you want," Allie replied. "That's not what I heard though, and from none other than Mike himself."

The blade twisted painfully, and Grace was sure she was bleeding internally. This wasn't like Allie—not even the crazy version of Allie. Did Mike really say that? She knew Mike had had a thing for Lucy, but Lucy had insisted their date over the holidays hadn't amounted to anything. Mike had told her the same thing, that's why Grace had finally agreed to go out with him. Had he been telling her the truth or glossing over the facts to keep Grace in the dark?

It wasn't like Lucy to do something like that. They'd jokingly called her a serial dater because she never ended up in a relationship; she always seemed to stay in a never-ending rotation of casual dates. How casual, Grace really didn't know for certain. Lucy never talked about that kind of private stuff.

"So you're saying," the producer smoothly turned back to Allie, "that Lucy likes to play with the boys but has never been willing to commit to any of them? Did any ever express an interest in having a serious relationship with her?"

"Oh sure," Allie glanced over as Grace made a choking sound. "Come on, Grace, you remember that guy, Danny Something? The one Lucy hung out with during homecoming our senior year? He was totally into her, and what happened?"

"I don't know," Grace mumbled.

"Exactly! Neither do I. Isn't that a little weird, us being her best friends and all? And that guy she met her sophomore year at Arizona State? She was all dreamy-eyed over him, and then boom! Nothing. And she wouldn't talk about that either."

"Maybe there wasn't anything for her to talk about. Maybe nothing happened, and she just moved on. She does that, you know."

"Yeah, she moves on *a lot*. Or maybe she does things she doesn't want us to know. Things a good little Mormon girl isn't supposed to do and wants to keep secret."

Grace couldn't believe it. They'd grown up together, she and Allie and Lucy. She knew Lucy. Of course, she thought she knew Allie too, but right now, she wasn't so sure. Did that mean she'd been wrong about Lucy all this time too?

She thought about Mike and how devastated she'd be if she discovered that he and Lucy . . . she couldn't even think about it.

Lucy was always so . . . so . . . straight arrow. She didn't make a fuss about it, but she'd left parties when alcohol, or worse, had shown up. Grace had left with her sometimes, although Allie had usually stayed behind.

And her clothes were always so . . . covering. She looked nice enough in them, but it had made helping Lucy pack for LA a big hassle. She and Allie had been pulling stuff out of their own closets. Grace had been annoyed because finding outfits Lucy thought were modest enough had been a royal headache, but it had really seemed to bug Allie, like she had taken it personally, like Lucy had been casting judgment on Allie herself because of her clothes.

"And," Allie continued, "you know she isn't going to tell anyone anything that will keep her from getting married in that temple of hers."

The producer sat up straight. "What temple?"

Grace tried to explain. "It's a thing with her church. They get married in a temple. Lucy has always said she is only going to get married in a temple."

Allie piped up. "Yeah. What do you think Ethan Glass will do when he finds out about that? What would bother him the most—finding out he can't even walk through the doors of a temple or finding out Spotless Lucy might not be as pure as she wants everybody to think?"

Grace opened her mouth to speak, but the producer lady put up her hand to stop her. She smiled. Grace was really, really beginning to hate that smile. "Thank you, ladies," she said, indicating to the cameraman that he could turn off his camera. "You've been very helpful. We'll let you know if we need anything else." She dropped money for a tip onto the table, and she and the cameraman left the coffee shop.

Grace watched, stunned, as Allie casually pulled out a compact and checked her lipstick. "What were you doing?" she nearly yelled. "You sat there and deliberately threw one of your best friends under the bus!"

The compact snapped shut. "Don't be such a fool, Grace. Do you really think Lucy is as innocent as she wants us all to believe? Do you really think all those guys she dated over the years have simply walked her to the front door and given her a tiny little kiss on the cheek, like she's their sister or something? Besides, she'll thank me! Ethan Glass isn't going to be upset about anything I said. He'll be relieved to hear it because you can bet he isn't interested in some holier-than-thou chick who doesn't know how to have any fun. This will push her a little, but they'll both be glad in the long run."

Grace shook her head. "I don't think so." She had to know the rest. She knew she was being weak, but it was eating her up inside. "Did Mike really tell you that he and Lucy . . . ?"

Allie stood and hiked the strap of her purse up onto her shoulder. "Oh, Grace, you're so pathetic. What do you think normally happens when two adults go on a date? Grow up."

Grace thought she might throw up. "Allie, please."

She shrugged. "He said their last date had been very, *very* interesting. But it was the *way* he said it. It wasn't hard to fill in the blanks." Then she smiled brightly at Grace. "So do you want to go shopping? I've got money to burn, and there's a little black dress with my name written all over it. Ben will flip when he sees me in it."

Grace was still reeling from Allie's callous comments and her own jealousy over what she'd said about Mike and Lucy. She could only stare dumbly at Allie.

"So are we going or not?"

"Huh?"

"Shopping!"

"Oh, sure, I guess so."

Grace followed Allie out of the coffee shop, but the bad feeling that had slammed her during the interview still clung to her with a vengeance.

CHAPTER 16

Lucy watched through the front room window as Andy and Brigham battled Ethan and Craig in a game of pickup basketball. Shortly after dinner, they'd bluntly told him he had an appointment outside, which meant running him through a gauntlet that included tough questioning with a competitive workout. The production crew was outside taping the rugged man game; a single cameraman remained inside to catch her every move.

Her mother came up behind her and wrapped her arms around her. "I don't know how they can stand to play in the heat like that. It's an inferno out there."

They watched Brigham take a shot that bounced off the rim. "It's an alpha male test of some kind, Kendrick style," Lucy said. "They won't be playing for long, anyway. There isn't enough time."

She snuggled back into her mother's embrace. "What are your impressions of Ethan now that you've met him?"

"He's not what I expected at all. He's nice and down to earth. And a handsome devil, even more so in person than in his pictures." She sighed. "I'll confess, I'm a little surprised. In a lot of ways, he's the kind of man I've always pictured you with."

"He surprised me too. And the more I get to know him, the more he keeps on surprising me."

Ethan blocked a shot by Andy. Craig snagged it and went in for the layup.

"He seems comfortable with your brothers, even knowing this game is only a warm up for the interrogation to come. I get the feeling he's up to the challenge."

It was true, Lucy realized. Ethan seemed to be taking everything about her family in stride. He hadn't even flinched as he'd walked through the front door and taken in the modest surroundings that included a painting of Christ and an artsy photo of the Mesa temple. Or the Book of Mormon on the sofa table . . .

Introductions had also gone better than she'd hoped.

She honestly hadn't known what her brothers would do. They were being friendly to Ethan, but it felt like the friendliness one might expect from pit bulls behind a chain-link fence—alert, wary, and looking for a weakness to exploit.

Craig's three-year-old son, Noah, suddenly dashed into the fray from out of nowhere, chasing after the loose ball, and ran smack into Ethan's legs.

Lucy gasped and flew through the front door, followed by her mother. But Noah bounced back to his feet, laughing and none the worse for wear. Definitely in the DNA, Lucy thought wryly as she staggered to a halt.

Then they all—even her brothers—stood and watched as Ethan Glass, millionaire *Soulmate*, picked Noah up by the waist and ran after the errant ball. Noah grabbed the ball and crowed with delight as Ethan ran him back to the basket and hoisted him high in the air so he could toss it into the basket. It had been a reflex on Ethan's part to do that, Lucy realized. There had been nothing calculated about his actions.

Ethan Glass liked kids. More surprises.

"Slam dunk!" Ethan yelled. Everyone clapped and cheered, especially Noah.

Craig walked over, grinning. "Thanks, man," he said to Ethan. "High fives, Noah buddy!"

As soon as the ritual hand slapping was over, Noah leaped from Ethan's arms into Craig's, then he twisted around and gave Ethan some kind of knuckle-bumping handshake.

And just like that, Ethan was officially one of the guys.

Soon her brothers herded Ethan to the backyard patio, followed by the production crew, for the thumbscrew session of the evening. David Kendrick wandered over to join Lucy and her mom. "I have to tell you, Lucy, your Ethan is not what I expected."

Your Ethan, he'd said. He wasn't her Ethan, and certainly her dad didn't mean it that way. Lucy and her mother exchanged a look; except for the *your Ethan* part, his comment was eerily similar to what her mother had said.

"I didn't expect this either, Dad. I didn't expect the answer I got to my prayers to involve him at all, you know?"

Before her dad could respond, Craig's wife, Becky, dragged a howling Noah over to them. "He wants to play with the big boys," Becky said.

Noah sniffed as Grandpa took him and settled him comfortably on his hip.

"Well, I'm a big boy. Let's go see what we can find to do."

Noah nodded morosely and plopped his head in defeat onto his grandpa's shoulder as they walked away.

"Speaking of big boys," Becky said, "do you suppose they have Ethan crying uncle yet?"

Lucy linked arms with her mother and sister-in-law as they started back to the house. "I think he can hold his own," was all she said. She'd learned to choose her words carefully the past few weeks with a camera nearly always present. At the moment, though, she'd give anything to be able to talk openly with her mother and sister-in-law. It would have been great to talk to Grace and Allie too, but Melanie had said no.

"So . . . ?" Becky said.

"So . . . what?"

"So what are you thinking? About you and Ethan?" Becky had that predatory look happily married people get that says they want everyone else to be happily married too.

Her mother was trying not to appear curious about Lucy's reply.

And the cameraman lurked.

"Well," she hedged, "I like him."

Two sets of eyebrows rose.

"A lot, okay? I like him a lot. But there are four other women still in this with me, and I honestly don't know how he feels about any of them. Or me, even. It's not the kind of thing you can casually bring up in conversation."

She hated it, but it was part of what she'd signed up for when she'd agreed to do *Soulmates*. Of course, at the time, she'd only been expecting a free trip to LA, not a painful journey through love, insecurity, and moral and religious priorities.

"I don't think I could do it, date a guy who was dating four other girls at the same time." Becky sank onto the living room sofa.

"There are so many things we need to discuss that if we were simply dating, we would have by now. There hasn't been time to bring them up. And yet, I don't know how far the relationship can go until I do bring them up." Lucy plopped her feet onto the coffee table out of habit before noticing the cameraman had reentered the living room. She started to move her feet off the table and then stopped herself in a small act of defiance. She hated feeling like she was under a microscope all the time. And there were a lot worse things than feet on a coffee table.

"I care about Ethan—more than I ever thought I would, and it scares me. But I know who I am and what's important in all of this. I pray all the time, and I have to trust that I'm on the right path." Lucy did believe it, but each step of faith in this process was terrifying.

Her mom took Lucy's hand and held it in her lap. "Well, if it helps, your dad and I pray for you every day too. And we're not the only ones."

Lucy brushed away an escaping tear and gave her mother a kiss. What was it with tears lately? She'd never been a crier before. "Thank you. I knew you would be, but it helps to hear it."

Linda squeezed her hand. "Now, you'd better go find that young man before the Kendrick boys carve him to bits."

* * *

Lucy made a detour to the kitchen, hoping for a few private words with her dad without the camera present. She found him at the table with Noah, who was popping M&M's into his mouth and scribbling with purple crayon in a *Shrek* coloring book.

"I tried to convince him that Shrek is green, but Noah's into purple these days."

Lucy smiled. It felt so normal and right.

"You heading outside to find Ethan?"

"Yes. He's tough, but people have to develop a fairly hefty immune system when it comes to exposure to the Kendrick brothers."

David chuckled. "They're not that bad. And they only want to know they can trust Ethan with their sister. I know exactly how they feel." He darted over to the counter to grab a paper towel for Noah, a very slobbery, very happy Noah, who'd given up coloring Shrek so he could pack as many M&M's into his mouth at one time as he could.

"Spit."

Noah shook his head.

Lucy, realizing the importance of supporting adult authority, bit the inside of her cheek and tried not to laugh. Her dad stuck the towel under Noah's chin and patiently but firmly repeated, "Spit."

Slimy brown goo flecked and marbled with bright colors slid down Noah's chin. Her dad expertly caught the blob and wiped Noah's chin clean. Then he hunkered down until he was face-to-face with her scowling nephew. "Noah, too much too fast is hard to swallow. Remember that."

Noah nodded glumly but still managed to pop a single blue M&M into his mouth with a degree of stubbornness that made David roll his eyes and Lucy choke.

David looked up. "Ethan's a good man, Lucy. I'll give him that much. Whether he's the man to make you happy in the long run, I just don't know."

"At this point, the *long run* is making it through the next elimination ceremony."

"You have to think further down the road than that."

"I know." Lucy sighed and looked out the kitchen window. Her dad followed her gaze. They could see Craig talking and gesturing wildly with his hands. "It looks like Craig's either talking pro basketball or giving Ethan the first missionary lesson."

"If that's the case, then good for Craig. Because you need to address the subject of religion with Ethan, and the sooner the better for both your sakes."

"I know that too. If I make it through this next elimination, I will. First thing."

* * *

Curt stood at the back of the large room they were using in Los Angeles to shoot the latest elimination ceremony and tried not to wring his hands while Dane yelled instructions at the crew.

Money was tight. Even with Ethan's financial backing and maintaining a tight rein on the budget, Curt was barely managing to keep the production in the black. He had mortgaged his condo and borrowed from his folks and anybody else he'd been able to sweet talk. Ethan had been willing to help Curt in this venture, which included the personals website and the television show, besides offering his name recognition by being the first *Soulmate*, and Curt knew he owed the guy. Big time.

Not that he'd asked Ethan for full funding. Curt had some pride, after all. But it meant that, while Ethan might feel a pinch if things went bad, Curt had everything to lose.

So the trick was to keep a close eye on the finances, wine and dine the network execs in style (which, unfortunately, cost money) to ensure a good on-air time slot, make sure the show had the kind of drama that drew viewers and pulled successful ratings . . . and make sure the drama wasn't the kind to alienate Ethan Glass in the process.

Simple. No problem whatsoever. Except . . .

Melanie had shown him footage she'd gotten from Lucy Kendrick's so-called best friends. She was convinced Lucy was the frontrunner, although Curt wasn't nearly as convinced as Melanie was.

But if Melanie *was* correct, Curt had to decide if he was going to allow her to proceed with her latest plan or not. He'd tried to squeeze some info out of Ethan, but the guy wasn't talking.

Curt rubbed his hands over his face. He and Ethan went way back. They'd been college roommates. They'd saved each other's backsides more than a few times, but Curt was no fool. He knew Ethan had bailed him out of trouble more often than he'd been called upon to return the favor.

And here he was again, dependent on the good graces of his long-time friend. He was grateful.

Why did it occasionally chafe, then?

He watched Rick go over his notes as the crew finished setting up. After the first night, they'd only brought Rick in to work on the actual days of the elimination ceremonies, tightly scheduling him for one-on-one interviews with the women and Ethan, and voice-over work. Rick was an easygoing guy who looked good on camera, and Curt had been lucky to get him—for a song, no less, largely because he was a virtual unknown.

Every little bit helped the budget and eased Curt's anxiety.

He noticed Melanie headed his way, so he slipped into character, aka Mr. Casual and Confident. He didn't know what it was about Melanie Carlton, but whenever he was within ten feet of her, he had the urge to run his hands through her perfectly styled, raspberry-pink hair and mess it up. Or run his thumb across her mouth and smear lipstick down her chin. Or kiss her.

The pressure of the job was definitely getting to him.

"What have you decided?" she asked.

"I've decided you're looking less tense these days. I'm either not giving you enough to do, or you must have talked Raoul into returning to the states with you." If he couldn't mess with her hair or lipstick, he could at least mess with her mind. Fair was fair.

Her foot started tapping.

"Fine. Let me see if I've got it straight," he said. "We have the best friends selling out poor, sweet Lucy. Except that poor, sweet Lucy isn't so sweet, according to them. She's playing hard to get with our *Soulmate*, because she somehow realizes it's the winning strategy. She's using the religious bit to convince everyone she's a paragon of virtue, but she's really just appearing on the show as a joke. She has never been in a committed relationship and has no plans for a long-term anything with Ethan whatsoever. She likes to win, and she sees this as a game."

"That's right."

"Makes perfect sense to me," he muttered sarcastically. "Out of curiosity, do you have a grudge against Lucy Kendrick?"

"Of course not. But I do have a thing against phonies, especially holier-than-thou phonies. If we've been duped by her, if *Ethan* has been duped by her, then we need to bring that out. Not only is it important for Ethan's sake, but it will also generate ratings like nothing else for this part of the show."

It will generate ratings. Curt felt his conscience sting him, but the lure was there as well, pulling at him.

"What have we got on the others? Keeping in mind that we can't afford to put all of our dramatic eggs in one basket."

She turned to face him, ready to do battle. "I'm telling you—Lucy is *the* frontrunner, Curt, and if he takes her to the end, you won't have your *Soulmates* happy ending. If she makes it through the elimination ceremony, we have to do something because Ethan will only have two other women to choose from at that point."

They did need a successful ending, or the entire *Soulmates* premise, and thus all of Curt's financial dreams, was sunk. No second season. No successful website. But he also wasn't convinced Melanie's plan was the way to go yet. Lucy's personal motives aside, if Ethan chose her, he could make a happy ending for the show and deal with the fallout later, after the website launch. Mel also needed to remember who was boss here. He gave her his most patronizing smile. "You were going to tell me about other dramatic eggs."

"Oh, all right." She heaved a sigh. "For what it's worth: We found Sara on the Internet. In a viral video someone made during a college spring break, if you know what I mean. I'm sure we could do something with that. Tiffany's extended hospital stay last year appears to have been a stint in rehab. And there is some question about the authenticity of Alison's master's thesis, but no proof as of yet. Denise's halo is untarnished so far, but we're still looking."

"The spring break bit could be used to generate publicity if we leak it before the show airs," Curt mused. "It's something to think about. The problem is that nothing is scandalous anymore. Nobody cares. Anything goes."

"Maybe you think nobody cares what anybody does anymore, Curt, but people care about betrayal. And that's the reason why using what we got from Lucy's friends is the way to go, because it's all about betrayal. It's about Lucy duping her friends into thinking she's been a saint all these years. Lucy cheating with some guy who's dating her best friend. Lucy going on the show and pretending to fall in love, knowing she never had any intention of marrying Ethan Glass. People will forgive a lack of judgment during a party weekend, and they'll empathize with the struggle of overcoming an addiction. But they resent feeling like they've been conned, and if they're watching the show, that's how they'll feel. Not only will they want to make sure Ethan comes through this betrayal with a happy ending, but they'll also want to make sure Lucy gets what she deserves."

"Quiet, everyone!" Esplin yelled.

Rick Madison smiled and spoke to the camera and then turned on cue to welcome the women to the elimination ceremony. After some glossy remarks about the importance of families in Ethan's search for his *Soulmate*, he invited Ethan to join them.

Ethan looked dashing and confident and slightly vulnerable all at the same time. Perfect. Curt couldn't have hoped for a better performance. Ethan's vulnerability didn't show up very often, but at the moment, it definitely added to his leading man presence. And in no time at all Ethan had selected his three remaining candidates: Tiffany, Denise, and Lucy. Melanie nudged Curt and mouthed, "We should have told him."

Lucy. Hmm. Maybe he'd look at the footage taken of her friends after all. Because really, why else would a childhood friend say the things she'd said unless she'd felt like she'd been conned for all those years, like Melanie suggested?

In the meantime, the crew needed to get two crying women on their way to the airport. Tomorrow they began a week shooting Ethan on romantic dates in the Pacific Northwest with the final three.

Those dates were going to wreak havoc on his beleaguered budget. Well, he'd worry about that tomorrow—because tonight he had a couple of network execs to schmooze.

CHAPTER 17

Lucy gazed out the limousine's window at the town of Sidney-by-the-Sea and its cheerful clapboard buildings and sturdy brick houses. Rows of masts, like motley sentinels standing at attention, rose from the sailboats docked at the marina. Seeing it all had been like stepping into a watercolor painting. There was a lushness here on Vancouver Island, a saturation of greens and blues that was intensified for Lucy after growing up surrounded by the stark, arid beauty of the Arizona desert.

Ms. Carlton and a cameraman sat facing her in the limo; Kyle rode shotgun and was slouched in the seat, probably asleep. They'd all had an early start. Lucy pulled a sealed envelope out of her bag and handed it to her. "This is the letter to deliver with the pig when you send him to the ranch."

Ms. Carlton tucked it into her tote. "Your pal Hamlet is being shipped to Montana at the end of the week. I'll make sure the letter arrives at the same time."

"Thank you."

"Now that we're underway, what do you say we make good use of the travel time with a few on-camera questions?"

Lucy reluctantly pulled her gaze from the beautiful scene outside the window. "All right."

Ms. Carlton nodded to the cameraman to begin recording. "What were your expectations when you decided to be on the show?" she asked.

Lucy thought about how to phrase her answer. "I'm not sure I had *expectations*, exactly. I hoped to have an adventure; you know, meet people and see places I might never have otherwise."

"What did you think of Ethan at the time? How did he affect your decision to be on the show?"

Lucy laughed. "I didn't think about Ethan at all. Or not much, at least. I figured I'd be out after day one, that he was going to pass right over me, that I wouldn't have anything in common with a millionaire playboy."

"Is that what you think he is? A playboy?"

"No, not . . . no I don't think that at all, not anymore. But at the time, most of what I knew about him came from celebrity magazines. There were lots of photos of Ethan with glamorous women. So I thought he was probably a player. I figured Ethan Glass wouldn't have anything in common with a small-town girl."

"A small-town, *religious* girl to boot."

"Yes," Lucy said.

"And yet, you're still here."

"I'm still here." She paused. "I'm glad I'm still here."

"You're very competitive."

Lucy rolled her eyes heavenward. "I know. I like to play to win; it's a fault of mine. It was beaten into me by my sweet, loving brothers. Everybody knows that. You know that. You've seen me in action, like when I caught that pig at the rodeo."

"And how do you feel about Ethan now? Are you playing to win him?"

Ms. Carlton was asking routine questions, but something felt off today. Maybe it was how she'd posed the question—*playing to win him.* "I would never play to *win* anyone, least of all Ethan." She looked straight at her. "I care about him. Anything more than that, Ethan deserves to hear from me first."

Ms. Carlton ended the interview because they had arrived at Butchart Gardens, their first destination of the day. Ethan was standing on the pavement, waiting, along with Mr. Esplin and the rest of the crew assigned to this part of the shoot.

Ethan greeted her with a hug and settled a kiss on her that held enough promise to be reassuring. Lucy felt a wave of relief. His continued ambivalence—open, then guarded—played havoc with her emotions. Her date with Ethan here on Vancouver Island was the last of the three romantic dates. Lucy wouldn't be human if she hadn't wondered how the other two dates had gone.

"What do you think of British Columbia so far?" he asked her.

The parking area was surrounded by the biggest trees Lucy had ever seen. It was also chilly. "It's beyond breathtaking."

He smiled. "Baby, you haven't seen anything yet. Come on." He noticed her rubbing her arms, removed his jacket, and laid it across her shoulders. It was deliciously warm and smelled faintly of his cologne and him. "Don't worry, desert girl," he said. "I'll keep you warm." Lucy's goose bumps instantly disappeared; now she was melting.

As they walked toward the entrance of the garden, he leaned toward her and spoke in a low voice. "Today's schedule isn't going to allow us to ditch the cameras. So we'll concentrate on enjoying the day together and save the serious stuff for this evening when we can actually be alone."

They spent the morning wandering the glorious gardens Jennie Butchart had created a century earlier. They strolled past carpets of manicured lawns, riots of tulips with frothy petticoats of alyssum, forget-me-nots, and the lacy white brilliance of spiraea and handkerchief trees in full bloom.

"I didn't realize so many shades of pink even existed," Ethan said as they wandered past a velvety cluster of English daisies, "let alone in one place."

"It's certainly more impressive than Cecily, Arizona," she replied, making him chuckle.

They passed a lilac bush bursting with flowers and fragrance. She stopped walking and breathed deeply. "More like the Garden of Eden."

"Does that make us Adam and Eve?" he asked, his eyes twinkling.

"Not if it means I have to wear fig leaves in this cold temperature." She gave a mock shiver.

He laughed. "Go ahead and keep wearing the jacket, Eve. If you're the only woman God has created for me, then I want to keep you healthy."

After a quick lunch, they enjoyed a tour of Victoria in a horse-drawn carriage, cuddled under a fuzzy blanket. Lucy felt a little fuzzy herself. She drank in everything around her: the stately Victorian homes, the joyful gardens, the gentle swaying of the carriage, the steady clop-clop of the horse. Ethan. The midday sun warmed the top of her head and her shoulders; the breeze on her cheeks was moist and cool.

They talked along the way for the camera's sake. Ethan told her stories of growing up on the ranch in Montana with his younger brother Jake and the housekeeper's son. How, as the oldest of the three, he'd led the others into and out of plenty of mischief over the years.

"There was one August when I was nearly thirteen that my mother and Terri, our housekeeper, spent the day bottling peaches. They also made fresh peach pies—several, in fact—for the family and enough to share with the ranch hands."

"Oh no." Lucy clapped a hand over her eyes. "As someone with three brothers, I can imagine only too well what you boys might have done."

He shot her a half grin. "Let's hear your best guess. I'll warn you now, though—you'll be wrong."

"Hmm." She studied his face for clues, but other than a twinkle in his eyes that he couldn't quite hide, he wasn't giving anything away. "You took the pies, hid in the barn, and ate until you were sick. No, wait. You took the pies, ate until you were sick, and then had a pie-throwing contest with the leftovers."

His lips twitched.

"Am I close?"

He laughed. "Well, we did take the pies. You got that much right."

Her brow knotted in concentration. "You didn't eat the pies? What red-blooded boys don't gorge themselves on pie?"

"Do you give up?" He casually waved to a couple of pedestrians who'd noticed the camera.

"No! Give me a minute. How old would the other two have been?"

"Jake would have been ten, and—they would have been about ten and seven at the time."

"So you were definitely the ringleader here. What would *you*, Ethan Glass, have done with pies, if not eat them?" She gave an unladylike snort. "You would have sold them on eBay, if it had existed at the time." His mouth twitched even more this time. "I'm actually close, aren't I?"

"Close enough. I allowed us to share one pie—telling them that, as the oldest, I got half and they had to split the other half between them. Then we put the other eleven pies in Jake's wagon and took them over to the bunkhouse, where we auctioned them off to the ranch hands they were intended for in the first place. We made good money that day, especially since I split up the profits the same way I split up the pie." He grinned.

"You're a natural-born entrepreneur, aren't you? Or would a more accurate term be *shark*?"

"Shark, definitely." He shot her an intense, dangerous look.

She didn't buy it for a minute. "There's more to the story though, isn't there?"

An eyebrow rose. "Yes. Want to try your luck there too?"

"Well, if I were your mother, we would have had a long talk about stealing, why scamming the ranch hands was a bad idea, and what you would be doing to make things right with everyone involved."

The breeze had teased a lock of her hair loose, and he brushed it from her face. "You know, not every mother is willing to go head-to-head with her teenage son, especially if he's strong willed and nearly a foot taller than she is. Maybe that's why we got away with taking the pies in the first place."

"Maybe, but I don't think so. You might be a natural entrepreneur, but I get the feeling you're an honest one. And that means your parents kept you in line when you were growing up."

"Okay, you're right. Mom's tiny, but she's tough. She never let us get away with much, not if she could help it."

"So what happened?"

"She was furious. I did get a lecture on honesty, you'll be happy to know. I also got one on leadership—how the two younger boys looked up to me and how that meant I had a responsibility to act wisely. We had to return all the money. The ranch hands razzed us about that for a long time. She also made the three of us pick peaches the next day. *All* day, though the other two got off easier than I did.

"Now, Old Jed's approach was totally different. After my mother got done ripping into me, he and I went for a ride on horseback to the far side of the property. He didn't say a word until we got there. I was shaking in my boots for the entire ride. But when he finally did talk, he proceeded to compliment me."

Lucy looked at him in shock.

"I know," Ethan said, catching her expression. "It wasn't what I was expecting either, not by a long shot. I expected to get my hide tanned and nailed to the side of the barn. Instead, he said he was impressed by the amount of money we'd gotten for eleven pies by coming up with the idea of an auction. He praised the fact that I gave myself half the money—saying that, as the brains of the operation, I'd deserved the largest cut. He said I'd shown—how did he put it?—'commendable self-discipline' by only eating one pie and saving the rest to sell."

She stared at him. "You're kidding."

"No. So not only am I thinking I've escaped serious damage to my backside, but I'm also reeling from the nice things my father's saying about me. He let it all sink in for a minute or two. Old Jed's a real expert at using silence effectively. And then he landed the zinger. He said, 'Son, you've proven today you can be successful at anything you choose to do. After today, I hope you'll at least choose to be successful at something honorable.'"

Silence.

"Wow," was all Lucy could think to say.

"Wow is right." He glanced at the camera with a pained expression. "And I'm sure all of our viewers will be expecting a PBS pledge break after that touching little story."

"I loved the story," Lucy said with feeling.

He trailed a finger along her cheek and gazed at her in a way that made her heart beat faster. He smiled. "I'm glad. But today is supposed to be about romance. How could I have forgotten?" And he kissed her.

It was a *wow* kiss. His fingers cupped her face and kept her close. She wasn't sure how long it lasted; she only knew that when she opened her eyes she had to blink several times before his face came back into focus.

"Next stop," Ethan murmured, "The Empress."

As Lucy's vision cleared, she noticed a magnificent old hotel elegantly draped in ivy, situated right at Victoria's waterfront. They were to have afternoon tea at The Empress, following a century-old tradition.

A private area had been arranged for the shoot, and when they arrived, Ethan held Lucy's chair for her and then moved to sit adjacent to her.

Their server was pleasant and professional, and once Lucy and Ethan were seated, she immediately brought a selection of little sandwiches and cakes. She turned to Lucy. "For you, ma'am, one of our herbal teas, perhaps chamomile with a touch of mint? Or hot cocoa?"

Obviously, her preferences had been taken into account. She doubted it would have been anyone on the television crew, certainly not Ms. Carlton, not the way she'd been acting toward Lucy the last few days. She looked at Ethan. He gave her a subtle wink back.

"Cocoa, please," she replied, beaming.

They said people fell in love, but Lucy didn't agree. She was soaring. And the more she discovered about Ethan, the more hope it gave her.

He was an amazing person—talented and bright and passionate. Honorable. She wanted him to have all of the blessings she had and too often took for granted. Listening to his story earlier, she knew she would willingly sacrifice any future they might have together if he would listen, have faith, and believe . . .

Who was she kidding? The part of her that climbed to the tops of pine trees and held her breath underwater wanted it all. Wanted to win. Not for the sake of winning but because she wanted to be the one at the end with Ethan. She wanted a life with the Ethan who teased kisses from her and told stories about stolen pies. She wanted the man who fit so nicely next to her in the carriage, who wore worn-out jeans as comfortably as he did tailored suits.

She was beginning to love him, and she wanted it all: Ethan Glass, his love. And eternity.

She needed to draw upon everything she'd learned from her brothers about winning because everything was at stake. She couldn't afford to lose when she spoke with Ethan tonight. She needed to believe in herself, she needed to be strong, and she needed to give it her all.

There could be no soft peddling when it came to her beliefs. To have Ethan and not have him forever was unthinkable. But to consider his rejection of her and her beliefs like so many others had done was terrifying this time around because this time it mattered.

She would have to let him know she'd fallen in love with him but that she loved the Savior more, that she had a testimony she would not deny. She was going to have to lay it all on the line.

She'd always known that sooner or later she'd have to do this. She had to have this conversation with Ethan before she could really know if they had a real future together. Surely he would listen to her when they talked that evening. Surely he cared about her enough to hear her out with an open mind and an open heart.

If he rejected her and her beliefs like so many others had done over the years, she would be devastated. Heartbroken.

It was a risk she was going to have to take. And it was going to have to be tonight.

* * *

As Ethan escorted Lucy to her hotel room, director, cameraman, and crew trailing behind, he explained, "We have a couple of free hours before dinner. I have some work to take care of before then, so use the time alone to relax and pamper yourself."

"Sounds good." A little downtime to collect her thoughts would be helpful.

He ran the key card through the lock and opened the door, and they all stepped inside.

"Ohhh!" she breathed. It wasn't the typical hotel room, that was for sure, not that she and her family had ever stayed in any swanky places before. The motel up by the Grand Canyon had actually gotten multiple stars from AAA, but it didn't hold a candle to what she was looking at now.

She was in an elegantly decorated, Victorian-style parlor. A sofa upholstered in burgundy velvet, embellished with carved woodwork, and piled with decorative pillows faced an ornate fireplace, above which hung a tapestry of a pastoral scene. An end table held a lamp with a deeply fringed shade. The walls were painted a deep myrtle green and were filled with paintings and old photographs, all in elaborate frames.

She ran her finger along the petals of a rose carved into the back of a chair and took in her fill of the room. "It's gorgeous." She beamed at Ethan. "I love it."

"Good. I told the producers I wanted something indulgent." He wandered down a small hallway Lucy hadn't noticed before.

"Indulgent?"

"Uh-huh. I wanted to spoil you." He opened a door on his right. There was an identical one to his left, and seeing it rang a warning bell in Lucy's mind. "Your suitcases are in here," Ethan continued. "You also have your own bathroom, and I think there's a walk-in closet . . ." He wandered farther into the room.

Momentarily alone, Lucy quickly opened the door on the left and peeked inside. It was another bedroom, and Ethan's luggage was just inside the door.

This was a two-bedroom suite.

She closed the door quietly, hoping no one had noticed. She had the sudden feeling that the camera's all-seeing eye was burning into her.

Lucy had a dilemma.

It was a fairly kosher—and respectful—arrangement, really, especially from the world's point of view, but it meant Lucy would be sharing a suite with Ethan on prime-time television, and that made a huge difference in her book.

Lucy pressed her hand to her stomach. Why had she not anticipated this? Was she that naïve? How could she not have realized that when the producers had spoken of a romantic date and time together off-camera it might have meant something like this?

Ethan returned to the hallway and immediately picked up on her change of mood. "Is everything all right?"

She swallowed. "I need to talk to you. Alone, okay?"

"Okay." His eyes didn't leave her face as he spoke to the director. "Dane, give us a moment, would you?" He gestured to the cameraman. "Off the record."

"Okay, we're alone," he said once Dane and the others had retreated back to the parlor.

She said a silent prayer and cleared her throat. "First, I want you to know I've had the most wonderful day. Because I've been with you." She persevered. "I want to spend every minute I can here with you. I hope you believe me."

"Okay, I believe you." He paused. "But . . ." He let the word hang, waiting for her to go on.

"But . . ." she could feel herself getting agitated, "I can't go on national television with it looking like we're sharing a hotel room. I can't. I know this is a suite," she added quickly, "with separate rooms, even. I know it means you understand a lot of things about me, and you're taking them into consideration. And I appreciate it more than you know. But, I just can't—"

"Shh. Hold on." He glanced down the hallway, so Lucy did too. Mr. Esplin appeared to be talking to the orange-haired cameraman. Ethan turned back to Lucy and then lowered his voice. "Lucy, listen. I promise you nothing is going to happen tonight, not if you don't want it to happen. I understand your religious feelings—I think. I mean, I don't understand them totally, obviously, but I get it, okay? No pressure here. But we need this time together; we need every minute away from the cameras we can get. And that means tonight. This is it. This is our time."

"Isn't there any other way?" she asked. "For us to have the time alone, I mean. If viewers know we're sharing a suite, they're going to assume . . . I *can't* have them think that. I can't have people thinking that the Mormon girl on the show is sharing a suite with the *Soulmate*."

"Lucy, honey, there's nothing to worry about." He was still speaking in a low tone, but now there was an edge to it. "We're both adults. No one watching will even think twice about it. Besides, I've given you my word. Isn't that enough?"

She sighed. This was turning out to be a lot more difficult than she'd thought. "No, Ethan, it's not. I'm sorry; I can't allow people to make those kinds of assumptions. How will I be able to explain that everything was innocent when it doesn't look that way?"

"Why should you feel a need to explain anything?" Now there was a definite edge to his voice. "You know, Lucy, I'm surprised. I didn't expect this to be a problem, not from you. Of all the women here, I thought you would be the one who was the least worried about other people's opinions, since you know your own heart so well."

"I'm not worried about their opinions of me, Ethan. I'm concerned about the example I'll appear to be setting for them. There's a difference. People in the public eye are held to a higher standard whether they like it or not, and like it or not, temporary or not, this show has put me in the public eye. I *have* to take that seriously."

He exhaled loudly. "Okay. Okay, I think I get it." After another quick glance at the crew in the parlor, he pulled out his cell phone and punched in a number. "Curt. I need you to book an additional room, preferably on this floor." He glanced at Lucy. She nodded, relieved, and smiled gratefully. "Great. And then can you find Kyle? I have something I need him to do. Thanks." He snapped his phone shut. "Done. Now, how do we address the issue of private time together? Do you have a curfew or anything else I need to be aware of at this point?"

His words sounded sarcastic, but a closer look at his face told her it was mostly good-humored resignation. "No actual curfew. Just good judgment."

"I can accept that, as long as good judgment allows input from the other party involved. Namely, me. Now," he added as he drew her in for a good-bye kiss, "I will see you in a couple of hours. Rest, relax. Indulge yourself. You now officially have your choice of two oversized whirlpool bathtubs. Have a nice soak. Have two."

"I'm sorry if it seems like I'm being difficult."

"I'm not." He gave her a wry smile. "At least not yet. I'll see you at seven."

* * *

"You're saying you got all that conversation?" Dane Esplin asked Rogan after they saw Ethan disappear down the hall.

"Sure," the cameraman answered. "Off the record doesn't mean squat with a signed release form on file. Don't these people know they signed a contract that allows twenty-four-hour recording rights?"

"Glass won't be happy if he finds out."

"He signed the same contract as everybody else."

"He's also the guy who signs your paycheck."

Rogan just shrugged. "I wish I'd had the time to get the hall camera into a better spot. I'm not sure how good the audio will be since they were whispering. But there's still usable stuff there, especially—" He stopped talking.

"Especially . . . what?" Dane asked casually. He'd seen Rogan and Melanie together a lot recently, and his sixth sense told him they were up to something.

Rogan looked at him blankly. "Especially . . . since it gave you more kissing footage to use. That's all."

Dane nodded. Ethan kissing Lucy Kendrick like she was his kid sister made for *especially* good footage. Oh, wait. Not really.

Rogan—and, more importantly, Melanie—was up to something, and Dane had been kept out of the loop.

But not for long.

* * *

Kyle knocked on the hotel room door and waited. Mr. Myers had sent him here but hadn't said anything else. He rocked back and forth on his feet and chewed on a hangnail.

The door opened. "Good. You're here."

It was Ethan. Definitely the last person Kyle expected to see today. "So are you," he replied.

"Change of plans. I need you to go up to the *Soulmates* suite and retrieve my luggage. Bring it here. And don't say anything to anybody."

Ah. Lucy had closed the door—literally and figuratively—on the romantic overnighter. Kyle gave him a mock salute. "I'll get right on it." He started toward the door.

"Wait." Ethan motioned him back. "Before you go, tell me again what happened when you went to church with Lucy."

Kyle leaned against the door and crossed his arms. "I told you everything. It was different. Lucy tried to explain things, but I finally pretended to be asleep so she wouldn't worry about me so much."

"I want details, Kyle. I need anything that can help me understand this before my date with her tonight."

"All right. Let me think. The sermons were on faith." He remembered something being said that he hadn't considered before, so it had stuck. "There was a scripture about not disputing what you can't see because answers don't come until after a trial of faith. Something like that. I looked for it in the Bible but didn't find it."

"That's because it's probably not in the Bible. They have other scriptures, I think."

"Oh." Kyle had seen something about that online but hadn't checked it out.

"Anything else?"

"Not really. Not about her church anyway. But . . ."

"But what? What is it?"

"Just a feeling I have, that someone might be up to something." He shrugged. "I could be wrong." But he didn't think so; he'd been feeling uneasy a lot lately.

"Go on."

"People whispering and then stopping when anyone comes around. Exchanging looks. I don't know. Even to myself I sound paranoid. Forget about it."

"What people, in particular?"

"Carlton and Rogan mostly." He'd sensed it with a couple more people today, which was probably why he'd decided to mention it. "Esplin. Maybe Curt."

"I'm sure it's nothing then. If anything was happening, Curt would tell me. He has more at stake in this than I do."

"Yeah, you're probably right." Kyle wasn't as certain. But he felt better telling Ethan about it. The uneasy feeling had been bothering him a lot lately. "Hey, Eth. You remember what I told you before, about the words Mom always says to me?"

"*Wa chay kay ya yo.* I remember hearing them a lot growing up."

"Yeah, that's it. *Wa chay kay ya yo, Hunka ate.*"

"I don't ever remember hearing that last part."

"No, I added it. It applies to you, from me."

Ethan's eyebrows rose. "That sounds deep. I assume you've brought this up now because you're going to end the suspense and actually tell me what it means."

Kyle nodded. "Yeah. I think you need it now. *Wa chay kay ya yo, Hunka ate.* May you seek wisdom from a higher power, chosen brother."

"Chosen brother. I like that. So, chosen brother, if we cut to the chase, are you suggesting that I pray about all of this and that this higher power will grant me wisdom?"

"Remember, I'm not what you'd call an expert," Kyle replied. "But I don't think it would hurt."

"I'll think about it. In the meantime, I am going to rely on good old-fashioned research to get through tonight." Ethan returned his attention to his laptop.

And in the meantime, Kyle thought as he left the room, *I'll seek the higher power on your behalf, brother. I think you're going to need all the help you can get.*

CHAPTER 18

A LEISURELY SOAK IN A tub the size of a small car might be just the thing after all, Lucy thought as she poured in extra bubble bath. She slid into the hot, fragrant water, soaked out as much tension as she could for as long as she dared, and then slipped into one of her favorite outfits—a creamy knit sheath with three-quarter-length sleeves. It flattered her shape and was comfortable, and Grace had found a terrific multistrand necklace and earring set that added a touch of glamour. Lucy hoped it would also bolster her confidence. She was going to need it.

She settled at the parlor desk to thumb through the Book of Mormon she planned to give Ethan. There were a few specific verses she wanted to mark for him. She also planned to give him a few—ok, several—Church brochures she'd originally brought along to share with the crew.

Her mind was a blur. How did one crystallize the entire plan of salvation into bullet points to be delivered in the space of a few hours? She wished she could talk to Craig or Andy and pick their returned missionary brains for a while, get the *Preach My Gospel* chapter breakdown, for starters.

She'd just finished listing everything she wanted to talk to Ethan about when there was a knock at the door. The mantel clock read barely six. She was sure Ethan had said seven.

"Ah, Lucy! Just look at you," Ms. Carlton said as she brushed past Lucy into the room, followed by Mr. Esplin and the creepy orange-haired cameraman. "Dane, didn't I tell you she'd look sweet?"

"Yes, you did," Mr. Esplin replied with a smile that showed too many teeth.

"And excited, I'm sure, about her *romantic* date with Ethan this evening," Ms. Carlton continued. "Aren't you?" she directed at Lucy.

"Yes," Lucy answered. She nonchalantly moved to the desk and shuffled her papers and brochures into a pile. "In fact, I still need time to finish getting ready. Was there something you needed? I thought we weren't doing any more interviews until Mr. Madison shows up for the elimination ceremony."

Ms. Carlton perched on the edge of the velvet sofa. "We thought so too. But we discussed it, and the consensus is that we needed to document your feelings going into this particular date." She smiled. Lucy hadn't seen that particular arctic smile of hers since day one.

It wasn't as if she really had a choice. "All right. Will it take long though? I really need to have some time—"

"We'll leave you plenty of time, Lucy. But tonight is a really big night. A deal-breaker night. It's crunch time—when you have to lay it all on the line. I can see that you know I'm right."

She pointed to a chair at a right angle to the sofa. "Why don't you sit there? Will that work, Dane?"

"It's perfect. How's the light, Rogan?"

Rogan opened the drapes as wide as they could go. Even at six o'clock, there was still a lot of summer daylight left.

They were all smiling at her . . . in the friendly way sharks smile at guppies, she thought. Mr. Esplin slid his laptop onto the coffee table in front of Lucy. She swallowed nervously.

"It's down to three now," Ms. Carlton said. "Tiffany. Denise. You. Think, Lucy. Did you expect to make it this far? It's exciting, isn't it? Do you love him? Do you think he loves you?"

She leaned forward, dropping her voice. "Do you think about the other two women, what he's like with them? Do you wonder how they feel about him? If they love him too? Do you wonder what it will take to convince him that your love is the strongest? What you need to do to prove that you're his *Soulmate*?"

Mr. Esplin clicked an icon and turned the laptop to face Lucy. A montage of video clips, raw footage from the show, began to play: Denise, legs a mile long, laughing with Ethan on a sailboat. Denise and Ethan walking down a tree-lined avenue, arms around each other. "He is the *sweetest* man!" Denise said with a syrupy sigh in the next shot. "I love him to pieces! I want to hug him and kiss him and spoil him and feed him homemade chicken and dumplings!"

Next up was Tiffany, poolside, wearing a microscopic swimsuit and smiling at Ethan—and the camera—like a Bond girl. Tiffany and Ethan clinking champagne glasses together, Ethan and Tiffany sharing a steamy kiss by the limo . . . Lucy turned away, but it didn't stop her from hearing Tiffany say, "Ethan is *fabulous*, the total package! How often does a man like him come along?" Next, Tiffany was on a balcony, a large city skyline as her backdrop. "I will do anything to be the one Ethan chooses as his *Soulmate*. I will do whatever it takes." She looked right at the camera. "*Whatever* it takes."

Mr. Esplin stopped the playback. They all looked at Lucy.

It was like taking a sucker punch to the stomach. But the idea of collapsing on-camera, let alone in front of these three, was unthinkable, so she lowered her head to her hands and took a few deep breaths instead.

She needed to get away from these people and regain her composure. She stood, relieved her legs hadn't failed her. "Will you excuse me for a minute?" She didn't wait for a response, didn't look back, until she'd shut the bathroom door behind her.

She braced her hands on the counter and stared at her image in the mirror. What were they trying to accomplish by throwing Tiffany and Denise in her face like that? What were they trying to do?

Obviously they wanted to provoke a reaction out of her on-camera, maybe provoke her into doing something rash that evening with Ethan as well.

Were they only targeting *her*, or had they done this to Tiffany and Denise too? Thinking of Tiffany and Denise and the vivid images she'd just been forced to witness had her doubled over, clutching the edge of the counter. Dealing with her feelings for Ethan was hard enough. But seeing the two remaining women with him like that . . .

She hadn't expected to fall in love with Ethan Glass. And based on the pain she was feeling, she no longer had any doubt that that was exactly what she'd done. She'd fallen in love with him.

She resented the fact that these people, for the sake of a few minutes of TV drama, would do such a cruel, manipulative thing as show her footage of Ethan with the other two women right before her date with him was scheduled to begin. And right now, they were out there in that fancy parlor, congratulating themselves for throwing her off balance. Expecting her to make a fool of herself in front of the camera.

Well, if they thought that, they didn't know her very well, did they?

They didn't understand that she'd graduated from the Kendrick School of Brotherly Torture. She was a lot stronger than they realized.

She took advantage of the facilities, washed her hands, checked herself in the mirror, did a little touch-up to her makeup, took several cleansing breaths to gain control of her emotions, and then added one final weapon to her arsenal, a prayer for inspiration, before opening the door and returning to the parlor.

Ms. Carlton stood looking out the window while Mr. Esplin paced the room. Rogan hit the record button on the camera as soon as he saw her. Big surprise there.

"Everything okay?" Ms. Carlton asked, almost sounding sincere.

"Yes. Thank you for asking."

"Now, where were we? Oh yes, how it feels to be one of the final three in Ethan's quest to find his *Soulmate*. What do you think it will take to win Ethan's heart? What will it take to convince him he should choose you rather than Tiffany or Denise?"

"Only Ethan can convince Ethan," Lucy answered. "Only he can decide who he wants as his *Soulmate*. Tiffany is dazzling. She knows what she wants and goes after it with all she's got. That's a dynamic quality. Denise is gorgeous and has a heart of gold. I will consider her a friend for life, whatever the outcome of the show. And Ethan—Ethan is an amazing man, and the more I learn about him, the more I care for him. I want him to be happy. I want him to find what he's looking for at the end of this journey."

"You saw the clips of him with the other women. Do you really think you're his soulmate, Lucy?" Ms. Carlton asked. "Do you think Ethan thinks you are?"

Lucy bit the inside of her lip, determined not to let the woman's jabs wound her further. "What does that mean? What *is* a soulmate?" she asked, hoping her voice sounded normal.

"Come on, Lucy. Are you deliberately being coy? What do you think this entire show is about? Ethan. Finding his *Soulmate*. Finding that person who is his other half, who makes him complete. His one-and-only."

"That's your definition. Is it Ethan's? Is it yours?" Lucy asked, looking at Mr. Esplin now.

"Sure it is. Of course it is," he said in a patronizing voice, showing all his teeth.

"Have either of you looked up the word *soul* lately? Done an Internet search? No? I did before I left home to be on the show. You might be surprised by how many definitions and philosophical viewpoints there are about what a soul is. And following that logic, it's safe to assume there are just as many definitions for *soulmate* too.

"I'm also absolutely certain that *my* definition of *soul*—and *soulmate*, for that matter—are not like either of yours. Am I Ethan's soulmate? Only he can say. Is Ethan my soulmate? I don't know. I hope I'm around long enough to find out."

"And how do you plan to do that?" Ms. Carlton prodded.

"By being myself and praying that it's enough for the moment."

"And your 'self' is as dull as a rainy day," Mr. Esplin muttered, loud enough for Lucy to make out the words. He wasn't smiling now, if that's what he'd been doing before. "We're done here," he declared, shoving out his arm and twisting it to get an obvious read from his wristwatch. "I think our time will be better spent setting up for this evening."

"May I ask you a question?" Lucy asked Mr. Esplin as he collected his laptop from the table. "Did you do this type of interview with Tiffany and Denise? I hope you didn't. You may call this reality TV, but ironically, it isn't very real at all, is it? Except it is to Ethan, Tiff, Denise, and me. What we're going through is real. And what you did today was wrong and hurtful."

He straightened and tucked the laptop under his arm. "You're right. Reality TV isn't real. It's a television show. And television shows need viewers and advertisers. If you were hurt, then I'm sorry, *really* I am, but you knew the odds of getting hurt were high before you agreed to be on the show. And my job is to make it a show that attracts those viewers and advertisers." He paused by her and patted her arm in a brotherly way. "I have a suggestion: loosen up, have some fun. Enjoy your fifteen minutes of fame. Let Ethan know you're into him. Put it all out there for him to see so there's no question in his mind. The guy has some big decisions ahead of him. Help him out a little."

He winked at her.

The door closed behind him with a click.

The wink gave it away. She knew the interview, complete with video, had been arranged solely for her, that when they'd knocked on her door, they'd been gunning for her, and they'd never considered doing something similar to Tiffany and Denise. She'd been down this road too many times before. It had to do with her religion and values. It had to do with her request for separate rooms.

She would accept it, then. It was part of the price she had to pay by holding to those values.

And yet, Ms. Carlton had treated her with what had bordered on contempt. And that was a pretty harsh stance, even for her. Especially since they'd managed to reach a point of friendly civility—until recently, that is. It didn't make sense.

She sighed as she glanced at the clock. She felt exhausted, and her nerves jangled. So much for the effects of a relaxing bubble bath. If she was going to be prepared to talk with Ethan that evening, she was going to have to put this all aside and get back to her notes. Ethan would be there any minute.

She was almost out of time.

* * *

"Our little Mary Poppins can sure carry the righteous attitude to new heights," Dane griped as the three of them walked toward the central bank of elevators.

"Yes," Melanie agreed as she pushed the down button. "She's a great little actress, isn't she? Too bad she doesn't know her BFFs spilled the beans on what she's really like. Rogan, where did you say those hidden cameras were? I tried to look for them but didn't want to be obvious."

"There's one above the fireplace, facing the sofa, and one in the hallway, but the angle's only so-so."

"Fine. I'm sure we'll get what we need." The elevator doors opened. It was crowded. "You two go on. I'll catch the next one." She was sick of Dane and Rogan anyway. Dane was an antsy little twerp who got under her skin. And Rogan would sell his own mother for the right price. She didn't want to spend any more time with either of them than she absolutely had to.

The stupid elevators were taking forever, so she opted for the stairs. It was only a few flights down to her floor.

That Lucy was something else. What an act.

Melanie was the first to admit she had an underdeveloped sense of trust when it came to people—heck, she knew people shouldn't exactly take *her* word at face value—but she'd actually started to like Lucy, believed she might be the real deal, that it wasn't all a big put-on for TV. When her friends Allie and Grace—best friends, *childhood* friends, no less—had ratted her out, Melanie had almost taken it personally, like she herself had been betrayed by Lucy.

It was time for Miss Perfect to get her comeuppance as far as Melanie was concerned.

* * *

"Alone at last!" Ethan exclaimed as the last of the crew filed out of Lucy's hotel suite. He closed the door with an exaggerated flourish and threw on the security lock. "I thought they'd never leave." He walked to Lucy, who was standing by the fireplace, and wound his fingers through her hair. "And I've been dying to do this all evening." He dipped his head and kissed her.

Lucy didn't want to think anymore. She wanted to lose herself in this kiss and forget they needed to talk. She wanted to forget that there were serious issues they needed to discuss. She didn't want to remember that he'd had romantic dates with two other women this week. She wanted to wrap herself in him, memorize the sound of his voice, the clean, spicy scent he wore, the subtle friction of his jaw against her cheek.

The rightness she felt when she was with him.

And how could that be? There were still too many unanswered questions.

Just another minute or two . . .

He ran his hands up and down her arms. "How was your dinner?"

"Wonderful." What she'd been able to eat of it anyway.

"I ask because I actually ate mine. I can't say the same about you." He chuckled as he took her hand and pulled her toward the couch. "Are we going to need to order room service in an hour or so? Get you a snack from the vending machine? Some Doritos maybe?"

"I guess I wasn't very hungry tonight," she said. "I can't imagine why."

He sank into the sofa and propped his feet on the coffee table, crossing his ankles, then settled her next to him with his arm around her shoulders. "Mmm, this is nice. Let's enjoy the peace and quiet for a while."

Lucy nestled next to him and actually breathed for the first time all evening. Despite the fact that she had been anxious at dinner, Ethan had done everything possible to put her at ease. He'd led the conversation, and she'd learned a lot about him as a result. They'd learned a lot about each other, actually—important trivial things, like their favorite colors (his was blue, hers was green). He liked to travel but hated flying, despite all the sky miles he'd logged. She'd confessed a desire to tour the cathedrals of Europe, which had gotten him talking about Renaissance art. They'd even sparred briefly over college football, comparing her Arizona State Sun Devils to his Trojans from Southern Cal before Ethan laughingly suggested they call a timeout.

It had been an important conversation for them to have and one that was relatively comfortable in front of a camera. When they'd arrived back at her suite, her nervousness had returned with the impending talk still to be faced. But once again, Ethan had sensed it and had helped her feel comfortable.

Right now, with her head against his shoulder, staring at the low fire crackling in the fireplace, she felt peaceful. She wanted to stay this way, wished they could stay this way and not talk. A few more minutes wouldn't matter. Just a few more minutes of this peaceful time with Ethan before she had to risk losing this, losing him, by sharing what she believed.

He kissed the top of her head then shifted her in his arms so he could reach her lips with his own again.

Just a few more minutes with Ethan, she thought. *Like this . . .*

* * *

"You brought all of this with you?" Ethan riffled through the stack of brochures Lucy had handed him, his brow furrowed. "When you left home to be on the show?"

Lucy knew what he had to be thinking. Religious brochures weren't the first things any woman he knew would make room for in her suitcase. "Just so you're not too weirded out, I don't normally run around with a mountain of Church leaflets in my purse. But when people find out I'm LDS—Mormon," she explained when an eyebrow rose, "they tend to ask questions. Mostly they're stuff like, have I met Donny and Marie? Or no smoking or drinking ones. But some people's questions are more in-depth.

"I didn't know how long I'd be around, but for some reason, I felt like I needed to be prepared for those kinds of questions."

"And have you? Needed to answer a lot of in-depth questions, that is?"

She smiled, recognizing the coincidence for what it was. "Not until this evening."

He thumbed through the Book of Mormon. She'd used torn strips of hotel stationery to mark specific pages. "And the significance of the underlined passages?"

"I thought some of them applied to our current situation. And some are just personal favorites."

He set the book down on the coffee table next to the brochures and turned to face her. "I have to be honest, Lucy. I'm not very religious. But I have no problem with a woman who is. In fact, Lindstrom told me that of the twenty-five women who came on the show, nearly two-thirds listed a religious affiliation of some kind. I guess that says something about me on some level, if all those tests of hers are to be believed."

He smiled gently and stroked her arm with the knuckles of his hand. "I'm trying to reassure you that I don't see this—this difference in religious perspective—as a problem for us. I would like to understand your beliefs a little better though. It's obviously a big part of who you are. So talk to me."

This was all she'd hoped for, for him to be willing to listen with the intent of understanding. Now she hoped she'd have the words within her that he could understand. She took a deep breath and dove in.

"Ethan, this show has made me think a lot about what I want in a marriage. I can't pretend to know what you want, but I do think I understand what you grew up with. You grew up with the kind of weddings where you hear ''til death do us part' and 'for as long as you both shall live,' right?"

"Yeah, I thought those were the only options," he said with a question in his eyes.

"Don't you think people—people who believe in a life after this one, because I do think a lot of people out there believe in an afterlife—would want the kind of promise that lasts forever in their wedding vows?"

Ethan nodded slightly but kept it at that so she could continue.

"Then why *wouldn't* the clergy have included forever in the vows?"

"Okay, why, if most people believe in an afterlife?"

She looked him straight in the eye. "Because they *couldn't.*"

He stared straight back at her.

She picked up the Book of Mormon and the pile of brochures and shuffled through them until she found what she was looking for. "Let's start with this one. It explains some of what I'm talking about. Then we'll look at this one . . . and this one after that . . ."

* * *

Ethan glanced at the mantel clock and rubbed a hand over his face. It was nearly seven in the morning.

He'd been reading all night.

He'd started with the brochures Lucy had given him, and when he'd had questions, she'd answered them for him as best she could.

He'd had a lot of questions. And, frankly, not all of them had been based on curiosity or the need for clarification. Sometimes he'd meant to challenge her, to debate the things she'd said because she'd made it all sound like it was some sort of gospel truth.

Sometimes he'd been flat-out argumentative.

She'd faced his challenging questions with backbone, he'd had to admit, but when he'd been inclined to nudge things into argument territory, she'd simply said she didn't want to fight, she just wanted to make sure he understood what he was reading.

How could anyone have a successful argument against a tactic like that?

So he'd turned to the next brochure. And then the next.

At some point after he'd picked up the Book of Mormon lying on the table, she'd kicked off her shoes and curled up next to him. He'd stopped asking questions and simply read.

By the time he'd read thirty pages, she'd fallen asleep leaning against him. He'd gently maneuvered her so she was situated more comfortably on the sofa and had tucked a decorative pillow under her head. She'd stirred a little but hadn't wakened. Not surprising, since the last few days had been long, busy ones. He'd felt more than a little tired himself.

By the time he'd read a hundred pages, he'd decided she'd be more comfortable sleeping in her bed rather than curled in a ball on the sofa, so he'd picked her up. He'd also brushed a kiss on her lips, not that she'd been aware of it.

He'd tugged back the bed covers and settled her among the feather pillows on the bed. He hadn't been able to resist planting another kiss on her. Her eyes had opened that time—just barely—and she'd smiled sleepily at him. "Ethan," she'd said in a scratchy, barely audible whisper, "love . . . forever . . ." and then her eyes had closed. So much for any princely awakening powers he could claim when it came to this Sleeping Beauty.

He couldn't be sure she'd even been remotely awake when she'd said the words, but they had pierced him nonetheless.

Now it was past dawn. Morning. He'd made it through the brochures, more than half of the Book of Mormon, and all of the verses she'd marked.

The last one was at the very end of the book, and at that point, he hadn't been the least bit surprised to find that it was about prayer. Prayer and faith. Recurring themes he'd read over and over again all night long.

I would exhort you that ye would ask God . . . having faith.

If any of you lack wisdom, let him ask of God . . . but let him ask in faith, nothing wavering.

Wa chay kay ya yo. Kyle had mentioned it as well.

May you seek wisdom from a higher power.

His thoughts were a mess. His eyes were blurred from lack of sleep and prolonged reading. His back hurt; his neck and shoulders were stiff.

He stood and stretched then went to splash cool water on his face in the part of the suite Lucy wasn't occupying.

He checked in on her on his way back to the parlor. She was still asleep, with an arm flung above her head and her hair a messy pool of bronze in the dark.

He wondered at the ironic circumstances of the past night.

She'd asked for separate accommodations for the sake of propriety, and he'd complied, despite thinking it was overly prudish in this day and age. He'd packed up his things and cleared out so she'd be able to maintain some sort of virtuous image in front of a national viewing audience. And he'd just spent the entire night in her hotel suite anyway, reading *religious* materials, of all things. *Alone*, while she'd slept soundly in another room.

Speaking of which, he needed to get back to his own room before any of the crew found out where he'd been all night. They would draw the wrong conclusions, which would be unfair to Lucy. He also wasn't in the mood to explain what he *had* been doing all night. He wasn't really sure *what* he'd been doing all night. Maybe after a few hours of shut-eye he'd be able to make more sense of it.

He had a raging headache.

He made it safely back to his own room unseen. After rummaging through his travel kit for aspirin, he set the alarm on the nightstand for ten. That would give him three hours of sleep—enough to take the edge off—and still give him time to sort through his thoughts before he said good-bye to Lucy at eleven, along with the rest of the *Soulmates* crew, who would be heading back to LA to set up for the next elimination ceremony.

How many aspirin could he safely take at one time?

He slipped his shoes off and fell onto the bed, dragging the bedspread partway over himself. He was too exhausted to care about doing any more than that.

Pray. Have faith. Pray. Have faith. The words pounded against his throbbing temples like sledgehammers. Self-reliance and hard work led to success. Not prayer. Not repeating some ancient litany that had nothing to do with the matter at hand. And not offering up wishes to some mythical, mystical being like a child would to Santa Claus. He could count on one hand the number of times he'd prayed in his lifetime.

The time he'd broken his arm as a kid, he'd prayed that Old Jed wouldn't kill him for messing with that colt. Since he was still alive and in one piece, he was willing to concede that the prayer had been answered. Anything else he could remotely call a prayer had occurred while watching sporting events, specifically during crucial plays, but he hadn't noticed them having any particular impact on the overall outcome of the games.

If he'd had a religious epiphany during the night, it was that while *he* might be able to compromise when it came to religious beliefs for the sake of a relationship, and while many people—possibly even members of Lucy's own faith—might also be willing to compromise, Lucy wasn't one of those people.

And that could spell the end for any future they might have had together.

* * *

Lucy walked the grounds of *Soulmates* House. She'd been back in Los Angeles since her date with Ethan. They'd said good-bye less than forty-eight hours ago. Today they were scheduled to tape the elimination ceremony on the back lawns of *Soulmates* House in a gazebo that was part of the landscaping behind the swimming pool.

It was nearly time for the ceremony to begin, but Lucy kept walking.

Ethan had seemed preoccupied when they'd said good-bye in Victoria; of course, considering everything she'd hit him with the evening before, she really couldn't blame him. She'd wondered how long he'd continued reading that night before giving up and returning to his room. She'd been too embarrassed to ask, embarrassed to think she'd fallen asleep with him sitting there.

"Lucy!"

Kyle was jogging toward her, so she stopped and waited for him to catch up.

He smiled appreciatively at her. "You look great!"

She sighed and smiled back as best she could, considering all the muscles in her face felt numb. "Thanks."

His expression turned serious. "Ethan's here now. It's time for the elimination to get under way."

Lucy's stomach tightened. "Okay."

He held out his arm like a gentleman. "Let's get you to the gazebo, then."

Lucy slid her hand into the crook of his arm. "Thank you, Kyle. For everything." He'd kept her company the past day or so after she'd returned to Los Angeles, and that had kept her sane. He'd also confessed, after he'd sworn her to secrecy, that he'd grown up with Ethan, which had been a huge surprise. And then she'd managed to extort a few stories about life on the ranch out of him.

He felt like a brother, and she'd told him so.

They were nearing the gazebo. Mr. Esplin was scurrying around like the rat he was, while the crew dragged cables and equipment into place. Tiffany and Denise were already there. "Good luck," he said. "Ethan's no fool. He'll figure things out in time."

Lucy nodded and gave Kyle what she hoped was a reassuring smile.

"You love him, don't you?" Kyle asked.

Lucy nodded again and felt tears threatening.

"I can tell. Right now, my mother, Terri—you'd like my mother, I think—would say something like 'not every step shows us the journey's end. Take each step, and trust the rightness of it.'"

Lucy had to smile. "Is that an ancient Native American saying?"

Kyle grinned. "Nah, just the words of Terri Gray Cloud with a little Kyle thrown in."

"Then your mother is wise, and she raised a good son. I'm sure I would like her." She glanced at the gazebo. The others were in place, and Ms. Carlton was glaring at her, of course. "I'd better go."

Kyle nodded. "This is just the next step in the journey for you, Lucy. And the next step for Ethan too. Trust it."

* * *

"I'm so nervous right now; my heart feels like a jar full of frogs," Denise whispered to Lucy after they'd shared a hug and moved to stand in position.

Lucy knew how she felt.

Tiffany had nodded a less than friendly hello and then gone to stand in place. Cameras were trained on them and running; Mr. Esplin had Rogan taping Rick over near the pool house.

And then there was Ethan, walking toward Rick and the camera, looking professional and serious and heartbreakingly wonderful.

And aloof.

Denise heaved a huge sigh. Lucy turned at the sound and took in Denise's big, dreamy eyes. Tiffany was shooting Ethan intense possessive looks. It was like watching a rerun of the video clips she'd seen in Victoria, compliments of Ms. Carlton and Mr. Esplin.

Ethan stood on the gazebo now and spoke to them. Lucy tried to pay attention. A few of his words made it through her fog of anxiety. *Honored, amazing, difficult.* She had no context in which to put them. Her ninja butterflies from the first day were nothing compared to how she felt now—like a Christian martyr waiting to see if Caesar's thumb pointed up or down.

And then Ethan was reaching to take a charm from the velvet case next to him. He paused. Lucy held her breath.

"Denise," she heard him say, "will you continue the journey with me?"

Lucy was pretty sure the squeal Denise made as she threw herself into Ethan's arms was a big yes, only to be confirmed by an, "Abso-*lutely,* sugar."

Denise floated back to her spot.

Lucy looked at Ethan.

Ethan looked at her. A muscle twitched in his cheek.

He turned to Tiffany.

And said Tiffany's name.

Lucy didn't hear him ask Tiffany about continuing the journey with him. The roaring in her ears was too loud.

The air was too thin. Everything in the gazebo disappeared down a gray tunnel.

And then Denise was hugging her and saying good-bye, and Tiffany was hugging her—even in her dazed state, Lucy knew that was weird—and Ethan was escorting her to the front of the house where a car was waiting to take her away.

Except, first Ethan detoured to a low retaining wall and urged her to sit down.

At least her vision was clearing. It was still difficult to breathe, but her hearing must have returned because Ethan was asking her if she was all right, and she could make sense of the words.

"I'm fine," she said.

She honestly couldn't feel a thing.

He took her hands in his. His were warm; she realized hers were cold. She was cold.

"Lucy, I'm sorry," Ethan said, sounding all business. "I wanted to understand your beliefs. I wanted to find the middle ground, the place where we could build a relationship. I wanted that relationship, wanted to see if it could happen between us.

"I know how important your religion is to you—that was obvious from the pile of pamphlets you dropped into my lap." He chuckled humorlessly. Then he sighed. "But what I realized about you was that, for you, it's all or nothing. And what I realized about me was that it was too much for me to take in all at once."

"Like M&Ms," she said to herself.

"What?"

She shook her head. "Nothing. Just something Dad said to Noah."

"I needed time, Lucy. More time than we had. That's what it boiled down to."

They sat on the wall without speaking. Lucy wasn't sure she could even move. She wondered vaguely if she should do something to bring this to its conclusion and end the miserable moment for both of them.

But then it would be all over.

This would be her last chance to speak to him.

A thought—but not quite a thought—flared through her then, filling her heart with tender emotion. Even now, saying good-bye to Ethan and feeling bereft, she hadn't been left alone. The Spirit was with her, comforting her.

But it was more than that. This was her last chance to share her deepest feelings, her testimony, with Ethan, and the Spirit was prompting her to do it. She took a deep breath.

"It *is* all or nothing for me, Ethan. You're right about that. If I had the chance to fall even more in love with you, then I would want that love to last forever. I would want you to be mine forever. I would want us to be two souls who weather the ins and outs of this life learning to be soulmates, loving each other even more in the life to come, and having our family with us too.

"I won't apologize for wanting that kind of love, one that offers the promise of eternity. It would be worse to love completely, believing there were time limits, always fearing the day when it would end. And eternity *does* exist, Ethan. At the very least, the stars prove it every night."

Ethan rubbed his hands over his face and then through his hair. His cool, businesslike demeanor vanished. In fact, Lucy realized, he was agitated.

"It's all too much, Lucy! Too *much*. I can't take it all in; I can't make heads or tails of it all. I'm reading about spirit worlds and visions in groves and apostasies and priesthoods and prophets and trying to decide which of three women I want to spend my life with, in addition to keeping my company running on all cylinders during my absence.

"There was too much riding on my decision today. Too much at stake. The show, Curt, the website, the sponsors. Too many people, too many things affected by what I decided today, not to mention my own life and future happiness.

"I've had to learn—spent years learning—how to evaluate risks. I'm not afraid of taking risks. But this one, Lucy, this one with you was just too big of a risk." He heaved a weary sigh. "I'm sorry. I'm so sorry. I had to make the best decision I could in the amount of time we had. And what we didn't have enough of . . . was time."

She nodded, resigned. "For me, it's too big a risk to love someone and know I won't have him with me forever. How funny is that? You don't have enough time, and I won't settle for anything less than forever."

He ran his thumb across her cheek then, wiping a tear away. When had she started crying? She hadn't realized she was.

She brushed his hand away and stood. His touch hurt too much.

"Let me walk you out," he said softly and placed his hand protectively on her back. It nearly killed her.

They walked in total silence now. Lucy had nothing more to say. What did one say at a moment like this anyway?

What we didn't have enough of was time, he'd said.

She'd handed him the keys to eternity, and he'd said they didn't have enough time.

She'd known that she had been taking a big risk, but she'd known she'd had to take it. She'd felt prompted to take it. It had meant really putting her heart on the line for the first time, for him and her love for him. He, on the other hand, had decided she was too big a risk because of the business investments involved. Oh, he'd said his life and future happiness were on the line, but really, was keeping Tiffany or Denise around instead of her such a huge guarantee of that future happiness? Hadn't she been worth keeping around for another week to find out?

No. That meant what he was really saying was exactly what all the other guys had said to her over the years. *You're a great girl, but you're too different. It's too much. It's not going to work out between us. Sorry.*

Well, she'd heard it before, and she'd survived it before. She would again.

In time.

They reached the limousine, and Ethan opened the door for her. The agony was almost at an end. She could hardly bear to look at him; she could see the regret in his eyes, the concern that he knew he'd hurt her. Best to make this businesslike, Lucy decided. It's what Ethan would do.

She raised her chin and attempted a smile. She cleared her throat. "Well, good-bye," she said and put out her hand for a handshake. That was undoubtedly a stupid move, but Lucy felt particularly stupid at the moment. Stupid and awkward and hurt and embarrassed, and all of it currently being caught on camera. Ethan took her extended hand and pulled her close instead, wrapping his arms around her for a final embrace. Held her there for what felt like a painfully long time.

She didn't want it to end. It would mean the end.

But eventually he drew back and brushed her hair from her face. "Good-bye, Lucy. My golden, radiant girl."

His words and tenderness finished her off. She slid into the limo, holding herself as still inside as she could. The door closed; the car pulled away from the curb and headed down the drive. She stared straight ahead, only vaguely aware that Ms. Carlton and the slimy cameraman were sitting across from her, shooting everything. She didn't care about the cameras anymore.

She buried her face in her hands and sobbed.

CHAPTER 19

ETHAN MOVED HIS HEAD FROM side to side, trying to work the kinks out of his neck and shoulders. Raphael was lathered from their morning run, and Ethan gave the horse plenty of time to drink his fill. He'd taken Rafe faster and farther than usual, but he'd needed to get away, far away, so he'd pushed his trusty friend to his limit. It shamed him. Even in Ethan's current state of mind, he'd known Rafe had been valiantly exerting himself, trying to please. But Ethan had felt pursued, and he couldn't seem to get far enough away—from the ranch, from the show. From his lingering thoughts of Lucy.

He hadn't been able to get out of Los Angeles fast enough. He'd arranged ahead of time to have a private jet take him to Montana immediately after the elimination ceremony. It had given him an extra evening with his family and precious hours away from the strain of *Soulmates* before it all started up again the day after tomorrow.

"I'll take care of that," a ranch hand said to Ethan as he started to remove Raphael's saddle. "Word is your ma's looking for you."

"Thanks," Ethan said and patted Rafe's neck. "Give him an extra treat, will you? I put him through the paces this morning, and he was a prince about it."

"Sure thing, Eth."

He watched as cowboy and horse ambled through the stable doors before turning toward the house.

He looked for his mother in the kitchen first. Terri, Kyle's mom, was there, measuring something mysterious into her food mixer. She'd been busy since he'd gone out riding that morning; there were pies cooling on racks near the window, and dirty dishes were piled in the sink, an unusual occurrence. Terri kept a spotless kitchen.

He came up behind her and started kneading her shoulders. "You're cooking up a storm in here."

"Sure am. We've got lunch tomorrow. Dinner tomorrow. All being shown on television too. You need to scoot now; I got work to do. Besides, your mama's looking for you. She's upstairs."

"Ethan? Is that you?" his mother yelled. "Come up here, honey. We need you."

"Get your hands out of that bowl!" Terri exclaimed, shaking her head and chuckling at him as he slid his finger into his mouth. The batter tasted wonderful. Just like always.

He found his mother emerging from the closet in his parents' bedroom, with his sister-in-law, Megan, and niece Brianna in attendance. The room was strewn with clothing. She held up the sweater she'd just retrieved. "What about this one?" she asked Megan.

Megan looked up from a pile of blouses on the bed. "You can't wear a winter sweater in June, you know."

"But it's lightweight, and the colors don't make me look as washed out. And I have to wear these slacks. They're the most slimming. The camera adds ten pounds, they say."

Brianna, with a sequined cocktail dress pulled over her play clothes, was posing in front of a mirror like a runway model and adjusting her Disney princess tiara, which was precariously anchored in place by the pigtails on either side of her head.

"Well?" his mother asked.

It took Ethan a second to realize the question had been addressed to him. "Well what?"

"What do *you* think?"

Brianna was making kissy faces at herself in the mirror, and Megan was tossing clothes and muttering something about pregnancy and baby fat and split ends. None of it made any sense to him.

"What do I think about what?" he asked.

His mother, the woman who'd given birth to him and had lovingly nurtured him into adulthood, gave him a withering glance that said she clearly thought her child was a moron.

"What about this?" Megan held up a skirt and blouse for her mother-in-law's review.

"But you're thinking about wearing your lavender sundress, Megan. We'll clash. Besides," she waved her hand dismissively in the direction of the skirt and blouse, "they're ancient. Out of style."

"I'm not sure about the lavender sundress though. My arms will look lumpy on camera. I think I should wear something with sleeves."

Ethan had finally reached his limit. He started to laugh, and he couldn't stop. He laughed as three pairs of female eyes glared at him. Brianna didn't even know what was going on, but it didn't stop her. She propped her hands on her sequined hips and gave him her best scowl before turning to admire herself in the mirror again.

When he finally got himself under control, he gave his mother a hug. "You're beautiful no matter what you wear. And who cares what anybody watching the show thinks anyway?"

"You don't understand," she protested. "I'm meeting two women my son is thinking of marrying. On *television*, for everyone to see. I want to make a good impression. I have to wear the right thing."

"As long as you're not wearing your birthday suit, you'll be fine," he muttered—

"Ethan!"

—obviously too loudly. "Sorry. Wear something comfortable. And if it helps, I vote with Megan. I've always liked that skirt and blouse on you too."

It was, apparently, the right thing to say. "You have?" she asked. "Well, then. Thank you."

He felt a tug on his pant leg. Brianna's pixie face beamed up at him, her scowl a thing of the past. He noticed her tiara was crooked and there was a streak of grape jelly on her chin. "Guess what! I'm going to be on TV, like a real famous person. Like a princess!"

He picked her up and settled her on his hip. He couldn't resist this kid. "Princess Beans."

She wrinkled her nose. "Not Princess Beans. That's a silly name. Princess *Brianna*. And everyone will know about me, and they'll smile and be my friend and want to play with me."

He lightly pinched her chin. "How about I play with you right now?"

"Okay!" She wriggled out of his hold to grasp his hand and tug him toward the door, eager for this new adventure to begin. "You can be the prince!"

He rolled his eyes and listened to his mother and Megan choke back laughter.

He can be the prince. "Let's go, then," he said, not without a little reluctance. He'd been thinking more along the lines of the swing set and teeter-totter out in back of the house.

Besides, he'd been playing make-believe prince for months now, and the game had gotten tedious.

* * *

Jed walked to the living room window and squinted as he looked out. "What in the Sam Hill is going on out there?"

Ethan joined him at the window.

A large van was parked in a gravel area near the corral, and Melanie Carlton had just stepped out of a black SUV that had pulled in next to it. Now cameramen were pouring out of the vehicle, following and taping her every step. The ranch hands, naturally curious, were beginning to congregate.

Curt hadn't mentioned anything at all that would account for this unscheduled—and unwelcome—visit.

"I don't know," he replied to Jed's question. "Let's find out."

The van's signage had been obscured by the crowd, but as he moved closer, Ethan could read it. It was a professional animal transportation service. Melanie saw him approach and moved to intercept.

"Ethan," she said. "Surprise! We have a special delivery for you." She produced a letter and handed it to him. "That's part one. Part two is in the van."

A man with the company's logo on his shirt had opened the van doors and was setting up a ramp, and everyone crowded around him trying to see inside.

Ethan could hear metal clanging and a snuffling sound. And then he watched in amazement as the man led a pig the size of Brianna down the ramp. But this wasn't just any old pig. This pig was decked out in full Shakespearean costume, with a frilly ruff around his neck, a lavender vest, and a pair of purple breeches that ballooned out on all sides. At the back was a slit for the pig's tail, which was tied with a wide satin bow. A tiny velvet cape trimmed in fake fur draped its shoulders, and the crowning touch, literally, was a matching velvet cap that was tied under the pig's chin and sported a jaunty white plume.

The ranch hands, who'd been quiet until the appearance of the pig, roared with laughter.

The pig squealed. Ethan wasn't sure if that meant the pig was trying to say he was delighted with his fancy duds or humiliated to be caught wearing sissy clothes. None of the pigs he'd ever known would have worn this stuff, he thought, amused despite his annoyance at having *Soulmates* intrude on his one free day.

Melanie nodded at the letter in Ethan's hand. "You can read that now."

He ran his finger under the flap and removed the letter, reading it silently to himself. *Ethan, This is our good friend Hamlet. He is my gift to you—a small memento of our time together. Or maybe not so small by now. He agreed to deliver this timely message to you:* To thine own self be true. *Fondly, Lucy.*

He refolded the letter and crouched down until he was nose to snout with Hamlet. "Well, pal," he said, "let's restore your dignity and get you out of these things." He nodded to one of the ranch hands idling nearby. "Take care of my friend here, will you?" The cowboy took the leash and ambled off to the barn, Hamlet trotting alongside, bow flapping, feather bouncing, cameramen following in his wake.

"Which of the two women we're meeting sent you that pig?" Jed asked, glancing at the letter still in Ethan's hand.

"Neither." He smiled, remembering Lucy at the rodeo, how she'd dashed after that greasy, smelly, squealing piglet, determined to come out the victor in the challenge. Her smudged face had glowed with triumph as she'd stood by the barrel that held Hamlet. Lucy—always glowing. He looked over at Old Jed, who was eyeing him too closely. He straightened his shoulders. "Neither," he said again. "I sent her home last week. Come on. Let's go back to the house."

* * *

Lucy had been home for a week when *Soulmates* premiered on television. During that week, she'd been approached by nearly everyone she knew, all of them eager to hear about her experience on the show. Neighbors had dropped by the house; ward members had approached her at church.

That had been hard enough, considering her emotional state. But when the local (as in Phoenix) news discovered that one of their own was appearing on *Soulmates*, Lucy's face started cropping up everywhere. Anonymity became a thing of the past. Strangers approached her, all of them curious and smiling and wanting her to pose for cell phone pictures.

She'd gotten a few replies to the job inquiries she'd begun before leaving to appear on *Soulmates*. And a few of those had actually been encouraging.

She'd spent a few days following up on them. It had kept her home and, to her relief, out of the glare of the limelight.

She hadn't seen or heard from Allie or Grace, which was strange. She'd considered dropping in on them at their apartment but hadn't done it. They'd push her for details, and because they were the sisters she'd never had, she'd end up crying, and she didn't want to cry. She'd done enough of that already. Besides, crying probably broke the confidentiality agreement on some level, especially with friends who knew her so well.

But it would be great to see them. She missed them like crazy.

She wondered how the romance between Grace and Mike Sessions was progressing. If she couldn't have her own happily ever after, at least Allie and Ben and Grace and Mike would. That would be nice.

She was busy on the computer the evening the show premiered. Her mother came into the room. "Are you going to watch this with me?" she asked as she sat down on the sofa.

Lucy wasn't sure she wanted to watch it. But she was even less sure how to answer and not violate the confidentiality agreement. "Sure," Lucy saved what she'd been working on and shut down the computer. "Of course I am."

"Dad set it to record. He had to go out for a while, but he didn't want to miss any of it."

Apparently her brothers felt the same because Andy and Brigham suddenly appeared with a bunch of their friends and plopped noisily around the room.

"Shh," Linda said. "The show's starting."

Soft music began playing, and Lucy watched Rick smile his Day-Glo smile for the camera. "Good evening. I'm Rick Madison. Welcome to *Soulmates* . . ."

And then he was introducing Ethan, and Ethan was meeting each of the women . . .

"There you are!" Brig and Andy hooted wildly, and one of Andy's friends wolf whistled. Lucy threw a pillow at his head.

"Check out the hottie!" one of the guys said.

"Hey! That's my sister you're talking about!"

"When did taping end?" Brig asked her, too smart for his own good.

"I can't tell you that," she replied.

"You just got home last week, so you must have been around for most of it."

"You don't know that for sure, and I can't tell you."

Before Lucy knew it, the broadcast had ended. She'd made it through. Her mother was watching her closely, though, so she smiled and pretended to listen as the guys did a postgame analysis of Ethan, Lucy's on-screen debut, the girls they thought were cute and the ones they thought were psycho, and who they would have sent home if they'd been Ethan Glass.

She went to bed early.

The following week rolled by, and Lucy had still not seen Allie or Grace. Allie's texted replies had said she was busy with wedding plans and she'd catch her later. Grace was on vacation and would call when she was back in Eagle Bluff. She must have been halfway around the world because she'd left the voice message in the middle of the night.

Episode two featured the sailing and rodeo dates, and the Kendrick family room had an even bigger crowd than before. Her dad was there; her brothers brought more friends, and her oldest brother, Craig, and his wife, Becky, were there.

Someone had even made popcorn.

Apparently *Soulmates* night was going to be a public event.

The kissing booth scene made everyone laugh. It was embarrassing to sit there and watch her family watch her kiss Ethan. But the horrible part had been watching the teasers showing Ethan and Denise kissing on the sailing date, especially knowing Denise was one of the final two women and possibly Ethan's *Soulmate* choice.

Everyone laughed again as Lucy and the others scrambled after greased pigs. Finally, it was the square dance and romantic picnic with Ethan.

Lucy left the room.

She couldn't watch her evening under the stars with Ethan while everyone else watched at the same time.

A few days passed, and life settled into a routine that didn't always revolve around *Soulmates*. She decided it was time to start earning her keep. Finding work in Eagle Bluff was her surest bet for now, so she borrowed her mom's car and drove into town.

She filled out job applications at a few places. She dropped by the *Daily Journal* to see if there were any positions open. While they didn't have any jobs available, the editor told her they'd love to do an interview with her. She declined.

On the return home, Lucy decided to stop at the resort Grace's family owned. Grace's dad had always liked her. Maybe he'd hire her to do odd jobs until she found something more permanent.

She pulled into the parking lot, surprised to see Grace's car there. Grace's car shouldn't be in the lot because Grace was on vacation. Maybe her dad's Porsche was in the shop again, so he was using it while she was gone.

She smiled and waved a greeting to Matt, the front desk clerk, who was busy checking in a guest. He flashed a grin and gave a quick wave back to her. She knew her way to the business offices.

Her smile lingered as she walked up to the receptionist's desk. "Hi, Jane, I was wondering if Mr.—"

"Lucy!" Jane crowed. "You were so *funny* last night! A three-date rule for kissing! And I nearly died watching you chase that pig!" She chuckled. "You must be here to see Grace. Go on in. I'm sure it's fine."

"No, I'm—did you say Grace was here? When did she get back from vacation?"

"She's been here every day, like always. Where did you get the idea that—"

Lucy didn't wait to hear the rest of the question. She headed back to the office where her good friend—her best friend—Grace, who was *not*, apparently, on vacation halfway around the world, was working and had been all along. Despite what she'd told Lucy.

Lucy intended to find out why.

The door to Grace's office was shut, and she could hear raised, angry voices. Lucy didn't care, and she didn't bother to knock. She walked in.

"Oh!" Grace exclaimed, her eyes wide with shock when she realized who'd just come through the door. She looked rigid and tense, Lucy thought. Mike Sessions sat across the desk from Grace, his arms folded across his chest, his face flushed. It looked like their little relationship—whatever it happened to be at the moment—had hit a rough patch. Tough beans.

"Hey, Lucy," Mike said, recovering his composure first. "I didn't know you were back in town. How was Hollywood?"

"I've been home a couple of weeks now," she said, ignoring his question. She looked pointedly at Grace. "How was your vacation? Where did you say you went?"

Grace at least had the decency to look embarrassed.

Mike just looked confused. "Grace hasn't been on vacation. Where'd you get that idea?"

"Yes, Grace, where did I?" Lucy asked her rhetorically. She turned from her tense, angry friend to Mike. "It looks like it's a good thing I showed up here today. I thought after everything I did for you over Christmas you'd be able to manage the rest on your own."

"Maybe you did a little too much over Christmas," Grace said sarcastically.

"What are you talking about?" Lucy asked, looking directly at Grace. When Grace wouldn't give her anything more than stony silence, Lucy turned to Mike. "What is she talking about?"

"I don't know! She won't talk to me. One minute everything's great and I'm thinking sure, yeah, I think I will ask her out. Then the big Hollywood production comes to town, and suddenly she's avoiding me here at work and sending someone else to get me if I'm needed on resort business somewhere. That's why I'm in her office right now, because it's getting in the way of work and it has to stop. And she *still* won't tell me why. Only that it's something to do with a confidentiality agreement so she *can't.*"

Grace glared at both of them. "Lucy's known forever how much I liked you"—she blushed furiously at her declaration but was too angry to stop what she was saying—"and friends just don't go behind friends' backs with the person they like. I just couldn't look you in the face, after I thought . . ."

Lucy huffed out a frustrated breath. "Grace, Mike invited me to a party with some of his friends when I was home over the holidays. You knew about that." She decided to lay it all out just to be certain she and Grace understood each other. "What you didn't know, and apparently still don't realize, was that I went because he's been friends with Craig since high school, so I've known Mike forever. I spent most of that party giving Mike a pep talk to call you, since I've known for a long time how you felt about him. I couldn't say anything to you because I didn't know if this lunkhead would actually call you or not."

Grace was silent for a moment, and then she turned to look at Mike. "Is that why you started talking to me a few months ago? But all you ever asked me about was Lucy. All you ever said was, 'Is Lucy home this weekend?' And then when Allie said—"

Mike relaxed with obvious relief when it became apparent Grace was finally willing to talk to him. He rolled his eyes. "Yeah, I know. I was nervous, I guess, since you're the boss's daughter. Lucy was the only thing I could think of to talk to you about. It's pretty embarrassing, actually."

Grace's face went into her hands.

The words *confidentiality agreement* Mike had mentioned were still ringing through Lucy's mind, and she hadn't missed the last part of Grace's comments—about something Allie had said. It had made her neck prickle. "'And then when Allie said'—what?"

Grace looked at Lucy with guilty eyes. "She said—So you and Mike were never—? You never—?"

"Mike and I went to a party together, where I shamelessly talked you up like I was doing an infomercial." Then the realization of what Grace had suggested hit. "Grace! How could you even think—?"

"What's going on?" Mike demanded.

"Oh, Lucy," Grace said, a look of horror on her face. "I think I owe you an apology. And you too, Mike. And then I'm going to tie Allie to a stake, pour honey all over her, and watch her be eaten alive by fire ants."

Mike gestured to Lucy to take a seat. "Maybe you'd better tell us exactly what's going on," he told Grace.

* * *

Ethan tossed his luggage into the back of the truck and climbed into the passenger seat. He'd said his good-byes and kissed his mother—and extricated Brianna from his leg, where she'd wrapped herself tightly and refused to let go, insisting she was going with him. Old Jed was already behind the wheel with the engine idling. Personally, Ethan had hoped that Jake would be taking him to the airport. Jake might try to get a few details out of Ethan, but he was too laid back to pry or push too hard.

His father, however, was a whole different kettle of fish. He wasn't normally the interfering type, but when he wanted something, he could be just plain stubborn. And Ethan had felt something brewing for the past week or so—ever since he'd returned to Montana from LA after taping the final episode and the selection of his *Soulmate*.

He buckled his seat belt and slid his sunglasses on.

Jed put the truck into gear.

Neither of them spoke. Ethan watched the scenery pass by—trees, cattle, a couple of barns. More trees. He glanced at his watch. He had pressing business matters to contend with that had been on a back burner for two months. Contracts and clients that needed attention. Ethan realized he was grinding his teeth. He consciously relaxed.

Jed checked his rearview. "Tiffany sure is a looker, isn't she? About gave the ranch hands fever convulsions just to see her. Knows what she wants too, that one. Not afraid to go after it either, from what I observed."

Ethan didn't reply. He knew firsthand just how fearless Tiffany was. It wasn't anything he particularly felt like sharing with his father.

"Now, that other one, Denise, she's a lovely woman as well. Sweet, lovely woman. I think I was bless-your-hearted almost to death in the space of a day. But very lovely, for all that."

More silence. Ethan really didn't need this conversation at the moment. The decision was made. He had his *Soulmate*. Curt had his show and his website. It was time to get back to business. Not to mention that he now had a relationship he had to make time for in all of this. He glanced at his watch again. He felt antsy, though he wasn't sure why. He had plenty of time before his flight was scheduled to depart, and there was plenty of time during the flight to review the contract he wanted finessed when he reached New York. But the ride seemed to be taking longer than usual. He glanced at the speedometer.

"You said you'd be out of the country how long?" Jed asked.

"I'll be in New York for a week then London and points beyond for roughly three more. Depending, of course, on what I find when I get there."

Jed grunted. "Have to say, I was curious enough to watch that TV show of yours for a bit."

Ethan hadn't watched either episode that had aired so far. He'd lived it. Watching had seemed redundant and a waste of time.

The silence resumed.

After several minutes, Jed pulled over onto the shoulder, parked, and put on the emergency brake. "Let's walk," he said.

Oh great.

Ethan walked alongside Jed and waited for the words that would follow. The gravel crunched beneath their feet. There was a rustling of wind and wildlife in the trees that lined the road. A pair of magpies scolded each other noisily before flying away.

Jed rubbed the back of his neck. "This isn't easy for me to say, but I'm going to say it anyway. You're making a mistake."

Ethan did *not* need to hear this right now. "What makes you say that?" he asked as levelly as he could.

"Maybe the fact that you've been my son for thirty years, give or take. Maybe the fact that, for a man who's supposedly found his soulmate or some such, you don't seem to be turning cartwheels about it."

"You're telling me you did cartwheels when you met Mom?" Ethan couldn't even imagine it. Branding cattle, roping steers, yes. Cartwheels, no. Not from the most taciturn man he'd ever known.

"Son, when your mother finally admitted she liked me more than a little and agreed to marry me, I didn't stop grinning for weeks. Months even. Probably did turn cartwheels at the time, I was that tickled."

"I'd like to have seen that." It would take seeing it to believe it.

Jed squinted in the direction they were headed. "I don't expect you to tell me what's going on with that show. I know all about how you're supposed to be helping that friend of yours. Nonsense way to find love, from my way of thinking, but that's neither here nor there at this point. But I'm going to speak my peace about what I see when it comes to my flesh and blood. And when I'm done, I won't say any more about it."

He looked at Ethan then. "Ethan, if this is what you're like when you're in love, you're about the sorriest piece of manhood I've ever seen. I've seen men face jail time with more enthusiasm."

"I'm under a confidentiality agreement."

"I'm not talking about some confidentiality agreement, and you know it. I don't have to hear the words to necessarily know what a man's thinking. You gave that pig in the silly getup warmer looks than I saw you give either of those two women."

Ethan shoved his hands into the pockets of his slacks and said nothing.

"I saw who was chasing that pig, son. I understand what's going on better than you think."

Ethan turned to Jed. "There were obstacles. Big ones that I know she's not going to compromise on, and I'm not sure I can either. And I didn't have the time it would take to find out."

"You have all the time in the world. You're not under some deadline here. You just think you are." Jed shook his head. "You're more like your old man than I thought. Stubborn. Listen, son, marriage lasts for a long, long time when it's done right. So make sure that when all is said and done, it's really what you want."

Ethan stopped walking and turned to his father. "How long, Jed? How long does it last? How long would you want it to last? I asked you before if Mom was your soulmate, and you didn't answer me."

It took a long time for Jed to reply. He scuffed at the gravel with the toe of his boot then studied the boot with apparent fascination before looking back at Ethan. With his coarse, dark hair streaked with gray and his leathery skin wrinkled and tanned from years in the sun, he looked like a tough old *hombre*. But his eyes were unnaturally bright.

"That woman," he said in a low voice, "gave me my boys. She gives me good company and peace when I need it. She also gives me a good piece of her mind every other day or so. I don't know anything about soulmates, as you call it, but I do know I've had a real partner who's stood by me through the good and the bad. And I'll keep her there with me always, if I'm lucky enough to have any say in the matter. I'd walk on coals if walking on coals meant I'd have her forever. I'd be that lost without her, and that's a fact."

Jed turned abruptly and headed back toward the truck. "We better get back on the road, get you on that plane." He brushed a hand quickly over his face as he walked.

Ethan stood, frozen. He was mortally afraid he might have just witnessed, for the first time in his life, Old Jed tear up.

He replayed the scene in his mind later that afternoon, at a cruising altitude of thirty thousand feet. He reached for his briefcase and, instead of retrieving his business notes, pulled out the stack of religious brochures he'd impulsively tossed into it that morning. And he began reading them. Again.

* * *

After the third episode aired, Lucy decided she would wait and watch the rest of the season online at a later date. Much later, like next year sometime, or next decade, maybe. Definitely not now.

She was still smarting from the conversation she'd had with Grace and Mike. A guilt-stricken Grace had confessed (despite the confidentiality agreement she'd signed) that she and Allie had been interviewed on camera by Ms. Carlton, which had surprised Lucy. She'd only heard Grace's side of the story so far, and she knew she needed to see Allie to get her side of things and set things right between them, but she was feeling hurt. The truth of the matter was, she'd been avoiding the issue; she didn't feel ready to deal with anything more at the moment.

If *Soulmates* had been some other type of reality show, one where she'd had to swim with sharks or survive in the Arctic with only a flashlight and a pack of chewing gum—or eat live bees—she would have been totally fine.

It was true that watching the first two episodes of the show with everyone else in the room—particularly her woof-woofing brothers and their friends—had been embarrassing but survivable. But watching the third episode, which included the trip to Mexico, had felt painfully similar to the time in sixth grade when Craig had found her diary and had read the part where she'd poured out all her innermost romantic feelings for Eric Sanchez—Craig's best friend and a major dreamboat—

to a laughing Eric Sanchez and the rest of their junior high buddies. They'd thought it was hilarious. She'd wanted to die.

Twelve years ago, she'd grabbed her diary, raged at Craig, and hidden in her closet for the rest of the afternoon, nursing her wounded pride and broken heart. At least this time she'd laughed and made jokes right along with the gang before excusing herself and going to her room. It wasn't quite like hiding in her closet.

She needed to get back to some semblance of normal life. The best way to do that was to ignore the show, keep herself busy, and make herself scarce on Tuesday nights. She also needed time to get her raw emotions under control. And the best place to do that for the time being, she decided, was at home.

She found projects around the house that would keep her busy. Each morning, she checked her e-mail, filled out a few more online job applications, and got to work. One day soon she might venture out of the house and talk to Grace's dad about a job. But not quite yet.

First she tackled the kitchen, reorganizing all of the drawers and cabinets, washing walls and windows, and cleaning every major appliance inside and out.

Next she attacked her bedroom. She laundered the bedspread and curtains and cleaned the carpet. She went through her closet and drawers, pulling out clothes she was unlikely to ever wear again and bagging them for charity.

That reminded her, she had things—shoes, jewelry, etc.—she'd borrowed for the show that she needed to return to Grace and Allie. She supposed she needed to call Grace and arrange a time to return them. Allie, too, of course.

On Friday morning, Grace called her instead and invited her to lunch.

"Dad told me to tell you he can keep you busy here at the resort as long as you want to be kept busy," Grace announced cheerfully. "Why don't you come here, and we'll have lunch in the coffee shop? I'll let Dad's secretary know you're coming, and she can pencil in some time this afternoon for him to talk to you about it."

"I'll be there," Lucy said. "And Grace—tell him thanks. And tell him he's getting a big hug and thank you from me this afternoon. Plus homemade cookies."

Grace laughed. "If you bring him cookies, you might even be able to negotiate a higher salary. See you in a couple of hours."

Lucy snapped her phone shut and smiled. She had a job! It was only a temporary fix, but it was a job nonetheless, and it bought her some time. It would give her something to look forward to each day instead of thinking about Ethan and wondering who his *Soulmate* was. Not that she was doing that, of course.

She headed to lunch feeling more optimistic than she had since she'd arrived back home. Life might finally be getting back to normal.

Grace was sitting at a booth near the back. She wasn't alone.

Allie was with her.

And . . . that was a *good* thing, Lucy firmly told herself as she approached them. Lunch with her two best friends, just like old times. The perfect way to clear the air and move forward.

"When I told Allie my date with Lucy had been *interesting*, it was because Lucy had spent the whole time telling me that *you* were interested in me," Mike had explained to Grace at some point that day in Grace's office. "That's what *made* the date so *interesting*. I knew how tight the three of you were, so I figured Allie was in on Lucy's little matchmaking scheme."

Then Grace had apologized again, and she and Mike had started a new chapter in their relationship, and Lucy had stared at her lap to give them some privacy—and found herself missing Ethan.

"Hey! Look at you, Hollywood girl!" Allie bounded out of her seat and gave Lucy a squeeze. "I hope you don't mind that I'm here," she continued as they both sat down. "Gracie said you two were having lunch today when we talked this morning, and I invited myself along. I have felt positively *guilty* for not calling you before now, but Ben's turning into a mean old bear when it comes to all the wedding plans. You can imagine how it is." She took a sip from her water glass and smiled at Lucy.

Luckily the waitress brought their salads right then and saved Lucy from having to reply.

The conversation eventually shifted away from Allie's wedding and traveled down a few safe roads before turning to the subject of *Soulmates*. Grace's confession to Lucy regarding the interview and her reluctant description about how it had gone down had concerned Lucy. She would never get a better opening to hear Allie's side of things, so she plunged in.

"Allie," she began, "Grace told me the two of you did an on-camera interview for the show. Right here in the coffee shop, in fact." She really wanted Allie to come clean with her. It would say so much about the true state of their friendship.

Allie stabbed at a piece of lettuce with her fork. "Yes, we did," she said. "So what was it like?"

"I'm sure Grace already told you all about it." She glanced at Grace.

"She has," Lucy said. "I want to hear about it from you too."

Allie shrugged and popped a bite of salad into her mouth. Her nonchalance didn't hide her sudden tension.

"Come on, Allie," Grace urged. "You said you wanted to talk to Lucy."

Allie toyed with her fork before setting it on her plate. She didn't say anything.

Grace huffed in frustration. "I told her you made the producers think she was only looking for a casual fling with a millionaire and that she's only pretending to have values. And that she did stuff with Mike behind my back."

Allie glared at Grace before returning her undivided attention to her salad.

"Why, Allie?" Lucy tried unsuccessfully to make eye contact with Allie. "Grace wouldn't even talk to me when I got home. You hurt Grace, and you hurt Mike. And you hurt me too. I don't understand. Can you at least tell me why?"

Allie looked up at her then. "They said they were looking for something exciting about you, something they could use in the show. What was I supposed to tell them?"

"The truth, maybe? Would that have been so bad?"

"Your version of the truth is boring. Ethan Glass is a millionaire who's used to dating glamorous women. I figured if I spiced it up a little so you'd sound more exciting and not as straight-laced as you want everyone to think you are, you might end up having some real fun for once in your life."

That explanation didn't ring true to Lucy. How could an interview Allie gave to Ms. Carlton affect anything Lucy did on the show or suddenly change her from being "straight-laced" to having "real fun," as Allie called it? Allie had always had a crazy side—Lucy had loved her for it and loved her in spite of it sometimes—but it had been after the hometown visit, after Allie and Grace had done the interview, that Ms. Carlton's attitude toward Lucy had taken a distinct turn toward ugly. She wished she could see the interview for herself so she'd know exactly what Allie had said.

"Oh, Lucy!" Allie sprang from her chair and threw her arms around Lucy in a tight hug. "Don't be angry. I was only trying to help. It's just that I don't understand you. I only wanted you to have some fun."

Lucy looked at Grace over Allie's shoulder as she reluctantly returned the embrace. Grace looked right back at Lucy. She wasn't smiling. She was shaking her head.

They ended the embrace and wrapped up their lunch. They'd known each other since third grade, Lucy thought as she said good-bye and headed to Grace's dad's office, bag of cookies in hand. The three of them. Best friends all these years. Nearly inseparable. Yet Allie didn't understand her. Allie hadn't wanted her to sound as straight-laced and boring as Lucy "wanted everyone to think" she was.

Lucy, on the other hand, was afraid she understood Allie only too well.

She would always love Allie. Bubbly, mischievous Allie. Lucy knew they could move on, and maybe on some level they could even remain friends, but things would never be the same. And for that, Lucy grieved.

CHAPTER 20

"Morning." Lucy's mom glanced over her shoulder at her while she scrambled eggs.

"Morning." Lucy kissed her mother's cheek and poured herself a glass of orange juice. Brigham was busy channel surfing on the small television set in the corner of the room. "What's he up to?"

He waved a hand absentmindedly. "Hang on a minute. Almost there."

Her mother set plates of eggs in front of him and Lucy and then sat at the table herself. "Apparently Ethan Glass is doing a live interview this morning. Eat some eggs."

Lucy picked up her fork, took a bite, and pretended not to care.

Andy, wearing sweat pants and a wrinkled T-shirt, entered the room. He plopped down next to Lucy and scrubbed a hand over his face in an attempt to wake up. "Morning," he rasped to no one in particular.

"After the break," the network news anchor said, "we'll be talking to Ethan Glass, star of the new reality show *Soulmates*, one of the surprise hits of the summer. And later in the hour, we'll continue our series on unhealthy food trends in the public schools."

"Have you seen any of the stuff they're saying online, Luce?" Brigham asked her when a commercial for antacids began.

"What stuff?" She managed another bite.

"*Soulmates* stuff. About that one blonde girl, Sara. Did you know her very well? Did she say anything about the video she was in while you were there? It's all over the Internet."

"No." Now there was a commercial for heavy-duty trucks. "I don't know what you're talking about."

"Oh," Brigham said, looking disappointed. "I wanted to know if it was true. But I wasn't going to search online for it myself. Mom would have killed me if I did."

"I wouldn't have killed you. I merely would have sat you down, reminded you once again about the dangers associated with looking for questionable videos, and then taken away your computer privileges for roughly twenty years."

Brigham gave a speaking look to Lucy. "Same difference, if you ask me."

"Searched for what?" Lucy asked.

Andy let out a noisy yawn and reached for the glass of juice Linda set in front of him. "Thanks, Mom. Your *Soulmates* pal Sara showed up in one of those wild spring break videos. And don't give me that look, Mom. I haven't seen it. Some of the guys at work told me about it, since they know Lucy's on the show. They were giving me flak. Wanting to know if Lucy's got a video out too. That kind of crap."

Lucy's mom glared indignantly at Andy. "I hope you told them your sister doesn't do that kind of thing."

"Shh, everybody," Brigham said. "Ethan's up next."

Sara was in a spring break video on the Internet? Lucy was still trying to wrap her mind around that one when the news anchor's words broke into her concentration.

". . . is joining us via satellite from London. Thank you, Mr. Glass. You must be pleased with the success the show is having. What makes *Soulmates* different from the other so-called reality dating shows on the air?"

"With *Soulmates*, we were committed to putting an intelligent match-making formula into place. To that end, we brought in an expert who created a thorough screening process, combining various personality tests, IQ and aptitude tests, interests, etc. In this first season of *Soulmates*, I am Dr. Berta Lindstrom's guinea pig."

The anchor chuckled.

Ethan was in London? What was he doing in London? London seemed so far away.

"So, Mr. Glass—may I call you Ethan? I understand taping for the show is complete. Are you a happy guinea pig? Can you give our viewers any hints about what they can look forward to this season on *Soulmates*?"

Ethan smiled. Lucy knew that smile—it was his corporate smile. She absently handed her fork to Andy as he slid her plate of eggs in front of himself and attacked them.

"I'm not going to give away any secrets," Ethan said. "But I have confidence in the process we put in place. Enough confidence to suggest that not only will our viewers be happy with the outcome, but they might also be hoping for similar results themselves when we launch the *Soulmates* personals website during the finale."

"You heard it here first, folks. A *Soulmates* website."

Ethan had said the *viewers* would be happy with the outcome, not that he was. Lucy knew Ethan well enough now to suspect that it was a deliberate choice of words. He looked happy, and, of course, she wanted him to be. But it was difficult to tell when he was wearing his CEO mask, and it was typical Ethan to be smoothly noncommittal in his reply.

The only time she'd seen the mask slip when he'd had it in place was when they'd said good-bye after her elimination. Lucy stood. "I'd better go get ready for work, or I'll be late."

". . . it must be a challenge to find time to be together with you presently in London. How long will you be there?"

"A few more weeks. And it is *definitely* a challenge to be separated from the woman I want as my soulmate." He paused as though for effect. "And thereby hangs a tale."

And thereby hangs a tale. Shakespeare. Lucy was beginning to hate Shakespeare.

"He seemed different in that interview. A little intimidating. He was more easygoing when he was here at the house," Lucy's mother said as the anchor thanked Ethan. "I really liked him then. More than I thought I was going to, if you want to know the truth."

"I liked him," Andy interjected. "He's a stand-up guy. Craig liked the way he dug in during our game of pickup but was okay with Noah being a part of the action."

The news anchor mentioned the next episode of *Soulmates* would air that evening. And Lucy found herself staring blankly at a yogurt commercial.

"Oh well, enough of all of this for now," her mother said, patting Lucy's shoulders. "You'd better go get ready."

"Yeah," Andy said, "instead of moping around the house all the time."

Lucy was indignant. "I haven't been moping." She looked pointedly at everyone in the kitchen. "I've been busy since I got back, cleaning my room, organizing the kitchen, looking for jobs. I haven't been moping."

"You're right, dear," her mother said, giving her shoulders a squeeze. "Bad choice of words on Andy's part. Wasn't it, Andrew?"

"And those were my eggs you ate!" Lucy added as she stood up from the table. She winced. As far as parting shots went, it was pretty lame, especially since she'd personally handed him her fork. But still.

"Sorry, Luce." He held up the empty plate, grinning and undermining his attempt to look sheepish. "Do you want them back?"

She growled at him and stalked from the room.

She wasn't moping. She must be doing something wrong if they thought she was. Because she wasn't. She was over Ethan. He'd chosen his *Soulmate* and was quoting Shakespeare in some sort of secret code to whichever one it was from London over the morning news. He'd moved on, and so had she.

Okay, so she hadn't. But she would. Somehow.

* * *

Kyle hurried into the living room of the cottage at the ranch he shared with his mom when he was home from school and turned on the television. Episode six of *Soulmates* was about to begin, the episode in which Ethan had sent Lucy home. Kyle had a real soft spot for Lucy. She'd been a friend right from the start. Kyle wanted to see for himself what he'd missed when he'd been helping behind the scenes. He'd known that Ethan had had strong feelings for her, and Ethan might have realized it too—if he'd only stopped thinking so hard about every little thing.

So far the show had been playing up Lucy's religious side big time—not in a bad way, but still obvious. It had included footage, comments from the other women, anything that made her sound like the ultimate good girl. The tactic had niggled at him at first, and then he'd shrugged it off. They'd been pushing several of the women into stereotypes, not just Lucy.

In last week's episode, Ethan had met the women's families; he'd gone seashell hunting in Florida with Sara, picnicking *Gone with the Wind* style with Denise in Georgia, and Chicago dog taste-testing with Tiffany along the shores of Lake Michigan in Chicago. Tiffany had ratcheted her siren act way up during the Chicago segment—and Kyle had been watching with his mom at the time. Seriously awkward.

"That girl's going to be a millionaire by the time she's thirty, just like Ethan was," Terri had said, right after Tiffany had managed to corner Ethan on a balcony. "Only she's going to do it by marrying and divorcing rich men. It won't be Ethan though."

Kyle had, for the first time in his life, been thankful for commercial breaks.

Next, they'd watched Ethan and Lucy explore an Arizona ghost town on horseback. Ethan had looked happier and more relaxed than Kyle had seen him in a long time. It had made knowing that he'd sent Lucy home even more of a puzzle.

He remembered he'd gone to the kitchen last week for a snack, since he'd known how the episode would end and that Alison and Sara would be the ones leaving. By the time he'd returned, he'd even missed the elimination ceremony. So he'd been caught totally by surprise when the little niggling feeling had struck him again. the teaser for this week's episode.

A brunette he hadn't recognized had come on and claimed, "Lucy's ambitious dating-wise. She's going after Ethan just because." A blonde had added, "She does things she wants to keep secret. Spotless Lucy might not be as pure as she wants everybody to think." Then Rick's voice-over had said, "Next week on *Soulmates*."

Teasers created a hook to bring in viewers and were often intended to be misleading. That's why they were called teasers in the first place. But after the way the show had been pushing Lucy's snow white rep the last couple of weeks, he'd gotten a bad feeling from this particular teaser.

His thoughts returned to the present. He was watching tonight's episode to prove to himself that he'd been worrying about nothing.

But less than an hour later, the bad feeling from last week returned with a vengeance. Kyle sat forward and stared in shock at the TV set. He couldn't believe what he was watching.

He yanked his phone out of his pocket.

* * *

The bad news—if it could be called that, Ethan thought as he loosened his tie after returning to his hotel suite—was that he'd had to stay in London longer than he'd planned. His business here had required some intense negotiations before everyone, himself included, had been satisfied.

Of course, anything that required additional time in London couldn't really be considered bad news.

The good news, if it could be called that, was that negotiations were now completed, he was going to make a ton of money, and he would be on his way home in a day or two. He'd be free to finally spend time with his *Soulmate*.

Except he already had a ton of money, and his *Soulmate* felt like a consolation prize.

He sat on the edge of the bed and kicked off his shoes. He'd chosen Denise. They'd spoken on the phone a few times while he'd been in

London, and he'd promised to arrange his flight home so he could stop in Atlanta to see her.

Denise was a beautiful woman, and once he'd gotten used to her over-the-top sweetness, he'd found he genuinely admired and cared about her. Their last evening together in LA they'd walked on the beach, and she'd clung to his arm and talked wistfully of the future. Their future.

He'd broken into a sweat, which didn't happen to him very often. And then the comments his father had made on the way to the airport had further unsettled him. *You're making a mistake*, he'd said. *Make sure it's what you really want.*

His father had been right on the money.

Because what he'd wanted was Lucy.

Not true. What he'd wanted was Lucy on *his* terms, but he'd also realized he couldn't have her on his terms or even negotiate terms because hers were nonnegotiable. So he'd told her that last day—at high volume—that he'd needed more time than the show would allow—and he'd let her go.

He'd had to make a decision and move on, like he'd done in more business deals than he could count over the years, like he'd done with the other contestants.

It had been convenient for him to blame his decision on the show. Easier on his ego because Ethan didn't think of himself as a coward. He'd faced angry steers and foaling mares, corporate bigwigs and sharks. Politicians. He'd been on a reality *dating* show, for Pete's sake, and he knew, as few men did, what kind of courage *that* took.

But if he was totally honest with himself, he'd been afraid after that night in Victoria. He'd been overwhelmed and afraid—because the thought he'd kept having was, *what if she's right? What if it's true?*

He hadn't wanted to find out. Because if he did, there might be no turning back. He hadn't been willing to take that kind of life-altering step.

So in the end, he'd chosen Denise, they'd taped the big moment, the show had wrapped up, and she'd told him how happy she was and asked him if he liked children and if she should relocate to be near him. He'd smiled—he thought he'd smiled—and had told her that, yes, he liked children and that he was happy too, and then he'd willed himself to believe it. He'd told her they had time to iron out the other details.

Time. It always seemed to come back to that.

And then Old Jed had used up an entire decade's worth of words telling him what he'd been unwilling to face. It had been the wake-up call he'd needed.

He unbuttoned and removed his shirt and peeled off his socks, tossing them in the general direction of his laundry bag. He'd reread the Church pamphlets on the plane. He'd started the Book of Mormon in New York and finished it by the time he'd arrived at Heathrow. Then he'd looked up the telephone number for the local branch of the Church. The person on the other end of the phone had promised to have someone call him right back.

An Elder Shaw had called him within minutes.

His two free evenings each week had been spent with Elders Shaw and McIntyre and had eventually expanded to include most of his free time on Sunday, attending church and spending time in discussion afterward.

He'd now experienced firsthand Kyle's warning that Lucy's church meetings lasted for three hours. He'd experienced it several times, in fact. It was a lot of time to give up every Sunday. It had been part of the apprehension he'd had realizing there might be no turning back. No turning back would mean a lot of time and commitment and sacrifice.

If it were true.

He walked into the bathroom and went through the motions of preparing for bed. He brushed his teeth and splashed cold water on his face and stared at himself in the mirror. Tonight Elder Shaw had challenged him, committed him, to pray about what he'd been learning. He'd known Ethan would be returning home soon.

Lucy had urged him to pray. Kyle had too, in his own way. The missionaries had been urging him to pray since their first meeting. In the last few weeks, he'd read more scriptures than he'd known existed on the subject. When Lucy had prayed on her pioneer trek, angels had come to help her. At least that was the impression he'd gotten. Were angels watching over him? Willing to help him if he asked? Did they even exist? He'd told Brianna angels kissed her good night, but he hadn't really meant it. It was like talking to her about the tooth fairy. Wasn't it?

He returned to sit on the edge of the bed and stared at his hands.

He didn't know how to pray.

He knew the Lord's Prayer and maybe a few others he could recite if pressed. But he suspected that wasn't what Lucy or Kyle—or Elder Shaw—had meant. Joseph Smith had said he'd offered up the desires of his heart. A man in the Book of Mormon named Enos had prayed all day long and into the night. He'd cried out so that his voice reached the heavens, though Ethan didn't feel comfortable doing that, especially in a five-star hotel. When Elder Shaw and Elder McIntyre had prayed with him, their words had been personal and pertinent to what they had talked about that evening.

Before they'd left, Elder Shaw had said, "Don't overthink it, Ethan. Just get on your knees and lay it all out."

All by himself, alone in his room, it still felt embarrassing to be talking to someone who wasn't there physically, even in a whisper. It was hard enough talking to Old Jed when he was standing right next to him, let alone God, who was somewhere in the unknown. But he'd promised Elder Shaw and Elder McIntyre he would do this.

He slid to his knees and rested his forearms on the bed. The room was quiet except for the low hum of the electric lights and traffic sounds in the distance. His sense of awareness was heightened; he found himself analyzing the bedspread in a detached way—the mix of colors, the details in the weave. He idly ran his finger along a line in the pattern and tried to collect his thoughts.

He could do this.

He dropped his head into his hands.

He'd faced bulls and battled corporate adversaries. And in the end, he'd never hesitated. He'd acted with confidence. But that was because he could see them and assess them and strategize. He took risks, but they were calculated risks. That was the difference.

What was he even supposed to say? He'd never "laid it all out" in his life. It wasn't how he'd developed his business; it wasn't how the men in the Glass family did things. But he'd given his word. He had to do it if he had any hope of moving forward with his life, now that he'd arrived at this crossroads. He had to do this if he ever wanted to be able to face himself in the mirror again.

So be it. He began, using the most familiar words he knew.

"Our Father which art in heaven, hallowed be Thy name." His voice sounded unnaturally loud, but he continued. It was definitely awkward at first, his words stilted, but gradually he became less self-aware, and his thoughts came more naturally.

He talked about what he'd learned about God growing up, the life decisions he'd made that had brought him to this point. He talked about his parents and how he wanted the same love and commitment in marriage that they had found with each other. He talked about his search for this so-called soulmate, the logical process he'd followed on the show, how hard he'd tried to make the best decisions. He talked about how struck he'd been by Lucy early on, how he'd thought she seemed different from the other women in some subtle way, how he'd wanted to know what that difference was and why. He went point by point through the information she'd given him, outlining what he'd read, summarizing what the elders had taught him, asking for clarification, posing his doubts.

By the time he'd finished, he thought he'd been pretty thorough. He wasn't sure how long he'd been on his knees. What was supposed to happen next? After an effort like his, he expected something to happen. In fact, the missionaries had assured him it would.

He glanced around the room and brought himself back to the here and now. He hoisted himself off the floor, sat on the bed, and waited.

Nothing.

Okay, that wasn't entirely true, he conceded. He felt pretty good. He'd given it his best effort, and he'd kept his word to Elder Shaw. It was unexpectedly helpful to verbalize all of those thoughts; he'd gotten clarity in a few areas, had little "aha" moments. Like the moment of glimmering insight that Lucy *was* different, even though he still wasn't exactly sure why. Like the sudden sense of just how deeply his parents loved each other.

But he had to admit that he'd hoped for more than a few little insights and a general sense of well-being.

Had he expected angels? Trumpets? Proclamations?

Had he really expected anything?

A glance at the clock told him he'd been at this business longer than he'd thought and he'd be lucky if he got more than a few hours of shut-eye. He crawled between the sheets and was asleep as soon as his head hit the pillow.

* * *

An annoyingly loud phone was ringing nearby. Ethan wished someone would answer it because he was trying to call Lucy on a bracelet charm shaped like a cell phone, and she hadn't picked up yet.

But the ringing didn't stop, and finally Ethan jerked awake and squinted in the direction of the sound. The light on his cell phone—the real one, not the charm bracelet one in his dream—was flashing. He fumbled for it, feeling an odd flash of disappointment that it wasn't a little silver charm.

"Glass," he mumbled. He threw his free arm across his eyes and settled his head more comfortably back into the pillow.

"Ethan, it's Kyle. Have you been—"

"Kyle." He yawned, nearly back to sleep. "You do realize it's"—he held the phone away from his ear and looked at the screen—"four in the morning here?"

"You didn't watch the show tonight, did you, man? I *knew* they were up to something. We need to do something!"

This wasn't normal, laid-back Kyle speaking, and Ethan dragged himself into a semisitting position, more alert now. "Slow down, okay? Who's up to something, and what something do we need to do?" It came out sounding funny, but he was too tired to figure out why.

"They deliberately threw her under the bus!" Kyle ranted. "I should have paid more attention. I should have done something to stop them."

Ethan's nerve endings weren't awake enough to handle Kyle's decibel level, he was irritated at being pulled from his dream, and he was annoyed that it was all happening at four in the morning. "Stopped who from what bus?" he growled.

"No bus! Lucy! Carlton and Esplin and Curt. You need to watch tonight's show. Watch it. And then call me. We have to act fast. The mess is already spreading like crazy." And he was gone.

Ethan switched on the lamp, wide awake and alert now. Any peace he'd felt after that prayer of his was gone, replaced by a cold sense of unease.

He threw off the covers and walked to the desk where his laptop sat. He'd deliberately avoided watching *Soulmates*, so he wasn't sure what was in the most recent episode. But something significant had to have happened to prompt this kind of reaction from Kyle.

He sat down to watch episode six of *Soulmates*, fast-forwarding through the scenes in Seattle with Tiffany and in Vancouver with Denise. Tiffany had made it to his third spot only because he'd known she'd land on both feet when this process was over. He'd been that confident in his decision to choose Lucy, even back then.

Denise would land on her feet too, he told himself now. He knew he was going to hurt her soon. But it wasn't fair to her to let things continue, not when he didn't see a future with her despite his best intentions. He'd thought he could maintain the relationship long enough for Curt to get his *Soulmates* ending, but that wasn't going to happen.

He focused back on the show as he found the spot he was looking for. Right before the segment in Victoria with Lucy was a scene with two unfamiliar women. He recognized the location as the coffee shop in the resort outside of Eagle Bluff, since that's where he'd stayed during his visit. Apparently, the two women were Lucy's best friends, but he would never have known it by what they were saying. The one named Allie described Lucy in such a way that anyone listening would think the worst of her.

Even Ethan found himself doubting Lucy as he listened.

That scene segued to their date in Victoria, now colored by what her friends had said about her. Every comment, every emotion from her seemed suspect. Doubts he'd never had about her snaked through his mind. He felt betrayed, foolish though that was. He'd been the one to send her home; he'd chosen Denise as his *Soulmate*. But it hurt to think she might have been less than honest with him.

It couldn't be true.

He paused the video and got a drink of water, got his emotions in check. If he, Ethan, who was in love with Lucy—yes, *love* was the word for it, he realized now—had doubted her character so quickly, what would people watching the episode think? People tended to believe the worst about others, and this episode had been crafted to get them to do just that.

He watched a flustered Lucy in their—*her*—hotel suite saying, "I can't go on national television with it appearing that we're sharing the same hotel room. How will I be able to explain that everything was totally innocent when it doesn't look that way?"

Wait a second.

He shouldn't be watching that scene at all. He had personally ordered the camera to stop recording at the time.

He watched himself relax on the sofa in the same suite later that same evening, his arm around her, the fireplace crackling in front of them. He watched himself kiss the top of her head and then turn her in his arms so he could kiss her like he'd really wanted to. Seeing it again, he could almost feel the warmth of the fireplace and the rightness of that moment. He frowned and rubbed a hand over his chest. He could definitely feel the warmth.

But again, there shouldn't have been any cameras present; that had been a clearly understood point between Curt and himself from the beginning. Yet here he was, watching his private time with Lucy, footage that shouldn't exist at all.

Then *Soulmates* history took a deliberate turn toward fiction.

After more on-screen kissing, the Ethan in the video stood and picked up a relaxed and pliant Lucy from the sofa. There was no indication that he'd spent hours reading in between and that she'd fallen asleep sitting next to him. Instead, the music track swelled to a romantic crescendo as he walked down the hall to the bedroom with her in his arms, kissed her again, and pulled back the comforter on the bed before laying her there.

He remembered distinctly what had occurred at the time: he had kissed her gently before leaving her to sleep while he resumed his reading in the other room. He remembered how she'd opened her eyes sleepily, smiled at him, and murmured something about love and forever. He still wondered what she'd been trying to say.

But unlike his memories, the scene in the video faded to black with him still in her room leaning over her, kissing her . . . leaving the definite impression that he had remained there with her. It was the exact image she'd been trying all along to avoid. He'd prided himself for being understanding and even noble toward her concerns, though he'd thought them unwarranted and a little naïve. He regretted those thoughts now.

He snapped his laptop shut and arranged for a car to take him to Heathrow. It may be four in the morning, he thought as he tossed his clothes into his suitcase, but he wouldn't be getting any more sleep tonight.

Twenty minutes later, after a quick shower and shave, he was in the back of a town car on his way to the airport. He pulled out his cell phone.

* * *

Lucy parked her car in the driveway at home and grabbed her gym bag. Working at the resort was a blessing in so many ways. It kept her mind occupied, it gave her a decent paycheck—and it gave her someplace to be when *Soulmates* aired. After work she'd hit the resort spa, sharing it with only a couple of the registered guests, until it was safe to go home.

Grace's father had offered her a permanent position, and she'd told him she'd let him know. She'd gotten a few positive replies from her online job search and was waiting to see what happened with them before giving him her answer. He'd told her he was in no hurry. Again, a blessing.

As she reached the porch, the door opened, and she was met by a grim-faced Andy. Definitely not the norm.

"Are you okay?" Lucy asked him.

"Not really," he replied, reaching for her gym bag. "Come into the family room."

"What's wrong?" she asked, suddenly panicked, trying to read his expression. "What happened? Was there an accident?"

"I'm thinking this was no accident," he said, leading the way. "And we've got a problem on our hands."

Her insides knotted. What had happened?

Her parents, Brigham, Craig, and Becky were there. The whole tribe was in attendance. Her mother looked strained, and Lucy thought her father's jaw might shatter if he clenched it any tighter. Brigham slid over on the sofa to make room for her and patted the cushion.

She sat.

"You need to watch this, honey," her father said. "And then we're going to have a family meeting." Her mother reached for her hand and squeezed it. Brigham pushed the button on the remote.

* * *

Melanie couldn't stop smiling. She took a swig from her water bottle and replayed the end of episode six, allowing it to keep her company while she crunched the latest numbers on the spreadsheet in front of her, her little pet project. Even before the premiere of *Soulmates* had aired, she'd kept track of the online interest in the show, from the minute the first promos had run, in fact.

The results weren't exactly scientific, but it was still satisfying to track the show's success this way. She'd identified which online celebrity rags had reporters and bloggers covering the show each week. She'd continually found herself adding to the list, and the number of sites had grown steadily. She'd also kept track of the comment boards. Curt would get viewer numbers from his network sources. She wanted to compare them with the online buzz about the show.

People commented on their favorites, but they commented even more on the women they hated and any controversy that arose. Sara and her little video had already been a goldmine of publicity. It proved once again that even bad publicity was good publicity.

She added another column of figures. *Soulmates* was going to make Curt filthy rich, and it was largely due to her. She planned to hit him up for a big salary increase.

She'd already watched this latest episode twice, and it had aired only this evening. There was something so . . . *gratifying* was the word . . . about seeing Lucy Kendrick knocked from her lily-white pedestal. She'd developed a steady following among the viewers with her kissing booth and pig-chasing antics. Dane and *Soulmates'* video editors had done such a good job punching up her good girl image that when the teaser with her friends had aired last week the comment boards had gone crazy. This week's spreadsheet numbers were the best ever.

They were going to top last week's numbers and then some. There wasn't anything in the remaining episodes—even the one in which Ethan chooses his *Soulmate*—that would be able to compete with the numbers they'd be seeing from tonight's "Episode Six: The Fall of Goody Two-Shoes," but it wouldn't matter. By now, enough people were hooked on the show that they'd stick to the end—and follow them into *Soulmates* season two.

It was a double victory for Melanie—her own professional success was assured, and Lucy was getting her comeuppance. Life just couldn't get any better than this.

Dane had managed to give Ethan and Lucy's final date the crowning touch—the perfect ending to Lucy's good-girl buildup. Melanie laughed again as she watched a worried Lucy explain that she couldn't share a suite—a suite of *rooms, plural,* for crying out loud—with Ethan. Not on national TV. No, siree. Gosh, Mrs. Brady, what would people think? But then, after some pretty convincing lip-locking, what had happened? Ethan had carried her down the hall and, well, what do you know? Fade to black.

The little hypocrite had it coming.

Melanie watched an angry Ethan lead a stunned Lucy to the limo of shame. It was an amazing moment, actually, since the guy had a repertoire of two when it came to showing emotion: cool charmer and corporate cyborg.

Now Lucy was in the limo crying. Melanie had been sitting across from her at the time. She was supposed to have interviewed her, and she'd tried to pose questions during the ride. But Lucy hadn't said a word to her. Watching her now, Melanie almost would have felt sorry for her if she hadn't learned what she was really like from her friends.

Her cell phone rang, and the ID said it was Curt. She'd only seen him a couple of times during postproduction. Her stomach did a flip. Why was he calling at this time of night? How could that guy have such an instant effect on her? It was so annoying. She shifted into producer mode. She would share the viewer numbers, play it cool. His show was a success, he was making a boatload of money, and Melanie was a big part of the reason.

She took a deep breath to settle her nerves and answered the call.

* * *

Allie: "Lucy said she was looking for adventure, and I thought, what better adventure than a romance with Ethan Glass, the most gorgeous millionaire in America, even if it doesn't last."

Grace: "Lucy's ambitious dating-wise. She's going after Ethan just because. She wasn't interested in him, she said. She wanted something that would get her out of Eagle Bluff."

Allie: "She does things a good little Mormon girl isn't supposed to do and wants to keep secret. Spotless Lucy might not be as pure as she wants everybody to think."

Lucy replayed the clip again. She'd watched it so many times she'd lost count. She'd had to watch it several times just to get over the shock she'd felt hearing Allie and Grace say those things about her.

The home phone hadn't stopped ringing. Reps from magazines and entertainment shows wanted her to comment. Even the local news affiliate wanted to do a spot. Well-meaning neighbors and ward members kept dropping by, but Lucy hadn't been in a mood to talk.

"Lucy?"

Lucy looked away from the television. Grace stood in the doorway. "I'm so sorry." She glanced over at the TV and winced.

"Me too," Lucy replied in a flat voice.

"Allie feels awful."

Lucy sighed. "I'm not sure if that should make me feel better or worse." She muted the TV.

Grace perched on the edge of the sofa. "Neither one. But I thought you should know that Allie does feel bad, for what it's worth." She turned her head to stare at the screen, where Ethan and Lucy silently galloped across the foothills of Eagle Bluff. "It's such a mess."

On-screen, Ethan reined in his horse, a look of pure joy on his face. Lucy couldn't watch it and turned the TV off. "Yes, it is."

"You need to know that as bad as the interview we gave was, *they* made it sound a whole lot worse. They chopped it all up and put it back together the way they wanted."

Lucy looked over at Grace. "What do you mean?"

"Like that part about you not being interested in Ethan? I wasn't even talking about Ethan when I said that. I was telling Allie that that's what you'd said to me about you and Mike. And that red-haired lady asked me if I thought Ethan was your type, and I told her maybe, that you were ambitious and worked hard at things, so you two might have that in common. She got all hung up on the word *ambitious*, and I said you *weren't* ambitious dating-wise. They cut out that part so it sounded like I said you were. I swear it was like that, Lucy. Allie said some stupid things that day, and you and I both know what she's like at times. I mean, it was her idea to fill out the *Soulmates'* application for you in the first place. But they made her sound even worse than normal."

Lucy could almost chuckle at that description of Allie. Lucy knew how true it was. If only it didn't all hurt so badly, this whole situation would be laughable.

"What are you going to do?" Grace asked.

"I don't know," Lucy replied. She thought of the scenes she'd just watched of herself with Ethan in the hotel suite, scenes she'd been surprised to learn existed. Using hidden cameras in her private hotel suite seemed like a cheap shot, even for a reality show. Funny how they'd failed to include anything that showed Ethan reading the Book of Mormon in any of it.

"Dad said to tell you not to worry about going into work tomorrow. He said to take a couple of days if you need to."

"Tell him thanks. I could probably use tomorrow to get a grip on all of this." She glanced into the kitchen. Her father was still on the phone with someone, and her mother was sitting at the table talking to a couple of neighbors. "But I'll be there the day after."

"Just keep it in mind."

"I will. Thanks again. Be sure to tell him."

Grace stood to leave, but she hesitated when she got to the door. "Lucy? What should I tell Allie?"

Lucy wished she had the words for a great line, a zinger that would put Allie in her place, something that would let her know exactly how betrayed she felt, that would hurt her like Lucy herself had been hurt. At the same time, she wished she were a bigger person than that and had the words to show Allie she could graciously forgive her. No hard feelings. But she was going to need more time before she could honestly and freely do that.

Why did everything about this *Soulmates* business always come back to the issue of time?

"Tell her whatever you think you need to, Grace. I'm not sure I know how I feel about things right now."

Grace nodded and turned away.

"Grace?"

She paused. "Yes?"

"Tell her I hope her wedding is wonderful. And that I'll miss being there."

"Oh, Lucy," Grace whispered.

Lucy fought against the tears that suddenly threatened to escape. They'd talked about their weddings, planned and dreamed about them together since they were girls. "Just tell her."

* * *

Ethan stood next to his office window and stared out at a hot and hazy downtown Los Angeles. He was sleep deprived, his head pounded, and he was in a foul mood.

He and a contrite Curt had spent the morning watching raw footage from the show.

Ethan understood the purpose of editing. When one had literally hours of tape to whittle down into one episode, it only made sense to choose moments that created the best drama and held viewer interest. But that wasn't what had occurred here. Production had deliberately and secretively gone about collecting and using footage to portray Lucy in a negative light.

He'd been adamant that hidden cameras were off limits. The fact that they'd been used was a huge breach of privacy and professional trust. On the other hand, it was ironically impressive that they'd been able to wade through hours of footage, string a few key moments together, and create something so believable—and so *opposite* of what had actually occurred that night in Canada. It took talent, but it also took premeditation and resolve to put together what had been portrayed in that scene. Otherwise, why go to all the time and effort? Why watch several hours of Ethan reading religious material to find something that could be used to suggest that more than reading had occurred that night?

He and Curt had also watched the complete interview with Lucy's friends. No one else's friends had been interviewed for the show. It had been a complete departure from the norm, obviously targeting Lucy.

He'd actually expected to find most of the misleading editing from the production team. But the blonde in the interview had attacked Lucy from both directions. Lucy was a prude; Lucy was a player. She hadn't wanted to be on the show; she'd used the show to make a break from her home town. She was virtuous to a fault; she wasn't as innocent as she wanted everyone to believe. She'd even deceived the brunette, who'd actually made an effort to speak well of Lucy until that bombshell had been dropped.

It wasn't anything like the Lucy he'd gotten to know. How could she be all of those things at the same time? Despite appearances, something didn't feel right.

So why would her friends say those things?

He didn't want to believe any of it, yet he couldn't help wondering whether he'd been duped by her somehow, which was ludicrous since, again, he'd been the one to end things and send her home.

But he also hadn't been able to forget her, despite trying to move forward. He'd met with *missionaries* for the last several weeks, and that was her doing as well. He'd been on the verge of calling Curt to figure out a way of putting things on hold, at least delay airing the final episode until he could sort things out better. And then this had happened.

He wanted answers. He needed answers. Fast.

Curt entered his office, shutting the door quietly behind him and remaining where he stood. "Everyone's here, Ethan. They're all in the conference room."

Ethan nodded. "Then let's do this."

"Eth," Curt laid a hand on his arm. "Honestly, I didn't know about the hidden camera, not at first. It doesn't say good things about me as executive producer, I know, and I'm sorry about that. They brought it to me later but not until we were in postproduction. By then you'd eliminated Lucy, and it was clear we could use it to draw viewers. And I have to say, the numbers support that decision. It's our best week yet by a long shot. The show's an honest to goodness success, man. We did it."

Honest and *goodness* weren't the words Ethan would pick to describe the show at the moment. He fought the urge to grab Curt by the necktie and throttle him.

"Curt," he said in a controlled voice, "I did not agree to be the pawn in some network *fiction*, manipulated to get ratings."

Curt tugged at his tie. Maybe he'd sensed what had been on Ethan's mind. "I know that."

"Do you need me to describe how it feels to discover that a camera has been *secretly* recording what is supposed to be my private time with a woman?"

"I get it, Eth. And I'm sorry."

"You're the executive producer, Curt. What your crew did was a violation of my trust and an affront to Lucy, and for that I should have your head on a platter. Lucy is the most moral person I know, and we're going to do whatever it takes to make things right."

And with those words, he suddenly realized he did know that about her. He did trust Lucy, and any doubts he'd had evaporated. "Let's go."

They headed down to the conference room, where Dane Esplin, Melanie Carlton, and Dr. Lindstrom were waiting. Ethan took his place at the head of the table. Curt slid into a chair next to Melanie.

"As you know," Ethan began, "I've been in London for the past several weeks." He'd downloaded every episode of the show and watched them all during his flight home. "But I understand that the show is a success. In fact, for a new summer show, the viewership is higher than our most optimistic projections. Amazing. How did you accomplish it?"

Esplin spoke up. "By hooking and keeping the audience. They cheer their favorites on and boo the ones they hate. But they watch because we have them hooked."

Ethan acknowledged his answer with a nod. "I noticed that info gathered from the ladies' applications was occasionally used to accomplish this."

"The women signed full disclosure agreements along with their applications," Ms. Carlton responded. "We worked with Dr. Lindstrom to gather information we could use to develop story lines for each episode."

"I did *not* allow access to my records," Dr. Lindstrom clarified. "They were only meant to be used to evaluate each contestant's compatibility with you, Mr. Glass. Ms. Carlton, Mr. Esplin, and I only discussed generalities about the women."

"Thank you, Berta," Ethan said. "Ms. Carlton, did one of those 'generalities' include Sara's Internet video that was conveniently discovered at the time the first episode aired?"

"No, Mr. Glass. I did additional research on each contestant to supplement what I'd learned from Dr. Lindstrom. We didn't post the video, but we were able to generate additional interest in the show by leaking it to the media. Online activity about the show went up a third immediately after."

"It was a collective decision, Eth," Curt said. "Esplin, Mel, and I discussed it and decided information in the public domain was fair game. If we hadn't pointed it out, somebody else eventually would have. By beating them to the punch, we were able to control that publicity and use it to the best advantage."

"I see," Ethan said.

"Look," Melanie added. "If it makes you feel any better, we learned that Tiffany had been in rehab, but we opted not to use it."

"Why?"

Esplin answered. "We weren't sure how it would play with people. It could have been 'Former addict overcomes life's challenges and finds true love on reality show.' Or it could have turned into 'Millionaire goes through elaborate matchmaking process only to end up with addict,' especially since she's been in rehab twice. It wasn't worth the risk, so we left it alone."

"There was also info on some of the others we decided wasn't in the show's best interest to use," Ms. Carlton added.

"'We' being?"

"Dane and myself. Sometimes Curt, although he delegated most of the day-to-day details to me."

Curt threw his hands in the air defensively when Ethan glanced his way. "I had my hands full schmoozing the network execs. The time slot they were threatening to give us would have been the kiss of death."

"Moving on," Ethan said, turning to Esplin. "Under what circumstances would you consider it justifiable to recreate history? Take an actual event and turn it into the complete opposite of the truth? Fiction. I watched this week's episode and saw a lot of fiction involving Lucy Kendrick and me . . . using hidden-camera footage, something that was agreed wouldn't happen. Care to comment?"

Dane Esplin hissed out a breath. "Sure, I'll comment. Lucy Kendrick was about as exciting as a car ride through Kansas, romance-wise. No one was the least bit surprised when you sent her home—or was that back to the convent? We had to do something. And I was given to understand that hidden cameras are allowed under the contestants' contracts." He gave Ethan a smarmy smile. Melanie, however, shifted in her seat and ignored everybody.

Ethan thought if he clenched his teeth any harder his skull would explode. He wanted to hoist Dane Esplin by his scruffy neck and hurl him through the window. Instead, he walked over to the window, looked out, and counted to one hundred. And counted to one hundred again. Allowed the people behind him to stew in the silence. When he'd cooled down enough to assure himself that Esplin would only land in the reception area of the offices across the street instead of the Santa Monica Pier, he returned to his desk, the CEO firmly back in place.

"Unfortunately," he said, "we now have two big problems we need to address."

"What big problems?" Curt frowned. "You're over the business with the hidden camera, right?"

Ethan shook his head. "I've decided I don't want Denise as my final choice. I want to reshoot the ending."

Three jaws dropped simultaneously. "Reshoot it how exactly?" Curt asked. "With Tiffany? No way. I've known you too long to believe you'd choose Tiffany." Curt's voice escalated with rising anxiety. "You're not planning to end the season by choosing *no one*? It will kill the entire premise of the show, not to mention the website! How are we supposed to end a reality dating show based on scientific compatibility screenings with you choosing no one?" He threw up his hands. "What are you thinking, man?"

"I want to go back to Lucy and persuade her to be my *Soulmate*. And until this episode aired, I was fairly confident I could persuade her. Unfortunately, a couple of you decided to implement a little character assassination. Now I have my work cut out for me. And that means you all do too."

He stood and leaned across his desk, his palms flat. "You have the remainder of this afternoon to put together a plan for the last two episodes, including the necessary steps to rescue Lucy's reputation." As the others stood to leave, he added, "Plan on a long night, folks. I'm still on London time, and as far as I'm concerned, that means your day just started."

CHAPTER 21

LUCY'S MOTHER PEEKED THROUGH THE kitchen curtains. "A van with a satellite dish is parked outside, and some people with cameras are standing across the street. The cameras have that long thing attached—"

"Telephoto lens," Lucy said in between bites of the yogurt she was forcing herself to eat.

"Telephoto lenses now. Honestly." She turned and looked at Lucy. "You need more than a yogurt. I'll make French toast."

"No thanks, Mom."

"Lucy," she warned in her stern mother voice.

"I can't. Dad will be down any minute to take me to work."

Her mother gave her a maternal stare before turning back to the window. "You'd think they'd have something better to do than camp in our front yard at seven in the morning. Like report on real news somewhere."

Lucy would have thought so too, even as recently as a week ago. But a week ago she hadn't been the topic of conversation on morning talk shows or the target of jokes on late night.

Her father, dressed in ancient jeans and an old shirt, walked into the kitchen and gave his wife and Lucy each a quick kiss. "You ready to hit the road? Andy," he hollered up the stairs as he pulled on a ball cap, "let's move it."

Lucy tossed the half-eaten carton of yogurt in the trash and grabbed her purse. Only a few days ago she'd watched, mortified, as her private evening with Ethan had played out on TV in a completely untruthful way. That had been bad enough. Then the phone had started ringing off the hook.

Early on the following day, Lucy had called the show's producers. The women had been warned to expect a few calls from the media when the show aired. But she hadn't expected to see her final evening with

Ethan turned into a lie on national TV, and she wanted to know what was going on before facing any reporters.

No one from *Soulmates* had returned her call.

"People are really worked up about the show," Andy had said, surfing the Internet that same afternoon. "There's a ton of stuff here. Check out this headline: '*Soulmates*' Lucy: Did She Have Us All Fooled?' Wait a sec—" He'd read silently for a minute then switched off the computer and glanced at Lucy. His face was flushed with embarrassment and anger. "I'm sorry, Luce," he'd said, giving her a quick hug. "Of all people, this shouldn't have happened to you." Then he'd stalked out of the room.

Lucy had immediately called the producers again. The receptionist had assured her that she'd passed along her message.

Andy's reaction had prompted Lucy to go online to see things for herself.

People hadn't held back on their opinions. It had hurt to read them. She'd seen people use scandal to make themselves into celebrities. She'd also seen celebrities make fortunes and then complain when caught in a scandal. *It wasn't their job to be a role model. They'd never asked to be a role model.*

The irony hadn't been lost on Lucy.

She'd fallen in love with Ethan and still thought about him too much. But she was tired of living with the pain and the what-ifs. So she'd immersed herself in the commentary, the speculations, the judgments. And she'd successfully replaced the hurt feelings with a different emotion.

She was angry.

And boy, did it feel good.

The anger kept her going, head held high, and she used it as her dad drove his truck past satellite vans and waving reporters and as she walked into the resort this morning. She could do this day if she stayed angry.

She nurtured her anger all day long at the resort, using it to build a fortress around herself.

At the end of the work day, her cell phone rang.

"Lucy! Melanie Carlton here."

"Ms. Carlton." *Cue the icy anger*, Lucy thought as she mustered her courage to face this call.

"So formal!" Lucy heard a soft chuckle. "I understand you've been calling. What a coincidence. We've been trying to reach you too."

Lucy didn't believe it for a minute.

"Listen, Lucy, it looks like there's a little more taping we need to have you do for us to wrap up the show. We'll be in Phoenix tomorrow morning, so expect us around noon."

Lucy felt stunned but indignant. Did they honestly think they could mess with her life like they had then simply announce they were coming back for more and expect her to roll over? "Sorry, Ms. Carlton, but that won't be convenient. I'll be working."

"I think you'll find it's in your best interest to rearrange your work schedule." Her voice carried the beguiling tone of someone dangling a carrot on a stick, but Lucy wasn't buying it.

"I'm not sure that anything I do for *Soulmates* is in my best interest," she replied. "So once again, sorry, but I'm not available."

Carrot on a Stick Carlton was gone, and the woman Lucy'd met on day one was back. "And *I'm* sorry, Lucy, but I need to remind you that you're still under contract. And we're on a very tight deadline for this shoot."

She was legally stuck. Trapped. "All right. Fine."

"Good." Ms. Carlton expelled a breath that, if Lucy hadn't known better, almost sounded like relief. "We'll see you tomorrow, then."

Lucy would see them tomorrow. Lucy was under contract. It didn't mean she was going to make it easy for them. In fact, she doubted they were going to like what they got on camera this time. She wasn't about to be taken for a fool again.

* * *

Melanie heaved a sigh and turned off the speaker phone. Two of the most handsome men she'd ever seen were giving her their undivided attention. It was her brand of luck that they were both looking at her as if she were a disgusting insect.

She felt like a disgusting insect. Not that she wanted them to know that, so she smiled as confidently as she could. "Mission accomplished. As you heard, she's agreed to the shoot." She swallowed.

"Yes," Ethan Glass drawled. "We could tell how excited she was about it too. Now you can schedule her two friends. And then you need to make sure you and Esplin have everything nailed down before we leave for the airport."

She glanced at Curt, gorgeous Curt. He only nodded, his expression blank.

Melanie nodded back and started punching in numbers on the phone.

* * *

Ethan felt edgy. He was always edgy before a big deal, so that wasn't anything new. If he was a little edgier than usual, it was because he was going to see Lucy again.

He was skilled at reading people. He'd made himself wealthy doing it. He'd read Lucy correctly as well. She'd fallen in love with him. It wasn't an arrogant statement; he'd known. But he didn't try to fool himself by thinking she'd simply run into his arms, everything forgiven. He had some convincing to do. But he was good at that too, confident in his skills of persuasion.

As they turned onto Lucy's street, Ethan noticed a van with a satellite dish parked nearby. "News media," he said.

"Not good." Curt pulled out his phone. "Mel, there are reporters here, and we don't want them involved at this point. Pass the word to the rest of the crew. And call Lucy to give her our new location." He looked at Ethan. "What's our new location?"

"The ghost town." There were good memories at the ghost town; Lucy would remember them.

"The ghost town," Curt said into his phone. "Right. Tell her thirty minutes, tops." He snapped the phone shut. "I hope this works, man."

"It will."

"There's a lot at stake here. If the show doesn't pull off a happy ending, it'll blow the entire venture to smithereens. No credibility, no show, no website. No nothing."

"It'll work, Curt. You'll have your *Soulmate*, one way or another. You'll have your show and your website. But when we're done here, you and I will be dealing with unfinished business."

"Understood."

* * *

Lucy couldn't stop fidgeting. Ms. Carlton had called and said they were changing the location of the shoot because of the news vans stationed outside the house. It only delayed the inevitable. Besides, the media were already involved, and the long drive to the ghost town was playing havoc on her nerves.

"We're staying with you," her dad said. All three of her brothers were crammed into the backseat. "We discussed this and made the decision."

Her faithful bodyguards. This morning her father had given her a blessing, and her brothers had been there. They, along with her mom and Becky, who'd stayed behind, were giving her all the strength they could, physically, emotionally, and spiritually. She loved them so much right now. She swiveled her head to look at her brothers. "You guys are the best brothers a girl could have."

Andy grinned. "Yes, I am."

"Who's the best?" Craig shot at Andy, eyebrow raised in challenge.

"I am," fourteen-year-old Brig said. "I let her boss me around, and it takes a real man to put up with that kind of crap."

Lucy smiled. For a moment, things felt normal. "You all know I need to do this on my own."

"Well," her dad answered gruffly, "we'll be nearby, just the same. Family solidarity."

Lucy blinked back the tears that suddenly threatened.

The ghost town came into sight. Cables, microphones, windscreens, and cameras were everywhere. People were dashing around. Dane Esplin was gesturing to the creepy orange-haired cameraman who'd taped her in her hotel room in Canada. Ms. Carlton and Mr. Myers were standing together conversing privately. Just like old times.

Ms. Carlton glanced her direction and said something to Mr. Myers then headed toward her. Mr. Myers went to a trailer parked several yards away.

Game on.

"Lucy!" Ms. Carlton was all gushing smiles. "Thank you for meeting us out here. Nasty paparazzi. I hope they haven't been giving you too much trouble."

"They haven't been my main concern, no."

"Well. Good. Follow me, and I'll explain what we need from you today." She pulled out her phone. "Is everyone set? Okay. I'm bringing Lucy now." She smiled brightly at Lucy. "Let's do this, shall we?"

Lucy didn't trust Melanie Carlton one bit. She'd been played before and didn't intend to be played again. "Before we do anything, I want to know exactly what you have planned here."

"I told you. Follow-up shooting we need to wrap the show."

Lucy didn't move. "You'll understand if I say that, based on past history, I don't believe that for a minute. So what's really going on here?"

"I told you," Melanie said again. "Follow-up shooting. How you're doing since leaving the show, that kind of thing."

"How I'm doing." Lucy's blood started to heat. "You want to know how I'm doing? I'll tell you. I'm coming to terms with the fact that this show decided that, for the sake of ratings, my reputation, my good name, was expendable." She was aware, despite the red haze clouding her vision, that people were gathering around them and that the creepy cameraman was shooting their conversation.

"Your good name?" Ms. Carlton snorted, actually *snorted*, at her. "Your best friends didn't even stand up for you. It didn't take much for them to sell you out for the little hypocrite you are."

That stopped Lucy. "Sell me out? What do you mean, *sell* me out?"

"Nothing. The point is, you made everyone believe you're this—"

"Stop. You said it didn't take much for them to sell me out. Take much of what?"

"Nothing!" Melanie insisted. She smoothed her skirt and her expression. "People just don't like feeling betrayed, that's all. Now, come with me so we can take care of this business." She started to cut through the crowd that had gathered to watch, gesturing for Lucy to follow.

Lucy didn't move. Taking a deep breath, tamping back the hurt and anger she felt, she shut her eyes and silently prayed for strength. She'd done everything she could during her time on *Soulmates* to make good choices, firmly believing she'd had a responsibility to be a role model. Somehow, she knew, it all came down to this moment.

She waited, eyes shut, praying, her silent words simple but pleading. *Help me, Father, help me, please help me*, over and over until they tumbled through her mind. And as they tumbled, they started pulling images with them: a den of lions, a fiery furnace, a jail in Carthage, Illinois.

This was nothing compared to those.

She made herself stand tall and looked at Ms. Carlton. And then the words came. "For some reason, you want to believe that I am not the moral person I claim to be. In fact, you went to a lot of effort to try to prove your point. Interesting, then, that you would be dishonest yourself in the process.

"All my life I have had to make tough choices. I believe what I believe, I make no excuses about it, and there is a price to pay as a result. If it has meant losing friends along the way because they couldn't accept who I am, then that was part of the price I had to pay. But they were my choices, and I accepted responsibility for them.

"You called me a hypocrite. Well, I'm the first to claim I'm not perfect. And being on *Soulmates* was difficult. Because along with dealing with my growing feelings for—With the situation, I knew that everything I did or said was scrutinized. I wanted to be a role model for others. In the end, I simply tried to be true to myself and trust that, while others would judge, the only judgment that really mattered was God's.

"You said it yourself. People don't like feeling betrayed. I know I don't. I've felt betrayed by all of you since the last episode aired. I was misrepresented in a very public way. Everywhere I turn there is gossip or a tasteless joke at my expense. It was hurtful, and I'm angry.

"But, you know, I realized just now that it doesn't matter. People will believe what they want to believe. Even you. You, who hid a camera in my hotel suite and caught me committing the crime of sharing my beliefs with someone I cared about. You, who turned that into something completely opposite of the truth.

"I'll fulfill my contractual obligations to the show. I have no illusions about how anything I say or do on tape today will be used, so do with it what you will. I will have a clear conscience."

She stopped speaking and looked around. Everyone was silent. Her dad and brothers stood like sentinels, watching and waiting.

"Lucy."

Lucy froze. Her heart started racing, and her legs threatened to collapse. She knew that voice. It was Ethan's. He was the last person she'd expected to see today.

He walked toward her, the crew parting to let him through like some biblical prophet. And then he was right in front of her, taking her hands in his.

Her only coherent thought was that she was afraid she might throw up on his shoes.

* * *

Ethan had never felt such pride. Lucy was magnificent. He'd been afraid he'd find some broken, weepy female. He'd been prepared to do battle for her, anything to assure her that he would right the wrongs that had been done. He still intended to.

But seeing her now, making no excuses, facing those who'd wronged her, had made his heart swell. If he hadn't been sure before, he absolutely knew it now. This woman, this strong woman, was his soulmate. He intended to make her his *Soulmate* as well. Right now.

"Lucy, you're even more beautiful than I remembered." He allowed himself a moment to drink in the sight of her. "I've missed you. A lot has happened since we said good-bye."

"That's certainly true," she replied flatly. It surprised him, especially after the impassioned speech she'd just made.

"I've had a lot of time to think since then, about you, about the things we discussed. Everything." He paused, waited for her to look at him. Over her shoulder, he could see her father and brothers move to stand closer behind her. He'd liked them when they'd met, appreciated that they'd made him feel welcome. Today, they were a wall of protection. For her.

Were they protecting her from him?

That idea didn't sit well, and their presence suddenly made him uncomfortable. So did the camera for the first time in a long time. So did the fact that Lucy wouldn't look at him. He needed to get her alone, where he could explain things better. "Will you walk with me?"

She glanced back at her father, then at the cameraman, and then faced Ethan, her eyes glued somewhere near his collarbone. "I'd rather not."

His stomach knotted. This was not going according to plan at all. "I'm only asking for a few minutes alone, in private, with you."

Now she looked at him. "Alone with a director, a producer, and a cameraman. And a hidden camera. I've done that version of private. No thanks. This time around I want witnesses, especially witnesses I know have my back."

It dawned on him. Her coolness toward him wasn't necessarily just because he'd eliminated her from the competition. She thought he'd been involved in the show's slander of her. Didn't she realize he'd been out of the country the entire time, that his role with the show was mostly that of investor? Didn't she trust him?

Apparently not, and what he'd expected to be merely a challenge took a deep turn south toward disaster.

But he would not give up. She was his soulmate. He believed that. So if she wanted this to happen with witnesses, she'd have them. He would do this her way. After what she'd gone through, she deserved it.

"All right. Witnesses it is." He cracked a smile and squeezed her limp hands. No response. "There's a reason I'm here today, Lucy. In Arizona, with you. Saying good-bye to you was the hardest thing I've ever done. From the first, you gave me something . . . I don't know. Different. Special. And for a long time, I thought, she's the one, the final one. The one who will be my *Soulmate*."

He braved the disbelief in her eyes and reached out to touch her cheek. "Until that last day in Canada, that is, when I realized how important your beliefs are. I hadn't expected that to be a complication. Just the opposite, in fact. My mother's a religious woman, and I wanted that for my family. It was one of the things that drew me to you.

"But it *was* a complication because it's a big part of you, and it requires so much, and I didn't know if I could commit to you and it too.

I didn't have the luxury of time to sort through it all. I had to make a decision, and it was a tough one to make.

"But I've had the time since then, and I've sorted through it all now." He smiled. "And I'm back. I want you in my life."

He hoped she couldn't feel his hands shaking in hers. He took a deep breath and dropped to one knee. "Lucy Kendrick, will you be my *Soulmate*? Will you continue this journey with me?"

She stared at him, her eyes huge. He could hear the murmurs of surprise from the crew. Curt and company must have kept Ethan's plans a secret. Maybe all the ghosts of Cecily, Arizona, had shown up to be her witnesses as well.

Why didn't she say something? He watched her face carefully. Where had his CEO skills gone? He couldn't tell what she was thinking.

A single tear threatened to escape, and seeing it nearly broke his heart. She blinked it back and raised her chin.

Not a good sign.

"No."

She said it so softly he almost didn't hear it.

He shook his head slightly. Maybe he didn't hear it. Maybe what she'd said was, "Oh." All she needed was more convincing, he was sure.

"It wasn't the same after you left. And that pig you sent—" he broke off, stifling a chuckle brought on by the vision of Hamlet in his puffy pants. "That pig made me miss you even more. We finished shooting, and I left for London. But London gave me the time—"

"This is a setup, right?" She looked around at the crowd, searching for someone. "This is their doing, isn't it? You finished shooting the show, but *now* you're here telling me *I'm* your *Soulmate*. I don't believe you. I can't."

She tore her hands from his and rushed through the crowd.

"Lucy! Wait—" Ethan pushed through the human wall and grabbed her arm, only to find her brother Andy's fist connecting with his jaw. He staggered and lost his hold.

"Ethan," she cried at the same time her father and brothers yelled at Andy to stop. He shook his head to clear it and moved his jaw gingerly from side to side. Nothing was broken, but he'd have a beauty of a bruise for a few days.

Lucy clutched his arm. "Are you all right? You're bleeding. Just a little, here on your lip."

He swiped his hand across his mouth. If he'd known one solid punch would get her looking at him like this, he'd have paid someone to do it

sooner. He had to make his move now, while he had her sympathy. "I'm
fine. But I'd feel a whole lot better if you'd walk with me and at least hear
me out." Her eyes clouded over again, and his heart sank. "Please, Lucy.
As repayment for your brother's violent behavior." He tried to smile then
winced. "Ouch." He rubbed his jaw gingerly.

She heaved a sigh, and he silently rejoiced. "All right. I'll hear you
out." She raised her chin. "But I still want witnesses."

At least she'd agreed to talk to him. He'd rather talk to her alone, but
he understood her reasons for distrust. He wasn't thrilled to be baring his
soul in front of an audience, but he'd taken risks all his life. He'd studied
his options and followed his gut and then taken the risks. It was what
had made him a success.

This was the biggest risk of all. For the first time, he was risking his
heart, and he'd never gambled with his heart before.

He led her away from the crowd, cameras rolling, noting that her
family was only a short distance away. He took her to a toppled tree trunk.
Sunshine filtered down through the pine boughs overhead and flickered
across her face like angel kisses.

Angel kisses. He thought of his niece Brianna, all freckles and fishing
poles and feminine wiles. He'd protect that kid no matter what. Through
the corner of his eye, he could see David Kendrick, arms crossed over his
chest, fatherly protection in full force. Ethan's own chest contracted at
the sight.

He sat next to her and took her hand. "Lucy, even though I've met
a lot of beautiful women, I think I'd given up on believing there was
someone for me, someone to build a life with. When Curt asked me
to be the *Soulmate*, I agreed on the barest chance that I might find that
someone. Even though I wasn't sure she existed.

"When you walked through the door that first evening, all golden
smiles, I knew something was different about you, something I had to
pursue and try to understand. You attracted me."

She interrupted him. "You never said anything. We would have
wonderful times together, and then you would close yourself off. I
couldn't tell what you were thinking or if our time together was any
different for you than it was with any of the other women."

He knew he'd guarded himself, kept his feelings close to the vest. "All
I can say in my defense is that I've never dated twenty-five women at once,
and the experience was daunting, to say the least. But it wasn't long before
I knew I was taking you to the end with me.

"But in Canada, I realized that by choosing you, I was committing to a life with different beliefs and practices, and more than that, I understood for the first time that you wouldn't settle for anything less than that. It was too much to absorb in too short a time."

"You could have given us that time, Ethan. You could have kept me there and given us the time."

"Give us the time now! Agree to be my *Soulmate*." He put his arm around her shoulders and pulled her in close. "I couldn't watch the show," he whispered. "I didn't want to be reminded that I had let you go, but I couldn't move on, couldn't stop thinking about you, no matter how I tried.

"I didn't know what happened until Kyle called me. And then I came straight back from London, furious that they could have done that to you. You have to believe that. And I vow I'll do everything I can to make things right." He kissed her tenderly, ignoring her resistance. "Be my *Soulmate*. Please, Lucy."

She pulled back, placing her hand on his chest as a barrier. "Ethan, a month ago I would have been thrilled to hear you say those words. I was falling in love with you; I know I was. It was terrifying because I knew I had to take the risk of telling you everything I believed in. When you let me go, I was crushed.

"I couldn't watch the show either. My family made me watch the last episode. They thought I needed to see it." She looked Ethan in the eye, and he caught his breath at the resolve he saw there. "My entire life I've tried to do what's right. It wasn't easy, and even friends I thought were okay with it weren't. It's all about choices, and I guess when we choose, we judge, and some people don't like that. But people judge me in return too. And now a lot of them, all across the country—how many people do you think watched that episode?—will judge who I am based on lies." She choked out a laugh. "Who would have thought that a lifetime of trying to live by my values could be undermined that easily."

He pulled her close again, unwilling to let go. "I'll do everything I can to make it right, Lucy. I won't let them get away with this."

"They already have." She shrugged her shoulders. "In the end, maybe it doesn't matter what anybody thinks. The people who really know me will believe the truth."

She looked him in the eye then. "I still . . . care . . . about you. It would be so much easier if I didn't. But the answer is no. It has to be. I've been treated badly—by you and by the show you helped produce. That's not something that a simple kiss and apology can make better, unlike your jaw." She kissed her fingers and touched them to his swollen cheek. "I'm sorry, Ethan, but my answer has to be no."

She stood, and the regret he saw in her face crushed him. He'd finally taken the time he'd told her he needed, in London, reading her scriptures, meeting with her missionaries, praying . . . and finally believing. And now, as she walked away, he was afraid the woman who was his soulmate, whom he wanted bound to him forever, was slipping from his grasp.

CHAPTER 22

CURT HIT THE STOP BUTTON on the DVD player. "Well, Eth, that's it. The reedit, the way you requested it. But I've got to ask, are you sure this is what you want to do?"

Ethan sat slouched, his chin on his fist, and stared at the blank flatscreen. "I'm sure."

"We kept a copy of the original version of the season finale. We can run it, and no one will be the wiser."

Ethan glanced over at Curt. "We're running this one, Curt."

He nodded, resigned. "I can't believe Denise has been so cool about this. Most women would throw a hissy fit after finding out they'd been chosen and dumped by you before the series even finished airing."

"Denise is a mensch."

"And easy on the eyes," Curt added.

Melanie looked up at Curt. She hadn't looked anyone in the face in more than a week.

"That too," Ethan agreed, noting Melanie's bleak expression before she returned her attention to her ever-present clipboard.

"I had to do a lot of talking to keep the network suits from nailing me to the wall." Curt raked a hand through his hair. "They're worried. It's not every day they premiere a reality dating show that's supposed to have a no-fail formula and ends up having no winner at the end. It defeats the purpose."

"I'm not changing my mind about this, Curt."

"Fine. Okay. This is the episode that runs tomorrow."

Ethan stood and headed to the door. "Good. I'll be watching."

"Hey, Eth," Curt said.

Ethan paused.

"Have you spoken to her? Lucy, that is."

"No." He'd not spoken to her at all after their encounter at the ghost town. Her refusal had stung. He'd initially blamed her hurt and refusal of him on the show's handling of her on-screen. Since then, he'd realized that their callous treatment had only added insult to the injury he'd inflicted on her himself.

She needed time to savor her victory over him, and as hard as it had been to not fly back to Arizona, he'd stayed in LA with Curt. Besides, he'd wanted to make sure this final, most important episode went according to his specifications. "No, I haven't spoken to her. But I will. Soon."

He had to hope, he thought as he strode down the hallway toward the lobby, that when she saw it, she would begin to believe him when he told her he loved her. He stopped, midstride. He did love her; he knew that now. But that wasn't what stopped him. It was the realization that he'd never said those words to her, even when she'd confessed that she'd been falling in love with him.

He groaned inwardly. For someone who'd been linked romantically with women over and over again, he was a bumbling fool when it came to the subject of love.

* * *

Melanie had busted her chops on this show, trying to prove herself a success. She'd done an amazing job—except for a few teensy details. But it had been a horrible week, and she couldn't take the suspense any longer. "Just say it."

Curt leaned back in his chair. "Say what?"

"Come on, Curt. I'm not a fool. And I know Ethan Glass is looking for someone to take the fall over this. He wants it to be me."

"Does he?" He was looking at her like she was a worm. Well, she felt like a worm, so she deserved to have him look at her that way. She'd lost any chance with him she may have had in her wildest dreams when she'd ruined the reputation of *his* boss's newly declared love. What were the odds of that? The kind of odds that had haunted Melanie her whole life.

Time to move on. Once again.

"It's my fault isn't it? The hidden camera, the suggestions to Dane Esplin, who, by the way, is an imbecile. Not that any of that matters right now," she muttered under her breath.

"You paid Lucy's friend to lie for us on camera."

"No! I—okay, the blonde friend was—Listen, all I did was slip her a couple hundred and suggest that we wanted some juicy details. I didn't ask her to lie. I certainly didn't know she'd lied. And if what she'd said was true, Ethan and the viewers had the right to know."

"You paid her friend. You arranged for a hidden camera when you knew Ethan had forbidden them. You helped edit the footage to show Lucy in the worst possible light."

"Okay! I'm a worm, I know! I get it."

He crossed his arms over his chest and stared at her. Even though she still felt like a worm, it gave her a shiver of awareness for him to be looking at her at all. She was pathetic. It was mortifying.

"The thing is, Mel, you're talented. You kept me organized, you kept Esplin in line, you kept the women from doing bodily harm to each other. *Now* what am I supposed to do? More than just Lucy and Ethan got hurt. You hurt me too."

"I already said I feel like a worm, didn't I?"

"Why, Mel? Tell me why."

"I thought Lucy was betraying Ethan. Don't make more out of this than it already is."

He was still studying her. Too carefully for her comfort.

Melanie could feel the blood rush out of her head, and suddenly Curt was next to her, looking concerned, and she felt even more pathetic. "What is it? Tell me," he said.

She sighed in defeat. What more did she have to lose, after all? "It was all a long time ago. I thought it was my big break. The dream job and the dream boss. Family man, straight arrow, chamber of commerce kind of guy. Except for the little illegal business he had on the side that he'd neglected to mention."

He pulled her into his arms. Great. She'd imagined something like this for months now, and it turned out to be the comforting-big-brother version. She choked on a sob and tried to stifle the embarrassing sound. Was invisibility too much to ask for? Apparently.

"Then what happened?" he asked softly.

"They eventually dropped the charges but not before I went through the ringer—he'd done a good job of covering his tracks by making them mine. It took awhile to get back on my feet. Lovely man." She was going to hate herself tomorrow for telling Curt any of this, but right now, his arms felt so nice. It had been a long time since anyone had even tried to be a friend to her like this.

Except for Lucy, that is.

She was lower than a worm.

"That blonde friend of Lucy's gave us a total one-eighty on her first interview."

Mel sighed again. "Yes, she did. Obviously, with my track record, it's easy to see that I'm a terrific judge of character." She braved a glance at Curt. "I hope we got enough from her to pull off the finale and start making things right for Lucy."

Now it was Curt's turn to sigh. "Yeah. The ratings have been great, and the network suits were right where I wanted them until this happened. We'll ride it out. But you're right. Someone does need to take the fall for this. Only it's the suits calling for a scapegoat, not Ethan.

"So," he said, giving her a quick squeeze before letting her go. "I'm afraid I've got some bad news and some good news."

Mel rubbed her arms, missing his warmth, and braced herself. Going for bravado, she gave a dry laugh. "There's good news?"

"I think so."

She couldn't decipher his expression, and the wait was killing her. "Give me the bad news first, not that I don't already know what you're going to say."

He nodded and pulled a paper out of his pocket. "Ms. Carlton," he said, reading from the paper, "based on the circumstances surrounding the use of hidden cameras against management's wishes, the false portrayal of contestant Lucy Kendrick, the lack of professional judgment resulting from personal bias that led to said portrayal, and the ensuing costs to the company as a result, your employment has been terminated, effective immediately."

That was that, then. Nothing more than she'd expected. "So, Mr. Myers, what's the good news?"

Curt gave a smile, one that brought her shivers back, and then he closed the distance between them. "I'm not your boss anymore. You see, I have a strict policy against dating coworkers."

And then he kissed her.

* * *

Lucy made herself watch the next episode of *Soulmates* with her family. She'd faced Ethan, and that had given her some peace. Some closure. Mostly. She'd told herself she'd be able to complete the process by watching the final two episodes.

In this week's episode, Tiffany and Denise were meeting Ethan's family at their ranch in Montana. She'd spent a lot of time telling herself in the bathroom mirror that she could watch this. She was pretty sure Ethan had chosen Denise—at least until a few days ago when he'd asked Lucy to be his *Soulmate*. Of course, Lucy had told him no, so she wasn't sure what he and the show were planning to do now.

And Lucy really loved Denise. She was beautiful, gracious, and kind. She'd become a friend for life. Ethan would be fortunate to have someone like Denise as his *Soulmate*. He absolutely would.

That's what she kept telling herself anyway.

They watched Rick interview Ethan and Ethan work on the ranch alongside his father and brother. And then a white van drove up to the ranch house. Lucy got a funny feeling that she knew what was going to happen.

"I think Ethan is about to receive the gift I sent him." She nudged Brigham with her elbow, trying to act cool and mysterious, but her stomach was fluttering.

Ms. Carlton handed Ethan her note, and then the van driver walked a larger version of the little piglet she'd caught at the rodeo over to Ethan. A significantly larger, extremely purple, Shakespearean pig that proceeded to squeal.

Along with her family.

"That's Hamlet," Lucy announced. "The pig I won at the rodeo."

Andy, doubled over with laughter, pointed at the television and hooted. "Even his hooves are purple!"

"Purple glitter," her mom added.

Ethan opened the note and read. Lucy watched his expression closely. He had always been so hard to read. His brow wrinkled for a minute before smoothing out again—and that was it. He crouched in front of the pig and said something to it before standing and walking away from the camera.

"What did the note say?" her mother asked.

"Thank you . . . that sort of thing," Lucy replied. "A few lines from the play *Hamlet* I thought were applicable at the time."

Her mother looked at her in question.

"'To thine own self be true.' Pretty funny, considering."

"Do you think Ethan was involved in what was shown in the episode last week?"

Lucy flopped her head back against the sofa cushions and squeezed her eyes shut. "He said he wasn't. But I'm having a hard time believing it right now. In *Soulmates* House, there was always talk about how he was the money behind the show. It's the classic Golden Rule: he who has the gold makes the rules. And it was obvious during tapings that he was the one ultimately making the rules."

Her mother got quiet, and Lucy went back to watching the show—in time to see Tiffany flirt with Ethan, flirt with Ethan's father, and flirt with Ethan's brother. Then they watched Denise gush and hug everybody within grabbing distance—although Lucy could tell Denise had scaled back the saccharin level to one that didn't automatically trigger a need for insulin. She liked Denise. Well, maybe not right at the moment, watching Ethan kiss her against the backdrop of a Montana sunset with sappy music playing, but she was only human, after all.

It didn't help knowing that what she was watching had occurred a month ago. It didn't help that he'd shown up here just a few days ago and asked her for another chance or that he'd seemed certain that she'd run right back into his arms—simply because he'd changed his mind after he'd had the *time* to *think*.

It really didn't help that running into his arms was exactly what she'd wanted to do.

It made her angry all over again. Angry at Ethan and angry at herself. Angry that she'd felt prompted to go on the show and the show had turned around and ruined her reputation on a national scale.

Rick Madison's voice-over announced, "Next week on the dramatic conclusion of *Soulmates*: Two women are in love with the same man, and now that man must choose. But before he does, a shocking twist—"

A clip of Allie, looking remorseful, broke into the running montage of Tiffany, Denise, and Ethan. "I wasn't a hundred percent truthful about what I said about Lucy—"

Rick's voice-over continued over a blurry shot of Lucy and Ethan in the hallway of her hotel suite. "Uncovered footage reveals what really happened. And Ethan finds himself faced with the toughest decision of his life. All this and more next week—on the dramatic conclusion of *Soulmates*."

Andy hit the off button.

"I hope they set the record straight."

Lucy hoped so too. She didn't for one minute think it would change what the world of television viewers thought of her, but it counted for something that Allie was trying to make things right.

"Hey, Lucy—"

She pulled herself out of her thoughts when she realized Brigham was trying to get her attention.

"There's a guy at the door. A FedEx guy or something like that. He says he has a package for you and you need to sign for it. Personally."

"Oh, okay." She headed toward the front door, trying to imagine what anybody could be bringing to her.

An official-looking man in a tan uniform stood at the door holding a large box. "Good evening. You're Lucy Kendrick?"

"Yes."

He set down the box and handed her a pen. "If you'll sign right here that you received the package—" She took the pen and signed where he indicated. "And there's your package. Have a good evening."

It was a fairly large box but, surprisingly, not very heavy. She hefted it into the kitchen and set it on the table. Everyone gathered out of curiosity.

"Who's it from?" Brig asked.

Lucy checked all sides of the box. "It doesn't say."

She tore through the packaging and opened the top flaps. Inside, nestled into packing peanuts, was something protected by a plastic bag. She carefully pulled it out, trying to keep the peanuts from escaping, and removed the plastic. "Oh!"

It was a stuffed toy pig sporting a goatee, dressed in a doublet, ruff, and velvet trunk hose. Her dad and brothers busted up laughing. "You're friend Hamlet's got a twin brother," Andy joked.

There was a card tucked into the band of the hat stitched onto the pig's head. Lucy removed it with shaking fingers and opened the envelope.

"It's from Ethan," she said. That wasn't a surprise to anyone, really, considering a pig in a Shakespearean costume had just shown up unexpectedly at their house.

The surprise was that he'd sent anything.

"What does it say?" her mom asked.

"'There is no comparison between that which is lost by not succeeding and that which is lost by not trying.' Sir Francis Bacon." After tossing Shakespeare quotes at each other, leave it to Ethan to one-up her *Hamlet* gift by sending her a pig with a quote from Sir Francis *Bacon*.

"I think Ethan's trying to tell you something, dear," her mother said as she stroked the pig's velvet cloak. "Did he say anything else?"

"'More to follow.' And he signed it." He'd signed it simply with a loosely drawn heart and his initials.

"Somebody went to a lot of effort to make this pig." Her mother was examining it more closely now. "The detail is amazing. He's even wearing an earring."

Lucy looked up from Ethan's note to study the pig again. Sir Francis Bacon's piggy ear was pierced by a silver hoop, and what dangled from it stopped Lucy short. "I'll be right back."

She dashed up the stairs to her bedroom and pulled open the top drawer in her dresser. Tucked beneath a stack of folded sweaters was a small, flat box she'd placed there the day she'd returned from Canada. She'd left it there, hidden, unable to reveal its contents to anyone and unwilling to have it remind her of the times it symbolized. Now she grabbed the box and flew back to the kitchen, where her family sat waiting, wide-eyed and curious.

"What does Sir Francis Bacon have to do with an old-fashioned clock earring, of all things?" her mother asked.

"It's not an earring," Lucy said. Setting the box on the table next to the pig, she opened the lid, revealing its velvet-lined interior and the charm bracelet that lay inside. "It's a charm." But it was more than a charm, she knew. Ethan Glass had given her time.

* * *

Exactly one week later, Lucy and her family were, once again, gathered around the television set.

"You know, Luce," a triumphant Andy said two inches from her face after pinning her down on the sofa, "you're not nearly as tough as you used to be."

Lucy pushed him hard, and he landed with a grunt on the floor but not before snagging her wrist and bringing her down on top of him. Brigham grinned from the computer desk and then dove on top.

"Ouch!" Lucy squeaked. "That's your . . . elbow . . . in my . . . kidney. Move!"

Before he could, Craig's family came through the door.

Noah shrieked, "Dog pile!" and leaped onto Brigham, creating a small earthquake from Lucy's perspective.

"Help!" Lucy croaked. "Can't . . . breathe . . ."

A laughing Andy at the bottom of the heap yelled, "Don't believe her! It's a trick!" But three-year-old Noah had rolled like a pill bug to the floor, so Brigham shifted off the pile himself and offered Lucy a hand up.

She was about to pummel Andy with throw pillows when her parents showed up, armed with bowls of popcorn. "Show's about to start," her dad said.

Lucy tossed the pillows onto the couch instead of at Andy. Time to get back to reality. She'd had the luxury of forgetting for a few minutes, thanks to Andy. Her family was doing everything they could to get her through tonight's finale of *Soulmates*. Even dog piles.

Boy, did she love them.

She made it through Rick's intro and through the segments of Ethan with Tiffany and Denise on their final dates, mostly by ignoring all of the surreptitious glances her parents and brothers kept giving her. They weren't being as subtle as they thought they were. She kept a serene look on her face.

She hoped it looked serene.

Because the ninja butterflies were back in full force.

Heading into a commercial break, Rick's voice-over teased about the "shocking twist" and "dramatic conclusion" again. Lucy took a moment to breathe.

"They always say that stuff," Brigham snorted. "It's lame."

"What do you think will happen?" her mother asked her quietly.

"I don't know. I don't have any idea how they'll decide to end things." Especially since she'd told Ethan no.

"What about the pig and the charm?"

She shook her head in reply. The charm had affected her more than the pig had. Ethan had told her he'd needed time and had given it to himself. Now she needed time, and he'd told her with the charm that he was giving it to her.

But he also had a show to think about, and she knew Curt Myers and company would make that the top priority.

The next segment showed a serious Rick explaining that they'd done a follow-up interview with former contestant Lucy's friend, who'd made some shocking confessions, followed by a clip:

Allie: "Lucy didn't have any serious dating relationships, and as close as we were as friends, I figured she would tell us more about the guys she dated than she did. I drew my own conclusions about what may have occurred on those dates."

It wasn't the most convincing apology Lucy had ever heard, but it was something, she supposed. The clip continued:

Rick: "You told your friend Grace that Lucy had cheated on her with her boyfriend."

Allie: "That was a misunderstanding. I found out after I did the first interview with you guys that nothing between them ever happened."

Rick: "What you're saying is, the Lucy we got to know on the show is the real Lucy."

Allie: "Yes. That's what I'm saying."

Rick: "Why did you lie in the first place? About one of your best friends?"

Allie: "I wanted her to be more like the rest of us, I guess. And I was encouraged to . . . I don't know . . . exaggerate, I guess."

Lucy gasped.

Rick: "Encouraged how, exactly?"

Allie: "One of the producers paid me cash."

That was the first bombshell.

Rick turned to the camera. "Later, we will hear from that producer. But first, Tiffany and Denise await Ethan's final decision. Who will Ethan choose? Let's hear from the *Soulmate* himself, Ethan Glass."

Ethan came on-screen and sat across from Rick. Lucy's eyes were glued to him.

Rick spoke. "So tell us, Ethan, what has this been like for you, now that you've reached the end of the journey?"

Ethan smiled, but it was his CEO smile. "It's been an amazing adventure. I've met some wonderful women, and I've learned a lot about myself in the process."

"*Soulmates* claims to be an advanced approach to finding love, with complex screenings of all kinds," Rick said. "In fact, a *Soulmates* personals website is being launched right after the finale. So, do you think you found your *Soulmate* on the show?"

Lucy held her breath, aware that the eyes in the room were glued to her. But she couldn't take her eyes off of Ethan and waited to hear what he was going to say.

"Yes, Rick. I found my *Soulmate*, my true soulmate."

Silence.

Then Andy exploded. "That jerk! Barely two weeks ago he was saying that to Lucy, and now he's spouting—"

"Shhh!" Lucy was out of her seat and standing in front of the television, watching Ethan as the episode continued. She studied his face, looking for anything telling. But his business persona was firmly in place as he took

Tiffany's hands in his and told her their journey was ending. His expression wavered as he told Denise in a separate scene that she wasn't his *Soulmate* and hugged her tightly.

And then it struck her.

He hadn't chosen either of them.

Her heart began to race, especially when Rick was back, announcing that they were about to discover what Ethan had meant when he said he'd found his true soulmate on the show. A montage of video clips of Lucy followed: stepping into the solarium doorway that first evening, attempting to outwit Ethan in the kissing booth, dragging herself through the dirt with a squealing piglet trying to wriggle free, snorkeling, on horseback, riding in a carriage through the streets of Victoria . . .

They were all clips of her, but Lucy's eyes were riveted on Ethan's face in each of the scenes. It had been his *real* face. She'd seen his expressions, his reactions to her. His smile of genuine interest when they were introduced in the solarium, his mischievous grin during their kissing booth exchange. The joy she could see as he made his way on horseback through an old relic of a ghost town. His look of absorption when she'd spoken of angels.

Rick Madison was on-screen again, saying something to Ethan about "what happened" and "Canada," but Lucy was too absorbed in her thoughts to catch all the words.

The next scene was in Victoria in her hotel suite, with her explaining that her concerns weren't about reputation as much as they were about being an example and role model. It was the same scene the show had used before as the setup to make her look like a hypocrite. This time, however, they showed what really happened that night.

She watched Ethan reading, with her by his side. Ethan reading, with her curled up, asleep on the sofa. Ethan tucking a pillow under her head and shifting to give her more space. Ethan carrying her to her room, tucking her in bed, and placing a kiss on her forehead before leaving the suite.

Rick: "That's not what we saw happen before."

Ethan: "You're right. Certain members of the production team were responsible for that editing decision. Those individuals have been fired."

Rick: "There's more to this though, isn't there?"

Ethan: "Yes. Had I known, I would never have allowed anything like this to occur in the first place, but I definitely draw the line when someone harms the person I have chosen as my Soulmate.*"*

Then Lucy watched herself in the ghost town as Ethan confessed his feelings for her and urged her to be his *Soulmate . . .* and his look of anguish when she told him no.

Rick: "That was tough for you to watch, wasn't it?"

Lucy nodded.

Ethan: "Yes." He cleared his throat. "Yes, very tough."

Rick: "Is there anything you'd like to say right now? To Lucy? To the viewers?"

Ethan: "The show's method worked. I found my Soulmate. *I also made a serious mistake by not recognizing her in time. Now it's up to her to decide if she found her* Soulmate *or not. I'll have to live by her decision. But whatever she decides, the show was a success."*

Before Lucy had any time to react, the doorbell rang. It was the same guy who'd delivered Sir Francis Bacon the week before. Tonight he brought her a small, square package and an envelope.

After thanking him, Lucy made her way to the living room sofa and opened the envelope first. Inside was a brief letter—longer than the note that had accompanied the stuffed pig but not by much. It read: "As you can tell from the enclosed pictures, I have taken the plunge. Literally. I have started a new journey. I wish you had been here to share this first step with me, but I also knew I had to do this on my own because it's right for me regardless of what happens between us. For that, I will always be grateful."

The first picture was of Ethan with two missionaries, all of them dressed in white. The second was of Ethan, again with the missionaries, but this time they were all wearing suits and ties. Ethan's hair looked suspiciously wet.

He'd been baptized.

He'd been baptized!

Her heart nearly burst. She handed the letter with shaking hands to her mother, who was hovering with the rest of the family nearby. Her fingers fumbled with the wrapping on the box and weren't much steadier when she opened the lid.

"Oh," she breathed.

He'd sent her another charm, this one a handcart filled with a sparkling cargo of tiny diamonds.

"Well," her mother said. "I wasn't expecting that to happen."

Neither was Lucy.

* * *

"Viewer numbers were up for the finale," Curt said, "thanks to the promos we tossed together at the last minute." He rested a hip on Ethan's desk and crossed his arms over his chest. He had relief written all over his face, despite his casual demeanor. "But I have to tell you, Eth, I was nervous. Really nervous. I wasn't sure how the new ending was going to go over, with you not choosing Denise or Tiffany. It was a huge gamble. But it got the numbers up. And the hits to the website have been steadily picking up. We're in the clear. So thanks, man."

"You don't have to thank me, Curt. I promised I'd give you a successful *Soulmates* ending based on Lindstrom's tools, and you got it."

"Speaking of Lindstrom, the doc was great. She streamlined her questionnaires so we can offer different levels of screening for different membership prices."

"Glad to hear it."

"Yeah." He wandered over to the window and fingered the leaves of a potted plant. "She's been meeting with Melanie, you know. Couple of times a week."

Ethan didn't reply. He turned his attention to the stack of reports on his desk.

"Mel's sorry, Eth. She's done everything she can to make things right. She arranged the interviews, helped with the editing. She even met with the media to make a formal apology."

And Ethan appreciated all of those things. If he'd been the only person who'd been hurt, he'd have moved on, especially now that he was sitting in church every Sunday and therefore continually being reminded to forgive others. But until he was sure that Lucy was all right, he couldn't absolve Melanie, or the others involved, for that matter. He knew Curt had been seeing Melanie since the finale had aired, and considering the sparks that had been flying off the two of them during taping, it wasn't a big surprise. But it was more than a little annoying that *Soulmates* had brought Curt and Melanie together, while Ethan's future with Lucy was still very much in question.

He repeated the words he'd told Lucy in Canada and that she'd eventually said to him, "Curt, some things take time. So for now, give it a rest."

Curt nodded but appeared hesitant. "Okay." He gestured between the two of them. "As long as we're cool."

"We're cool," he assured him. "Everything will be fine." And eventually it would be too, in one form or another. He had to believe that.

Curt nodded again. "Okay. I guess I'll be seeing you." But he remained by the potted plant.

Ethan picked up a report from the stack on his desk. "Was there something else you needed?"

This time Curt shook his head. "Nope. Nothing I need. But what about you, Eth? What are you going to do?"

Ethan rested his head against the back of his chair and squeezed his eyes shut. "I don't know. I promised to give her time, but the wait is killing me." He squinted at Curt. "All I know is that now that I understand what she was telling me, about soulmates and eternity and really being together forever, I can't imagine any of that happening without her."

He loved her. She challenged him, she made him laugh, he could relax with her and be himself. With her, he could envision what his parents and his brother had in their lives. And she'd opened his heart not only to love but also to faith. He'd always believed in himself and his ability to succeed at anything. Now he believed in the rightness of life, in its purpose, and in a loving Father who wanted what was best for him. He prayed that having Lucy by his side was what Father in Heaven wanted for him too.

And then it struck him like a flash of fire through his chest.

He knew what he needed to do. It was inspired. Literally.

He'd prayed over and over that Lucy would change her mind. He'd also promised her that he would give her time. That didn't mean it had to be time away from him. He would never have been baptized if she'd only prayed for him. No, she'd given him information, books, and writings to study. He'd followed that up with missionary discussions and church attendance. He'd asked the tough questions and demanded the answers. And then he'd prayed. But even the answer to that prayer had taken time.

How could he expect Lucy to gain her answers with time alone? She needed tangibles, like he'd needed. She needed to *know* Ethan, really know *him*—the new and improved Ethan—before she prayed and received her answer concerning their future.

His heart was pounding. He felt light and happy. But not confident—that was how the old Ethan would have felt.

No, he didn't feel confident.

But he did feel hopeful.

He noticed Curt eyeing him warily. "What's up? What are you thinking?"

He grinned. "I'm thinking that Lucy can have all the time she needs, as long as it's time with me. Curt, old pal, can you get me the number for the resort in Eagle Bluff? I have a reservation to make."

Curt's eyebrows raised as comprehension dawned, and he grinned back. "Sure thing. And if I'm thinking what you're thinking, you'll be packing for an extended stay in Arizona."

Ethan stood and clapped Curt soundly on the shoulder. "That, my friend, is exactly what I'm thinking."

* * *

When Lucy arrived at work on Monday morning, Matt, the front desk clerk, flagged her down and told her to go directly to Grace's father's office. That was strange. Since she'd returned home and started working at the resort, he'd had her reporting to the resort manager or his assistant.

She walked down the main hallway toward the resort offices. Maybe Grace's dad needed her for an urgent assignment; he'd had her do things like that occasionally before. She hoped whatever it was didn't require much concentration. She'd found it difficult to focus on much of anything recently. Except Ethan.

Brigham and Andy had kept track of news online. Comment boards that before the finale had been harsh toward Lucy had turned more favorable the past couple of weeks.

"It's like this," Andy had said. "People think you were either a victim or a willing participant in a show that manipulated things for hype. Not everyone is going to trust a reality show to do anything sincere, especially apologize on the air."

Lucy wasn't sure she even cared anymore, and she caught the irony in that. She'd worried so much about what to do, what to say, what to wear when she'd been on the show. What people would think. What example she set. In the end, she'd had no control of the outcome. Like Shadrach, Meshach, and Abednego, she'd gone through a fiery furnace. And while, like them, the experience hadn't killed her, she did feel singed around the edges.

And Ethan had gotten baptized. She knew him well enough to know he wouldn't have done it for her. But did he really understand what a life-changing decision he'd made? Did she dare to really hope?

As she continued down the hall to the resort's business offices, she hoped Grace's father wasn't going to have her do anything involving numbers. She might cost him a fortune today if he did.

Jane, his assistant, was busy at her desk, her phone cradled between her ear and shoulder. She murmured, "Never mind, she's here," into the phone and hung up. "There you are," she said to Lucy. "I was just checking with the front desk to see if you'd arrived."

Lucy glanced at her watch. "I'm not late for anything, am I? I don't remember a meeting being scheduled, and I usually don't arrive—"

"No, no! You're fine. Right on time." She smiled.

Something was up.

"They're waiting for you. Go on in." She winked at Lucy, a reassuring wink that only added to the mystery.

"Ah, there she is!" Grace's father said as she approached the open doorway. "Good morning, Lucy, come in and have a seat. We've been waiting for you."

Lucy smiled at him as Jane shut the office door behind her. "Good mor—" She stopped. Ethan stood in a back corner of the office. He was dressed in slacks and a dark polo shirt, his hands shoved deep into his pockets, and he looked wonderful and intense and a little less confident than she'd ever seen him before.

"Have a seat, Lucy," Grace's dad urged her again. "I've been getting acquainted with Mr. Glass, here. He asked me to arrange this meeting," he added in explanation. "I also told him I wasn't going to leave you two alone unless it was okay with you."

"Thank you," she said, still staring at Ethan. "And thanks for looking out for me."

"I watched the show too, honey." Grace's dad stood, assuming correctly that the look she was giving Ethan was his cue to go. "Well then, if you're okay with this, I'll leave now. Jane's right outside if you need anything."

Lucy managed to nod her approval, and he gave her a quick fatherly hug and left.

She was alone with Ethan. She was still standing by the door. He hadn't moved from the corner either; his hands were still in his pockets. She waited for him to speak first.

"I've become a believer," he said.

"A believer," she echoed.

"A believer in Einstein's theory of relativity."

That wasn't what she'd expected to hear. She frowned.

He moved toward her. "It's been two weeks since I've seen you, but it feels like ages."

Her heart skipped a beat. "I don't think that's what Einstein was talking about."

He walked closer. "Whatever. All I know is that the past couple of weeks are all the time you get. At least all the *alone* time you get. Because I've also become another kind of believer."

Taking her hand, he led her to a sofa and sat beside her. He looked directly into her eyes. Lucy saw determination in them but something more too. Vulnerability?

"The scriptures say that you're supposed to study things out in your mind and then pray, right?"

She nodded.

"I did that while I was in England. I expected to get an immediate answer, but I didn't." He huffed out a laugh. "It made me angry. I'm new to this whole prayer business. I like my answers straightforward. I also had no idea how to even recognize an answer. But answers started to come, little by little."

"They did? How did you know?"

He smiled. "Because I felt them. Here." He placed her hand over his heart and covered it with his.

She could feel its solid pulse beneath her fingers. "What answers did you get?" she whispered.

"The first was that I was being unfair to Denise for the sake of the outcome of the show. I didn't love her, and she deserved better than that. The second was to find missionaries when I arrived home and continue what I'd been doing in London."

"You met with missionaries while you were in London?"

"Elder Shaw and Elder McIntyre, my new pen pals. And when I got back, they were replaced by Elder Rivera and Elder Liu, currently serving in Montana. The third answer was that I wanted to be baptized, because, like I said earlier, I've become a believer. A real believer, Lucy. The gospel's true.

"And finally, I realized that the time I needed to give you was time with me, if you want it. So, here I am. I've arranged for a suite here at the resort. One of my assistants is thrilled with the idea of spending the next few months at an Arizona resort with all the amenities. But no one makes a move unless you give the go-ahead. What do you say? Will you let us have this time together?" He got serious. "Please say yes."

It was all just beginning to sink in. He was here, staying here in Arizona, to be close to her. Staying at the resort. He'd joined the Church. "Ethan, I— you really *do* believe? You really were baptized?" She could hardly grasp it all. "Do you know how long I've waited for someone to care enough about me to do this? All these years, every guy I met . . . It wasn't worth it to them—*I* wasn't worth it to them—"

"Lucy, sweetheart, I wasn't baptized for you. You need to get that straight right now. I read what you gave me for you. That's all. I was baptized for *me*.

Come here." He pulled her onto his lap. "I don't have a tissue, but you can use my shirt."

She laughed through her tears and rested her head on his shoulder. She felt him relax. "Does this mean I get to stay?" he asked.

"Yes," she replied. "I would love that more than anything." She settled onto his lap and wrapped her arms around him. He rested his head against hers. It felt peaceful. And right.

"Lucy," he whispered. "I want you to be my soulmate. Not with a capital *S* or a big reality TV ending. My soulmate, the one who really continues this journey with me. Like my mother has been for my father." He turned to look at her suddenly. "You haven't met them yet. I want you to meet my family."

She smiled through tears that wouldn't stop streaming down her face. "I'd love to meet your family."

"Good. That's good." He rested his head against hers again. "Lucy?" he murmured again.

"Hmm?"

"I love you. I understand forever now and what that means, and that's what I want with you. But I've promised you time, and I intend to keep that promise."

Lucy smiled and hugged him tighter. "Oh, Ethan, I love you so much. But you're right. We need time together. I need to get to know the new Ethan Glass."

"New and improved Ethan Glass. I think you might like him."

"Only time will tell," she teased.

He chuckled right before he kissed her.

CHAPTER 23

IT WAS A PERFECT AUTUMN day for an Arizona wedding. The air was warm and dry, the scorching heat of summer only a memory, the sky a breathtaking, cloudless blue. The ballroom at the Eagle Bluff Resort glittered like a jewel. Chandeliers sparkled, flowers imported just for the occasion spilled elegantly from urns and arbors and tabletops. The hum of conversation blended with the melodious strains of a string quartet. The bride wore a frothy confection of a gown that puffed and billowed around her as she hugged each guest in greeting. The groom stood next to her in a tailored dinner jacket and a tight smile.

Ethan squeezed Lucy's hand in reassurance. She smiled even more reassuringly back.

"Are you sure you're okay being here? We can leave."

"I'm fine." Her eyes swept the room, taking it all in. There was a lot to take in. "Allie's finally getting her dream wedding. By the way, Grace said we need to check out the cake."

"I'm not sure this is the groom's idea of a dream wedding."

"Allie's hard to stop when her mind's made up." She and Allie had talked a couple of times, and Lucy was trying to let go of the past. Making the decision to attend the wedding had been a first step, but Ethan was still protective of her.

"I'm so glad you're here!" Grace hugged Lucy. "You're supposed to be standing next to me wearing an identical hideous dress though. Hi, Ethan."

"Hello, Grace. You look stunning."

She grimaced. "Stunning would be an accurate description, but thank you for making it sound complimentary."

Ethan laughed. Lucy smiled and relaxed. She could do this.

They greeted Allie and Ben. Allie hugged Lucy tightly for several long minutes. "Thanks for coming. It means so much to me to have you here."

Lucy smiled but said nothing.

"I was so worried that you wouldn't forgive me, but here you are, right? The two of you together. Happily ever after and all that, just like me and Ben." She tossed her groom an indulgent smile. "But I knew you'd forgive me. I got you two together, right?"

"Right," Lucy managed to say.

Allie hugged her again. Lucy felt suffocated. "Well. Congratulations. To the both of you."

Ben hugged her briefly and shook Ethan's hand. "Thanks for coming tonight, Lucy. It means a lot."

She nodded.

Ethan grabbed her hand and pulled her none too gently toward the exit. "We're getting out of here."

"What about the cake?"

"You want to see the cake? Grace takes pictures of everything. She can show you pictures of the cake later. We're gone."

She stopped arguing and followed him.

"She doesn't even get it, does she?" he asked as he helped her into his car. "Allie, I mean. She gets that she told some lies and that you got angry at her as a result. But that's it. She doesn't see that her lies started the whole chain reaction with Melanie and the show's editing and the media feeding frenzy that came about as a result. And Ben still had the guts to marry her. I pity the guy."

Lucy cupped the side of his face and kissed him. "I love you. And you're right; she doesn't get it. I understand that about her though. Deep down, I really think she believes she's the reason we're together, and maybe she's right. She did fill out the show's application for me. I wouldn't have met you otherwise. But don't pity Ben. He understands her too, and he loves her. And if anybody can get her to toe the line, it's Ben."

Ethan kissed her and put the car into gear. "And now we're out of here. We have a very important engagement, and we're almost late."

"We do?" They hadn't discussed any plans for after the reception.

"Mmhmm. But I'm not saying any more about it. You'll have to wait to find out."

Ethan had turned playful since his arrival in Arizona. Occasionally, when she'd drop by his temporary offices at the resort during her breaks, she'd see the CEO face he'd worn most of the time when she'd gotten to know him on the show. But it was rare these days.

They'd spent a lot of time together. Quality time. They took advantage of the resort facilities—the horses, in particular. He jokingly referred to Cecily, the ghost town, as their "personal haunt." She always rolled her eyes at the terrible pun, but it did seem like it was theirs. They'd spent hours there over the weeks, talking and really getting to know each other.

He'd also attempted to teach her to golf. She'd never been a great golfer, but the old competitive spirit she'd had with her brothers had reared its head again. By this time next year, she'd told him, her handicap would be lower than his. He'd only laughed at her. The following week she'd beaten him by shooting better than her handicap. He'd stopped laughing.

They'd spent time at the resort pool, where she'd impressed him with her diving skills. Then he'd taken to the diving board and put her to shame.

He'd also gone to church with her and her family. That had been the best part for Lucy. She'd watched him absorb what he'd heard there and listened to him as he'd posed questions and digested the answers. He'd had several gospel discussions with her parents and returned missionary brothers.

She was convinced that his baptism had been for himself and was not something he'd done as a concession for her.

They pulled out of the resort parking lot and headed down the street.

"What possible engagement could we have at"—she glanced at the car's digital clock—"seven forty-five on a Wednesday night?" she asked.

He smiled at her and wiggled his eyebrows at her. *Wiggled* his eyebrows! "Did I just happen to give you an enigmatic smile filled with intrigue and mystery?"

She snorted and pretended to be out of sorts. "No. You gave me a silly grin and a corny answer filled with redundancy."

He laughed and drove the car around the block and into another of the resort's parking lots, one that was closer to his suite of rented rooms. "Too bad. Still not saying."

She could only laugh and shake her head at him.

He made her stay put while he sent a brief text—he wouldn't tell her to whom—then practically dragged her through the lobby and down the hall toward his suite. "Come on, come on, we need to hurry."

What could be so urgent? She chuckled, confused but delighted by his playful antics. She really loved him. She'd told him she loved him more than once. He hadn't repeated the words to her, not since he'd told her he loved her the day he'd arrived back in Arizona. Three months had passed since then. He was still giving her time, she suspected. She didn't need any more time though. She was ready.

He unlocked the door and led her directly through the suite and onto the balcony. Darkness had fallen, but he didn't turn on any outside lights. They had the stars and a quarter moon to see by, and candles in hurricane lanterns flickered on a nearby table. It took her eyes a moment to fully adjust, to see what lay on the table next to the candles.

Strawberries. Chocolate-dipped strawberries. Ethan led her over and pulled out a chair. She sank gratefully into it because her legs had failed her. "Oh, Ethan," she managed to get past the tightness in her throat.

He gave her a lopsided grin. "I thought about frying up some bacon," he said as he sat in the chair next to hers, making her laugh. But then he got serious. "Do you remember that first night? After the rodeo? We had strawberries then as well. And you introduced me to the concept of eternity. The vastness of it. The realness we can see with our own eyes." He gestured toward the sky, a deep blanket of diamonds.

"I remember."

"That was the night I discovered that Lucy Kendrick was not like the other women there. She didn't drink champagne," he said as he poured a glass of ice water from a carafe and handed it to her. "She didn't like to lose, even if it meant taking on somebody bigger and tougher than she was. She challenged me. She still does. And she didn't kiss on a first date." He chuckled.

Lucy could feel her cheeks heat up, even after all this time with him.

He picked up a strawberry and held it to her lips. She took a bite. The berry was sweet, but the kiss that followed was sweeter. "She kisses me now, thank goodness," he murmured. "I was afraid for a while there that she never would again."

He reached into his pocket, pulled out a small velvet box, then handed it to her. Lucy's heart nearly stopped beating, and her fingers felt clumsy as she opened it.

She gasped and looked at him in surprise. It wasn't what she'd expected. "It's a charm."

"It's a lot more than that." It was, in fact, a heart cut from clear glass. The facets that helped define its shape caught the candlelight, and it flashed with fire and color. "It's supposed to represent my heart. And it's glass, so please don't break it."

She wrapped him in her arms. "Who would have thought Ethan Glass, millionaire entrepreneur and celebrity extraordinaire—a man who sparks fear in others with only a glance—would turn out to be such a softie?"

"Yes, well. Don't spread that around. I'll only deny it." He reached back into his pocket and retrieved her *Soulmates* bracelet.

"You and my mother have been conspiring together, haven't you? Does my entire family know what you had planned for tonight?" Her family had all grown to love Ethan over the past few months. It had taken a few long one-on-one conversations with her dad and a few intense pickup games with her brothers to get there, but Ethan had eventually won them over.

Right along with her.

"She dipped the strawberries, I confess. But I think Brigham actually searched your room for the bracelet."

Lucy put her hands over her face and groaned. The idea of her teenage brother riffling through her drawers . . . She wouldn't think about it right now. Especially since Ethan was reaching into his jacket pocket again. His breast pocket this time.

He held a diamond ring, and his fingers shook slightly. "Lucy," he said, "I love you. I want you to be my wife. But . . ."

"But what?" Ethan sat there holding a ring, and he was saying *but*? Lucy panicked and didn't even realize she'd asked the question out loud.

"But I want you to be happy. You've always wanted to be married in the temple. You've made that clear ever since I've known you. I don't want to take that from you. So if you'll agree to marry me, I'll agree to wait. I was baptized four months ago, so in eight months I can—"

She put a finger over his lips to silence him. "Ethan, I trust you. And I want our life together to begin as soon as possible. Of course I want to be married in the temple. That would always be my first choice. But I also didn't expect to fall in love with a brand-new member."

"You really love me," he said.

"Yes." She smiled up at him. "I love you like crazy. And I trust you."

"Does this mean—?"

She laughed now. "Yes. So this is what I suggest. Together we discuss the pros and cons of waiting to marry next year in the temple versus marrying now and going to the temple a year later. And then we—"

"—study it out in our minds and pray for guidance." He grinned at her. "It doesn't take me long to figure things out."

She beamed at him as he slid the ring onto her finger. It fit perfectly.

* * *

They married a month later. That was the nice part about marrying a wealthy businessman, Lucy thought as she snuggled into the sofa. He had clout and connections, and they'd been able to pull the simple wedding together in record time. They'd prayed and had decided that getting married quickly would be the best plan for them.

It had enabled his family to see them get married, and Lucy knew that had made them happy. She adored Ethan's family. His mother had been fun and feisty, his brother, Jake, had teased her, Jake's wife had hugged her and promised to let her in on all the secrets for understanding the Glass men. Brianna had formed a major crush on Brigham and trailed after him constantly. And Old Jed had even shed a tear or two during the ceremony. If Lucy hadn't glanced over just at that particular moment and seen it for herself, she wouldn't have believed it.

Kyle and Terri had been there too. Ethan had started to explain his "adopted" brother and his reasons for being part of the production crew, but Lucy had replied that Kyle had informed her of that fact before she'd been eliminated from the show. Ethan had immediately grabbed her hand and dragged her over to Kyle, where he'd lectured Kyle (at great length and with much hilarity) about the dangers of violating confidentiality agreements in contracts, making all of the guests laugh. She was thrilled that her good friend Kyle was now an official part of her family.

Grace had been her maid of honor. Lucy had invited Allie and Ben, but they hadn't attended.

That had been the one cloud on an otherwise perfect day for Lucy. That and the cameras. Curt, who'd been invited as a guest, had brought Melanie—it blew Lucy's mind to think about it—as his date. He'd also brought a new director and a few cameramen and crew members, having convinced Ethan and Lucy that a happy follow-up in the form of a TV special would do wonders for the website, not to mention the upcoming season of *Soulmates*, which was scheduled to begin shooting a few months after their wedding. Ethan had drawn the line on allowing the actual ceremony to be televised though. Lucy had agreed 100 percent.

They'd honeymooned on the beach in Mexico, where he'd shown her the starfish, and then traveled south to Cabo. Ethan had decided to make his temporary office in Phoenix a permanent one, at least for the time being. Working out of Phoenix meant he'd had to do some additional traveling, but they'd decided Lucy would travel with him. She'd been thrilled at the prospect. And he'd been taking temple preparation classes and had even contacted the temple to schedule their sealing, although it was still a few months away from actually happening.

"Hurry!" she called from the sofa. "It's going to start any minute."

Ethan showed up almost before she'd finished calling him and settled into the sofa next to her, pulling her close and wrapping an arm around her. He plopped his stockinged feet onto the coffee table in front of him, next to the bowl of popcorn he'd brought from the kitchen. "Ah, this is living. A nice, cozy evening at home."

Lucy smiled. "No limos."

"No spotlights," Ethan countered.

"No cameras."

"Mmm. With my wife at my side and butter on my popcorn—"

"Our popcorn."

"Oh, all right. I suppose I can share. Our popcorn. With my wife at my side and butter on my popcorn, there's only one thing I can think of that could make this evening any better than it already is—"

"*Shush*. It's about to start." Lucy giggled.

"I'll shush you," he said and kissed her soundly. "Mmm, that definitely made the evening better," he whispered, looking at her in a way that still managed to melt her heart. "But, as I was saying," he added mischievously, "there is one *more* thing that could make this evening even better." He gestured toward the flatscreen TV. "And that one thing would be . . ."

"Welcome to a new season of *Soulmates*. I'm your host, Rick Madison. A lot of you watched last summer as handsome businessman Ethan Glass went on his search to find love . . ."

"Did you pay him extra to say *handsome*, you sneaky—"

Ethan shushed her again the same way—not that Lucy was complaining.

". . . It's time to welcome this season's *Soulmate*. You may remember her from last summer. She nearly won Ethan's heart, and now it's her turn to find love. Please welcome Denise Pendleton . . ."

Lucy couldn't help it. She squealed. "Did you know about this? What am I saying? Of course you knew about this."

Ethan only laughed. "Careful, you'll wake the neighbors." He set the popcorn bowl in his lap and dug in.

". . . And I'm absolutely positive that *Soulmates'* unique method of matchmaking will find me the *loveliest* man in the country, the man who will be my *Soulmate*."

Lucy sighed with contentment. She'd found love with Ethan. He was her husband, and very soon he would be her eternal companion. They were becoming each other's soulmates, one day at a time.

Now if only he would stop hogging the popcorn . . .

ABOUT THE AUTHOR

KAREN TUFT WAS BORN WITH a healthy dose of curiosity about pretty much everything, so as a child she taught herself to read and play the piano. She studied composition at BYU then graduated from the University of Utah in music theory as a member of Phi Kappa Phi and Pi Kappa Lambda honor societies. In addition to being an author, Karen is a wife, mother, pianist, composer, and arranger. She has spent countless hours backstage and in orchestra pits for theater productions along the Wasatch Front. She also has a 75 percent success rate when it comes to matchmaking and is a big believer in happy endings. Among her varied interests, she likes to figure out what makes people tick, wander through museums, and travel—whether by car, plane, or paperback.